I0612892

SHADOWS & STARLIGHT

B Wills

Golden Light Publishing House

Cover design by: Kayla Vaught
Library of Congress Control Number: 2018675309
ASIN: B0DYYZ8YWF
ISBN: 979-8-9928401-0-0

TRIGGER WARNINGS

Shadows & Starlight is a non-stop thrilling adventure containing acts of violence, gore and magical related injuries, sexually explicit scenes, mentions of domestic and family violence, torture, praise kinks, assault and attempted rape. Magical tropes with mentions of blood magic, succubus, fae, dark kings and magical prophecies. This book is intended for mature audiences.

If you are sensitive to the above mentioned elements, please take note and protect yourself. Then prepare to join Ophelia, Nova, and Seraphina on their journey to restore balance to their kingom.

There's fuckery to be had!

Welcome, to the Eternal Darkness Chronicles... we've been waiting for you.

BOOK PLAYLIST

) ··) ·) · ● · (· (·· (

1. Dirty Thoughts - Chloe Adams
2. Fuqboi - Hey Violet
3. You Need To Calm Down - Taylor Swift
4. All Good Girls Go To Hell - Billie Eilish
5. Castle - Halsey
6. You Should See Me In A Crown - Billie Eilish
7. Cake By The Ocean - DNCE
7. So Hot That It Hurts - Hey Violet
8. Cut Deep - Matt Maeson
9. Woman - Kesha
10. Gasoline - Halsey
11. Phoenix - League of Legends, Cailin Russo, & Chrissy Costanza
12. Honestly - Gabbi Hanna
13. Cinderella's Dead - Emeline
14. Constellations - Jade LeMac
15. Ordinary - Alex Warren
16. Lights Down Low - Max
17. Taste of You - Rezz, Dove Cameron
18. Heavy Is The Crown - Linkin Park
19. Nightmare - Halsey
20. 7 Minutes in Hell - Chrissy Costanza, Viola
21. Boyfriend - Dove Cameron
22. Voodoo - Viola

"Oh good, you're still here. Now, join me on an epic journey that will leave you weak in the knees... and probably cussing me out. Oh! By the way, thank you for not killing me for that last chapter."

CONTENTS

PROLOGUE: DARKEST DAY & BRIGHTEST NIGHT

The cries of labor echo through the chamber, a relentless sound that shakes the walls and threatens to break my composure. A sharp crack splits the air, and I look down, realizing I've torn the armrest from the chair. With a grimace, I pull my hand away and twist my fingers nervously in my lap.

I'm stationed in the small sitting room just outside the birthing chamber. Knowing she's bringing another child into the world should be joyful. But the weight of the seer's prophecy hangs over me, making the entire ordeal unbearable. Nausea rises in my throat at the thought.

Another scream pierces the air, sending my nerves spiraling. My mother, High Priestess Niahm, appears at the door, her silver eyes flashing in worry. "Esmyra!" she calls, her voice edged with urgency. "Come quickly!"

Fear coils in my stomach like a wild animal, thrashing for release. I leap from my seat and immediately move toward the oak doors, my heart pounding.

"Hurry, it's almost time," she urges, grabbing my hand, pulling me inside, and shutting the door behind us with a snap.

Inside, the room is bathed in rich purples and blues, the four-poster bed at the center. There, struggling with every ounce of strength, is my mate, Queen Siofra. She clutches Jade's hand, the maid's knuckles turning white from the pressure.

"Come now, she's been asking for you," my mother chides, waving me forward.

I step toward the bed, smoothing out the creases in my silver bodice, the fabric swishing with each step. "I'm here now," I whisper, gently prying Siofra's hands away from Jade's.

Siofra grips my hands with desperation as another wave of pain crashes over her. My mother moves to examine the queen's progress, her hands shifting beneath Siofra's gown. "Push hard on the next one, Your Majesty. I see the head."

As the next contraction hits, Siofra pushes with everything she has, a scream ripping from her throat as she bears down. She seizes my hand, her grip strong enough to bruise, and I bite my lip to hold back my cry.

A newborn's wail fills the room as Niahm catches the baby, her face glowing triumphantly. Siofra collapses back on the bed, exhausted, sweat beading on her brow. "Well?" she demands, her voice shaky. "Is it a girl?"

The baby's cries answer her, the tiny limbs flailing, and Niahm nods, a smile tugging at her lips. "Yes, Your Majesty. A healthy, beautiful girl."

Tears fill Siofra's eyes, her chin trembling as she gazes at her daughter. Her voice quivers as she christens her: Princess of

Shadows.

Niahm lifts the baby, allowing Siofra to take in the sight of her. I watch, my heart breaking as tears streak down my cheeks. The cruelty of it all weighs heavily on me.

I had prayed to the goddess, begged her for another son, and made countless offerings at the altars. But the fates, those cruel, unforgiving fates, have chosen otherwise.

Siofra gestures toward Jade, who hurriedly rushes across the room and opens the curtains to reveal the full moon hanging high in the sky. It's an omen—one I feel deep in my bones.

When Siofra gasps, I look up, catching sight of a falling star streaking across the heavens. Mother's breath catches beside me. She murmurs a single phrase, just above a whisper, but it chills me more than the night air.

"Shadowbound Blossom."

"I knew it," Siofra whispers, her voice raw with grief. I hold her hand, a chill settling in my chest as I kiss her knuckles softly. Her sobs still fill the room, but for a moment, she's calmed.

We sit in silence, each of us lost in our thoughts, the weight of what's to come pressing down on us.

"You know what you must do," Siofra says, her voice sharp with resolve.

It's not a request—it's an order. And though it will tear my soul to pieces, I know there is no choice. "Yes, my queen," I whisper.

She nods, her face hardening with determination as she sinks back into the pillows. The room seems to stretch, time warping in a haze of confusion and dread. Then, Siofra's grip tightens on my hand again as another contraction hits, a soft groan escaping her lips.

"Mother!" I call, my voice tight with panic as I turn to her.

Niahm hands the swaddled infant off to Jade and rushes to Siofra's side, her eyes widening in shock. The queen's scream rings through the room again, sending tremors through my body. "There's another one, Your Majesty," Niahm says, her voice filled with surprise. "It's crowning. Push on the next contraction."

"Twins..." I murmur, my heart lodging in my throat as the second baby's cries fill the air, a new life joining the first.

CHAPTER 1: S.O.S.!

Nova

It's a foggy, gloomy morning that mirrors the impending doom lodged in the pit of my stomach. I hastily pack my travel satchel with an assortment of potions and herbs, grabbing the ones that will cause the most damage.

It's not that I intend to cause trouble. I just need to be prepared.

A missive from my third-in-command, Galean Hawthorne, arrived this morning. Now, it sits atop the growing pile on my desk, untouched since I read its damning contents. The old and worn desk occupies a corner of the lower level of my rented townhouse in Bevan. Next to it, an open bay window with cherrywood trim houses a plush lavender bench. I often sit there to read, basking in the natural light that floods the space. It's usually a peaceful place where I have my morning tea.

Not today.

I shake my head, wondering after all this time if we're going backward instead of forward. I've made so many mistakes lately, and in this game...mistakes are not something I can afford.

Our magic system is spread across five realms, each group responsible for its part in keeping Eventide running as a whole. Seven years ago, something shifted, and our illustrious king decided he had a personal vendetta with elemental witches and the blood magic we practice.

Eventide is made up of a diverse community. Home to fae, witches, warlocks and humans, making it unique in more ways than one. Rumor has it the king has a secret, and his plans stem from fear and paranoia. We plan to use this to our advantage. He's going too far with his reach for power, and it's time to stop this madness.

It's undeniable that magic seems to be growing more powerful each decade, producing equally powerful fae, witches, and warlocks. In the days of Queen Siofra, magic was celebrated. Her Majesty's misson was to blend the communities, creating a utopia for all of Eventide.

She brought together Mystic Shores on the west coast, our prestigious Water Realm, and Wildwood Haven between the mountains in the middle of Eventide. The Earth realm grew exponentially. So quickly that the two have been conjoined at the hip ever since, working in tandem to keep our country thriving. From there, she reached out to Dragon's Roost, the most significant den of dragon shifters in the Fire Realm, creating a bridge between them and the snow-capped tundra of Winterhaven Hall, our Air Realm. The relationship she built between them created an entirely new grimoire that is still used today to teach the new students of the Winterveil Citadel, the most prominent school of magic in the country.

Bringing together the original nine houses was her idea of cultivating the future she believed Eventide desperately needed. It's a damn shame it never came to fruition. All because of a spineless creature hellbent on destroying everything she worked so hard to build.

How can the king claim to worship the goddess Astraea when she blessed us with this power? How can he despise our magic so abhorrently when magic is a part of our everyday life? Magic is in our blood. It's who we *are*.

I scowl, still in disbelief of the turn of events that brought us here. My eyes roam over my desk, locking onto the missive once more, forcing my thoughts back to the present. My brother nearly blew our cover—fifteen years of careful work— because he couldn't follow orders. I told him to get close, not to infiltrate the goddess-damned palace.

It's bad enough that he got caught. Worse still, King Elrond plans to make an example of him today in Eventide Square.

I exhale sharply, and grab my dark navy cloak, securing it tightly around me. The fabric settles over my shoulders and shrouds me in much-needed anonymity. I pause by the oblong mirror near the mantle, checking my reflection. My face is little more than a shadow beneath the hood.

Good, it's time to make some noise.

Stepping out into the alley, I barely reach the end before a vortex of red energy crackles through the air. The sight draws a smirk to my lips. As the final wisps of Galean's portal dissipate, I step through, knowing he'll be waiting for me on the other side.

Sure enough, when my feet touch the cobblestones of Eventide Square, I find him standing there—arms crossed, an unim-pressed scowl fixed firmly in place. Raking a hand through his chestnut-colored hair, he snaps his gold pocket watch shut.

"You're late, Duskweaver."

I nearly sigh. "I'm not late. I'm right on time."

"Three minutes late. Which means you're already screwing up our not-a-plan. All for the sake of your *reckless* and *idiot* of a brother." He sniffs, arching a brow.

"Galean," I warn, stiffening under his glare.

"Fine. Nothing better to do, anyway, than march to my death on this glorious morning."

The sarcasm isn't lost on me.

As we weave through the crowded market, I take in the scene. Eventide Square—normally a bustling marketplace—is unrec-ognizable. The usual vendors have been pushed into the alleys, their stalls stripped away to make room for the king's spec-tacle. The scent of sticky buns lingers, making my stomach mewl in protest.

I wonder, not for the first time, why King Elrond insists on such public executions. It isn't just about punishment. He enjoys this—flaunting his power, watching his subjects trem-ble in fear. I shiver at the thought of a man looking into his people's eyes as he takes one of their own from them.

Nervous energy flutters in my stomach, erratic and unwel-come. I take a steadying breath, forcing myself to focus before my thoughts spiral further.

Galean catches my eye, then leans down close to my ear. "Are you sure?" he asks, guiding me toward the west corner of the square.

"No," I whisper.

From here, the wooden stage is fully visible. The gallows

loom, dark and waiting. Dried blood stains the planks, remnants of yesterday's execution, the thought sending another round of nausea swirling through my belly.

And then I see him.

Skalanis stumbles as he's half-dragged toward the stage, his clothes dirt and blood stained, hands bound in iron chains. My palms sweat at the sight of him. He looks terrible—his steps sluggish, his body swaying. A tall, muscular man with pitch-black hair walks beside him.

He yanks him forward when he slows but reaches out a steadying hand when he stumbles.

The sight of my brother—caked in blood and dirt—sends me over the edge. Violent thoughts, tremors, and heat flood my veins.

Galean's grip tightens around my waist, his fingers pressing hard enough to bruise.

He knows. He knows exactly where my mind is going.

"Be still," he murmurs, his breath hot against my ear. "The warlord is present, and Ryvvik's in position."

Onstage, the Prince Warlord yanks Skalanis upright by his chains, locking them behind his back. He moves with chilling efficiency, adjusting the noose before slipping it around my brother's neck.

"Where *is* he?" I whisper furiously, my eyes darting across the platform, searching for my target.

"There." Galean hisses the word through clenched teeth, nodding toward the right of the stage.

King Elrond emerges, looking ever the victor, his smugness sending a ripple of anger through me.

He walks slowly and deliberately toward the podium, standing tall despite his hunched grip on the pommel of his cane.

His silver hair flows down his back, and the obsidian crown of stars resting atop his head gleams under the morning suns. Every movement is measured and designed to command attention.

A predator surveying his prey.

I clench my fists as his shrewd silver eyes sweep the crowd, hunting—searching—for the rest of the rebel forces. Then, his voice booms through the square. Cold. Unyielding.

"I stand before you today, as your king, deeply saddened and distressed by the current state of our kingdom."

A calculated pause. He lets his words settle and allows their weight to press down on the gathered masses before continuing.

"I come before you, asking those present to bear witness." His gaze drifts across the crowd, ensnaring them one by one. "My royal guards have uncovered a traitor among you—a worthless criminal determined to see me assassinated. Determined to drag this kingdom into the depths of anarchy!"

Murmurs ripple through the crowd, and tension sweeps through the area. The aroma is potent, laced with a sense of dread.

King Elrond's voice rises, prickly and commanding. "I ask you—should we allow this *filth* to plague our streets?"

"No!!!" The roar of the crowd is deafening, sending a bolt of panic through my chest. My stomach lurches, as a wave of terror grips me in it's wake. *The fools*!

The king's lips curl in satisfaction. "No, we should not."

His hands tighten on the podium as he continues, his voice thick with righteous fury. "When Astraea blessed the Morningstars, she chose us as her voice—the arbiters of justice in this earthly realm. And so we will fight fire with fire! We will stamp out all who seek to harm this kingdom and its people! We will not rest until the rebel forces are on their knees, begging for mercy!"

The crowd erupts, their cheers a frenzied, feverish chant.

I snort, tuning out the rest of his sanctimonious speech as I reach into my satchel. My fingers close around a small glass orb—a particular favorite of mine. Earth and fire magic swirl within, a volatile blend of destruction and chaos. Perfect for creating a distraction.

Beside me, Galean slips the orb into his palm, then moves away, taking his position near the right of the stage. He stops just behind the prince, blending effortlessly into the scene.

The prince notices him, shooting a sly grin in his direction. A whisper passes between them, and Galean smirks. His expression is all cocky bravado, hands moving in animated gestures as he speaks.

The prince listens, then turns—pausing just shy of the stairs leading to the podium. "Prince Warlord, step forward." The king's voice rings out, crisp and commanding.

Galean tosses me a cheeky grin, before casually letting the orb slip from his palm. It rolls across the cobblestone, nearly bursting when it clips a sharp rock. I hiss through my teeth, tension rippling through me, but the orb settles—right at the podium's edge, exactly where I wanted it.

King Elrond lifts his chin, his expression carved from ice. "I condemn you, Skalanis Duskweaver, to death by hanging."

A condescending grin stretches across his face, and I nearly snarl at the sight. My fingers twitch at my side as I send a silent prayer to the goddess, begging for her guidance.

Fire stirs in my core. It coils, waiting for the perfect moment to strike.

The prince moves toward the stage, preparing to execute the prisoner, and then… I strike.

"Incendio."

The explosion rips through the square, igniting fear in the crowd. Screams fill the air, sending a bolt of trepidation through me. The podium *shatters*, sending pieces of wood and metal flying everywhere. A shockwave slams into me, licking my cloak with heat.

A dark shadow flits in my peripheral, snaring my attention and a grin tugs at the corners of my mouth. Ryvvik is soaring overhead when the dust clears, his dragon form impressive as he dives through the sky.

"Dragon!!!" The panicked cry spreads like wildfire. People shove past one another, desperate to escape the chaos.

I hiss, dodging the mayhem. A commotion catches my attetnion, satisfaction curling in my chest as the guards scramble to drag the false king from the stage. Then, my stomach lurches.

The prince's shift catches my attention, a dazzling array of blue energy swirling like a vortex.

His dragon form bursts into existence, streaking cobalt fire through the sky as he collides with Ryvvik. They spiral, snapping jaws and slashing claws, and their flames clash in blinding arcs of blue and gold.

The square erupts into sheer madness all over again. It's complete pandemonium, and I spy several people who've fallen–only to be trampled on. I cringe, shoving the thoughts away as I scan the square.

I spot an opening as the last of the guards clear the stage. I raise a hand, summoning a surge of energy, and hurl it toward the temple at the square's edge. The stone shudders—then crumbles. The collapsing structure sends up a cloud of dust, scattering what little order remains.

I bolt, charging forward with reckless abandon.

A dagger whistles past my ear, sending a shiver snaking down my spine. Instinct takes over and I whirl, thrusting my hand forward. "Terrae motus!"

The ground rumbles, cracks splintering outward. Roots burst from the earth, twisting and coiling like serpents before striking their target. They wrap around my attacker, pinning him in place.

Another rushes me, but I don't break my stride.

Yanking a light orb from my satchel, I hurl it at the ground. "Clara lux!"

Blinding radiance floods the square, sending guards stumbling, their hands flying to shield their eyes.

I leap onto the stage from the left, landing behind Skalanis. Power hums at my fingertips as I lash out at his chains. The first strike weakens them. The second sends cracks skittering along the metal. The third—they snap.

Skalanis lets out a breath, rubbing his raw wrists. "Thanks, sis," he mutters, accepting the spare cloak I shove at him. He grins, shameless despite everything, and quickly kisses my temple. "I knew you could do it."

"You shouldn't have done it in the first place," I seethe, shoving him toward the edge of the stage.

"Later!" he hisses, yanking me aside as a guard crashes beside us.

We weave through the chaos, dodging blades and bursts of magic, our path a frantic blur of motion. Overhead, Ryvvik is still locked in combat, flames streaking through the sky.

I reach into my satchel—*fuck*, one last orb. Better make it count.

Twisting, I hurl it high into the air.

Galean, ever the opportunist, catches my movement. A wicked grin flashes across his face before he sends a lightning bolt straight into the orb.

It detonates, sending shrapnel flying. It rains down, striking —right into Prince Arax's chest.

He falters, banking to the far left and almost crashing maw first into a nearby building.

For a breath, he hangs suspended, wings losing momentum. Then he plummets, falling hard into the earth.

Ryvvik seizes the moment, surging upward and away, racing toward the horizon.

"SEIZE THEM!!!" The shout tears through the square, thick with fury.

I smirk and grab Skalanis, yanking him toward the nearest alley. We tear through the maze of Eventide's backstreets, twisting and turning, lungs burning with exertion. The shouts behind us fade, swallowed by the labyrinth.

Finally, we slip free.

I sag against the stone wall, my breath coming fast. Skalanis grins at me, all mischief and exhaustion.

"Admit it," he pants. "You missed this."

I scowl, blowing a stray hair out of my face in irritation.

He just laughs, giving me another lazy grin.

"What were you thinking?!" I whisper sharply, pushing myself off the wall and taking another right turn, mentally counting the twists and turns as we navigate the maze of back alleys.

"Well, it worked, didn't it?" Skalanis replies smugly, his breath still coming fast from our sprint. He snorts when I shoot him a glare. I turn up the ice, making it cold enough to freeze hellfire. Still, he smirks.

It's enough to make me want to wring his neck!

"Yes!" I hiss, barely keeping my voice down. "That's not the point."

"Sure it is!" He smirks, utterly unbothered by my apparent anger. "You needed an inside look at the king's personal guard, and now you have it." He squeezes my shoulder as if that makes up for the near-disaster he orchestrated.

I huff, filing away my irritation for later. We're not safe yet, and it would be foolish to berate him here. I take the final turn, leading us into the last alley. "How many?" I ask, my voice quieter now. I'm not ready to forgive his recklessness, but we need the intel.

"Ten." His tone turns serious. "At all times. Two were stationed inside the king's chambers, a personal food taster, his valet, and six more guarding the outer perimeter. After today? He'll double, maybe even triple security." He shrugs as if discussing anything *but* the fact that he nearly got himself executed.

A familiar crackle of energy shivers through the air, announcing Galean's arrival. He steps from the portal with an air of exasperation, barely sparing us a glance before stating dryly, "Are we done playing chicken with the entire military force of Eventide?"

Skalanis snorts a laugh, his pale blue eyes dancing with amusement. "*Done*? My friend, we're just getting *started*!" He flashes a grin, reaching for my hand once more.

Galean runs a hand down his face, clearly vexed, "Try not to get caught next time, will you? I can't keep rescuing you like some damsel in distress." His lingering smirk betrays the trace of amusement lurking beneath his frustration.

He extends his palm toward the sky, waiting. I press my

hand into his, our energies twining together, magic sparking between us. Potent and wild, the power hums through me, weaving into something entirely new—a cloaking signature strong enough to mask our departure. The portal before us flickers and solidifies, revealing the familiar streets of Bevan. The triple suns hang high now, and the morning fog has long burned away.

Galean releases a slow breath. "Next time you plan a reconnaissance mission, let's agree on a real plan before you pull another ridiculous stunt." With a huff, he shoves Skalanis through the portal before he can argue.

I cackle, throwing a middle finger up at Galean. "Then, whatever would I do for entertainment?"

His scowl is priceless. Laughing, I step through the portal, leaving the chaos of Eventide behind as I join my brother in the streets of Bevan.

✳ ✳ ✳

"Skalanis Bayne Duskweaver, get your ass back here!" I holler through the apartment, slamming the door before tossing my cloak onto the nearest hook.

Silence.

So fucking typical.

"I swear on all things unholy, I'm going to throttle that brother of mine," I grumble as I take the stairs two at a time, my boots striking the wood with sharp, angry thuds.

By the time I reach the second floor, I'm already scanning the rooms. The bathing chamber door is slightly ajar, steam curling from the crack. I shove it open, and there he is—relaxed by the clawfoot tub, arms crossed along his chest, wearing the smuggest expression possible as he waits for the water to fill up.

"This conversation wasn't over," I snap, planting my hands on my hips.

Skalanis barely lifts a brow. "And this couldn't wait until *after* my bath?"

The room is warm, the scent of eucalyptus lingering in the air. A cool breeze stirs the green curtains framing the open window, but I barely register any of it. I'm too furious.

"No, it could not," I seethe, whirling on him. "You completely ignored my orders! I said don't get close, and what do you do? The. Exact. Opposite." My voice rises, and in a second I'm across the room and swatting at him.

Skalanis dodges, hands up in defense. "Stop it!" he yelps, backing up against the linen closet. "Damn it, Nova Rayne, this is ridiculous!"

"No! You *disappeared!*" My voice cracks, but I don't stop. "Three goddess-damned weeks, Skalanis! Do you even realize how worried I was?"

This time, my hand connects with his cheek.

He swears, rubbing his jaw. "You're worse than Mom, you know that?"

"Oh, please. I didn't hit you *that* hard."

His scowl deepens as he leans against the white marble sink, crossing his arms. "Are you done now?"

"That depends."

"On what?"

I fold my arms, my voice quieter now but no less sharp. "Why did you go off script? Does everything we've worked for mean so little to you?"

His expression softens, guilt flickering across his features. He swipes a hand through his hair, scratching his beard—a nervous tell. "Look, I know how important this is to you. Nova, I promise, I want that bastard to pay just as badly as you do for what he did to our father. I'm sorry, okay? I didn't think it through. I should've sent a raven."

"You're damn right. You should've sent a fucking raven," I mutter, shaking my head.

He sighs. "I saw an opportunity and took it. My only regret is that the king's taster got to the goblet before I could slit his throat."

For a heartbeat, I don't process his words. And then—

"You tried to poison the king?!" My vision goes red. "Are you insane?"

I lunge for another hit, but Skalanis catches my wrist mid-swing. His grip is firm but not painful, his pale blue eyes locking onto mine.

"Stop it," he says, his voice dipping low. "We're not kids anymore, Nova. I know you're worried, and I've already apologized. Let it go."

I hiss, jerking my wrist free. "Fine," I mumble, my anger finally cooling into something more exhausted than furious. I swallow hard. "Just... send a raven next time, will you?"

His eyes soften, and in the next breath, he pulls me into a tight hug.

"Dad would be so proud of you," he whispers, resting his chin on my head.

I squeeze my eyes shut. "I hope so."

"He would." Skalanis pulls back slightly, smirking. "And he'd love that you still give me as much hell as you do."

"Damn it, Lani." I snicker, the nickname slipping out before I can stop it. I'd been two when I first called him that, unable to pronounce his full name. It stuck, much to his chagrin.

"There's my sister." He grins, ruffling my hair like I'm still a child.

I swat his hand away, rolling my eyes as I turn for the door.

"Nova," he calls.

I glance over my shoulder.

His expression is earnest now, all teasing set aside. "I missed you too, sis."

A small smile tugs at my lips before I slip out of the room, closing the door softly behind me.

CHAPTER 2: HUNGER & LUST

<u>Ophelia</u>

I'm ravenous again.

It's a constant ache I've long since grown accustomed to. You'd think, after all these years, I'd have learned to curb the appetite of my fae form.

But as luck—or misfortune—would have it, I can't remember a time when I wasn't starving.

And I'm not talking about the mundane gnaw of human hunger. No, this is something far more insidious, a hunger that festers in my bones and thrums beneath my skin. A craving that can only be sated by lust, by the siphoning of raw, electric energy. It's madness and bliss wrapped into one, a fever that never truly breaks. The scent of it alone is enough to drive me wild.

I lick my lips at the memory of my last meal. The hunger flares instantly, twisting sharp and demanding in my gut. I need to *feed.*

Shaking off the haze, I scan the bustling market, seeking my next indulgence.

The rectangular square is packed with vendors, all poised for a long day of haggling. I'm tucked into the south corner, near Margo's Confections—my favorite bakery. It's warm, saccharine aroma is already teasing my senses. I make a slow pass through the new stalls, admiring bolts of fine silk, towering stacks of poorly written romance novels, and—

I nearly laugh out loud.

An actual Hippogriff flits about in the market, its owner boasting about the beast's impeccable breeding. It shrieks, snapping its beak at shoppers, stomping its shoe'd hooves and flapping its wings in irritation.

"As if anyone would buy that temperamental menace," I chuckle, shaking my head.

Then I feel it—heat curling in the air, a thread of desire so potent it tastes like honey on my tongue.

My lips curl into a slow, knowing grin as my gaze lands on her.

She radiates longing, the kind that sings to me and draws me in like a moth to a flame. Even from across the market, I feel it pulling, a thread of anticipation thrumming between us.

And she feels it, too.

I see the moment it catches her, the way her body stills, the slight parting of her lips. My particular brand of siren call has taken hold.

Casually, I drift closer, weaving effortlessly through the throng of bodies. I pause at a nearby stall, feigning interest in a delicate glass figurine of a dancing girl. My fingers brush over the cool surface, but my attention remains fixed on my actual prize.

The scent of Margo's bakery swirls through the air again—chocolate-covered éclairs, strawberry truffles, and her signature apple pie. My stomach clenches in response, my mouth watering at the thought of indulging before I head home.

Not yet.

Instead, I shift toward a stall displaying an array of finely crafted blades, plucking one up to test its balance. It's a sharp and well-weighted blade, but even my fascination with knives pales compared to the scent of vanilla-sweetened hunger lingering in the air.

I place the blade back down, nodding absently to the vendor, and turn—

And there she is.

My breath catches, anticipation thrumming through my veins as my eyes drink her in.

She's petite yet curved in all the right places, wrapped in a cerulean velvet gown that pools past her ankles. A silver diadem sits atop her soft silvery-golden curls, its diamonds catching the sunlight. The ringlets spill down her back, and my fingers itch to tangle in them, to tilt her face toward mine.

Then there are her eyes—pale blue, impossibly deep, watching me with the same intensity I watch her.

And those lips... full, plush, tempting.

She looks ravenous... but, *so am I.*

I drag my tongue over my bottom lip, and her gaze tracks the movement—a delicious feeling skitters down my spine, one that can only be described as lust.

This is going to be fun.

Her caravan is stationed at the south corner of the market square, tucked beside a vendor's stall overflowing with trinkets and an almost absurd number of plants. A quick scan of the counter reveals baubles, dried herbs, and potions neatly arranged, each promising some form of remedy or enhancement. A weathered wooden sign boasts in bold script: *Cures for Every Ailment.* I snort at the claim.

An herbalist *and* healer, then. How *fascinating.*

The caravan is made of rich oak, and its navy blue awning stretches outward to provide a sliver of shade. She's not one of the usual vendors I've seen in the market before, which tells me she's either part of a traveling troupe or entirely on her own. My instincts lean toward the latter—not that it particularly matters.

What does matter is the way she looks at me.

Her pale blue eyes flick over my body, taking in the long onyx curls cascading over my shoulders, the deep crimson of my lips, and the sharp, otherworldly glow of my violet irises. There's heat in her gaze–a slow-burning invitation.

One I gladly accept.

I close in—like the vulture I am—and take her outstretched hand in mine. Her fingers are warm and delicate. She smiles, launching into a soft, melodic spiel about her wares.

"I have a great deal on these tinctures—they pack quite a punch if you're traveling alone. My mugwort is on sale, and this sage bundle is infused with lavender and eucalyptus for extra potency."

She moves fluidly through her sales pitch, polite and poised, but I barely hear a word. Her scent—goddess, her *scent*—is intoxicating. Lust rolls off her in a sweet, heady wave, a fragrance so pure and untainted that it makes my mouth water.

I wonder if she feels this pull as intensely as I do.

She finishes speaking, waiting for me to respond, but I see

the moment her composure falters. Her lips part slightly, her pupils dilating just enough to betray the storm brewing inside her. Her breath hitches, her eyes burning with intensity.

I lift a hand to her cheek, my fingers tracing down the soft curve of her jaw, lingering at the hollow of her throat. A flush creeps up her neck. Her pulse stutters beneath my touch.

Beautiful, just...beautiful.

"Do you want me to stop?" I murmur, though we both know the answer.

She shakes her head, gripping my cloak like an anchor, silently urging me closer.

I oblige.

The moment our lips meet, her sweetness crashes over me, and my hunger roars to life. Energy flows from her, rich and electric, and I drink it in, feeling the gnawing void within me finally—*finally*—begin to quiet. Pleasure coils in my core, sharp and exquisite. But I take only what I need, never more. I have learned control. I *must* have control.

Still, the temptation is always there.

I force myself to break away, letting her energy settle as I press a softer, lingering kiss to her lips. She gazes at me, dazed, her fingers still curled against my neck as if unwilling to let go.

Now that my hunger is sated, I allow myself to indulge in the *other* pleasures she has to offer.

Her hand trails down my chest, her nimble fingers teasing at the fabric of my tunic, and a quiet moan escapes her lips. I tangle my fingers in her curls, tilting her head back for another kiss.

"Should we take this somewhere more private?" I murmur against her skin, my lips tracing a slow path down the delicate slope of her neck.

She whimpers—a sound that sends fire straight through me—before nodding in agreement. The moment my tongue grazes the curve where her neck meets her collarbone, she shudders, her body responding beautifully.

Her grip tightens on my hand as she pulls me toward the caravan door. With a quick flick of her wrist, she flips the wooden sign over, effectively closing her stall for the afternoon.

Or at least for the next couple of hours, I think with a smirk as I follow her inside.

She moves quickly, clearing a small bed of colorful scarves and discarded clothing, but something shifts when I reach the threshold.

A jolt of energy snaps through the air, putting my senses on high alert.

I freeze.

The familiar crackle of magic tingles against my skin—not the pleasurable kind, but the *wrong* kind. The kind that makes my blood run cold.

"What the…" The words barely make it past my lips before the sensation intensifies.

A fucking force field.

The haze of lust is gone, replaced by something wilder, something brimming with anxiety. It rolls off her in waves, suffocating in its intensity.

My instincts scream at me.

Get. The fuck. Out.

She catches me off guard as I turn to leave, slamming me back against the door, her dagger pressing into my throat.

"WHO SENT YOU?!" she yells.

A sharp sting blossoms at my neck, warm droplets of blood

trickling down as she digs the blade in deeper. The message is clear—silence isn't an option. Neither, unfortunately, is my self-preservation because my smart mouth gets the better of me.

"Look... I don't know what kind of kinky shit you're into, and I certainly don't kink-shame, but no one sent me." My voice is a low growl.

She yanks my hair, forcing me to meet her gaze. Her blue eyes are glacial now, narrowed with pure disdain.

"WHO. SENT. YOU."

I sigh dramatically. "Do I need to repeat myself? No one sent me. Do you need your damn ears checked or something? I'm sure there's a potion for that."

The dagger presses in just enough to sting, stealing a small gasp from my lips. Pain can be a pleasure if done right—but this is different. This is a fucking *psychopath* holding me hostage.

"I won't ask again," she hisses. "Who the fuck sent you? Ryvvik? Galean? Fucking Skalanis, for the goddess's sake? WHICH ONE WAS IT?! The timing couldn't be worse—I'll kill them all if they sent you into my goddess-damned—"

"Oh, for fuck's sake, I already told you! No one sent me!" My frustration boils over, my voice rising to match hers. "I'm a succubus for crying out loud! I was just trying to feed!"

Silence.

She stares at me, her grip on the dagger wavering, her wide eyes betraying a flicker of uncertainty. And then—she laughs.

I blink in shock as she drops the knife entirely, clutching her stomach as hysterical giggles spill from her lips. Tears streak her cheeks, and she's shaking her head, gasping between peals of laughter.

"Y-you're a succubus?" she wheezes. "Astraea has a goddess-damned sense of humor. Damn, those *blasted* fates!"

I stand there, seething, waiting for her to get a fucking grip. When she doesn't, venom laces my words before I can stop them.

"Oh, for fuck's sake. I was not sent here. Haven't you ever met a succubus before?" I snap, brushing off my cloak and straightening myself after her minor assault.

She wipes her eyes, still grinning. "I'm so sorry—" a hiccup, another giggle. "I'm not normally so jumpy. Well, isn't this rich? Fate really does have a twisted sense of humor. I'm Nova, and clearly, there's been a misunderstanding."

"You don't say." My tone is flat, punctuated with an eye roll.

She smirks. "You can never be too careful. I've never felt so drawn to someone before; or had my energy drained like that. I thought you were a witch who cast one of those awful amore-mortem spells. And when you were zapped entering my caravan, I thought—well. You saw how that turned out."

Something about her explanation feels... *incomplete*. My jaw clenches, heat flushing across my cheeks. Wrong place, wrong time—the story of my fucking life. And suddenly, the whole thing is so absurd that laughter bubbles up in my throat before I can stop it.

The sheer ridiculousness of it all—her paranoia, my hunger, the fucking dagger at my throat—it's too much.

I practically cackle as I duck my head under the caravan door, ready to get the hell out of here.

Before I can escape, she's beside me again, catching my hand in hers.

"I *am* sorry..." Her voice is softer now, almost sincere. "Would you like a cup of tea? You still haven't told me your name, and I suppose I owe you an explanation." She tilts her head, all wide-eyed innocence.

I know better.

"Ophelia," I say, my tone sharp as I tug my hand free. "No. I have to go."

This time, she lets me. I stride away from her caravan, putting as much distance between us as possible.

"Do come back some other time...Ophelia," she calls after me, her voice tinged with something unreadable.

A shiver runs down my spine.

"I have a feeling you'll be back sooner or later."

"Not likely," I mutter, slipping into the shadows as our three suns begin to set.

✳ ✳ ✳

Nova

Ophelia stalks away, leaving me standing there, strangely bereft. My gaze lingers on the sway of her hips, the effortless grace of her movements. She is, without a doubt, one of the most breathtaking creatures I've ever seen.

I absently brush my fingers over my lips, still feeling the ghost of hers against mine. The heat, the hunger.

I sigh, forcing my thoughts back to the present. Everything hangs in the balance, and if I'm wrong about this—no. I can't afford to be wrong. Not now. Not with her.

Ophelia *is* the one I've been searching for.

Guardian of Bevan.

If the fighting leathers weren't enough of a giveaway, the sheer number of blades strapped to her body would have sealed it. She's a warrior through and through.

A succubus, though—I didn't see that coming.

Does she truly have no idea how rare she is?

It certainly doesn't help that I'm already drawn to her in ways I shouldn't be–more than I have any right to be. There's something about her—something crucial, something I can't quite name yet. She is a piece of a puzzle, one I plan to uncover.

So, I let her go.

But not without a parting shot.

"Do come back some other time... Ophelia," I call after her, my voice laced with teasing. "I have a feeling you'll be back sooner or later."

"Not likely," she mutters, her irritation evident.

A grin spreads across my face, tugging at the corners of my mouth.

Such a feisty little thing.

✳ ✳ ✳

Ophelia

Fury and embarrassment linger, a red-hot flush that creeps up my neck and across my chest. I push forward, determined to distance myself and Nova's caravan as much as possible.

Lost in my thoughts, I weave through the crowded market square of Bevan, practically shoving past humans, witches, and fae alike. It's not fast enough for my liking. The scent of roasted vegtables and smoked fish clings to the air, making my stomach growl, but not enough to sway my path. I take the next alley, ducking into a narrow corridor that reeks of fish from the Celestia Sea.

Leaning against the brick wall of someone's home, I take a moment to catch my breath.

Quickly, I assess my belongings—my velvet pouch of coins is still tucked in my hidden pocket, and both daggers remain sheathed at my back. I reach up, fingers grazing the spot on my neck where Nova's dagger bit into my skin, but the scratch is already healing. The magic of my fae form hums beneath the surface, knitting me back together.

"Fucking crazy herbalist," I mutter under my breath, straightening out my clothing before releasing a deep sigh.

Satisfied that she hadn't managed to rob me blind, I summon the magic of my succubus form. A familiar sensation shudders through me as my body shifts—horns pierce through my onyx waves, my ears elongate to sharp points, and my dark wings unfurl. The veins threading through my obsidian wings shimmer with violet and lilac hues in the last rays of sunlight.

Night has finally fallen. With it, my power swells to its full potential.

I launch into the sky, biting back a laugh when the wind

catches my wings, lifting me higher. The weight of the day loosens its hold as I ascend, rising above the rooftops and tree-tops, soaring toward the stars.

Up here, I can almost kiss the constellations.

The ache of embarrassment eases the longer I stay aloft. In the open sky, I am my most authentic self—untouchable, un-shaken.

I beat my wings hard, angling toward the distant mountains. My home isn't far from Bevan, and as I near the valley, the sight of the lake nestled between the hills calls to me.

I dive, my wings tucked tight against my back; plummeting toward the water, as the wind roars in my ears. My pulse thrums with exhilaration. The lake rushes closer—closer—closer—

At the last moment, I snap my wings open. The wind catches me, yanking me into a glide just above the water's surface. I skim my hand across the lake, fingers trailing through the rip-ples, laughter bubbling from my lips.

Water lilies drift in my wake, their delicate petals gleaming under the moonlight. They take over the lake every summer, and I can't help but smile as cherished memories race through my mind. Seraphina loves them as much as I do.

As I near the dock, I'm unsurprised to find my sister waiting for me, hands on her hips, her silver eyes gleaming with mis-chief. The manor looms behind her, and the scent of dinner lingers.

"There you are," she says, a knowing smirk curling at the cor-ner of her lips.

In all the ways I am dark, Seraphina shines. She radiates warmth, joy, and calm—an effortless siren's gift. Even without magic, people are drawn to her and I consider myself lucky that fate saw fit to bind us together.

I cringe as I remember my earlier encounter. "Sorry, Sera, I lost track of time," I reply, omitting the part where a deranged herbalist nearly slit my throat. I tuck a strand of hair behind my ear, studiously avoiding her gaze.

She chuckles at my expression. "And I'm the damned queen of Eventide." Her eyes narrow in suspicion, molten steel flashing. "What kept you?"

I sigh, relenting, and recount my run-in with Nova. By the time I'm finished, Seraphina is laughing, shaking her head in amusement. I suppose, in hindsight, I did scare the poor woman half to death.

No wonder she fought back.

Still, Sera's laughter fades into quiet contemplation. She picks at the loose threads of her lilac gown, then twirls a strand of silver hair around her finger—a telltale sign that something is troubling her.

"I'm curious, though..." she murmurs, her voice thoughtful. "Not many can resist the pull of a succubus. Or a siren, for that matter."

I arch a brow. "You want to try your luck with the little spitfire?" I tease, tugging playfully at her hair.

She swats my hand away with a laugh. "No, thank you. I think you've convinced me to steer clear. Siren song be damned."

I roll my eyes. "Alright, what's running through your big, beautiful brain?"

She bites her bottom lip—another nervous habit—and exhales. "Nothing. I'm probably just imagining things." She shakes her head again, brushing off whatever thought had taken root. "It's getting late. Dinner's cold by now."

I know better than to press. If something's genuinely bothering her, she'll search for answers on her own.

And she does.

Dinner is a quiet affair, and afterward, as we bid each other goodnight, I watch her head straight for the ancestral library. Predictable as ever. She'll spend hours scouring old texts while I retreat to my room, curling up with a terrible romance novel.

The irony of today's events is not lost on me.

Yawning, I climb the midnight-blue carpeted stairs to my bedroom, practically throwing myself onto the plush mattress. My canopy's dark purples and blacks cast a soothing shadow over me.

I kick off a few pillows, burrowing under my soft black duvet. I don't even care that I'm still in my clothes. Luca will undoubtedly have something to say about the state of my sheets in the morning.

But exhaustion claims me too quickly for it to matter.

The scent of lavender incense drifts through the air, wrapping me in familiarity.

It smells like home.

And with that comforting thought, I surrender to sleep.

✳ ✳ ✳

<u>Seraphina</u>

I'm brooding again. That much is obvious.

Lazily sprawled across my mother's old velvet-covered burgundy chair, I swirl my brandy in its goblet, watching the amber liquid catch the firelight. The desk before me—an heirloom of my ancestors, or so my mother claimed—is a silent witness to my growing bitterness.

With an irritated huff, I push my long silver hair off my chest and rise, stalking to the stone fireplace. I brace my hands against the mantle, staring into the flames, searching for answers that refuse to reveal themselves. The feeling won't leave me. A persistent itch beneath my skin, a whisper at the back of my mind. No matter how much I drink, how many times I tell myself to let it go, it lingers. Guilt always does.

If only Mother had listened.

My gaze drifts back to the desk, to the journal lying open atop scattered scrolls and tomes. Not one of my mother's, but one I found tucked away in our library—a book filled with things she never spoke of. And within its pages, the prophecy that haunts me.

I don't need to reread it. The words are permanently seared into my mind.

One child blessed in moonlight.
One anointed as the morning star.
One locked away, bound 'til she came of age.
In duty, She is bound by great sacrifice.
Truths hidden shall be uncovered.
Her Kingdom stolen by a ruthless crown.
Injustice, strife, and scorned are they.
Long forsaken, a hope-filled whispered dream.

When darkness meets light.
Earth will meet fire.
Water will meet air.
When a Shadowbound Blossom blooms.
A mistake is made.
An offering given will break Her bonds.
Her rage unleashed will set them free.

Queen of Night, She will be crowned.
Bathed in darkness and starlight.
Swathed in death and deep eventide.
Death dispatched, they will cry!
Righteous Morningstar, Astraea chosen!

— Oracle Niahm, High Priestess of Astraea

I shiver.

It's been seven years since we fled Morningstar Palace on the eve of my twentieth birthday. Seven years of questions without answers, of rage and resentment festering in my heart, of guilt that refuses to loosen its hold.

I swipe at the few stubborn tears slipping down my cheeks. There's no time for regrets.

Slamming back the rest of my brandy, I drop into my chair, setting the goblet down with a sharp *clink* against the desk's polished wood. "What am I missing?" I murmur to the empty room.

My fingers move on instinct, flipping through old journals and scrolls filled with the scribbled accounts of priestesses, histories of the fae, and their magic. I know what I'm looking for. And when I find it—a delicate tome bound in deep purple—I skim through the pages until my suspicions are confirmed.

Snapping the book shut, I toss it onto my growing pile of research.

Leaning back in my chair, I prop my slippered feet up on the desk, my mind churning. An elemental witch in Bevan... how curious.

If she is who I think she is...

If the prophecy is what I *fear* it is...

Then, it's only a matter of time before King Elrond comes knocking.

The thought keeps me restless. I linger by the fire until the embers die, unable to shake the feeling that the world I know will change forever.

Eventually, exhaustion drags me to my room, but sleep does not come quickly. I slip beneath the covers, comforted by their familiar warmth, yet my mind refuses to quiet. The day's events loop endlessly in my thoughts, and I nearly reach for the brandy again.

It's a long time before the tension in my body unwinds, before the weight pressing on my chest eases.

And when sleep finally claims me, it is mercifully dreamless.

CHAPTER 3 - CAT & MOUSE

Elrond

"**W**hat do you mean, they've disappeared?" The words leave my mouth in an acidic snarl, curt and visceral. My guards stammer, practically shaking in their armor.

Good.

They should be worried.

"Well?" I tap my fingers against the desk in the center of the room, my gaze cutting across today's security detail. They shift uneasily, twitching under my scrutiny as they wait for judgment.

Bromwick, the newest among them, eyes his comrades warily before stepping forward. "Your Majesty," he begins hesitantly, "we found traces of portal use, but the signature is cloaked. The priestesses are working to track the source, but it's slow going."

I stalk toward him, deliberately slow. He gulps, his already pale complexion darkening with a flush of nervous pink.

Rage simmers beneath my skin, boiling over until I see red.

"Find them! Useless fucking fools!" The snarl that rips from my throat is guttural, reverberating against my study's burgundy and gold-striped walls. "Well? Don't just stand there—*do something!*"

Bromwick flinches, such a pathetic response. It does nothing except further incite my fury.

"Incompetent wretches," I mutter, turning back to my desk. "Must I do everything myself?"

Seating myself in the plush wingback chair, I seize the feathered quill to my left and scrawl out my orders.

"See to it that the square is locked down. No one comes in or out."

Folding the missive, I press my signet ring into the pool of hot wax, sealing it. "Take this and go." I thrust the missive toward Bromwick, who remains an absurd shade of pink. Fucking gingers.

"Oh, and Bromwick?"

"Yes, Majesty?" His pale blue eyes flick nervously to mine.

"If you come back empty-handed, I'll see to it your body is sent to your family in pieces."

I smirk as the delicious scent of his fear wafts through the air. He looks ready to piss himself.

"Do hurry. My patience is wearing thin."

Bromwick nods stiffly, bowing as the rest of his company quickly follows suit. Without another word, they leave me to my thoughts.

The study falls silent, save for the crackling of the fire in the hearth. The quiet feels foreboding, like a chill I can't quite shake. I sink back into my chair, my fingers steepled as I think.

I'll need to tighten my grip on this kingdom. These pathetic displays of defiance are becoming wearisome.

My half-filled glass of brandy catches my eye. I lift it to my lips, taking a long swig, savoring the flavor of crisp apple and spices.

"Father."

I glance up as my youngest son strides into the room. "You wanted to see me?" His midnight-blue eyes furrow with concern.

"Where's your brother?" I don't bother answering his question. Arax should know better than to show up without Lorne—insufferable children.

"He'll be along momentarily." His tone is clipped, gruff.

Childish. Not the behavior I expect from my warlord.

"Fetch him." I ignore how his jaw tightens and his fists clench at his sides.

"Yes, Majesty."

He turns sharply, but not before I catch the flicker of frustration in his expression.

I let him take two steps before I lace my voice with venom. "You and Lorne need to settle your differences once and for all. I'm sick of this infighting."

A beat of silence.

"This is beneath you. Morningstars are supposed to set an example." My gaze hardens. "So—set one."

He jolts—like I've struck him. His gaze hardens, jaw clenching as if he has more to say. Instead, he straightens, clasping his hands and widening his stance.

"It's more than a petty squabble," he says carefully. "Lorne is vicious—ruthless at times—and it's escalating. Covering up his transgressions is becoming harder. It's a problem that could cause bigger issues for the Morningstar name."

"Ruthlessness is key to successful leadership," I snap, narrowing my gaze at my wayward son. "We must flush out the vermin who would see me unseated—assassinated. Lorne's behavior is the least of our concerns."

Arax nods stiffly, bowing once before leaving to search for his brother.

"Oh, and son?" My voice drips with disgust. "Don't forget where your loyalties lie. I would hate to have to use you to set an example. The Morningstar name does not make you immune to consequences."

He stops dead in his tracks. His fists clench at his sides—like he's fighting an instinct he knows better than to indulge.

A beat of silence. Then, without a word, he strides out the door.

Foolish boy.

I exhale sharply, sinking back into my chair. I'm sick of this petty shit. The squabbles, the self-righteous indignation, the fucking childish grudges.

If anything, I admire Lorne. At least he's not afraid to get his hands dirty. Arax, on the other hand? He's overdue for a lesson. Clearly, he's forgotten the rules of being a Morningstar.

My gaze drifts to my desk. The unfinished brandy calls to me —a moth to flame. Then, my eyes settle on the journal I've dissected repeatedly.

I reach for the brandy with one hand, flipping through the journal with the other, taking slow, deliberate sips. There's got to be a way to quell the dissent brewing.

And then—it comes to me—a devilish thought, curling through my mind like smoke. A ripple of pleasure rolls down my spine.

Anticipation is such a bitch.

"Barnaby!" I snap.

The pocket door to the servants' passage cracks open. "Majesty?" my valet answers, peeking inside.

"Summon the council. It's time we put an end to this little rebellion."

Barnaby bows and disappears without another word.

I glance back at the journal, my fingers ghosting over the ink-stained pages. This may hold the key to turning the citizens of Eventide into putty in my hands.

* * *

In no time at all Barnaby has escorted Asmodeus Stormsong, Victor Fintvale, and Elivandria Emberweaver into the room. Each of them looked particularly pleased with themselves.

Imbeciles.

Elivandria steps forward, her black hair glinting in the light of the study. Her burgundy robes swish as she walks toward me, her gray eyes glued to mine. "Majesty." She says, her voice lilting. She bows, followed suit by Asmodeus and Victor.

"Rise," I say sharply. "I called you here to discuss our failure in the square earlier today. Do any of you *fools*—have a contingency plan to get this under control? I looked *weak* out there today!"

I slam my hands down on the desk, startling my council. Each of them flinches, and a smug satisfaction creeps across my face.

The three look at one another, each nervously twitching in their own way. Elivandria's eyes dart, while Asmodeus strokes his graying beard, and Victor? Well, the sniveling fool constantly jerks and twitches, his hands shaking so violently at times he's no longer permitted to drink anything in my presence.

It's tedious—really.

"Well, don't just fucking stand there! I need a solution. This dissent spreads like wildfire, and I grow weary of this cat-and-mouse game. I want action! I demand results!"

My words slam against the walls, the sheer force of them sending a visible shiver down their spines.

Victor, the fool, dares to speak. "Your Majesty—your guards are already searching for the rebel who escaped. Action has already begun. Your men are capable, let them—"

I don't let him finish.

The glass vase shatters against the wall with an angry, splintering crack. Shards rain down in glittering fragments, a satisfying destruction that hardly puts a dent in my rage.

"Am I not a *benevolent* king?" My voice drips with rage, my hands curling into fists at my sides. "Have I not given my time, my resources—my own blood—to this kingdom? The people have no reason to revolt! They walk around freely, their heads stuck in the fucking clouds." I sneer. "It's time to wake them up. I want the rebels rounded up immediately and sent to the gallows."

Silence, infuriating silence.

They stare at me, dumbfounded—mouths slack, eyes glazed, bodies rigid with fear. It's as if they don't even dare breathe.

Finally, Elivandria speaks, her voice unsteady. "Your Majesty, I'm not sure that's such a good idea." She wrings her hands, hesitating, testing me.

Wrong move.

"I didn't ask for your fucking opinion. See that it's done!" My snarl cuts through the air as I lean over the desk, snapping my teeth.

They scatter like frightened mice, nearly tripping over themselves in their haste to flee.

A deep, devilish chuckle rumbles from my chest. Good. Let them be afraid.

Fear is an excellent motivator.

And I plan to shake this kingdom to its very foundation.

CHAPTER 4 - AFTERMATH

Nova

Sunlight filters through the curtains, dappling the hardwood floors in a soft, golden glow. It should be calming, but it isn't.

I sit perched on the lavender plush bench in the reading nook, my fingers curled tightly against my lap, the storm inside me raging far louder than the quiet morning. Sighing, I nervously smooth out the crinkles in my teal-colored gown, turning my attention back to the task at hand.

My eyes scan the parlor, its tan walls sparsely decorated with rich tapestries. Shades of emerald and rich blue, embroidered with golden and silver threads, depict brilliant scenes of our kingdoms.

The tapestries are filled with moments of our history, some long forgotten. My eyes trail down the emerald tapestry, noting it's displays of our goddess, Astraea, and her three beautiful daughters, their hands filled with magic, turned upward toward a solar eclipse. It's a stunning sight, though it does nothing to quell the anxiety filling my body.

Galean will be here soon. Any moment now he will be striding through the door with an update.

Another wave of nausea rolls through me, twisting low in my belly, and I exhale slowly to keep it at bay. I still can't believe Skalanis was so reckless. I can't reconcile it or make sense of it, and the more I turn it over in my mind, the more it frays at the edges, unraveling into something far more dangerous.

I need to tell Galean my suspicions. Need to find out what he knows. Need to figure out exactly what the king is planning.

The weight of it all presses against my ribs, heavy and unrelenting.

It's enough to drive me mad.

As if on cue, Skalanis enters the room, his eyes downcast, his entire posture weighted with the knowledge of just how badly he's fucked up. He doesn't look at me, and I don't blame him.

"Good morning," I say, the words slipping off my tongue like silk, smooth and unreadable despite the fury still clawing at my insides.

"Morning," he mutters, sinking into one of the deep green high-backed chairs. His fingers rake through his dark locks before moving to his beard, a nervous habit I recognize all too well. The silence between us is thick, charged with the tension of everything left unsaid.

We wait, tethered in silence, both of us consumed with our thoughts.

True to his word, at the first chime of the bell, Galean strides through the door. His entire frame is tight with strain, and dark marks shadow the skin beneath his eyes—a sure sign of another sleepless night. He doesn't have to say a word for me to know—things have only worsened.

Galean sinks into the chair across from me, tucking his head into his hands, his entire frame sagging in defeat.

"Galean," I say, my voice laced with concern, the sound echoing through the room. "How bad is it?"

"It's bad." His words are flat, lifeless. He doesn't bother to lift his head and instead groans discontentedly.

Skalanis swears under his breath, stoking the fury already simmering beneath my skin. Anger flares, hot and biting, begging for release. Not now. He's already been chastised. Nothing good will come from reopening that wound.

"He's already sent orders to round up anyone suspected of having ties to us," Galean continues, his voice heavy. "It's only going to get worse. Just last night, twenty people were sent to the dungeons. He did a search-and-sweep of Astra, Nova." He pauses, his tone thick with grief. "I've never seen so many families turn against one another, all just to save their own fucking skins."

I suck in a sharp breath, tears pricking at the corners of my eyes. "Astraea's sake..." I mutter, swiping furiously at my face before they can fall.

Skalanis shifts uncomfortably in his chair, guilt twisting through his expression. I must remind myself that he's already feeling the weight of his choices. But frustration still claws at my insides, making it damn near impossible to focus on Galean's words.

"Skalanis's description is *everywhere* now... there's no chance in hell we're getting him in the palace again," Galean says, his gaze flicking to Skalanis, watching his reaction.

"That's not ideal..." I murmur, heavily sighing as I turn my gaze toward the window.

No good will come of this. I can feel it deep in my bones, an unshakable certainty, raging and relentless—a reminder of how badly this has all gone wrong.

Sighing, I speak, my voice edged with bitterness. "And what, pray tell, do you suggest we do *now*?"

"We're going to have to lay low for now. There's no other course of action. I suggest we pause any more reconnaissance of the palace and the king's movements. Arax is already growing suspicious, and we can't afford another display of recklessness. I've been in this game longer than anyone else... because I *follow* the rules and play my hand at the appropriate times."

He shoots Skalanis a biting look that sends a shiver down my spine.

"I've already apologized..." Skalanis grits out, gnashing his teeth together.

"Apologies mean nothing when lives are at stake. You've set a chain of events in motion that I'm not sure we can stop. If anything, it's only heightened his paranoia," Galean snaps, his patience obviously wearing thin.

My own patience is wearing thin—threadbare and ever-shifting—as I listen to these two fools bicker like children.

"There's no reason to snap at one another! What's done is done." My voice is razor-sharp, cutting through their tension. I narrow my eyes at both but linger on Galean the longest.

"Save it for the war, you two. Are we agreed? We lay low for the foreseeable future? Skalanis, your days of reconnaissance are *over*."

"Agreed," Galean says.

Skalanis eyes me with scrutiny, hurt and frustration etched

across his face. He nods once before looking anywhere but at me.

Fine. If that's how he wants to play it.

"Good," I say, the words edged with irritation.

"How is your progress with the letters?" Galean asks quietly, as if he's gauging my reaction.

"I've studied them, and they seem promising. That's why we're here. Ryvvik is still busy with some mysterious errand, so for now... Skalanis and I will have to be enough."

Galean's jaw clenches, annoyance flickering across his face. "When can you expect his return?"

"Not for some time," I admit.

He considers this, worry creasing his furrowed brow. "Be careful," he says at last, like he's turning the words over in his head before speaking them aloud.

"Always," I mutter, though my focus has already shifted to the one thing that's probably going to send Galean's pulse skyrocketing. "I think I've found her."

"Excuse me?" His voice is sharp, incredulous. His amber eyes glowing with disbelief. "And you're just *now* relaying this information? Why the fuck didn't you tell me sooner?!"

"I've only just met her, for starters, and I'm not convinced it's her. I just have a good feeling, that's all. At the very least, she might be a potential recruit. Only Astraea knows the path she will take." I shrug, feigning a nonchalant attitude.

"Only Astraea knows the path... Do you hear yourself, woman? You sound fucking ridiculous. You've just met her and have no insight into who she is... I swear, you're as reckless as your damn brother." He swipes a hand down his face, exasperation radiating from him.

"Galean..." I warn, displeasure seeping into my bones.

"No! You both are bloody fools. You need to figure out who the fuck she is before you start trusting her with information. I'm not watching this happen. I fucking refuse to go down with the two of you and would rather live a life of servitude to a monster than fail because of misplaced trust. *Get it together, Nova.*" His voice is biting, and volatile.

"Get it together? I haven't given her the first fucking inkling of who I am. I'm not a goddess-damned imbecile," I snap, growing weary of the course of this conversation.

He chuffs, shaking his head as if he's holding back something he's itching to say.

How is it that *my* motives are being brought into question? I'm not the one who fucked up here. I grit my teeth, forcing the words out. "I've done nothing wrong. I haven't given her anything."

He laughs, though the sound is devoid of humor. "If you two keep going down this path, you're going to ruin the carefully laid game we've spent fifteen fucking years working toward. Does their death mean so fucking little to you, Nova?"

I suck in a sharp breath, the words cutting deeper than any knife ever could. "Watch it, Galean." My brother's voice slices through the air, heightening the tension in the room.

Galean shrugs before turning his attention back to me. He studies me intently like he's trying to decide if his words hit their mark.

Smug bastard.

It's enough to make my fingers itch, the urge to slap that self-satisfied look right off his face nearly unbearable. Exhaling sharply, I stand, pacing back and forth in front of the window. Below, the streets of Bevan bustle with shoppers, oblivious to the danger lurking just around the corner.

I sigh, frustration lacing every word. "You have no right to question me, especially not about that. Do you really think their deaths didn't matter? That I'm that callous, cold, and uncaring? If that's what you believe, then you don't know me at all, Galean."

"It's a fair question. You're not the only one who lost someone, Nova." His voice is taut with anger as he shoves himself out of his chair, closing the distance between us in just a few strides until he's inches from my face.

"Galean..." Skalanis warns, his posture rigid with unease.

"You're right," I concede, the irritation in my voice palpable.

He blinks, like I've just slapped him with my admission. So, I say it again. "You're right. You've lost people too—all *good* people who didn't deserve the fate they were given. I'll take everything you said into consideration."

"That's all I ask," Galean says, eyeing me with something that almost resembles newfound respect. "I'll send a raven should anything change."

With that, he gestures to Skalanis, beckoning him forward. I sigh, turning my attention back to the street, knowing full well Galean is about to give Skalanis an earful.

It can't be avoided. It needs to be said. And even I have to admit it's better coming from him than from me. Skalanis never takes me seriously.

So, I sit once more on the plush bench, wringing my hands in my lap. The stakes have risen, and I'd be a fool to think we'll make it through this unscathed.

"Astraea, help us..." I mutter, sending a silent prayer to the irksome creature, begging her to keep us safe.

CHAPTER 5 - SHENANIGANS & THE BOMB

<u>Ophelia</u>

I woke the next morning with a crick in my neck and a drool-soaked pillow.

"Yuck," I mutter, inching toward the edge of the bed.

I feel hungover—an unfamiliar sensation, one I've never formed an acquaintance with. I must have taken more than intended, meaning I'll be nursing a splitting headache for several hours.

Just. Fucking. Fantastic.

Energy drunk—the appropriate term. It only happens when a succubus feeds on a particularly powerful witch or shifter, but—

"Well, fuck me," Sera's voice cuts through my thoughts, making me jolt upright and immediately regret it. The room tilts dangerously. "You look like a herd of hippogriffs ran you over and left you for dead in a pile of shit."

"For the goddess's sake, Sera!" I clutch the sides of my head, trying to steady myself. "Way to give me a damn heart attack!"

I squeeze my eyes shut, willing the room to stop spinning. This shit is for the birds.

"What? Just. WHAT?" I groan, pleading with the universe—or the temperamental goddess who's probably laughing her ass off at my misery—to make it stop.

"Astraea, give me strength," Sera mutters.

Before I can brace myself, she's within arm's reach, swatting at me like an overzealous nanny and ordering me downstairs. Every movement makes my headache worse.

"Move your ass. I'll make a healing tonic for your... mishap," she says, far too smug for my liking. "Someone overindulged last night."

"I didn't *overindulge*." My voice is pure indignation. "I'm not some goddess-damned newly gifted succubus."

She just grins, infuriatingly smug. "You most certainly did if you're in this state."

"I did *not*," I growl.

Her only response is to shove me unceremoniously out of bed. I land with a graceless *thud* on the floor.

At least the rug is comfortable.

"Oh... that's nice," I murmur, sprawled out like a pathetic wretch. The shaggy fabric is soft under my fingertips, and I inch forward until my forehead touches the hardwood floor, relishing the incredible relief.

"For the love of the fates and all things divine," Sera groans, and I can practically *hear* her pinching the bridge of her nose. "You're going to be worthless and wretched all day, aren't you?"

"Yep," I emphasize the *p* for good measure.

She sighs in exasperation before stomping out of my room, finally leaving me alone in my misery. I bask in the quiet, switching sides to cool the other half of my face.

I have no idea how long I lay there, stroking the damn rug like some lovesick lunatic, but I don't even hear her return.

Then—*splash.*

Ice-cold water crashes over me, and I shriek, flailing like a wet cat as I scramble to my feet.

The room spins again.

"For fuck's sake!" I groan, clutching my head. "Was that *necessary*?"

"Yep," Sera replies cheerfully, gleeful as ever. "Totally worth it for that scowl on your face."

I glare, or at least attempt to, but my vision is still swimming.

Exasperation clings to me like my now-*soaked* clothes, squelching with every movement. I *hate* being wet. The way fabric clings, the damp chill, the awful squishing sounds—it's enough to make me gag.

Before I can complain, Sera plops a small vial into my hand. It reeks of something vile, and I grimace, already dreading it.

"Ugh. Bottoms up," I mutter, tossing it back in one go. The taste is *atrocious*, but at least it's over quickly.

"That. Was. Gross." I shudder.

"You'll be thanking me in about ten minutes! Besides, I wanted to talk to you about something, and I think you've just confirmed my suspicions," Sera says in a ridiculously cheery tone for someone who drenched me in ice-cold water.

The audacity.

"Alright. Out. Get out of my room." I point toward the door, already feeling marginally better—though I'd rather die than admit it, especially with her looking so smug. "Let me dress in peace, asshole."

Smirking, she takes her victory and leaves, leaving me to peel off my soaked clothes with a dramatic sigh, as I mourn the state of my favorite leathers. I slip into a pale yellow tunic and simple breeches, tugging on dry boots before grabbing a comb from my dresser. Working through the tangles, I tame my wavy curls into something presentable, my fingers weaving them into a braid that rests like a crown atop my head. Loose tendrils frame my face, giving it a softness befitting a lady.

The room's gas-lit sconces no longer feel like daggers to my skull when I finish. "At least that nasty shit is good for something," I mutter with an eye roll, hurrying downstairs before Sera gets impatient.

I nearly barrel into poor Luca, our ever-suffering lady's maid. Grinning sheepishly, I steady her, mumbling a quick apology before darting past. Luca mutters something under her breath about wild children and propriety, which only makes me snicker.

Moving light-footed through the burgundy-colored hall, I pass towering portraits of my ancestors, their eyes seemingly tracking my every step. It's a ridiculous thought, but I've never quite shaken the feeling. I don't spare them a glance.

At the end of the corridor, I push open the heavy oak doors of our ancestral library. The familiar scent of parchment and leather washes over me, a comforting presence. Towering bookshelves line the circular room, cradling centuries of knowledge —family histories, priestess accounts, and tomes painstakingly collected through the ages.

And in the center, right where I expect her to be, sits Seraphina.

A small smile tugs at my lips; there's something endearing about Seraphina's predictability.

She's hunched over an ancient scroll, absentmindedly twirling a lock of hair between her fingers, so engrossed she doesn't notice me. The candlelight catches on the delicate engravings of the wooden desk she sits at—an heirloom passed down from Lady to Lady of Aetherlight Hall, its corners adorned with intricately carved roses and ivy. Our signet. Seraphina's mark as Viscountess.

While the four territories of Eventide are largely patriarchal, our kingdom is not. Titles pass to the eldest daughter, which —thank the fates—is Sera's problem, not mine. As the second daughter, my duties are different. I serve as Bevan's guardian and second-in-command to my sister, with no desire to wed for prestige or money. Let Sera handle the nobility—I'll stick to my battles.

She's so deep in thought she doesn't notice when the sleeve of her pale pink gown drifts dangerously close to the candle beside her.

I clear my throat. Loudly. "AHEM."

She startles, her quill slipping from her fingers. Wide, bewildered eyes snap up to meet mine.

"I suppose that's payback for this morning," she mutters, clutching at her chest as if to steady her racing heart—utterly oblivious to the fact that she nearly went up in flames.

I smirk knowingly. Her heartbeat is loud, fast—thump-thump-thump-thump—clear as day over the crackling fire and the rhythmic ticking of the grandfather clock in the corner.

Succubus hearing has its perks, sometimes.

"You rang, Your Highness?" I dip into an overly dramatic curtsy, my voice dripping with sarcasm and amusement.

She rolls her eyes at me and spreads several scrolls and leather-bound books across her desk. "Oh, hush... now where did I put—aha! There you are, you sneaky little bastard." She snatches a dainty, journal-sized book wrapped in delicate purple binding.

Curiosity gnaws at me, and I inch closer as she flips through the pages, her fingers tracing the words like she's handling something sacred. "Here it is! Succubi are the strongest at mental persuasion of all fae, though sirens and their call rank a close second. Their power feeds on lust and desire, drawing energy from their prey's life force. Often associated with dark magic, fire, and flight—though that depends on ancestry—"

"Sera, if I wanted a history lesson, I'd have asked Luca for another tutor." My voice is more piercing than intended, thick with impatience.

She lifts her gaze just enough to shoot me a withering look. "Be patient and hush! Now, where was I—ah." Her lips move silently as she finds her place again. "Only the strongest shifters and magic users—particularly elemental witches—can resist a succubus's persuasion. If they're distracted or already thinking lustful thoughts, they're even more susceptible, able to break free only behind strong wards."

She snaps the book shut with a satisfying thud, a triumphant gleam in her eyes.

The weight of her words settles in my chest. I exhale slowly. "You're saying—"

"Yes." She sighs. "Your mystery woman yesterday? Not just any witch. An Elementalist." Her fingers tighten around the book's spine. "And that's rare. I haven't seen one in over seven years. Kind of odd, don't you think? An Elementalist roaming Bevan, of all places."

Damn her. I didn't want to be more curious about Nova than I already was. But now, the questions won't stop turning over in my mind.

"Maybe I should go back and—"

Sera's chair scrapes against the floor as she jolts upright. "For what?" Her voice is a low hiss. "You know as well as I do that if King Elrond doesn't already know about her, he will soon. Don't go looking for trouble; neither of us needs it." Her hands press against the desk, her knuckles pale. "It's not like we're in his good graces. I mean, for fuck's sake, I've avoided court for seven years! The last thing I want is to be summoned, forced to attend, only to be paraded around like a prize mare for some noble bastard to marry. Do not call any more attention to us than we already have."

The way she says it—the sheer, unfiltered exhaustion in her voice—makes something in me twist.

"Astraea be damned..." The words barely leave my lips as I stare at my sister. I knew she hated the idea of marriage. She's always preferred her books, the quiet of the manor. But avoiding court? *Entirely*?

"Sera, you've never..." I trail off, my throat tightening. I'm not sure I want to finish that sentence.

Because I don't want to hear the answer.

For all these years, I understood my role. I traveled, trained, passed my trials and became what our family needed me to be. I thought she had done the same, fulfilling her duty while I fulfilled mine.

Astraea, help me.

She exhales sharply and turns to the fire. The glow flickers over her face, casting soft shadows beneath her eyes. She looks... tired. Heavier. It's like she's been carrying this weight alone for far too long.

And truthfully? She has.

A lump forms in my throat. She never asked for this. No one expected her to take over so soon. No one could have foreseen our mother's death—except, perhaps, one person. I have no proof. Only a gut-deep certainty that he is to blame.

They called it an accident, a careless mistake, one that cost us our mother's life. Our mother's taster was late that night. A mere oversight, they said.

A moment of negligence.

But I know better.

Poison disguised as cinnamon. The very thing she was deathly allergic to. The one thing her cousin—now the King of Eventide—knew better than anyone.

The court whispered of foul play, but whispers mean nothing without proof. And proof is all that matters.

But knowing doesn't change the fact that she's gone.

It doesn't change the image burned into Sera's mind—the sight of our mother writhing, gasping for breath as her throat closed, as her body failed her, as no one—not the healers, not the guards, not the gods themselves—could save her.

It doesn't change the hatred I feel toward the man who now sits on the throne.

And it doesn't change the fact that Sera is playing a dangerous game.

"How could I... after Mama?" Her voice is barely a whisper, small and fragile in a way that cuts me to the bone. "I can't even stand to see his face. I see it all the time. It haunts my dreams, that night, that awful night. He took everything from me, and I know—"

Her breath shudders, catching on a sob, and before she can collapse under the weight of it, I'm there. Wrapping her in my arms, holding her together as she trembles apart.

Seven years. Seven years of survival, of clawing our way forward, just the two of us against the world. And all this time, she's carried this unbearable guilt, an unrelenting ghost that lingers in every unspoken word, every sleepless night. I feel the tight bands of fear constricting my ribs, the icy panic of what this means for us, but I shove it down. She needs me.

"It wasn't your fault," I whisper, my words fierce and unwavering, willing them to be true for her if nothing else. "It never was."

She shakes her head violently, even as she hiccups through another sob, clinging to a belief that is slowly destroying her. Every strangled cry is another crack in my chest, another piece of my heart shattering into dust. She has to know, yet she refuses to release herself from this torment.

So I stay. I wait, letting her grief run its course, holding on as tightly as I dare.

"Thank you… for sitting with me." Her voice is hoarse when she finally speaks again, quieter now, as though exhausted by the weight of her sorrow. She curls against my shoulder like she used to when we were children, seeking comfort where she can find it.

"I know." I rest my chin against the top of her head, closing my eyes. "And I meant what I said. It's not your fault."

She doesn't argue this time. Instead, she nods against me as if conceding just for my sake, as if she no longer has the energy to fight me on it. But I see it in her eyes—the burden she bears, the way court life stole the girl she used to be and left behind a woman drowning in duty. She was never meant to be this. It was never supposed to be her.

There were nights, so many of them, when I returned from Raven's Hall—broken, bruised, barely holding myself together —only to collapse into her arms and sob until there was nothing left of me. She was my one bright spot, my only anchor. And now, I will be hers.

When she finally pulls away, something shifts inside me. Watching her like this, so hollow and grief-worn, my sadness burns away, leaving only one thing behind.

Rage.

As the pieces fall into place, it simmers under my skin, slow and deadly. My silent vow to myself is reckless, dangerous, and utterly inevitable.

I will set this right.

No matter the cost.

CHAPTER 6 - RETRIBUTION, OR SOMETHING LIKE THAT.

Ophelia

I stalk the streets of Bevan with purpose, weaving through the throngs of midday shoppers, my destination clear in mind. Nova's stall is precisely where I expect it—nestled in the south corner of the market, close to an alley I know well. She hasn't spotted me yet, and I intend to keep it that way.

Slipping into the shadows, I press my back against the worn brick, scanning the bustling square with sharp, practiced eyes. My black cloak—crafted by the finest tailor in Eventide—shrouds me in near invisibility. Its enchanted weave allows me an unobstructed view while keeping me hidden from wandering gazes.

She's with a customer wearing an ever-present, disarming smile on her lips as she offers suggestions. I should focus on the conversation, piecing together why she's here and what she might want. Instead, my gaze betrays me, tracing the soft silvery blonde waves of her hair as they catch the sunlight, the delicate way they frame her face like a halo. The pale blue gown she wears clings in all the right places, the bodice catching the light, gemstones winking like tiny stars along the generous swell of her breast.

My breath hitches, heat curling low in my belly. An ache—unwelcome, insistent—stirs beneath my ribs.

I grit my teeth, tearing my gaze away. Fucking hell.

Desire coils through me, my succubus instincts stirring in restless hunger, demanding to be unleashed. My beast—silent but no less present—growls in agreement, thoroughly unsatisfied with yesterday's fleeting encounter. I hate that she has this effect on me. Hate it more that I don't know if I want to fight it.

I force myself to focus.

For several minutes, I watch as she serves customer after customer, her voice warm and confident as she recommends tinctures, spell components, and remedies for ailments I don't bother committing to memory. And then—of all things—I am enthralled by her lecture on jackalope antlers. The damned things are an incredibly potent healing agent. Who knew? Not me. But Nova does, and she speaks of them with such passion that, for the briefest moment, I almost forget why I'm here.

The bells chime in the distance, marking midday. Vendors begin shuttering their stalls for lunch, and Nova waves off her last customer before closing her own. She still hasn't noticed me as she turns, moving briskly through the marketplace, weaving past merchants and street performers.

I follow.

She makes her way toward Trix's Bistro, one of the finest

cafes in Bevan—a good choice. Beatrix Hayfield is a gifted chef, and her establishment is an extension of the more prestigious restaurant she owns, The Trix. It is a perfect spot for an afternoon meal.

I should turn back... but I don't.

She enters the small café, and I linger by a nearby building, watching as she orders her lunch. One of Beatrix's best qualities—at least from my current perspective—is her love for open windows. It makes my job infinitely easier. Through the large panes, I can see Nova's interaction with the owner; her movements are brisk and efficient as she pays before heading to the pickup counter. There's an easy familiarity with how they speak, which only comes from routine. She's a regular, then.

I barely have time to slip into the alley before she exits, her parcel in hand, calling a cheerful goodbye over her shoulder.

Once there's enough distance between us, I follow, taking mental notes of every vendor and shopkeeper she greets. She moves with purpose but not urgency, stopping at her favorite stalls—Margo's Confections and Twila's Fabrics & Necessities. Twila Nightwood, a fae woman nearing her second hundredth birthday, lights up at Nova's approach, and they chat like old friends.

Then there's Marcus Banewood's shop. The old cobbler beams as Nova steps inside, and when she emerges minutes later, she's burdened with several delicately wrapped boxes of slippers. She thanks him with a soft kiss on the cheek, and he pats her shoulder in return, his expression full of quiet fondness.

Nova is well-liked. Respected. Trusted. The realization settles uneasily in my chest.

Given yesterday's encounter, I don't know whether to be

grateful for her help—or wary of it.

But I don't have time to dwell on that.

She moves fast, slipping down an alley I don't recognize. I quicken my pace, my steps light and soundless, shadowing her as she strolls through the narrow passage. There's something intentional in how she moves, like she's trying too hard to appear casual. She finally stops at a plain, unremarkable, brown wooden door that blends into the background.

She smooths her skirt, takes a deep breath, and knocks—three times in quick succession.

I barely have time to react before she turns, scanning her surroundings.

My pulse stutters.

I dive behind a set of wrought-iron stairs to an apartment bathed in soft ecru and ochre. My breath catches in my throat, and my ears strain against the silence. The alley is so quiet that the tension vibrates against my skin, heavy and suffocating.

Damn it. I was careless, and I never get caught!

I hold still, forcing my heartbeat to be steady. There's no way she heard me... right?

After a few agonizing moments, I risk a glance. Nova exhales, seemingly satisfied she's alone, and then—

She slips inside.

I move swiftly, emerging from my hiding place and making my way to the door, but before I can reach it—

A shimmer of light, bright and unnatural, flashes across the wooden surface.

And then—poof.

The apartment vanishes.

I freeze, scowling at the now-empty space where the building stood just seconds ago. A concealment enchantment. Clever.

Whatever Nova is hiding in there, it's something worth protecting.

And in Eventide, secrets are rarely harmless.

* * *

The bells chime again, and I nearly groan. Two hours have passed, and Nova *still* hasn't emerged.

I'm hungry. Irritable. Frustration claws at me, relentless and insistent, tightening around my patience like a noose. I hate waiting. Worse, I hate waiting with nothing to do but think.

The gnawing hunger festers inside me, my succubus stirring beneath my skin with a purr of discontent. She wants energy. I want answers. Neither of us are getting what we need.

Another set of bells rings, signaling three hours have passed.

What the fuck is taking so long?

I grit my teeth, forcing myself to stay put. Every instinct screams at me to move, hunt, and claim what's mine—except nothing here is mine. Not the answers. Not the elusive herbalist wrapped in secrets. And certainly not the warmth of her body pressed against mine, no matter how much I still feel the ghost of it from yesterday.

The fourth chime breaks me. My restraint, and my patience —shattered.

A growl rumbles low in my chest as I storm down the alley back into the thrumming heart of the market. Shadows no longer matter. Caution no longer matters. The beast inside me is prowling, restless, desperate for release.

I move through the crowd like a predator scenting blood in the water.

Lust. Desire. Wanting.

It clings to the air, thick and sweet, winding around me in invisible tendrils. The market is alive with it, bodies pressing close, hands grazing in fleeting touches, heated glances exchanged in passing. It's intoxicating. Overwhelming.

And then—

A familiar scent beckons me forward. Vanilla, thick and warm, tinged with the sharp bite of pomegranate. I knew it before I even saw her.

Nova.

She's standing at her stall again, that same smirk playing at her lips, eyes locked onto me like she was expecting this and expecting me.

Damn her.

I don't stop. I don't think. And I certainly don't give myself a chance to second-guess the primal urge roaring inside me.

One second, I'm striding forward. The next, my hand is tangled in the back of her hair, and my mouth is on hers.

She doesn't hesitate. Doesn't flinch, and meets every punishing kiss. Every nip and bite, she matches with equal ferocity. Her hands grip my tunic, pulling me in until there's nothing left between us—just heat, just the heady rush of power crackling in the space where our lips meet.

It's maddening. Suffocating.

I hate how good it feels, how right it feels.

And I hate how, for a split second, it feels like I might actually need this.

I break away, breathing hard, my forehead pressing against hers. Her fingers are still clenched in my tunic, her breath just as ragged as mine.

"Feel better?" she asks, voice teasing, but there's something else beneath it. Something unreadable.

I exhale sharply, raking a hand through my hair. Damn her. Damn me. Damn this.

"As—illuminating—as that was," I say, clearing my throat, heat creeping up my neck, "I'm not here for... that."

The corner of her lips lifts. "I know."

I blink. "You know?"

She studies me for a long moment, searching, weighing something in her mind. Then, as if she's found what she was looking for, she takes a deep breath and meets my gaze with quiet resolve.

"Yes." A pause. Then, "And I need your help."

* * *

The Ghost

I pull my cloak tighter. It's worn fabric shields me from the elements and prying eyes. Pressed against the rough stone of an apartment building, I angle myself just enough to keep a clear view of the market and the woman who runs the caravan.

She's deep in conversation with a dark-haired warrior, a woman clad in battle-worn leathers, blades strapped across her back like second limbs. Even from this distance, there's a charged energy between them, their gestures sharp, their expressions tight. Though I can't make out the words, it seems as though they're arguing.

I remain still, waiting. Watching.

The herbalist has something I need, and patience has been my closest ally. But as the two women step into the caravan, I grit my teeth, watching my opportunity slip through my fingers.

Damn it.

A quiet curse escapes my lips, the kind that would have earned me a sharp look from my mother. Frustration coils in my gut, but I can't afford to linger.

I turn sharply on my heel and disappear around the corner, my strides purposeful as I head toward Earthtide Alley. The commander should be waiting across from *The Trix*. If he's made progress, I need to know.

The streets are thick with bodies—merchants haggling, shoppers chatting—blissfully unaware of the dangers lurking beneath the surface of this world. They drift from stall to stall, their biggest concern the weight of their coin purses, while I weave through them, moving with the kind of practiced ease that ensures I remain unseen.

When I reach Earthtide Alley, I pull my hood lower, its shadow concealing my face. I lean against the rough brick and wait.

It isn't long before I see him.

The commander moves across the square with the subtlety of a boulder rolling downhill. *The damned fool couldn't blend in if his life depended on it.* He towers over the crowd, his broad frame making him an undisguisable presence. The sight is almost enough to make me laugh—almost.

He stops beside me, adjusting his cloak in a poor attempt at nonchalance.

"Did you manage?" he asks, voice low but gruff.

I sigh, biting my bottom lip. "No. She went inside before I could get close. I'll have to find another way. What about you?"

His jaw tightens, eyes flicking toward the crowd before *The Trix*. "Lost sight of the dragon. He gave me the slip down Night Hawk Street."

I pinch the bridge of my nose, a pulse of frustration throbbing behind my temples. *This has to work. We don't have the luxury of failure.*

"We need a new plan." My voice is sharper than I intended, but the weight of urgency coils tight inside me.

The commander nods. "I know." His tone is solemn, and for a moment, I wonder if he feels it too—that pressure, the ever-narrowing window of time.

I push off the wall, my boots making no sound against the damp stone beneath me. "Let's go. There's no point in standing around now."

I don't look back. I don't have to. The commander follows without question—he always does. He'd follow me to hell and back if I asked him.

We slip through the labyrinth of streets, twisting and turning through alleys known only to those who operate in the shadows. A right. A left. Another right. And then we stop in front of a dead end.

The commander moves without hesitation. His hands rise, fingers weaving intricate symbols in the air, too fast for my eyes to fully track. I've tried to master the motions myself, but they still elude me even after all this time.

Within seconds, the air in front of us shimmers and folds in on itself, a portal rippling into existence. Its surface glows like stardust caught in a swirling current, tendrils of light stretching outward as if beckoning us forward.

The commander turns to me, extending a calloused hand. "Ready?"

His storm-gray eyes flick over me, the molten silver catching the light. There's heat in his gaze, something unspoken but palpable. It rushes through me, unexpected and unwelcome, leaving my pulse slightly unsteady.

I swallow the feeling and place my hand in his, letting his warmth ground me.

"Let's go home," I murmur, stepping into the waiting portal.

CHAPTER 7 - QUESTIONS.... MORE FUCKING QUESTIONS.

Ophelia

I must have misheard her. There's no way she could be this reckless.

"You *what*?" My voice is sharper than intended, my stomach twisting as I hope—no, *beg*—for a different answer.

"Before you interrupt me, you wear your emotions and thoughts on your face. It was easy to read." She lifts a palm in reprimand, giving me a knowing smile. "Yes, you heard correctly, as much as it pains me to admit it. I do, actually, really need your help. But for the love of Astraea, can we please take this inside and away from listening ears and prying eyes?"

A jolt of energy shoots through me, sharp as a lightning strike, but beneath it is a thread of unease. I hesitate, but curiosity tugs harder, pulling me forward. As I step inside the caravan, that familiar zap prickles over my skin—Nova's wards.

The space is larger than it should be—another clever enchantment. She leads me to a sitting area, where a beautifully upholstered settee and chaise lounge sit beside a table already set for tea.

I take a seat across from her, relaxing on the chaise. She pours, and I politely ask for one scoop of sugar and three for cream when she offers. We both nurse our cups, taking slow sips. The blend is perfect—nutty and sweet, with hints of lavender. It's better than anything I've ever had.

"I suppose I owe you an explanation," she says as if reluctant to break the quiet. But I didn't come here to leave empty-handed. So, I nod once.

"I *know* who you are."

The words land like a hammer. My breath stills, my body tense, but she continues before I speak.

"I knew the first time I saw you. But I had to be sure you could be trusted. I don't know how far *his* reach extends, and I couldn't take that risk, you understand?"

"I do." I grit my teeth in response, swallowing the sharp retort burning on my tongue.

Damn this elemental witch.

"I know, that's... sneaky of me, and I suppose it doesn't exactly aid my case. But I had to be sure. I needed to know you were the right choice. When you followed me, I realized today that I can't deny it anymore—you *are*."

She meets my gaze, eyes pleading, her voice thick with emotion.

"I won't pretend or mince words. I'm drawn to you more than I've ever been with anyone else. You do things to me—things I haven't felt in over fifteen years. But this? It's important. Lives are at stake, and this secret I carry will either save us or damn us all if we fail."

I stare at her. My mouth hangs open so wide I could catch flies with it. A secret so big it could *damn us all*? The weight of her words settles over me, heavy as a storm cloud.

What the fuck did I get myself into?

She rises from her seat and moves to a dark cherrywood bookcase, pulling a red book down to rest on its spine. A series of clicks and whirs break the silence as hidden mechanisms come to life. The bookshelf glides effortlessly to the left, revealing a concealed entrance. She gestures for me to follow.

And, unsurprisingly, I do.

We descend, earthen steps spiraling beneath us. The descent is short, leading to a circular chamber at the bottom. Intricate tapestries cover the walls, each a masterpiece of woven history. One shows humans, fae, and witches dancing in worship. Another depicts magic wielders and the Eventide dynasty—a bookcase lines the far side, sparsely filled with leather-bound journals and trinkets.

She pulls a small wooden box from the shelf and places it in my hands. It's plain, unassuming—just simple pine, smooth beneath my fingers.

But it's light. *Too* light. And somehow, that unsettles me more than anything else.

She fidgets with the lock, fingers deftly flicking open the clasp to reveal a pile of letters. "I received these not long ago," she says, unusually solemn. "And I believe they may be from the Queen."

The words slam into me like a physical blow.

"The Queen?" My throat tightens.

Nova nods, then adds, "She was half elemental witch."

I gasp, but her sharp look instantly silences me. There's an unspoken plea in her gaze—*let me finish.*

"She took that secret to her grave," Nova continues, softer now. "Goddess, bless her. She protected more than a thousand of us. But she didn't just die for the elemental witches." A pause, weighted, heavy. "She died protecting her dynasty."

I swallowed thickly as she handed me a letter dated more than twenty years ago. The parchment is aged and brittle, and the ink is faded, but the name it's addressed to is unmistakable.

Esmyra.

My mother.

My fingers tremble as I scan the contents, my stomach twisting into knots. "She was writing to my mother… but why?"

Nova exhales, the answer visibly paining her. "Your mother was her closest ally, and dearest friend. Perhaps… even more if these letters are to be believed. Their bond was a secret —kept that way for their protection. Court politics would have twisted it into leverage." She hesitates, her following words carrying the weight of something irreversible. "And so, your mother did something unthinkable in the service of her Queen. Something forbidden. Something punishable by death."

My pulse stutters. My vision narrows.

The weight of those words sinks into me like lead. There are only a handful of crimes in our realm worthy of execution. We live for centuries, sometimes millennia. Death isn't a punishment doled out lightly. And during Eowyn's reign, darkness had festered like a disease.

I think of The Rising—the chaos, the war, the desperate, brutal power struggles. I think of the atrocities that marked that era; the blood spilled to keep dynasties intact. But none... none could be as unspeakable as what I now fear my mother has done.

My breath turns shallow, and my knees go weak.

Changelings.

A tremor starts in my hands. My stomach churns violently.

The treaty was supposed to have put an end to it—to the practice of stealing human children and replacing them with fae-born ones. The council declared it an abomination, a crime against the natural order, punishable by death.

And yet, I know. Deep in my marrow, I know.

My mother took a child. A human child.

A strangled sound escapes me, half gasping, half sobbing. A pain so sharp rips through my chest that I feel like I'm being split in two.

"Why?" My voice is barely above a whisper, raw and broken. "Why would she do something so... monstrous?"

Nova sighs, stepping closer, taking the box from my hands, and setting it aside. She reaches for me, pressing her forehead gently against mine. It's meant to ground and soothe me, but I can't find my footing in the storm raging inside me.

She pulls back, her fingers trailing my cheek before fully cupping it. Her touch is warm, but there's grief in her eyes.

"I'm so sorry," she murmurs. "But if my assumptions are right..." She hesitates, her brows drawing together before finally forcing out the words. "I believe she saved Queen Siofra's newborn daughter. I believe she rescued the princess from being drowned at birth by stealing a human child to take her place."

The room tilts, but Nova doesn't stop. "I believe she saved the Princess of Shadows—the one blessed with starlight, the savior of the realms, the savior of the elemental tribes. Saved her and hid her all this time."

I can't speak, and I can't move. I can only stare at her.

Nova watches me, waiting and giving me time, letting me process the enormity of what she's just said.

But it feels impossible. Like the world I knew had just shattered at my feet.

Finally, after what feels like an eternity, I manage to force out the question, clawing at the edges of my mind. The one that burns like wildfire through my chest.

I already knew the answer before I asked. I see it in the tension in Nova's shoulders, her jaw tightening, and the way she braces herself.

"I'm assuming," I say, voice hoarse, "you know who this mysterious savior is?"

Nova nods once. "Yes."

She exhales, grimacing before she says, "And you're not going to like it."

*   *   *

My hands are clammy, and my head pounds. It sounds like I'm underwater, voices muffled and distant, like echoes bouncing off the walls of a dream. Someone is calling my name, but the words don't make sense. My mouth is a desert, my tongue dry and heavy, stuck to the roof like sandpaper.

I crack an eye open, only to shut it again as a blinding light sears through me. "What happened?" I groan.

"Oh, for fucking goddess's sake! You're awake." The voice is sharp, somewhere between relief and exasperation. At least, I think it is—everything feels too much. "You fainted. Then you fell and hit your head."

"I. Do. Not. *Faint*," I growl, the mere suggestion chapping my ass more than the pain in my skull.

"Well, you did," she snaps. "And scared the hell out of me while you were at it! Here, you awful wretch, let me apply this. Stay still."

Something cool presses against my forehead, soothing but unwelcome. The grumpy voice is annoyingly familiar.

"Can you stop yelling? And get rid of that light—it's too bright," I mutter.

More rustling. Curses muttered under her breath—quiet movements in the background.

When I open my eyes again, only a few candles flicker. The world is dim and merciful. Nova sits beside me, and I realize I'm lying in her bed.

Of course, it's Nova.

Everything rushes back at once—the hidden stairs, the secrets, the weight of what she told me—the impossible, monstrous truth.

"No," I say, forceful and final.

"Phe…" Her voice is careful, as if I'm something fragile.

"Ophelia." The correction is sharp and biting. Her use of that nickname tastes bitter. "It's not true."

Despite the piercing ache in my head, I glare at her.

Nova sighs, watching me with something close to pity. Then, without a word, she stands and retrieves a single letter. She hands it to me, her expression unreadable. "Read it," she says, her voice thick with disappointment. "And then maybe you'll believe it."

She walks away, giving me space. Space that I desperately need to calm the storm that's raging within me.

I hesitate before gingerly touching the parchment, my fingers unsteady. The letter is addressed to my mother.

I scan the top, searching for anything that might prove this is a forgery. But there's nothing. The fine parchment bears the royal insignia, the ink rich and unfaded. Even I can't deny its authenticity.

It's hers.

I force myself to read.

My dearest Esmyra,

I can never thank you enough for your sacrifice, not just for me but also for Eventide. How will I ever repay you? I am forever indebted to you, the heart of my heart, the light of my life, and the soulmate of my destiny.

You must hide her far from his reach and keep her magic bound. What I ask is monstrous—I know it. A part of her will always be missing; my heart shatters at the thought. But I cannot change course—not now.

Please, do this last thing for me, my love. Her life, and the lives of so many, depend on it.

Without your help, without your sacrifice, Eventide will fall.

She is the last of my line. My little prodigy. Not even he suspects the depth of the power buried beneath her skin.

I have arranged everything. New identities. A haven hidden deep in the mountains, far beyond his reach.

I know you will despise what I say next, but I cannot let you go without protection. Arenhold will travel with you as your guard. I can already hear your rage as I write this, but I beg you—endure it. This is our most dangerous game yet.

This deception must save you. It must.

He has never seen your true form. Our last trick. Our only chance. Aetherlight Hall and this charade will keep you safe. But you must never let your glamour slip. Never.

I am so sorry.

To fake your death is an abomination, but it is the only way.

You are, and always have been, my most precious secret. My beautiful wife, what will become of us?

I am afraid—for you, for me, for my people.

I should have listened. I should have never taken Elrond as a consort. I should have seen it sooner.

I thought I was securing an alliance, appeasing the council with an heir. But now I see—he will never stop until I am his. He already has two strong sons and a fine daughter, which is insufficient. Armies, wealth, land—I have given him more than any Queen before me would've dared; still, he hungers for more.

And he despises my daughter. He fears her because she will inherit this kingdom.

Wretched fool.

His greed will consume us all.

I know, just as surely as I know I love you.

Our deception must hold. It must buy me time to give her a fighting chance—my Princess of Shadows.

I pray you can forgive me. You, and you alone, now hold everything dear to me. My fate, the fate of Eventide—all of it rests in your hands.

Go swiftly, and know that my heart is yours. Now and always.

Even in another life, I will find you. And in the next, I will love you still.

Your heartbroken wife,
Siofra

The letter falls from my fingers. I don't even feel it slip.

My heart shatters into a thousand pieces, and I don't know where to begin picking them up.

Everything has been a lie.

My entire life. Every moment.

It's a cruel joke—some twisted cosmic deception. And I'm the fool who never saw the game for what it was.

Nova's voice comes back to haunt me.

"It's one of you."

One of us is the lost princess, heir to Eventide.

One of us is an elemental witch.

One of us is King Elrond's greatest enemy, and her very existence is treason.

It's too much. Too impossible to believe—yet something flickers at the edges of my mind, a memory from that terrible, fated night.

Mama's tension—the way she wrung her hands as she helped Seraphina prepare for her debut. The clipped, hushed tones between them. The warning for me to behave at my initiation into the guild. A tight hug, a zap of energy, whispered words I couldn't make out. Seraphina's rigid expression as she told me goodbye, the way she pulled away from me and locked me out of her mind.

The pieces snap together, one by one until they form a picture I don't want to see.

"She knew," I whisper. "She knew, and she didn't tell me."

Betrayal crashes over me, raw and unrelenting. The pain in my chest tightens, stealing my breath, and the sobs break free before I can stop them. They come in waves, dragging me under.

Then—vanilla and pomegranates flood my senses.

Nova.

She gathers me into her arms, holding me tightly as I shake apart. "Shhh. I'm so sorry. It's okay. You're okay," she murmurs, pressing her face into my hair. I cling to her, crying harder, cursing her in the same breath. She takes it all, tightening her hold, one hand stroking down my head, fingers threading through my hair.

"You're still you," she whispers. "You're still the person you were ten minutes ago, an hour ago, a day ago. You're still Ophelia."

I don't know how long we stay like this—her singing softly, me wrapped in the safety of her arms. Time warps. Slows. Disappears.

I don't want to leave this moment because I know what waits outside of it. Truths I'm not ready to face.

Nova gently cups my chin, tilting my face toward hers as if sensing me slipping away. Her expression is raw, unguarded. Something unnamed stirs in my chest.

"Ophelia... talk to me," she pleads, tears slipping down her face.

I pull back, shifting to sit at the edge of the bed, my back to her. "I need... time," I murmur. "It's almost too much." I swallow hard, the lump in my throat nearly unbearable.

"To think that Sera—" I choke on her name, pain lancing through me all over again. I take a slow breath, forcing myself to push forward. "I think she knows something," I admit, barely above a whisper.

Nova says nothing at first. The silence stretches, heavy with unspoken thoughts. I can feel her sympathy like a weight between us.

I bristle. I don't want her pity.

"If she does…" Nova finally says. "If she knows already… then she knows he won't stop until the princess is dead."

She hesitates at the last word but doesn't need to say more.

It doesn't matter which of us it is.

We're both in danger. And King Elrond will show no mercy.

My hands curl into fists, fingernails biting into my palms. Beneath the grief, something else simmers—hot, unrelenting, dangerous.

I rise abruptly, striding toward the door.

"What will you do?" Nova asks.

I don't hesitate.

"I'm going to find out the truth." I glance back at her, voice steady, unwavering. "And then, I'll help you. Whatever you're planning—I want in."

CHAPTER 8 - SMILE IN MY FACE
WHILE YOU TWIST THE KNIFE.

<u>Ophelia</u>

Once again, I stalk the streets of Bevan, a singular mission burning in my mind as I leave Nova's caravan behind. I pass my favorite haunts in a blur, too consumed to offer even a nod of acknowledgment.

Fury roils inside me, tangled with confusion, doubt, and the gnawing sense that this is some cruel joke Astraea—the ever-fickle goddess—is playing on me. A princess? Me? For fuck's sake, I live and breathe weaponry and combat, curse better than most men, and wouldn't know what to do with a ball gown if my life depended on it.

"This is insanity," I mutter, shoving past a family of humans. They eye me warily, a mix of caution and fear flickering across their faces, but I don't bother sparing them a glance. My mind is stuck in an unrelenting loop.

Princess of Shadows.

The title echoes through me, relentless and unshakable. It drags me back to a distant memory—to whispers in the shadows, faint voices that once called to me. I haven't heard them in years, not since the eve of Seraphina's twentieth birthday.

The realization stops me cold.

A witch curses as she stumbles into me, but I barely register it. My pulse pounds in my ears. "It doesn't mean anything... does it?" I whisper, my breath hitching. My heart slams against my ribs. "It can't. Please don't let it mean something. For fuck's sake, Astraea, I'll give you anything."

The prayer tastes like desperation on my tongue.

The rest of my time in the market is a haze of turbulent thoughts. No matter how hard I try to suppress them, they coil back, unrelenting, dragging me deeper into memories I had either suppressed or forgotten.

When my boots hit soft soil, I realize I've walked beyond Bevan, past the outer fields. A weary sigh escapes me as I surrender to the familiar shift, letting my power rise. My wings unfurl, and my senses sharpen as I take to the sky. Maybe the flight will clear my head. Perhaps the crisp air will strip away the doubt.

But it doesn't.

It only feels like a cruel twist of fate.

Another silent plea escapes me, thrown into the vast sky like an offering. *Let me be wrong. Let Seraphina be innocent. Let her not be keeping secrets from me.*

My stomach knots, twisting tighter with every beat of my wings. I dip low, skimming the outskirts of the lake surrounding our land. My thoughts are too loud and too consuming.

So much for clearing my head.

As I land, my boots slam against the dock, and I'm already storming toward the house. Anxiety bleeds into anger, and I let it consume me, feeding the fire inside.

If Seraphina is hiding something, I will uncover it.

The truth always comes out. Nothing can stay buried forever.

* * *

She's sitting at her desk again, wholly engrossed in the scroll before her, oblivious to the storm brewing in my chest. I step closer, fists clenched at my sides, rage simmering beneath my skin.

She looks up, excitement shining in her eyes. "You're back! I've already taken care of our invitations to the Celestial Light Festival. You only have to choose your cloak and gown. I know, but we haven't attended one in ages—it'll be good for us to be present. Besides, it's an age-old tradition and the perfect ceremony to ease back into the rhythm of things—an important time to reflect on the fruits of our labor as we move toward the harvest. Or something like that."

I nearly snort. As if I give a damn about some festival or a gown, I'll wear once before it collects dust in my closet. She moves a few things on her desk, but my silence and scowl are likely forgotten. I don't acknowledge her plans. I don't move. I simply wait.

"Ophelia..." She trails off, finally registering my rigid stance, the tension radiating from me.

A frown. Confusion next. Then, for the briefest flicker of a moment, fear.

"What's wrong? What happened?" she asks, her voice unsteady as she drops the scroll onto her desk.

"How long?" I ask, my voice low and controlled.

"Ophelia—"

"HOW. LONG?" I demand, each word razor-sharp.

She looks away, walking straight to the fire, and her back turns to me.

The roaring in my ears nearly drowns out her whisper.

"You went to see her again, didn't you?"

"You don't get to ask questions. Not about *that*." My voice is a snarl, my succubus purring in agreement with my fury. "How. Fucking. Long?"

She sighs, then turns, fresh tears spilling down her cheeks. The grief rolling off her is suffocating.

"I can't explain it," she admits. "It was more of a feeling. Things about our life here never fully made sense. Haven't you ever noticed? We never had friends in town. It was just you and me. Mama kept us so secluded that we never went to school or entered Bevan's markets without those ridiculous cloaks and face coverings. Yet, we had the finest tutors the best education money and status could buy. I understood that. But something still felt... wrong."

She pauses, blinking away tears before continuing.

"So I searched. I scoured every scroll, tome, and journal I could find in our archives. And I found the scriptures years ago —hidden, tucked away. I think she meant to protect us from them. They spoke of the power of children blessed by moonlight, death, shadows, and the goddess herself. Of one child, bound by magic, who would one day break the curse and wield it all."

She swallows hard.

"That night," she whispers. "That goddess-damned awful night. I knew something was wrong. Mama was more anxious than usual, obsessing over my debut, pushing you to leave. I asked her about my suspicions—about a passage I'd found. And she lied! She lied right to my face, knowing I'd feel it. She told me I had a wild imagination. That tonight was meant for joy. That we'd be reunited with the court by the king's demand, his cousins finally returning. A beautiful match, she said. A wonderful celebration."

Seraphina laughs, but there's no humor in it.

"But I *felt* it. The rage she tried to hide. The heartbreak. The disgust."

She turns, pulling a book from the shelf, flipping through the pages with practiced precision, stopping at a marked passage. "It's a prophecy," she says, extending the book toward me.

I don't take it right away. The weight of the last few hours presses on me, and every word I've read today only seems to unravel everything I thought I knew. I stare at the open book, pulse-pounding, hesitation gnawing at my gut.

She inches it closer, sensing my reluctance.

Finally, I take it, my hands trembling as my gaze catches the words.

"One child blessed in moonlight.
One anointed as the morning star.
One locked away, bound 'til she came of age.
In duty, she is bound by great sacrifice.
Truths hidden shall be uncovered.
Her kingdom stolen by a ruthless crown.
Injustice, strife, and scorned are they.
Long forsaken, a hope-filled whispered dream.

When darkness meets light.
Earth will meet fire.
Water will meet air.
When a Shadowbound Blossom blooms.
A mistake is made.
An offering given will break her bonds.
Her rage unleashed will set them free.
Queen of Night, she will be crowned.
Bathed in darkness and starlight.
Swathed in death and deep eventide.
Death dispatched, they will cry!
Righteous Morningstar, Astraea chosen!"

—Oracle Niahm, *High Priestess of Astraea*

I slam the book shut with a violent force, the sound cracking through the room like thunder. My heart races, and my stomach twists. Every word burns, like a truth I can't swallow, a future I can't bear.

"This is insane," I snap, my voice tight with disbelief. "Do you see this? This is the stuff of legends, not our reality. We can't—"

"It's not just a fairy tale, Ophelia," Seraphina interrupts, her voice sharp, her gaze unwavering. "I can feel it. Mama was terrified. This is more than some ancient myth. It's real."

Her eyes are wide, and I can see it in her—a flicker of something deep, the weight of too many thoughts she doesn't want to voice.

"I don't care if it's real or not, Seraphina!" I lash out, the words coming faster than I can think. "Look at it! Look at what it says. You think this applies to us? That this nonsense somehow makes sense for what we're going through! This is a curse written in riddles, not something we can just… interpret!"

Seraphina flinches, and I regret the harshness in my tone, but I can't stop the anger bubbling up. The anxiety too. I'm nervous that this prophecy means something, scared that it doesn't. Nervous, about all of it.

"You don't get it," she spits, her voice rising with equal force. "We can't just ignore it! What if it's the key to everything? What if it explains why all of this is happening to us? Why we keep… walking into things we don't understand?"

"I don't know!" I shout, throwing my hands up. "Maybe it's a warning. Maybe it's a curse from gods we don't even know, written to screw with our heads. We don't—" My voice cracks, and I stop, my breath coming too fast. "We don't even know what it means yet."

"I don't care what it means!" Seraphina's voice breaks, her hands gripping the edge of the table as she leans in, eyes fierce. "You can't just dismiss it like that. Mama was terrified for a reason, and I—" She stops, swallowing hard, trying to hold herself together. "I think it's about us."

I shake my head violently, backing away from her. "No. No way. This isn't us. I won't—"

"You're scared," she accuses, her voice low but sharp as a dagger. "You don't want to believe it, because that means we're part of something bigger. Something we don't control. But I'm not ignoring it. I'm not pretending this isn't real."

I want to scream. To shake her and make her understand that I'm not truly scared. I'm angry. I'm angry that this whole mess—this entire fucking nightmare—is coming to us with no warning, no understanding, and we're just supposed to *accept* it?

"I'm not scared," I say through gritted teeth. "But I'm not going to stand here and let you drag me into this bullshit."

Seraphina's face hardens, her eyes burning with frustration and confusion. "You don't get it. I'm not dragging you into anything, Ophelia. I'm trying to find a way out of this madness. But you... you're refusing to see what's right in front of us."

The words hang between us, sharp and cutting, both of us breathing hard, on the edge of something neither of us wants to face.

"I can't ignore it," Seraphina says softly, her voice strained, but firm. "I can't just pretend we're not involved. And if you won't see it, I will. I won't let this prophecy destroy us. I can't."

I want to snap at her again, push her away, and deny it all. But I can't. Something in her voice, in her eyes, makes me falter. It makes me wonder if she's right and if they're *both* right.

"I don't know what to believe anymore," I mutter, shaking my head in frustration. "But I'll be damned if I let this define us."

We stand there in silence, each of us breathing heavily, staring at the book between us. Neither of us is willing to back down.

✳ ✳ ✳

After a long night of disbelief, frustration, tears, and reluctant forgiveness, Seraphina finally granted my request. I'll send a missive to Nova, inviting her to tea—though even that small concession came with heavy reluctance. Seraphina barely tolerated my decision, her lips drawn tight, her gaze filled with doubt. The tension between us still crackles, thick with unspoken words and a deep, gnawing suspicion that refuses to let either of us rest.

She's not telling me everything. I can feel the way her energy shifts, the undercurrent of fear that laces her words whenever I mention Nova's name. And I can't deny the nagging doubts of my own, a seed of uncertainty about Nova that I've been trying to ignore. The tension from our earlier argument lingers in the air, and the remnants of anger and fear are still heavy between us. But it doesn't matter. She can't stop me, not when I've already made up my mind.

The letters Nova carries will convince her of our mother's treason, and whatever fears she harbors will soon be put to rest. Or so I tell myself, though doubt lingers—doubt that I'd rather not acknowledge. A flicker of that same uncertainty burns in my chest, but I force it down.

Faint bells chime in the distance, signaling the end of another day in the market. Nova will be here soon. The thought should bring some semblance of relief, but it gnaws at the back of my mind like an unhealed wound, reminding me of the things we haven't resolved.

Listlessly, I make my way back to the library of Aetherlight Hall, drawn there by habit more than anything else. But as I step inside, I can't shake the feeling that everything is teetering on the edge of unraveling. The air is heavy, thick with anticipation and unresolved tension—one breath away from shattering completely.

How often have I walked through these doors, never knowing the depths of my mother's secrets?

Countless hours were spent at her feet as a child, playing as she wrote her endless missives to the palace. Years of watching her pace before the fire, lost in thought, her fingers absently skimming the spines of ancient tomes.

I thought I knew her.

I settle at the grand desk that has served generations of Aetherlight Hall. *Was that a lie, too?*

My fingers trace the intricate carvings—roses and thorns, curling leaves kissing the edges of the wood. A sharp ache twists in my chest. *No longer of roses and thorns, but of shadows and death.* The thought stabs deeper than I expect like a piece of my soul is fracturing in two.

It's astonishing how something so simple can shatter even the most ironclad convictions.

Anger flares in my gut, hot and unyielding. Fire licks at my fingertips before I realize what's happening. A startled yelp escapes me as I snatch my hands away from the desk, and the flames sputter out almost instantly.

What the hell was that?

I look down, my breath catching. A scorched mark mars the wood where my palms had rested. But something else catches my eye—a tiny sliver of raised wood, like a thorn protruding from the desk's surface.

I reach for it, carefully peeling the thin panel away, nearly gasping at the sight. I've uncovered a hidden drawer, one that stirs something deep in my soul at the sight of it. Instinct begs me to push it in, and I do, watching in fascination as it springs open. I reach my hand inside, feeling around slowly.

A handful of objects rest inside the hollow space. I first pull out a miniature portrait of Seraphina and me as children.

A lump forms in my throat.

I set it aside and reach for the next—my breath stutters, and I nearly drop the frame.

My mother.

But not as I remember her.

In this painting, she is radiant, her long, blonde waves cascading past her waist, her pale blue eyes tinted with silver. Her once angular features are fuller, and her cheeks are soft with a rosy glow.

My fingers tremble as I press them to my lips, then lightly to the painting, tracing the mother I thought I knew.

Then, my gaze shifts to the second woman in the frame.

My stomach drops.

I don't need anyone to tell me who she is. I already know.

Queen Siofra.

She stands beside my mother, clad in an indigo gown strewn with stars, her dark raven hair wound into intricate coils. A diadem of moons circles her head, a crown of celestial silver.

But it's her eyes that steal my breath.

They are almost identical to mine.

Lilac-colored irises stare back at me, and my heart thunders so violently that I almost drop the frame.

No! No, no, no.

I force myself to look again, my fingers gripping the portrait like a lifeline. But the truth doesn't change.

"Fuck," I whisper, my voice shaky. I set the painting down on the desk as if it burns.

Panic surges inside me, but I shove it down, forcing my mind into order. I reach into the drawer again, determined to uncover every last secret.

My fingertips brush against something soft. A neatly folded slip of paper was buried at the back of the drawer—a letter.

I break the seal with trembling hands.

My dearest Ophelia,

I write this on the evening of your departure to Raven's Hall.

I'm sorry, my love—what I'm about to tell you will surely break your heart and shatter the illusions you've held your entire life.

There is no easy way to say this. None that will make your pain easier to bear. So, I will rip the bandage off quickly.

You are not who you think you are.

You are not Ophelia Aetherlight, Lady of Aetherlight Hall.

You, my darling girl, are so much more.

You are the daughter of my heart but not of my blood.

Your real name is Princess Ophelia Xamira Morningstar–heir to the throne of Eventide. Princess of Shadows. Heir to the Morningstar line, and future Queen of Eventide.

I know, my love. This is a bitter tonic to swallow. I know the questions must be swarming in your mind, the betrayal you must feel.

But this truth—however painful—can never change my love for you and your sister. It does not diminish you. It does not define you.

I may not have given you life, but you are still my daughter. You always will be.

I had prayed that I would have time to tell you this myself.

But I fear I have made mistakes. I have misplayed this game, and the time has come to pay for it.

If you are reading this letter, then I have failed.

By now, the news of my death will have spread across the land.

Daughter, listen carefully.

Follow the shadows.

The whispers you pretend not to hear, the darkness that calls to your soul—follow it.

It will lead you to the royal cemetery, a fountain revealing itself under the full moon's light.

There, you will find some of the answers you seek.

I love you, my Ophelia, more than life itself. I am so proud of the woman you are becoming and the leader I know you will be.

All my love,

Mom

The letter falls from my hands.
Silence rings in my ears, deafening and vast.
I squeeze my eyes shut, my breath coming fast and shallow.
Princess of Eventide.
Future Queen.
The words coil around my throat like a noose.
The world tilts beneath me, shifting on its axis, and I know—
nothing will ever be the same again.

CHAPTER 9 - REBELLION & LEGIONS

<u>Ophelia</u>

I've been staring at the fire for what feels like hours. Maybe it has been. Time seems to have stopped.

This feeling—this crushing weight—is familiar, yet more profound than I've ever known. The pain is raw, an open wound I can't begin to mend. I don't know what's real anymore. Is this what insanity feels like? One moment, the reality is solid beneath your feet. The next, it crumbles, piece by piece.

The heavy doors creak open, but I don't turn my head. Footsteps echo softly against the stone floor, drawing closer. The scent of vanilla drifts into the room.

Nova.

I barely react when she sinks to the floor, leaning against my legs. The simple, grounding gesture unravels me. Tears spill over, silent at first, then unstoppable. In an instant, Nova and Seraphina are in front of me, their voices urgent, their questions a blur. I can't hear them. It's like I'm underwater—distant, detached.

A sharp crack snaps me back. My head jerks to the side before the sting even registers.

"What the fuck was that for?" I snarl, a growl rising in my throat.

Nova meets my glare without flinching. "Now that I have your undivided attention, I'll remind you that you invited me here. Remember? Tea in the library? I was to bring important letters—"

"Oh, fuck you and your damn letters!" I snap, pushing out of my chair and storming away.

A hand clamps around my wrist, yanking me back. I stumble into another chair, and before I can react, Nova's hands are gripping the armrests, caging me in. Her blue eyes burn with fury, ice-cold and unyielding.

"I don't know what the hell happened in the last twenty-four hours," she hisses, "but for the love of the goddess, get a fucking grip."

I say nothing.

A sharp inhale from Seraphina draws my attention. I follow her gaze—straight to the letter.

The letter I didn't burn.

Shit.

I was supposed to watch that goddess-damned thing turn to ash—to carry that secret to the grave. Let the world go on believing the princess died as an infant.

"Ophelia..." Seraphina whispers, rushing toward me. She wraps me in a fierce embrace, but everything inside me screams to escape—run, fly, and disappear.

Nova swears under her breath as she paces, skimming the

letter. I pry Seraphina off and exhale sharply. I should have burned it.

A minute passes. Then another. When Nova finally looks up, I see the understanding and the sympathy.

A humorless laugh escapes me. "Well," I murmur, "looks like you've got your long-lost princess after all."

Their exchanged glance spells out my future. I see it in Nova's eyes—what she wants, what this means for her people. For *all* of our kind. Restoring me to the throne would change everything.

"Can you two stop looking at each other like that?" I snap. "I know exactly what you're thinking, and the answer is no."

"You don't understand—"

"No, Nova, I do understand." My voice is steel now, edged with a bitterness I didn't know I possessed. "And I don't want it. I don't want a throne. I don't need a fucking crown. So no. We burn that letter, and we forget this ever happened." I sink lower into the chair, arms crossed like a petulant child.

Seraphina whips around, silver eyes blazing. "We are NOT burning that letter, Ophelia."

Her conviction startles me.

"You'd rather I... what?" I throw my hands up. "March into the palace, kill the king, and take a crown I didn't even know existed until yesterday? Do you hear how insane that sounds? How impossible?"

The silence stretches between us. Another glance flickers between them—one I can't decipher.

Nova sighs. "It's time you knew everything. What's really happening. What's out there."

I pinch the bridge of my nose, already exhausted. "I won't like what you're about to say, will I?"

"No," they say in unison.

I groan, letting my head fall back against the chair. "For the love of the goddess."

* * *

Nova

I pour the tea mostly because I need something to do with my hands. One scoop of sugar and three spoonfuls of cream for Ophelia, two for myself, and three for Seraphina. I grimace, handing Seraphina her overly sweet tea.

Luca, the feisty redhead of Aetherlight Hall, has outdone herself again—biscuits, sandwiches, and cakes arranged in perfect rows. She fusses over Ophelia, piling her plate high and murmuring she's too thin. Ophelia humors her, taking a bite of a biscuit with a soft thank you before Luca finally departs, leaving the library in expectant silence.

Ophelia's eyes find mine the moment the door clicks shut. Those violet irises—so striking, so relentless—hold me in place, stripping me bare. No one has ever made me feel so exposed, as if she sees past my words and walls straight into my soul. Heat pools low in my stomach, and I must remind myself to breathe. Focus, Nova.

I tear my gaze away, fidgeting with my teacup. I know what I'm about to say will change everything. Maybe even destroy whatever fragile trust we've built. But there's no turning back now.

I sigh and start at the beginning.

"After the Queen passed, things... worsened. I'll never under-stand why she chose him as her consort, not when the man despises our kind. More than that, King Elrond fears us—fae and witch alike. He's spent years trying to erase magic. The last five years have been the worst." I glance between them, gauging their reactions.

"He can't possibly ban magic use," Seraphina says, disbelief furrowing her brow. "Why would he even try?"

"If my sources are right..." I hesitate, but only for a moment. "The Queen cursed him the night she was murdered. A power-ful curse—one so potent it took her life as payment. It's only a rumor, but Elrond was one of the strongest warlocks in the realms before that night. That's how he rose to power and se-cured his place as consort."

Ophelia's gaze sharpens, flicking between Seraphina and me. Neither of them knew. I shouldn't be surprised. They've been away from court for too long.

"The curse stripped him of his magic," I continue, "and it set off a ripple effect. He's aging faster than he should be. A man who should be in his prime is now a decrepit husk. My source tells me he weakens by the day. His son, Prince Lorne, is al-ready preparing to take his place."

Ophelia's eyes narrow. "Your source?" Her voice is laced with suspicion, her fingers curling around the arms of her chair.

I meet her gaze and hold it. "Galean Hawthorne."

Recognition flashes between them. Their full attention is mine now.

"Galean is my informant," I explain. "He's in my faction of the rebellion, stationed inside Morningstar Palace. We gained a foothold in the courts, slowly turning nobles against the king. The goal was simple—gain Prince Arax's favor, convince him to help us overthrow Elrond, and… remove the firstborn from power." I keep my voice even, but the weight of the words presses on my chest.

"But?" Ophelia demands, her grip turning white-knuckled.

"But that was before the killings started." A bitter laugh escapes me. "Not random at all, despite how they were made to look. Each victim had something in common—magic, an animal form, abilities beyond the ordinary. He's making a statement. A warning. He's preparing for war."

Seraphina stiffens, the blood draining from her face. "So that's what's been happening…"

I catch the shift in Ophelia's expression, the storm building behind her eyes. She's putting the pieces together—realizing Seraphina knows something.

"You've heard about the killings?" I challenge, tilting my chin up, daring her to lie. The protectiveness in my chest takes me by surprise, but I shove it down.

Seraphina hesitates, then nods. "Whispers in the markets, in the women's cottages when I help with childbirth. I thought it was just rumors. You know how people talk in Bevan."

"I wish it was." I exhale slowly. "A month ago, Galean left a box of letters on my doorstep. He wouldn't tell me where they came from, only that I needed to read them. I thought he was losing his nerve. Before I could confront him, he vanished back to the palace." My voice tightens. "So, I read them. Devoured them, more like. And when I saw what they contained, I had no choice but to come searching for you."

Ophelia holds my gaze, something shifting in her expression. I press forward before I lose my nerve.

"We need you. Eventide needs you. You don't want the crown, and that's exactly why you should have it. You've always protected the people of your town. When the time comes, you'll do it again. Your power is waking, Ophelia. I can feel it." I flick my gaze to the desk—its charred edges a stark reminder. "You feel it, too. It's whispering to you, waiting to be released. The binding—"

"The letter all but confirmed that." She cuts me off, voice tight. "You read it." She exhales sharply. "Doesn't change the fact that I don't want the damn crown."

"No," I say softly, "but if nothing changes, people will die. Magic will die. He will burn everything to the ground."

She shakes her head, refusing to accept it.

Frustration flares in my chest. I slam my cup down, tea sloshing over the rim. "You don't understand what's coming. What I've seen—" A violent shiver rolls through me, the vision clawing at the edges of my mind, sickening and relentless. My breath shudders.

Ophelia and Seraphina exchange a look, concern bleeding into the silence. Then Ophelia turns back to me, her voice low. "What have you seen?"

I swallow hard, the words like iron on my tongue.

"Death itself."

* * *

Ophelia

The room was so silent that I could hear a pin drop; the air was charged with something I couldn't name.

"Death itself?" I echo, the question slipping past my lips before I can stop it.

A gray pallor washes over Nova, and shivers wreak havoc on her body. She seems distant, detached, as if something unseen has its grip on her. Her eyes glaze over, the weight of whatever she's seeing pressing hard against her.

"What do you see?" Seraphina asks softly, her voice laced with concern. She steps closer, compelled by an innate compassion, and takes Nova's hand.

When Nova speaks, her voice is almost spectral and layered, as if she carries the echoes of many within her.

"Darkness. Death incarnate. Destruction and chaos reign freely. Creatures consume us, and our power—extinguished. They take many shapes: winged, scaled, furred. All of them, inky darkness, spilled from a fissure in their world—one caused by a curse. A curse that lingers over the Queen of Night, over the imposter King who sits on a stolen throne. Only when the debt is paid will peace and balance be restored. Five realms, five lands to protect."

A groan escapes her, and she bends forward, her body contorted at an unnatural angle. Seraphina gasps as Nova's fingers tighten around hers with inhuman strength. Her eyes snap up, solid black, locking onto me.

The hair on the back of my neck rises.

A distant wind howls, thunder rattles the manor, and lightning streaks across the sky, illuminating the room in an eerie flash. The temperature plummets and my breath is visible in the frigid air.

Then Nova smiles—a twisted, sinister thing.

She lifts a single finger and points at me.

"Morningstar, hear us. We shall have you. We will lay waste to everything you love. We will cross oceans, time, and space to hunt you. Princess of Shadows. Queen of Night. Your blood will taste sweeter than our vengeance. We are death, and we are legions. You cannot stop us. Join us. Wield us. Lead us, Queen of the Damned. Lead us, and you will know power without limits. Lead us and destroy the usurper. JOIN US, OR WE WILL DESTROY YOU!"

The last words rip from her in a scream so chilling it feels like the walls themselves recoil.

She gasps, her chest heaving as though she's drowning in the return of her breath. Her eyes roll back, and her body collapses into the chair.

My heart slams against my ribs, but I can't move. Fear has turned my limbs to stone.

Seraphina is already in motion, breaking a vial of smelling salts, waving it under Nova's nose, cursing under her breath as she does. Nova stirs, her face an alarming shade of green, and then—

She retches.

Right onto my boots.

I curse under my breath, kicking them off and shaking the bile into the fire before setting them by the hearth.

"Sorry," she mumbles, slumping back into the chair, the first traces of color returning to her cheeks.

Seraphina gives me a pointed look that all but says *quit being an asshole.*

"It's fine," I say, though the smell still lingers.

Seraphina moves to fetch ginger water, but not before making a few *obscen*e gestures at me, urging me to get over myself.

I roll my eyes but kneel beside Nova anyway, though sickness is far from my domain. She sags against the chair, exhaustion weighing heavy on her.

I smooth a hand over her brow, fingers threading into her damp hair.

"Are you okay?" I whisper, careful not to speak too loudly. Just in case she has a headache.

"I'm fine." Her voice is hoarse. "Weak from the vision, but I'll recover." A flush of embarrassment colors her cheeks. "I really am sorry about your boots."

I huff a soft laugh. "Those old things? They'll be fine."

She sighs, nestling against me. I allow it, though the feeling of her warmth against me is dangerous in ways I refuse to examine.

After a moment, she speaks again.

"I'm almost afraid to ask... about what I saw. After I blacked out..."

A chill creeps down my spine, the phantom sensation of spiders skittering over my skin. The memory of her voice—of *them*—still coils tight in my chest. But I know she needs to hear it.

"You were... possessed," I say finally. A shiver racks her frame. "And there's truth in your vision, as much as I hate to admit it. You spoke of legions of death."

She pales again, swallowing hard. "The stench of decay is still in my nose. I can *feel* the remnants of that thing that stole my body. I've never felt anything like it—the weight of death and darkness pressing in. I don't know what it was, and I never want to meet one. Ever."

Her fingers clench my arm, her fear pouring off her in waves. I say nothing. I don't *need* to. Whatever those things are, whatever she saw—it's real. And it's coming.

The stuff of nightmares.

And it's then that I realize—*freedom means nothing if we're all dead anyway.*

I exhale, pulling her tighter against me.

"I'll help you," I whisper.

She laces her fingers through mine, squeezing once in acknowledgment. "Looks like I should welcome you to the rebellion," she murmurs drowsily. "What a fine introduction you've had."

I snort at that, smoothing a hand down her back. I should move her, should keep a safer distance, but I don't. She's quickly becoming my favorite distraction—a problem, though not one I can afford to dwell on.

So, instead, I hold her. Press a lingering kiss on her forehead, her temple, her hair. Another trinket for another box, to be examined when the world isn't on fire.

I close my eyes, exhaling sharply.

"Well, Astraea," I mutter under my breath, "you fickle bitch. I suppose I'll play your games after all."

CHAPTER 10 - SHADOW GATE'S
& NEW FRIENDS

<u>Ophelia</u>

The following week passes in a blur. At Seraphina's insistence, Nova has taken up residence in one of the guest rooms—one of my favorites, bathed in deep black and midnight blue. The two of them have become fast friends, a development I'm still not sure I entirely like, considering the amount of mischief they've managed to stir up in just a few days.

Our days remain much the same, but I find myself anticipating our evenings in the library most. Hours spent pouring over old texts, searching for any clue about the deathlings—what they are, where they came from. The good-natured bickering between us feels effortless like the missing piece of a puzzle slipping into place. Nova is the missing piece.

Then, there are the stolen moments—time spent worshipping one another, losing ourselves in sweet torment I never want to end. It's madness. She is madness. And yet, she is the best distraction I've ever had. Even now, I feel the phantom touch of her fingers trailing over my skin, seeking that one spot that unravels me. My breath hitches, the memory sending molten heat rushing through me.

Across the room, she smiles—wicked, knowing—and winks. The wretch. She knows exactly what she does to me, and I'd wager she does it on purpose.

Suddenly, a vision crashes through my senses, unbidden and all-consuming.

Us. Tangled together before the fire. Her mouth and tongue claim me, her fingers digging into my hips to hold me in place. I hear my own gasps and feel the shuddering waves of pleasure as she tears me apart, only to put me back together again.

My fists clench at the phantom sensation. My breathing sharpens, my body tightening with need. And yet, even that pales in comparison to the heaven and stars she led me to last night.

The vision vanished as swiftly as it came, leaving me shaken, my chest rising and falling in uneven breaths. I find her eyes again, and she's still smirking. The challenge glitters there, unmistakable.

Before either of us can speak, Seraphina lets out a horrified squeal.

"Ew, gross! I can *feel* your lust from over here! I'll finish my research in my chambers—because at this rate, I'll never get anything done while you two are fucking."

She snatches up her books and storms out, leaving Nova and me clutching our sides in breathless laughter.

* * *

The air crackles, thick with lust and desire. One moment, we're laughing; the next, silence falls between us. My fingers itch in anticipation, my pulse racing at the intoxicating scent of Nova's arousal.

Then she moves. A blur of heat and need as she closes the distance, seizing me in her arms, her mouth crashing down on mine.

She tastes of pomegranate and vanilla, sweet and decadent, and I swear I could drown in her. Her scent lingers between us, dizzying and heady. I slide my hands into her hair, fisting the soft strands as I yank her head to the side, exposing her throat. My lips trace a path along the curve of her collarbone, each kiss burning hotter than the last. She answers with her own assault, dragging me closer and biting down on my shoulder. A groan rumbles in my chest.

I return the favor, teeth sinking into her neck just enough to make her gasp. Her body trembles against mine. My name is a whisper on her lips—needy, demanding.

I want more. I want everything.

Somehow, between breaths, I manage to unlace her gown, stripping away the layers until she stands before me—bared, breathtaking. A growl rips from my throat, hunger twisting through me, primal and unrelenting.

As if she could hear my thoughts, she quickly worked my corset, yanking loose my tunic and breeches. Then, for a moment, we just look. Devouring each other.

I reach out, tracing the swell of her breast with the tip of my finger before lowering my mouth to follow. She sighs, her fingers tangling in my hair, guiding me—demanding more.

Then, her hands move lower. A teasing graze along my hip—a slow descent to the heat pooling between my thighs. I suck in a breath, parting my legs as she brushes over my slickness, her fingers featherlight.

The first stroke is torturously slow—the second firmer.

My head falls back, pleasure curling through me.

I yank her hair, dragging her mouth to mine, swallowing the moan that slips past my lips. My hips move with her rhythm, chasing the pleasure, needing the release only she can give me. She quickens the pace, her fingers relentless, knowing exactly how to unravel me. The tension coils tighter, higher—until it snaps.

White-hot pleasure crashes over me, shattering me apart. Her lips swallow my cry, the waves of my orgasm still pulsing through my body as she holds me through it, her breath ragged against my skin.

But I'm not done. Not nearly.

I push her back onto the lounge, my mouth never leaving her skin. I trace the soft curves of her body, leaving a path of kisses from her breasts to her stomach, lower still—until I taste her.

She gasps, her hips jerking against my mouth.

I pin her in place, dragging my tongue over her with agonizing slowness. She moans, head falling back, hands clutching at my hair. I savor every sound, every shudder, working her higher, faster, until she's writhing beneath me, lost to the pleasure I give her.

"If this is payback for my little illusion earlier—oh!"

Her words break into a cry of ecstasy as I push her over the edge. Her release floods me, and I won't stop. Not until she's shaking, her thighs trembling, her breath coming in ragged gasps.

Finally, I crawled up beside her, pulling her into my arms. Our bodies were slick with sweat, and our heartbeats were still racing in tandem.

For a while, we just lay there, wrapped in each other.

"Have you heard from the others?" I ask eventually, my voice rough from exhaustion and pleasure.

"I have," she murmurs, fingers tracing lazy circles on my back. "Ryvvik and Skalanis are due to arrive next week. I received their ravens this morning."

"Good."

A heavy silence falls between us. It's not uncomfortable but weighted.

I know it. She knows it.

The hourglass has turned.

Nights like these, filled with nothing but touch and longing, will soon be replaced by strategy, scheming, and treason.

I shift, pressing closer, needing her again, needing to lose myself in her before reality catches up to us.

She kisses me, a hand coming around my throat—possessive, claiming. I let her, let her take control, let her guide me as she pulls me on top of her, shifting me until my thighs straddle her mouth.

Then she moves, tongue flicking, teasing, setting fire to my every nerve.

I shudder, grinding against her, the pressure, the heat driving me higher—the glow of my magic flickers over my skin, reflecting in the sweat-slicked surface of hers.

She doesn't stop. I won't stop.

I splinter apart, pleasure consuming me, galaxies bursting behind my eyes as the very foundation beneath us trembles.

Damn this witch and the spell she's woven on me.

∗ ∗ ∗

The next day, we stumble upon a hidden entrance in the library—entirely by accident.

We were fucking again, as we seem to do more often than not these days. I had Nova pinned against a bookcase, her leg draped over my shoulder as I devoured her. Somewhere in the haze of pleasure, she reached for balance, her fingers catching on the spine of a random book. Her grip slipped the moment she came, yanking it free.

The entire bookshelf groaned, then swung open.

We had just enough time to exchange startled looks before we tumbled through, landing in a heap on the musty stone steps beyond.

I admit, that was not my finest moment.

Later, after fetching Seraphina, we returned to the entrance, lanterns in hand, ready to explore. Shadows stretched down the stairwell, vanishing into the unknown.

"I'm surprised you didn't know this existed," I mused, stepping carefully down the uneven steps.

"Not too hard to believe." Seraphina snorted, raking a hand through her hair. "The book she pulled was *The Wonderment of*

Matrimony."

I let out a bark of laughter, the sound bouncing off the stone walls. Nova huffed beside me, muttering something about *fate and having a sense of humor.*

At the bottom of the stairwell, we stopped in front of a door covered in selenite. The air around it thrummed, pulsing with an energy that settled into my bones like a whispered promise.

"Was Esmyra an elemental witch?" Nova asked suddenly, stepping forward to trace her fingers along the crystal.

"Not that I'm aware of," I said slowly. Seraphina frowned, mirroring my expression. The same thought flickered between us.

Could the queen have cast this?

Nova exhaled sharply, her palm hovering just above the surface. "This isn't just a door. There's a woven spell here, an energy signature left behind by an elemental witch." She studied it for another beat before turning to us. "One of you will be the key to unlocking it."

Her gaze flicked to me. Without hesitation, I stepped forward and pressed my palm against the handle.

A sharp crackle of energy licked over my skin, leaving behind a sensation like thousands of tiny needle pricks. Then, with an audible click, the lock gave way. The door swung open.

Nova turned to me with a triumphant smirk, smug satisfaction written all over her face.

"Don't go getting a big head," I teased.

She snorted but wasted no time darting through the entrance. Seraphina followed, and I stepped in last—only to stop dead in my tracks.

"Holy shit," Nova whispered.

Before us stretched a sheer obsidian pathway polished

smooth as glass. Towering pillars of solid onyx flanked the path, their surfaces gleaming in the dim light of our lanterns. The air felt thick, charged with an ancient power that prickled against my skin.

"I've only ever read about shadow gates," Seraphina murmured, awe coloring her voice. "Never in my wildest dreams..."

"I know," Nova agreed, her expression alight with a scholar's glee. "I've never seen one in such pristine condition."

I sigh, planting my hands on my hips. "Would someone like to explain to me what the fuck a shadow gate is?"

Seraphina and Nova exchanged a glance before Nova turned to me.

"They're rare," she said. "Kept secret for a reason. All records agree that only a powerful elemental witch can create one. Think of it as a bridge between time and space."

"So, it's a portal," I said.

Nova shook her head. "More than that. A shadow gate doesn't just lead to another place—the wielder's intention shapes it. It could be as simple as stepping into another kingdom or as dangerous as a doorway to an unknown dimension. Some believe they can connect all the realms, but no one knows for sure."

"Why not?" I asked.

"Because the moment you cross one," she said slowly, "you might never return."

I stared at the shadow gate, a cold weight settling in my stomach.

"Well," I muttered. "That's just wonderful."

✳ ✳ ✳

The next few days pass in a whirlwind; before I know it, another week has come and gone. Today, Nova's allies arrive. I don't want things to change, but I know they will.

We stand at the entrance of the great hall—an old ballroom that hasn't seen use in years—waiting. A battered carriage rattles up the lane, pulled by two sturdy brown horses. The vehicle looks like it's seen better days, the wood worn and the wheels creaking under the strain of the journey. It halts at the foot of the steps, the horses snorting as if relieved to stop.

Nova moves gracefully down the stairs, the frills of her midnight-blue gown swirling around her ankles. The moment two burly men step out, she lets out a delighted squeal and rushes to them, throwing her arms around their necks in a fierce embrace.

The first man is tall and broad, exuding a quiet but dangerous confidence. His golden skin glows in the afternoon light, and his tousled blonde locks frame a face that is striking and warm. His emerald-green eyes sparkle with mischief, and a dimple carves into his cheek when he grins. He radiates effortless charm, the kind that makes people gravitate toward him despite their better judgment.

My gaze drifts lower, taking in the tattoos covering his right arm and creeping up his neck. Golden dragons twist and coil across his skin in soaring, striking, and resting poses, each one intricately detailed. Nova introduces him as Ryvvik, her first in command. I incline my head in acknowledgment, already sensing that beneath his playful exterior lies something far more lethal.

The man beside him is a stark contrast. Where Ryvvik is

easygoing and inviting, this one is all sharp edges and cold calculation. His piercing blue eyes sweep over us, taking everything in with an assessing stare. Jet-black hair falls just past his shoulders, framing a face that is both severe and unreadable. His stance is rigid, his aura giving nothing away. Unlike Ryvvik, he wears no grin—only the ghost of impatience flickering across his otherwise unreadable features.

Nova introduces him as Skalanis, her brother and a Demi-Fey general. *Interesting.*

I glance at Seraphina and immediately bite back a laugh. She's staring at Ryvvik with barely concealed lust, her expression caught somewhere between intrigue and irritation.

I grin knowingly. *To be fair, I can't blame her. He is pretty to look at.*

Catching my amusement, Seraphina scowls at me, her cheeks darkening. I take the opportunity to open a telepathic link, letting my thoughts brush against hers.

"Quit staring at me like that!" she shrieks through our connection, her embarrassment flaring.

I wink, chuckling softly. But when I glance back at Ryvvik, I notice something interesting—his gaze has also found Seraphina, his body unconsciously drawn toward her. The air shifts, and I catch the mingling scents of sandalwood and brandy, meeting a haze of sea and sunlight. Their unspoken desire hums between them, unnoticed by the others but evident to me.

A slow smirk tugs at my lips. *Oh, this will be fun.*

Before Seraphina combusts from sheer mortification, I decide to intervene. "Should we go inside and get this party started?"

Ryvvik turns his attention to me, flashing that damn dimple

again. "I like you already." He slings an arm around Nova, dragging a visibly uncomfortable Skalanis into his embrace. "Now, what are we drinking? Oh! You all remember that time we—"

"Shut the fuck up, Ryvvik," Skalanis growls, his voice a low rumble of warning. "We are not playing that game again."

Ryvvik's laughter booms through the courtyard, deep and unbothered. "Oh, but it was *so* much fun last time! The look on your face—priceless."

Nova rolls her eyes while Skalanis glares, looking every bit like a caged animal caught under Ryvvik's arm.

I don't even try to stop the laughter bubbling up from my chest. It spills out of me, wild and unrestrained, and within moments, the others are laughing, too—Ryvvik's infectious joy breaking through the meeting's initial stiffness.

And just like that, I decided I liked him, too.

CHAPTER 11 - RYVVIK'S QUEST

<u>Ophelia</u>

O nce our guests had settled into their rooms, we gathered around the grand dining table, the scent of roasted meat and herbs filling the air. Luca and the dining staff moved efficiently around us, setting down trays of food that sent my stomach into a riot of anticipation. If the hint of rosemary was any indication, she had once again snuck one of my favorite dishes onto the menu.

The rich, savory aroma of braised venison enveloped me when I lifted the cover from my plate. My mouth practically watered as I took my first bite. The meat was tender, bathed in a reduction of cognac, mushrooms, rosemary, and a splash of red wine that added depth to the flavors. It melted on my tongue like butter. Luca had outdone herself again.

"This is delicious, Luca. Thank you," I told her as she passed, refilling my goblet with more wine.

"My pleasure, my lady," she replied brightly.

"You've outdone yourself. This venison is better than my ma's cookin', but don't you tell her I said so." Skalanis shot Luca a wink, his usual brooding demeanor momentarily replaced with a teasing grin.

Luca turned a shade of pink so deep it nearly rivaled the wine in our goblets. She almost knocked over Seraphina's drink in her flustered state, catching it just in time. I coughed into my hand, failing miserably to hide my laughter. Across the table, Ryvvik caught my eye, a knowing grin playing on his lips.

I smirked in return, watching Skalanis lean toward Nova, whispering something undoubtedly scandalous in her ear. She rolled her eyes in exasperation but didn't suppress her smile.

Something was fascinating about these two men—how they had become integral to the rebellion and earned Nova's loyalty. I made a mental note to unravel that mystery later, but before I could dwell on it, Ryvvik clapped his hands together, drawing everyone's attention.

"So... Are you sure I can't convince you to play a round of Ryvvik's Quest?" His grin was boyish, a mischievous expression that usually preceded terrible–or highly entertaining–decisions.

Skalanis groaned, running a hand through his dark hair before downing the rest of his wine in two long gulps. "Fine," he muttered. "But I swear on all things divine if you cheat again —"

"I did not cheat! It's not my fault you're a terrible listener. The rules are simple. Anyone can follow them, for goddess's sake." Ryvvik huffed, looking thoroughly offended.

"Oh, this I have to see. What are these mysterious rules you speak of?" I asked, taking another slow sip of my wine, intrigued.

Nova started laughing, a wicked glint in her eyes. Skalanis shot her a glare that clearly said, *I told you so.* Ryvvik ignored them both and straightened in his chair.

"The rules are simple," he began, his voice taking on the tone of someone about to impart great wisdom. "Four cards hold the most power. The ace is worth thirty-three points and guarantees an automatic win—play it, and the round is yours. The king is worth thirteen, the queen twelve, and the jack eleven. Any numbered card carries its face value, regardless of suit. Rule one, as I said, is simple, so let's move on. Rule two: if you lose a round, you drink. You have thirty seconds to finish, or you take an additional drink. Rule three: every card played must add up to thirteen or thirty-three. Fail to make the number? Drink. Rule four: no identical pairs are allowed. Rule five: you cannot use the same number combination twice in a row. If you do—" he grinned wickedly, "—you lose."

Skalanis groaned again, slumping lower in his chair, his scowl deepening. "See what I mean? Impossible."

His obvious suffering only made Ryvvik's grin stretch wider, and I couldn't help but laugh at their dynamic.

Seraphina, who had been quietly observing, leaned forward, her gaze flicking appraisingly to Ryvvik. "I'm in," she said smoothly.

Ryvvik's expression lit up like a firework. "That's the spirit! What about the rest of you? The bet starts at ten flamecoins. Who will lose the first round?"

"Wait..." I squinted at him, amusement bubbling up. "What the hell is a flamecoin?"

"It's a dragon thing, baby." He winked, throwing another exaggerated wink at Seraphina, who narrowed her eyes in suspicion.

"Don't worry. Mooncoin will work just fine," Nova interjected with an exasperated sigh. "Ryvvik just likes to think everyone in all five realms should carry flamecoin."

I snorted, casting another glance at Skalanis, who still looked like he was contemplating the meaning of his existence. Seeing such a formidable warrior pouting like a child was too much— I lost it, laughter spilling from my lips.

Ryvvik arched a brow, his grin turning knowing. "Oh, why the hell not," I finally said, lifting my goblet in a mock toast.

And with that, the game began.

✳ ✳ ✳

As the evening wears on, two things become abundantly clear. One: Ryvvik's drinking game is pure chaos. The endless ways to fuck up keep everyone confused, which means we all end up belligerently drunk. And two, Seraphina and Ryvvik are more than intrigued with each other. He hasn't let her stray more than a foot or two from his side all night, his gaze practically stripping her bare across the table. Even now, his hand rests on her exposed thigh.

Okay—maybe I owe Seraphina an apology.

Sheesh. Get a room.

Make that three things. Skalanis's icy exterior? Total front. The man might just be the biggest teddy bear I've ever met.

We've all just lost yet another round of *Ryvvik's Quest*—as he so grandly named it—to the man himself. Another round, another groan, and another pile of coins slipped into his possession. "Another?" he asks, his left hand absentmindedly grazing my sister's leg. Her cheeks flush, her eyes darkening with desire.

Nope. I'm not watching that happen.

"I think I'll call it a night. You've cleaned me out anyway, you fiend!" I say with a slight slur, my head swimming from too many shots of cinnamon whiskey. I wiggle my brows at Ryvvik before giving Seraphina a pointed look. She grins, all sass and heat, but her face betrays her—flushing even deeper as his hand undoubtedly moves higher.

Shuddering, I lean into Nova, my lips brushing her ear as I whisper, "Come to bed."

We both say our goodnights, leaving the three of them to their game.

"I'm convinced Ryvvik cheats," Nova giggles as we clumsily climb the stairs.

"What the hell was in that whiskey?" I laugh, tripping over the train of her robes.

"Oh, if I had to guess… I'd say it was spiked with sprite dust."

"Sprite *what*?" I ask, blinking in confusion.

She's a few steps ahead of me now, grinning from ear to ear. "I'm just messing with you. I'm *pretty* sure the whiskey wasn't spiked—this time." She giggles and darts up the last few steps, nearly tripping as her sleeve slips, exposing bare skin.

"This time?!" I repeat incredulously.

Then, all thoughts of whiskey and mischief vanish.

The air shifts.

Vanilla desire curls around me, thick and intoxicating. Even in my drunken haze, I can feel the heat of her arousal mixing with my own, an electric pull tightening between us.

Her eyes glint with challenge. Then comes the smirk.

Before I can react, she's off—bolting down the hall toward my bedroom, laughter echoing as she disappears through the door.

"Wicked thing," I murmur, giving in to the chase.

* * *

<u>Seraphina</u>

I hear their laughter as they disappear down the hall, leaving me alone with Ryvvik and Skalanis—a fact I'm not sure I'm ready to face. The warmth of his hand on my thigh is already too much, and when his grip tightens, a slow heat flushes through my entire body. I should move, break the moment before it spirals, but I don't. I can't.

His fingers slide higher, the ghost of a touch brushing against the drenched silk between my legs. My breath catches, my body tightening at its sheer audacity. He barely touches me, yet I feel it everywhere, my pulse hammering, my skin burning with the need for more. This is reckless. I barely know him. But I want him—want this—and I don't think I've ever wanted anything more.

"Another round, brother? Or do you grow tired of losing—again?" Ryvvik's voice is casual and teasing, but the way his fingers press more firmly against me, slow and deliberate, is anything but.

I bite my lip to hold back a sound of pleasure, my fingers digging into the armrest of my chair as Skalanis groans in frustration. "You're insufferable," he mutters, pushing up from the table.

Ryvvik doesn't even acknowledge him. He's focused solely on me, his touch never faltering, his smirk deepening when he feels my body shudder beneath him. I barely register the sound of footsteps leaving the room. All I can think about is the way he's touching me.

"Finally..." His voice is low, filled with satisfaction. "Now I have you all to myself."

The scent of him—sandalwood, cinnamon whiskey, and the crackling heat of fire—wraps around me, intoxicating and dangerous. The moment his lips crash against mine, I'm lost. There's nothing gentle in the way he kisses me. It's raw, consuming, the kind of kiss that steals the air from your lungs and demands surrender. I groan, my hands fisting his shirt as I pull him closer, as if he isn't already invading every inch of my space.

His free hand slides up to my throat, tilting my head back as his tongue claims mine, each stroke punishing and possessive. I whimper against his mouth when his fingers push inside me, slow but relentless, his palm pressing just right. He's playing me like an instrument, knowing exactly which notes to pluck to make me come undone.

"You have bewitched me," he murmurs against my lips, his voice rough with need.

A broken cry escapes me as he drives me higher, my hips bucking against his hand, chasing the pleasure he so easily gives and withholds in equal measure. When I finally shatter, he swallows my moan with another devastating kiss, his growl vibrating against my lips.

"Good girl." His praise is hushed and reverent, sending another shiver through me.

He doesn't give me a moment to recover. His hands grip my thighs, spreading them wider as he kneels before me, his breath ghosting over my heat. My mind flashes back to Luca's teasing words earlier in the evening—*You'll tempt the devil in that dress.*

I shivered, realizing just how right she was.

Then his mouth is on me, and I swear I forget how to breathe. His tongue moves with deliberate slowness, lapping up my release like a man starved, his deep hum of satisfaction sending jolts of pleasure through my already shaking body. I arch into him, greedy for more, but he tuts in disapproval, landing a sharp smack against my clit.

"Greedy thing," he murmurs, his voice thick with amusement.

"Please," I gasp, my pride long gone, my body burning with the ache only he can soothe.

He grants my plea, his tongue working me over with agonizing precision. The pleasure coils tight, unbearable, and just when I'm on the brink, he stops. I barely have time to curse him before he flips me onto my stomach, pulling my hips up before sinking into me in one deep, punishing stroke. I cry out, my fingers clawing at the floor as he stretches me, fills me, and consumes me.

"Not yet," he growls, gripping my throat as he pulls me up against him, his thrusts deep and unrelenting. His other hand snakes around to rub slow, lazy circles over my clit, tormenting me even as he drives me closer to madness.

His teeth sink into my shoulder, his tongue soothing the sting a moment later. My body is trembling, the pleasure unbearable, my release hovering just out of reach. "Please," I gasped, my voice breaking as he thrusts deeper.

"Come for me," he commands, his voice dark and possessive.

He angles his hips just right, and I shatter. The orgasm rips through me, so intense that I swear I see stars. I scream his name, my body convulsing around him, and the sound only seems to drive him wilder. His rhythm stutters, his grip tightening before he thrusts one last time, spilling himself inside me with a growl of satisfaction.

We collapse together, our bodies tangled, our breaths uneven. I lay sprawled across his chest, his strong arms wrapped around me as if he had no intention of letting go.

His emerald eyes meet mine, and something in them makes my chest tighten—something unspoken, something dangerous. He looks like he has so much to say, but I can't let him. I'll lose myself if I acknowledge it and let myself believe this is anything more than a fleeting moment.

I avert my gaze, but he's too damn observant. He tilts my chin back, his lips brushing mine in a kiss so soft and gentle that my throat tightens. His kiss isn't a demand this time. It's a promise. A question. A claim.

I can't let him claim me.

The kiss turns urgent again, filled with need, and I surrender, knowing it will be my downfall. I feel it in my bones—this man could ruin me.

And yet, when he flips me onto my back, sliding into me once more, I meet him thrust for thrust, willing to drown in the distraction for just one more night.

Just for tonight.

Because if I let this become more, I might not survive it.

Though, as his hands grip my hips and his lips devour mine, I think—maybe, just maybe—it wouldn't be such a bad way to go.

CHAPTER 12 - DRAGONHEART

Seraphina

S unlight spills through the window in delicate rib-
bons, painting warmth over my bare skin. A weight
—solid and grounding—anchors me to the bed, and it
takes me a moment to realize it's Ryvvik's arm wrapped possessively around my waist. His body is flush against mine, heat radiating from his skin like a low-burning fire.

I blink, my mind still tangled in the haze of sleep, and then
last night rushes back in a flood of sensation. His hands, his
mouth, how he unraveled me piece by piece.

A flush blooms across my chest, embarrassment war-
ring with the deep, bone-deep satisfaction still thrumming
through me. I barely know him. And yet, it felt as if he knew
every hidden part of me—every unspoken desire, every place I
longed to be touched.

Carefully, I shift, attempting to slip from his grasp, but the moment I move, his fingers tighten around my wrist. A lazy, satisfied grumble rumbles through his chest as he pulls me back against him.

"Trying to slip out on me, little witch?" His voice is thick with sleep, husky and teasing, like silk laced with embers.

I swallow hard. I had been trying to do just that.

He tuts, brushing his lips against my temple, his hold on me firm but gentle. "You were sleeping so well," I murmur, grasping for an excuse, "and I have things to do today."

"No."

His denial is simple, absolute.

"Yes," I argue, though it comes out weaker than I intend. "I can't stay in bed all day. Especially not in your bed."

"There is nothing you need to do today except let me ravish you..." He nips at my shoulder, his fingers skimming over my hip. "And feed you."

A shiver licks up my spine.

"Last night..." I begin, needing to say anything before I lose myself again.

"Don't you dare." His voice dips lower, dark and possessive. "Last night was fucking heaven, and you know it."

I scowl, but he only smirks, seeing right through my feigned indignation.

"You're insufferable," I huff.

"And you're in denial."

The look we exchange is electric—challenge, frustration, something far deeper neither of us dares name.

"I'm not in denial," I insist. "We had fun—"

"You call that fun?" he scoffs, his nostrils flaring. The wounded pride in his expression is almost amusing.

I bite my lip, enjoying the flicker of irritation in his eyes.

"Wasn't it?"

His fingers trail up my arm, lazy and knowing. "Say what you want, little witch, but I felt you trembling beneath me. I heard you beg for more."

My breath stutters. His touch is feather-light, moving down my belly, then teasing lower. He doesn't touch me where I need him most, only ghosts his fingertips across my inner thigh.

"You want this," he murmurs, pressing a kiss to my jaw. "Us. Me."

I do. Stars help me, I do.

As if sensing my surrender, he dips his head, his lips a whisper against mine as his fingers find my clit. The tease is maddening, slow strokes barely enough to satisfy. My hips shift toward his touch, instinct taking over.

"What do you say, little witch?" His voice is liquid heat, a promise and a demand. "I want to hear you say it."

My pulse pounds, heat flooding every inch of me.

A sudden smack against my thigh has me gasping. "I won't let you come if you don't," he warns, his tone laced with wicked amusement.

"Please," I whisper, breathless.

"Please, what?" Another slow stroke, devastatingly light.

I swallow my pride. "Please, make me come."

The second the words leave my mouth, he rewards me—fingertips pressing, circling, working me toward that sweet, inevitable edge.

"Good girl." The praise is a caress, sliding over my skin like silk.

I arch against him, my body surrendering to his touch, and when my release shatters through me, I don't hold back the cry that slips from my lips.

His lips brush against my temple, and I feel him smile.

"You're mine, little witch."

I should fight the claim in his voice, should resist the way it settles into something deep inside me. But I don't. Not right now.

He pulls me into him, fingers tracing the curve of my back as he murmurs, "My dragon heart."

The words send a pang through my chest, an ache both sweet and terrifying. I tell myself this is temporary—just a stolen moment before the storm ahead. Soon, we will be fighting for our lives, and nothing about this can last.

But as our energies intertwine, my silver threads tangling with his gold, I can't help but wonder... what if?

For now, I silence the thought.

For now, I let myself sink into him, into this feeling, into the fragile illusion that, just for today, we belong to each other.

* * *

Much to my surprise, Ryvvik has stayed by my side every night since that first one. And while part of me craves solitude, I won't lie—I like it. Too much.

We've fallen into a routine.

Sex. Arguing. Food. Arguing. Sex.

It's infuriatingly good. Even the bickering. Especially the bickering.

I don't know what's worse—that I want it or that I find myself picking fights just to start another round.

Like now.

He's sitting in a plush chair by the fire, going through a scroll for me, focused and unbothered, and all I want is to capture his attention, just for a moment. Just to feel the heat of his gaze on me.

"Go any slower, and we'll never understand how that gate works," I tease, watching him carefully.

A corner of his mouth twitches up, but he doesn't rise to the bait. He simply drags a finger over a particular line, studying the text as if my words were nothing more than the crackling of the fire.

I sigh, turning back to my journal. I read the same paragraph three times before snapping it shut, irritation curling in my stomach.

Fine. New tactic.

I shift, hiking up my skirts—a lilac chiffon number that whispers against my skin when I move. Slowly, I massage my thigh, running my fingers from my knee to my ankle. My hair spills over my shoulder, pooling around my waist as I stretch, deliberately exposing the bare skin of my legs.

I hear the rustle of the scroll.

Then, a quiet, sharp curse.

Biting my lip to suppress my satisfaction, I let my hands wander, trailing up the tops of my thighs, slipping beneath the sheer fabric, exposing more skin. He swears again, louder this time.

Good.

I drag my fingers higher over the bodice of my dress, grazing the swell of my breasts.

The temperature in the room spikes, the air thick with heat, and I know damn well it's his magic. Still, I pretend not to notice, kneading my shoulders, rolling my neck—an innocent stretch that just so happens to arch my back in a way he can't possibly ignore.

I don't hear him move. I just feel him.

His heat presses against my back, his fingers replacing mine, working into my temples, neck, and shoulders. I shudder as warmth seeps into my skin, his magic unraveling every knot of tension in my body.

"Looks like you can be useful after all," I murmur, tipping my head forward to grant him better access.

I know I've won when his fingers tighten in my hair.

He yanks, tilting my head just enough to bring my ear close to his lips.

"Careful, little witch..." His deep, sinful growl sends a ripple of anticipation down my spine.

His free hand wraps around my throat, applying just enough pressure to make my breath hitch—my pulse pounds beneath his fingers. My body knows this game.

It craves it.

I shift, pressing my hips back against him, and nearly gasp when I feel the hard, undeniable proof of his arousal.

Ryvvik hisses, his grip tightening, his body coiling against mine. His other hand slides down, splaying possessively over my waist before traveling lower, his caress feather-light. He nips my earlobe, his teeth sharp, his lips soft, each contrast making me burn hotter.

"You're going to be the death of me," he murmurs, his hand skimming over my hip, his fingers teasing just below the waistband of my skirt.

"And you're going to be the bane of my existence," I counter, my voice breathless but sharp.

He chuckles, low and dark. "Oh no, my dragon heart. I'll be

much worse than that."

His fingers slip lower, brushing against the slick heat of my core, and I bite back a moan.

"You won't want anyone else," he continues, his voice a promise, a curse. "I'll ruin you. Just like you've ruined me."

"Ruined you?" I manage, though the words are barely more than a whisper.

"Yes. Ruined." His strokes turn deliberate, teasing, maddening. "You've ruined me from ever looking at another. From craving anyone else's touch. I will burn for you alone, forever needing, possessing—"

"If I didn't know any better," I breathe, fighting the way my body trembles against his touch, "I'd say you're distracted, Nightflame."

His fingers are still.

For half a second, silence thickens between us.

Then, his grip tightens.

"As if you don't know exactly what you're doing," he rasps. "Silverhorne."

The name hits me like a slap.

I stiffen before I can stop myself, every nerve recoiling at the lie I've tangled myself in.

Ryvvik doesn't notice.

But I do.

The name doesn't belong to me. Not really. It's the one I gave him in a moment of panic, the one that kept me safe. But my real name? The one hidden in ink, tucked away in a fragile blue journal?

Morningstar.

I'm a fucking Morningstar, like Ophelia.

Unlike Ophelia, though, there's no record of my birth. Just a name, scrawled in delicate script, buried in the depths of my mother's desk, waiting for me to find it.

Two days ago, I did.

And ever since, its weight has sat like lead in my chest.

I don't even realize I've gone rigid until Ryvvik's hand loosens around my throat. He turns me gently, forcing me to face him, his golden-flecked emerald eyes scanning mine.

"Where'd you go, Sera?" His voice is softer now, edged with something dangerously close to concern.

I hesitate. Just long enough for guilt to sink its teeth into me.

How much longer can I keep this secret?

I stumble through an excuse, gripping the closest truth I can offer. "Of all the things I could've found, I found that instead. My true last name. It's not exactly useful."

His thumb strokes my cheek. "Dragon heart…"

I hate how much comfort those two words bring me.

"You're already being helpful," he says, watching me closely. "You've been tearing through every journal, every scroll, every book. There's not much else we can do right now, and you know it."

I open my mouth to argue.

He doesn't let me.

"Let's cut the shit."

Despite everything, I snort.

His mouth twitches. "We've been at this for hours. You're hungry. I'm hungry. Let's eat, take a break, and return to it later."

Before I can protest, he takes my hand, leading me toward the library doors.

I let him.

Only because my stomach chooses that exact moment to

howl its grievances.

Fucking Astraea's sakes.

CHAPTER 13 - THINGS BEST LEFT FORGOTTEN

Seraphina

The scene starts the same as always. It's so real that, at first, it's hard to discern that it's just a dream. When I catch sight of my mother wrapping Ophelia in a tight embrace, I don't question it. The warmth of their hug should be comforting, but something is wrong. The longer I watch, the more I notice how Ophelia's body remains too still, as though she's been carved from wax. A flicker of something dark ripples at the edges of my vision, but when I turn my head, there's nothing there.

I descend the grand staircase, my gown of deep plum chiffon whispering around my legs—only, at one point, the sound *disappears.* The fabric moves, but it makes no noise, and the silence stretches too long before the rustle returns, out of sync with my movements. I hesitate mid-step, gripping the railing, but the moment passes.

"Leaving so soon?" I call to Ophelia, forcing my steps forward to reach the bottom.

When I do, my mother slips an obsidian crystal into her pocket, its surface carved with runes I don't recognize. She's muttering under her breath in a language that skates just beyond my understanding, the syllables curling through the air like smoke.

"Please do your best to behave," she says, smoothing Ophelia's hair. "I'm sure you'll clash with some of your instructors; you've always been headstrong."

Ophelia grins. "Probably some of my superiors, too."

Mother sighs. "Just... try. Will you?"

Ophelia chuckles, pressing a kiss to our mother's cheek. "Of course, anything for you, mom."

I frown at our mother's trembling hands. The conversation from earlier lingers in my mind, gnawing at me.

Before I can speak, Ophelia turns to me with a teasing smirk.

"Well? Are you just going to stand there? Come tell me good-bye, you asshole."

I force a tight smile. "Of course, forgive me." I steel myself, locking my mental shields as Mother taught us long ago. "Please be careful, and write often. I'm going to miss you, little sister."

Ophelia's expression flickers. Her brows pinched in confusion for a moment, but the look vanished too quickly, like a ripple in still water.

"I'll miss you too," she says. "Can you have Gabriel send my trunk out? I need to go and ready Blaze for the journey. I hope you have a wonderful debut, Seraphina. Twenty is such a special time in your life, and what better way to celebrate than at the palace? Truly, you deserve it." She plants a final goodbye kiss on my cheek.

I open my mouth—to say what, I don't know—but the scene *shifts* before I can stop it.

I'm back in the library, seated at Mother's desk, fingers flipping through the delicate pages of her journals. I know what I'm searching for—the scripture, the prophecy—*the truth.*

The air changes. A thick, suffocating stillness settles over the room, pressing in from all sides.

Mother storms in, her silver eyes flashing in ire.

"Seraphina, what is the meaning of this?" Her voice is more angry than I remember. She plants her hands on her waist, here eyes glinting with something unreadable.

I hesitate. For a split second, the room *breathes*—the shadows stretching unnaturally long along the bookshelves, the candlelight flickering too erratically. I blink, and everything is normal again.

"I was looking for a particular passage," I say carefully. "The one I spoke to you about earlier tonight."

Mother's expression shutters. "Seraphina... I told you already. There's nothing to that prophecy. It's simply something I found intriguing from my time in the palace, nothing more."

She won't meet my gaze. Instead, she picks at imaginary lint on her gown.

"I can't help but feel like you're keeping something from me —"

"Seraphina, enough! Let it go." Her voice cracks through the air like a whip. "Now, go and finish packing the rest of your belongings."

The room tilts. No. *The world tilts.*

The next moment, I'm standing at the library's threshold again. I don't remember moving.

I should leave. The carriages are waiting. But something is *wrong.*

A bookcase that should be whole is ajar, revealing an opening I've never seen before. The air beyond it is black as ink.

"That's odd," I murmur, stepping forward.

Nothing but silence greets me.

A weight presses against my chest, but curiosity wins. I descend into the darkness, fingertips skimming the stone walls as I feel my way down.

Halfway down, a low, *humming* sound fills the space, growing louder.

A whoosh—then *scuttling.*

Something is coming straight toward me.

My pulse spikes. I lurch back, scrambling up the stairs, my breath catching in my throat. At the top, I snatch the fireplace poker from its stand, grip tightening until my knuckles ache.

The darkness stirs, shadows coiling behind a figure that bursts through the hidden passage.

"Mom!"

She startles, silver hair gleaming in the dim firelight. "What are you still doing here?" Suspicion laces her voice.

"I—I came to tell you the carriages are ready." I swallow the unease sticking to my ribs. "We must leave now if we're going to make the ceremony in time."

She studies me for a beat too long before nodding. "Right. Let's not keep the queen waiting."

The world *fractures.*

Suddenly, I'm back in my chambers, my ladies' maid lacing my corset until my breath is a shallow whisper in my chest.

The scent of lavender and candle wax clings to the air.

Mother's voice drifts from across the room.

"Did you manage to get a hold of the kitchen maid?"

I blink. "I did. I can't wait to see the king's surprise when he receives his special treat! It's sweet how close you two are, Mother."

"Good." A pause. "You've done well, daughter." A longer pause. "You've attracted a lot of attention, darling. The Stormsong family has already inquired about your hand."

I exhale sharply. "Can we save the wedding planning for another time, Mother?"

She laughs lightly. "Of course, dear. I'll wait for you in the sitting area."

The moment she leaves, the air shifts. A *wrongness* slithers beneath my skin.

The grand ballroom is *too bright.*

Everything is dipped in gold, the chandeliers casting fractured prisms of light. The royal family sits at the head of the table, horizontal to ours. When Queen Siofra raises her glass, her voice rings *unnaturally loud.*

"To the future of Eventide!" She cheers, toasting the room with her goblet held high.

The words *echo,* stretching longer than they should. My ears ring.

At my side, Mother stares at her plate, seemingly oblivious. The king meets her gaze across the room, and mother seems to fill with tension.

Something cold coils in my stomach.

The dessert arrives, servants placing generous helpings of cake in front of us on golden plates. Mother takes a bite, chewing and murmurs her approval.

I do the same. The sweetness spreads over my tongue.

Then—a choked gurgle. I turn, my breath catching.

Mother's face is turning *blue.*

I scream as she clutches my hands, her nails digging into my skin. Her gaze is wild, fixed on something behind me. I whip around, searching for the source. The king narrows his gaze at me.

He nods, tilting his golden goblet toward me in mock salute.

Mother convulses, her grip tightening.

"Mom," I sob, shaking her. "Mom, please, tell me what to do! Mom—"

Her body stills. The light in her silver eyes flickers—then *dies.*

I scream, the sound shrill as it fills the room.

A cold *hand grips my shoulder,* and I jerk awake.

* * *

I wake thrashing in the bed, my throat raw from screaming, my body drenched in sweat. The nightmare still clings to me, thick and suffocating, like smoke in my lungs. My mother's lifeless eyes. The king's chilling smirk. The way my hands had been useless to save her. It all lingers, tormenting me even as my conscious mind fights to return to the present.

"Sera!"

The deep voice rumbles through the haze, grounding me and tethering me back to reality. Strong arms wrap around me, firm yet careful, a steady heartbeat beneath my ear. Sandalwood and brandy fill my senses, warm and familiar, pulling me out of the nightmare's grip.

I gasp, still caught between two worlds, but Ryvvik holds me tight, cradling me against his bare chest. His fingers stroke through my hair, down my spine, and over my trembling shoulders. He murmurs soft reassurances, his lips pressing against the top of my head. His breath is warm and steady, as if willing me to borrow his calm.

"You were having a nightmare," he says, his voice rough from sleep but unwavering. I whimper in response, and he tightens his hold. "Shhh. It's okay. I've got you now."

The tension gradually leaves my body, but the ghosts of the past still whisper in the corners of my mind. I burrow closer to him, seeking more of his warmth, his presence—anything to drown out the lingering echoes of that night.

After a long silence, he speaks again. "Want to talk about it?"

I hesitate, but with his arms around me in the dark, I feel safe enough to let the words slip free. "It's the same nightmare I've had since my mother's death. I relive it over and over. Sometimes, it's just flashes, like I'm watching it from the outside. Other times... like tonight... I live it all over again." My voice is barely above a whisper. "Like I never left."

His arms tightened around me, and he exhaled sharply through his nose as if trying to push down whatever emotions were rising in his chest. "That's rough," he finally says, his voice quieter now. "Is there anything I can do?"

I don't have to think about it. "Just hold me."

He shifts slightly, kissing my temple, and murmurs, "Of course, my Dragonheart."

He keeps his promise.

Throughout the rest of the night, he doesn't let go. He holds me against his chest, his warmth chasing away the cold remnants of my nightmare. And for the first time in a long time, I don't feel so alone.

CHAPTER 14 - OOOOO, YOU'RE SO SCARY!

Elrond

Musk, decay, and death greet me as I descend the stone steps into the catacombs of the dungeons. Arax waits for me at the bottom, ever the warlord with his rigid stance and brooding expression. If he didn't remind me so much of his bloody mother with his coloring, he'd be the spitting image of me in my prime.

"Report," I snap, not bothering to wait for him as I stride down the dank corridor.

"The rebel is in the torture chamber, waiting for you, Father." Arax matches my stride with ease, his voice steady, unreadable.

The flames flicker, the gas-lit sconces casting long, shifting shadows that do little to illuminate the passageways. "I see.

Only one? I'm disappointed." The words cut through the stale air, leaving my mouth in a snarl.

The atmosphere is charged with something unreadable. His posture stiffens beside me, taut with frustration. "The only one we determined without a doubt had a connection to the rebel forces, Your Majesty," he says finally, deferring to formalities.

I smirk, knowing damn well the fear I still invoke, relishing in the anxiety pouring off him in a delectable haze.

"Are they not *all* accused of treason?" I snap.

Arax pales, his jaw clenches, and he eyes me warily before saying, "Yes, Majesty."

"Then should they not be interrogated and given the same exact treatment as our *friend?*"

"As you wish, Majesty." He says, ushering me to a heavily warded wood and iron door. "Aperta."

The door snaps open without so much as a click, the magic of the warding dissipating seamlessly to allow us entry into the torture chamber.

Decay hits my nostrils first, followed swiftly by the foul, dank odor of trickling water creeping like sludge along the stone walls. The air is thick, oppressive.

There, tied to a chair, bound and gagged, sits the rebel. My eyes narrow at the sight of him—disheveled blonde hair, dark brown eyes, a taut jaw set with determination.

Shouldn't this man be trembling? Doesn't he know who I am?

A defiant gaze stares back at me. One I know will take time and effort to break. A small matter in the grand scheme of things.

"Release the gag," I instruct, slowly removing my leather

gloves. A rage coils inside me, one that won't be tamed with idle chit-chat.

The vermin spits at my boots, but I don't give him the satisfaction of a reaction. Instead, I smile, acting as though his filth is nothing more than a minor inconvenience.

"Well, that's one way to greet your sovereign. What is your name, boy?"

He grunts, chuffing indignantly. "Why would I tell you a single thing?" He spits on the ground again, the corners of his mouth tugging into a smug smile.

"First, because I'm the one holding all the power. Secondly…" I trail off, allowing Arax to take the lead. His mere presence sends a ripple of unease through the rebel's body.

"Your king asked you a question." Arax's words are sharp, tinged with an edge of frustration.

The rebel has enough sense to look wary—not that it will do him any good. "Talon," he says, suspicion lacing his voice. "Why am I here?"

"I think you know exactly why you're here," I say, moving toward him, my fingers grazing the table lined with an assortment of torture devices.

He shakes his head, denial etched into every tense line of his body.

"Yes. You do." I snarl, nodding in Arax's direction.

"Allow me to refresh your memory," Arax says, shadows spilling from him like silk in a spider's snare.

The shadows are relentless, probing for every piece of information he wants to keep buried. I watch, enraptured by Arax's performance—such raw, beautiful power wielded with precision. A twinge of regret strikes my chest, sharp and unyielding.

No matter. He will do what must be done.

The shadows coil tighter, slipping into the rebel scum's mind, gripping him in unforgiving scrutiny. There is no escape, no mercy—only the inevitable unraveling of his secrets.

It's euphoric—the way the screams fill the room, sending a shiver down my spine, a tingling rush that settles all the way to my toes. They're remnants of a long-forgotten itch, one that begs to be scratched. I gnash my teeth, like an opium addict craving their next fix, barely restraining the urge to sink deeper into the pleasure of it.

Clenching my fists at my sides in a poor attempt to hide my reaction, I stalk to the edge of the table housing weaponry that makes my blood sing in anticipation. Idly, I run my fingers across the blades, hammers, whips, and maces, savouring the cool caress of metal against my skin.

"Father." Arax's voice is tinged with concern. "I've got the information."

"That quickly?" I muse, turning my attention back to the rebel.

Sweat drips from his dampened golden locks, beading across his furrowed brow. "That's disappointing," I mutter before sparing a glance in Arax's direction.

"Father!" He hisses, grabbing my arm with such force that my brow raises in question.

"You should remove your hand... *son*." The words are poison-tipped, edged with raw anger.

"Apologies," he mumbles, giving me a cursory once-over before continuing, "There are no ties to the rebels from this man, Sire."

"Impossible," I mutter, my gaze snapping back to the prisoner. "You obviously didn't dig deep enough."

Arax grips my arm again, pulling me toward the chamber

door. This little act of defiance will not go unpunished. But for now, I'll tolerate the distraction.

He drags me out of the chamber, slamming the door behind him. "Father, I'm telling you, that man is innocent," he snarls, crossing his arms over his chest.

Rage spills over, and I snap. My hand strikes him hard across the face, the sharp crack echoing through the corridor before I throw him to the ground. "You must've misheard me," I sneer, punctuating the words with a vicious kick to his ribs. "I told you, *you* didn't go deep enough."

"Father, please!" he gasps, his arms shielding his ribs as I send another flurry of kicks to his chest. Satisfaction curls through me as my boot connects with his face, blood splattering onto the cold stone floor.

"Finish this," I command, my voice low and dangerous, "or I swear you'll be strapped to that chair faster than you can pray to the fickle bitch herself."

"If I do this, nothing will be left of his mind. Please, don't make me do this." Arax begs, blood dripping down his split mouth. "Father, please. This man has children!"

"Then perhaps he should have thought of the consequences before aiding the rebellion." My voice is cold, unwavering. "I'll hear no more of this. Finish it, or I swear I'll drain your power like I should have done ages ago."

I snap the edges of my black cloak, dusting it off before straightening my emerald green doublet. "I want a full report when you're finished."

"Father!" He calls after me, desperation laced in his voice, but I've already turned, already begun my ascent out of the dungeon, leaving him writhing in pain.

Foolish children. Will they ever learn their parents always

know best?

CHAPTER 15 - MYSTIC SHORES
& CELESTIAL LIGHTS

<u>Ophelia</u>

"Why are we doing this again?" I ask Seraphina for what has to be the hundreth time in the last hour.

Luca stands behind me as I sit at my vanity, her hands deftly working through my hair. The vanity is delicate, carved from cherrywood, its settee swathed in black velvet fabric. Its drawers and shelves hold all sorts of powders and cosmetics —things I've never so much as touched. There's even a special nook for heated tongs, which Luca used earlier to shape my waves. I nearly snorted at the sight of them as if I'd ever willingly let those monstrous things near me again.

"You know it's going to be fun!" Nova chimes from the couch at the foot of my bed, her voice excitedly lit. "Just imagine the festival tonight, the lanterns glowing as they float into the sky." She sighed, clasping her hands together as if she could already see its magic. "It'll be beautiful."

From behind the dressing screen, Seraphina giggles. "You're not getting out of this, so stop trying. You were right—I must start behaving as Lady of the Manor. This is the safest way for us to ease back into society."

"Fine," I huff, crossing my arms like a petulant child.

Nova stifles a laugh and moves to help Seraphina with her gown while Luca turns back to me, her expression all business. My hair is finished—half-up, woven into two soft braids that meet at the crown, while the rest cascades in loose curls down my back. Luca slides a diadem of glittering stars onto my head, the cool metal pressing gently against my scalp. Matching teardrop earrings dangle from my ears, swaying as I move.

I gulp and quickly avert my eyes from my reflection, warmth rushing to my cheeks.

Luca clicks her tongue and tilts my chin up, her left hand steady, her right wielding a kohl pencil. "Hold still. Close your eyes, and don't open them until I say."

I obey begrudgingly, sitting stiff as she sweeps the pencil along my lids, darkening my lashes and tracing delicate lines into the creases of my eyes. It's over in seconds, but I still feel her fingertips gently smoothing the edges.

"You can open them now, Lady Ophelia." Luca steps back, assessing me.

I blinked, glancing at the mirror. The effect is striking—subtle, yet undeniably alluring. The rogue she pats onto my cheeks is barely visible, just enough to highlight my cheekbones. I swallow hard, shifting uncomfortably at how unfamiliar I look.

Luca, satisfied, turns her attention to Seraphina and Nova,

helping lace up the final details of their gowns.

Seraphina steps out first, and momentarily, I'm speechless. My sister looks stunning.

Her gown is a deep, velvety indigo that clings to her curves in all the right ways, flowing like liquid silk as she moves. Two high slits climb her legs, stopping just below her thighs, revealing glimpses of toned muscle. Tiny constellations of silver thread and sequins swirl along the fabric, matching the sheer, glittering cloak trailing behind her. The neckline plunges daringly, accentuating her collarbones and the smooth expanse of her skin. A thin silver headpiece rests atop her silver curls, a single indigo gemstone glittering at its center.

She looks... celestial.

Nova emerges next, just as breathtaking. Her gown is the deepest shade of cerulean, with a modest neckline that leads into a sheer, open-back panel. A luminous full moon is embroidered at its center, surrounded by tiny stars that seem to shimmer as she moves. Though the gown is sleeveless, a sheer, cape-like train cascades from her shoulders, rippling behind her like a river of stars. Her golden curls are swept to one side, a crescent moon comb securing them in place.

She twirls, grinning. "What do you think?"

I shake my head, finding my voice. "You look beautiful."

Nova beams, a soft blush dusting her cheeks.

"Your turn!" Seraphina calls, and my stomach knots.

Nova chuckles as she pulls me up, steering me toward Luca's waiting hands. I grimace, bracing myself as she guides me into the gown.

The moment I see myself in the mirror, I go still.

The gown is deep purple silk, the bodice structured with a boned corset that cinches my waist. The neckline dips daringly low, framing my collarbones and the curves of my chest. The flowing skirt is adorned with silvery moons in every phase, from waxing crescents to full, luminous orbs. Two slits climb high up my legs, revealing hints of lean muscle as I shift. A delicate belt of silver stars wraps around my waist, adding to the ethereal effect.

The back is what stuns me the most.

A sheer cape flows from my shoulders, whisper-thin and barely noticeable, except for the embroidered moons that line my spine. The fabric is almost weightless, pooling onto the floor behind me like a star-kissed veil.

"Wow," I murmur. It's all I can say.

I never cared for dresses, but this one? This one, I might keep.

Nova steps beside me, pressing a kiss on my cheek. "You look beautiful."

Seraphina joins us, her gaze warm. "You look like a princess..."

I let out a breathy laugh. "I would argue, but... I'm kind of speechless."

Seraphina leans in conspiratorially. "Finally."

Nova snickers.

And just like that, we fall into an embrace—Nova and Seraphina wrapping their arms around me, pulling me close. I don't resist. For a moment, I let myself sink into the warmth, the comfort, the quiet, unspoken love between us.

A pang of sadness wells in my chest, reminding me I'll be leaving soon.

Who knows when we'll have a moment like this again?

✳ ✳ ✳

The pristine white beaches and crystal-clear waters of Mystic Shores are breathtaking, especially bathed in the soft glow of the evening summer light as our triple suns make their descent on the horizon. Its renowned shores make it a prime destination for visitors, particularly in the warmer months. We port just outside the city, blending seamlessly into the crowd as we pass through the tall, beige-toned gates.

As we walk the lively streets, Mystic Shores is an assault on the senses in the best way. The vibrant energy, the scent of salt and citrus in the air, the warm glow of lanterns lining the cobblestone streets—it's almost too much to take in at once. Stalls stretch endlessly along the road, each offering something unique: shimmering fabrics, intricate jewelry, handcrafted trinkets, and exotic foods.

To our left, a bakery stall releases the mouthwatering aroma of fresh pastries. The scent of lemon and sugar is nearly intoxicating. A painted wooden sign proudly reads: Mooncakes. Stacked neatly behind the counter are delicate tarts shaped like crescent moons, their golden crusts glistening under the lantern light.

Nova doesn't hesitate. She ambles over and purchases enough for all of us, passing them out with a grin. One bite, and I'm confident I've died and gone to the stars. The buttery pastry melts on my tongue, the citrus tang lingering perfectly. It's gone far too quickly.

"I think I need another one," I mumble, eyeing the stall again.

"You'll survive," Seraphina teases, looping her arm through mine as we continue down the street.

A few stalls over, a boisterous vendor waves us down, his

excitement contagious. "Thirsty?" he calls, gesturing to an assortment of glowing bottles. "You won't find better than this tonight! A fresh batch of Faerie Fizz—here, have a taste!"

He holds out a tray of tiny cups filled with an electric-blue liquid that shimmers as it moves. His brown eyes gleam a little too mischievously for my liking, but Nova shoves a cup into my hand before I can argue.

"Bottoms up," I say, tossing it back.

For a moment, nothing happens. And then—

Oh.

Everything sharpens—the world hums. The colors around me are suddenly brighter, the air sweeter, and the fizz on my tongue somehow warm and cool at once. It's delightful, euphoric.

"Oh, that's *dangerous*," I murmur, licking the lingering sweetness from my lips.

Seraphina hums in approval, already ordering full glasses for all of us.

We settle at a nearby table, only a single shot in and already pleasantly tipsy. Seraphina and Nova are whispering, giggling behind their hands as they not-so-subtly eye Skalanis.

"Oh no," I mutter, recognizing that look in Seraphina's eyes. "This is gonna be *good*."

"Nova, I swear—" Skalanis growls, already scowling.

Nova rolls her eyes, before cutting him off. "I'm doing you a favor. *How long has it been again, brother?*"

"None of your damn business, that's how long." He chuffs, taking another swig of his drink.

I catch on immediately. Seraphina has decided that since the rest of us are... *occupied* in that department, Skalanis should be, too. It's a solid plan in theory, but considering we're all already halfway drunk off Faerie Fizz, I'm not sure it's our best idea.

"Oh, *she's* pretty," Seraphina muses, nearly sloshing her drink into Nova's lap as she points to a stunning brunette across the square.

Ryvvik follows her gaze, then smirks. "She doesn't swing that way, sweetheart," I tell him, giving him a cheeky grin.

He chuckles, leaning in close. "I know. And I wouldn't have her any other way," he murmurs. "Besides, I'm a possessive dragon. And I *bite*."

The words have me smirking, but before I can respond, he shifts his attention back to Skalanis—who is still glowering at Nova.

"Oh, but *her*—" Ryvvik nods toward a beautiful blonde who has been casting Skalanis not-so-subtle glances for at least ten minutes. "She's practically making heart eyes at you, mate. *Sly dog*."

He waggles his eyebrows.

Skalanis snarls.

I choke on my drink, sputtering loudly as Nova thumps my back in amusement.

"For fuck's sake," I mutter, wiping my chin.

This night is about to get *interesting*.

CHAPTER 16 - BABY, YOU'RE A FIREWORK!

Ophelia

We down our drinks in unison, and a moment later, we unanimously decide to send a very surly Skalanis to fetch another round.

"Okay, so what's his deal?" I ask, giggling as I lean in closer to Nova. "It can't have been that long, right?"

"Oh, but it has!" she exclaims gleefully, her breath warm in my ear. "Far too long. He's so rigid, so tense—he needs a proper romping to straighten himself out. Once that happens, he'll be back to his old self."

"That settles it," Ryvvik says, his gaze sweeping the crowd with a calculating glint. "We have to get him a date. Tonight."

Four identical grins spread across our faces, and I nearly cackle when Skalanis returns, balancing our drinks with a suspicious glare. He knows we're up to no good—even if we're only trying to play matchmaker.

"There's something different about this drink," he mutters, eyes fixed on the pier as he takes a slow sip.

We stifle our laughter, exchanging conspiratorial glances but offering him no explanation. Instead, we sip our Faerie Fizz and watch the early evening crowd drift past. It's still quiet —too soon for the festival's main spectacle—but the air hums with anticipation, a current of magic and mischief.

Then it happens—a shift in the air, a pull like the scent of a crackling fire catching on the wind. Desire.

"There!" I hiss, swinging around, my finger pointed at a stunning brunette beside her equally gorgeous red-haired companion. "Woah!" I yelp, nearly toppling out of my chair. Nova's steadying grip saves me, her right hand snatching my seat before I meet the cobblestones. In thanks, I plant a quick kiss on her cheek.

"Oh, yes. She will do nicely," Seraphina says, eyes gleaming with mischief.

"Yes, isn't she perfect?" Ryvvik practically purrs, batting his lashes at Skalanis.

"Alright, I'll talk to her for you, brother dear." Nova rises smoothly, already eyeing her mark. "Once I point you out, I'm sure she'll be over here faster than you can say 'Faerie Fizz.'"

"I swear, Nova Rayne, I will flay you alive," Skalanis hisses, his eyes blazing with preemptive mortification.

"Pfft. Please. Our mother would have plenty to say about that," she counters, hand on her hip. "Now tell me—one good reason why I shouldn't be your wingwoman right now."

"How about the fact that it's bloody pitiful having your little sister play matchmaker?" he groans.

"Wingwoman," she corrects smugly. "Oh! Now's my chance."

She saunters off before he can protest further, leaving

Skalanis slack-jawed and the rest of us in stitches. His scowl deepens—then flickers with something resembling intrigue when Nova returns, triumphant, the brunette in tow.

She introduces herself as Bridgette, a priestess from the Temple of Astraea in Astra. Warm brown eyes, a smattering of freckles across her nose and cheeks—a quiet charm to her, a sweetness matched by the silver star belt cinched at her waist. Her tunic-style deep crimson gown sways as she fidgets with her sleeve, her hood drawn back just enough to reveal a delicate moon-and-star circlet nestled in her tawny ringlets.

"Thank you for inviting me to watch the light portion of the festival with you," she says softly, a flicker of worry in her eyes. "I wonder where my friend has gotten off to, though."

"I'm sure she's found some company of her own," my sister teases with a giggle, her steps slightly unsteady from drink.

I don't bother suppressing the cackle that rises in my throat nor the grin I toss Seraphina's way. Instead, I grab Nova's hand and race ahead, the festival's magic crackling in the air around us.

The suns are setting fast. Soon, the true purpose of the festival will be revealed.

At the entrance of the long pier, I stop short, momentarily breathless.

The night is alive with beautiful chaos—songs and laughter intertwining with the shouts of merchants calling out their wares. To my left, the Artisan Quarter boasts this year's most powerful artifacts, a dazzling array of magical creations.

One, in particular, catches my attention—a device capable of illuminating the entire Water Realm.

As the light warlock who presented it explains its mechanics, I can't help but marvel at its potential. A relic capable of brightening an entire city? That's a miracle in itself.

I stare, entranced, but only for a moment before Nova tugs at my hand, leading me away.

"Come on," she urges, grinning. "We're going to the Rainbow Gardens."

And just like that, we're swept deeper into the night, the festival unfolding around us like a dream waiting to be lived.

The others trail behind us, each paired off, arm in arm, falling in easy conversation and quiet laughter. When I glance back, I catch Skalanis nestled beside Bridgette, their heads tilted slightly toward each other. A grin spreads across my face, and I nudge Nova with my shoulder.

"They look cozy," I murmur in her ear, my voice laced with amusement.

"I should hope so." She smirks, a wicked glint in her eyes. "If your lust radar is as sharp as you claim, they'll be in each other's arms before the night is over."

I chuckle, letting the teasing slip into the twilight as we reach the garden's edge. The air is thick with the scent of fresh blooms, and the entire space glows with enchanting displays. Floral arrangements sculpted into moons and stars shimmer with soft luminescence, while hedge animals—rabbits, deer, and even foxes—are lit by an array of vibrant colors. The shifting hues of blues, purples, pinks, and oranges cast a dreamlike glow over the festival, making it feel like we've stepped into a realm untouched by time.

"I think my favorite is the floral bunny," I declare, admiring the intricately woven figure standing proudly near a hedge.

"The bunny? Seriously?" Ryvvik gasps in mock horror. "Did you somehow miss the fire-lit dragon? It's right there, Ophelia. Right. There."

"Oh, the dragon is impressive," I concede with a grin. "But something about the bunnies tugs at my ice-cold heart."

"That's it—no more Faerie Fizz for you." He snatches my cup before I react, downing the rest in one gulp.

I gape at him. "Did you just—"

"He did." Skalanis lets out a laugh, shaking his head. "Damn, Ryvvik. We could've gotten you another drink. You didn't have to resort to theft."

"She's delusional if she thinks a bunny tops a fire-breathing dragon. I was doing her a favor." He grins, looking far too pleased with himself.

Bridgette giggles, her warm brown eyes lighting up. "You all are a wild crew! Tonight has been incredible, and these gardens —just look at them! Are you staying for the lantern dedication?" She clasps her hands together, practically glowing with excitement. "It's so romantic under the light display. You absolutely must stay!"

I arch a brow at Skalanis, enjoying how he shifts under Bridgette's eager gaze. "See? It's so romantic, Skalanis. We *have* to stay."

His scowl flickers, and though he tries to mask it with reluctance, his expression softens when he meets Bridgette's hopeful eyes. With a heavy sigh, he offers her his arm. "As you wish."

Bridgette beams, slipping her hand into the crook of his elbow as they stroll ahead.

Nova stifles a laugh. "On a scale of one to ten, how much trouble are we in?" I whisper.

"This has long surpassed the one-to-ten scale." Nova smirks. "Skalanis will seek revenge of *catastrophic* proportions the first chance he gets."

"She's not wrong," Ryvvik chuckles, his deep laughter blending into the festival's hum.

We fall into step behind the oblivious pair, giving them space while weaving through the crowd. The pier is energetic —vendors call out, music spills through the night, and lanterns gently bobbing overhead. The scent of the ocean mixes with the faint aroma of spiced treats, wrapping the festival in warmth.

At the edge of the pier, the path opens to the beach, where logs and blankets are scattered in a welcoming sprawl—people from Mystic Shore and beyond gather, their voices an undercurrent of anticipation.

"What's next?" I ask as I settle beside Bridgette, and the rest of our group follows suit. The boys cluster together while the girls take up the rest of the blanket.

Bridgette sighs wistfully, her gaze drifting toward the sky. "A breathtaking dance display," she murmurs, her voice tinged with reverence. "And then...the Celestial Light Ceremony."

As the last of the crowd settles, the air vibrates with anticipation. A single drumbeat shatters the hush, followed by another and another—deep, rhythmic, and commanding. The sandy stage fills with men, their bodies painted from head to toe in glowing hues of blue and purple. The paint catches the moonlight, making them look like celestial beings summoned from the ocean's depths.

They strike their drums in unison, weaving a hypnotic harmony that ripples through the festival. At the center of the clearing, two figures emerge—opposites in color but equal in stature. The man on the right is striking, with bronzed skin, golden sun-kissed hair, and piercing ocean-blue eyes. His crown, a dazzling creation of opal and glittering shells, catches the light as he moves. Dressed in a deep navy tunic embroidered with silver, he radiates effortless power.

Beside him, the woman is his mirror in contrast—pale, with cascading golden hair and luminous amber eyes. Adorned with miniature golden suns, her crown sits atop her head like a halo. The silk of her gown flows like liquid gold around her as she steps forward, her voice clear and commanding.

"Welcome to the Celestial Lights Festival!" She grins, drinking in the crowd's energy. "For those who don't know me, I am Lady Aurora Aetherlight, one of your hostesses this evening. Lord Stormsong's family has played a pivotal role in securing tonight's entertainment, so without further ado, I leave you in his capable hands."

The crowd erupts into cheers as Lord Ronan Stormsong steps forward, his roguish grin sending a ripple of excitement through the festivalgoers. "Thank you, Lady Aurora. We have something truly special for you tonight—a performance as breathtaking as the stars themselves."

He claps his hands and turns toward a group of figures standing at the edge of the stage. "I give you—The Dancing Songweavers!"

The moment the words leave his lips, the music bursts to life. The Songweavers take the stage, clad in flowing skirts and sheer bodices, their movements fluid as water. They twirl, leap, and spin in perfect synchronicity, their glowing bracelets leaving streaks of light in their wake.

One dancer breaks away, launching into a dazzling display of backflips before landing in a perfect spin. The crowd goes wild, their cheers blending with the pulsing drums. I can't tear my eyes away, utterly captivated by how they move—graceful, fearless, and mesmerizing.

As the performance climaxes, the dancers weave together one last time, their movements painting a story in the air. Then, with a final, dramatic twirl, they freeze—chests heaving, faces glowing with exhilaration—before bowing low. Applause crashes over them like a tidal wave, the energy infectious.

Lady Aurora steps forward again, her golden eyes luminous even in the dark. "What a spectacular performance! We are blessed this season with abundance, creativity, and prosperity!" Her voice carries effortlessly, weaving through the crowd.

The waves roll gently against the shore as she speaks, a rhythmic backdrop to her words. "The Celestial Lights Festival is a celebration of growth, a tribute to the seeds sown earlier this year. It is a moment to honor our ingenuity, our creativity, and the boundless potential that still lies ahead. Now, as we move to the beach, take care when choosing your lantern. Find one that speaks to your very soul."

A hush falls over the crowd as her gaze sweeps over them. "Paint your dreams upon them, let your wishes take form. And when they rise, may the goddess Astraea hear your prayers and guide you to your destiny." Her lips curve into a knowing smile. "Merry meet, merry blessed, and may the fates grant us a fortuitous year!"

She tosses a handful of shimmering paper into the air, the tiny flecks catching the light like falling stars. Then, without hesitation, she turns, grabs Lord Stormsong's tunic, and pulls him into a kiss.

The crowd erupts once more, laughter and cheers echoing across the beach.

I barely had time to register the moment before I noticed Bridgette. She's moving—toward Skalanis.

Oh, this is going to be good.

Her intent is obvious, and her posture is sure. But before she can reach him, Skalanis moves first. His eyes widen for half a second before he quickly steps forward and presses a chaste kiss to her cheek instead. "Are you ready to head to the beach?" His voice is smoothly composed—only the deadly look he shoots in our direction betrays his true feelings.

I barely smother my laughter, coughing to cover the sound. Grabbing Nova's hand, I pull her toward the shore before I lose it entirely.

We trip over our skirts in our haste, breathless giggles tumbling between us. The sky above ignites in a burst of color—the first firework of the evening exploding in a dazzling display of silver and blue.

"So this is the light show Bridgette was talking about," I murmur, staring up in awe.

"They're stunning," Bridgette sighs, stepping beside me, her gaze soft with wonder.

The fireworks continue, each display more elaborate than the last, illuminating the festival in a kaleidoscope of color. A peaceful hush settles over us when the final explosion fades, anticipation thick in the air.

We make our way to the lantern stations, where rows of delicate paper lanterns wait, each uniquely shaped. I select a star-shaped one, running my fingers over its smooth surface before picking up a brush. Dipping it into a pot of black paint, I hesitate—just for a moment—before writing the words that come to me first.

For Eventide.

Simple. Honest. The biggest dream I've ever dared to claim.

The moment stretches around me, filled with possibility. For the first time, I can see it—the future I want. A world I would fight for—a throne I would take, not for power, but for something far greater.

We gather at the water's edge when the others finish, lanterns in hand. We wait for the signal, holding our breath in collective silence.

Then, in a moment of pure magic, my lantern lights on its own.

I gasp, watching it lift from my palms, weightless, floating higher and higher. Thousands of lights rise alongside it, a shimmering river of hopes and dreams ascending into the heavens.

I should be watching them. But instead, my gaze drifts to Nova.

Her pale blue eyes catch mine, reflecting the golden glow of the lanterns. Without thinking, I lean in—slow, deliberate. Our lips meet in a kiss that speaks louder than words.

We break apart, breathless, foreheads resting together.

"What did you wish for?" I whisper, brushing my lips against the tip of her nose.

Her cheeks flush, her gaze full of something so real, so unguarded, it steals the breath from my lungs.

"You," she whispers. "I wished for you."

CHAPTER 17 - ONE BIG HAPPY FAMILY

<u>Nova</u>

The afternoon light filters through the parlor room's windows, casting golden hues across the polished floors and plush seating. I sit by the fireplace, fingers drumming idly against the armrest, waiting for the others to arrive. I called this meeting to introduce Ophelia and Seraphina to Galean, though I doubt he'll be thrilled. Still, Ophelia needs a crash course in how our world operates if she's to ascend the throne.

She won't like what she hears—of that, I'm certain—but we don't have the luxury of sugarcoating reality. I've given the others strict instructions on what topics to discuss and, more importantly, what to avoid. The last thing we need is to send them running before they've even had time to process the depths of Galean's depravity. Speaking of which, he's the only one I haven't warned. Mostly because I didn't bother telling him they'd be here.

The door swings open, and Ophelia strides in with Seraphina and Ryvvik close behind.

"I told you not to let me drink so much," Seraphina groans, pressing her fingertips to her temples as she collapses onto the couch. "Now I'll never be able to look those people in the face again."

"It wasn't that—okay, maybe it was—bad," Ophelia admits with a grimace.

Seraphina groans louder and buries her face in Ryvvik's shoulder.

"Dragonheart," he murmurs, amusement in his tone. "You recovered well enough. It will be fine."

I force a reassuring smile. "I'm sure Lady Aurora will assume it was nerves. It was your first formal meeting, after all." It's a blatant lie, but she doesn't need to question it right now. The fae are relentless when it comes to decorum.

She only groans again, clearly unconvinced.

I glance at the clock and mutter under my breath, "Come on, Galean."

Right on cue, a shimmering portal splits the air in the center of the room, and Galean steps through precisely at two o'clock.

"You're late," I say, arching an eyebrow.

He huffs, rolling his eyes. "I am precisely on time." He snaps his ridiculous pocket watch shut, fully satisfied with himself.

"My mistake." I flash him a saccharine smile. "Galean Hawthorne, meet Princess Ophelia Morningstar and Lady Seraphina Silverhorne-Aetherlight, Viscountess of Aetherlight Hall."

He barely glances at them. "Pleasure." The word drips with insincerity as he drops into a chair near the couch where Ophelia and I sit.

The door swings open again, and Skalanis stumbles in, looking like he got precisely no sleep. "Apologies," he mutters, running a hand through his hair before collapsing into the last open seat.

"Now that we're all here..." I shoot my brother a pointed look before turning back to Galean. "We need a diversion to get into the royal cemetery. Can you make that happen?"

Galean leans back, crossing his arms tightly against his chest. "Say I have those connections—when would this execution need to take place?"

I exhale sharply, my patience dwindling. "A simple yes or no will suffice."

Ryvvik shifts uncomfortably beside me, bracing for whatever acidic remark Galean will throw next.

"Yes," he finally says, stiff as ever.

"Perfect." I don't give him the satisfaction of a reaction. Instead, I turn to Skalanis. "Bring everyone up to speed."

He scowls but gets straight to it.

"As I told you, he has ten guards total, though I imagine that's tripled since my grand escape." His lips curl in a smirk at the memory. "There were six guards posted outside his chambers at all times. They rotate shifts three times a day—same three sets, always. Same with his valet and taster. They never change."

Ophelia frowns, and I brace myself. I already know what comes next, but hearing it aloud is another matter entirely.

"There have been thirty more executions in the last six months. All shifters. All with some magical ability. The so-called transgressions were so insignificant it's almost laughable that they even made it through the proper channels."

"Thirty..." Ophelia whispers, gripping the couch's armrest so tightly her knuckles turn white. "He's killed thirty of them..."

"Well, what did you think was happening out there, Princess?" Galean snaps. "It's not all sunshine and daisies in the real world."

"I never said it was!" she shoots back, her eyes flashing with warning.

"No, of course not," Galean says with an eyeroll.

"I didn't know!" Her cheeks redden, each second fueling her frustration. "I didn't know any of this was happening."

"Wake up, silly girl! You've been safe in the countryside while everyone else has bled for you."

"How was I supposed to know when it was kept from me my entire fucking life?! How dare you—how dare you, you spineless sack of—"

"That's enough." My voice slices through the room, brokering no argument. It's a tone that commands attention and ends discussions before they even start. "Galean, I'll see you in the hall."

He knows better than to protest. Without another word, he storms out, and I follow, sparing Ophelia a withering glance as she sputters in indignation. My patience is *gone*, and I refuse to entertain any more petty squabbles.

Galean is already waiting for me outside, his jaw tight with frustration. "She shouldn't even be involved in this," he hisses the moment I step into the hall. "Why the fuck did you have me meet her in the first place? If I'd known she would be here, I wouldn't have come."

"I have to give her something, Galean," I whisper back, barely containing my irritation. "She's too damn smart for her own good, and I'm not ready to drop the biggest bomb yet. It's enough that she knows I'm involved in the rebellion. She insisted on meeting you before the journey. It's called a compromise."

"She wants to be involved?" He scoffs. "It's her damn goddess-given right? Nova, are you hearing yourself?"

"Why wouldn't I be serious?"

"Because of who she is! Have you lost your ever-loving mind? I don't want her anywhere near this."

"Well, tough shit. We're going to need her—"

"No." His voice is final, his amber eyes blazing with rage. "This is where I draw the line. I'll get you into the grounds, but only you. Take it or leave it."

I hold his gaze, my mind already made up. "Fine."

I have zero intentions of following his ridiculous rules. I can't get into the royal cemetery and retrieve what we need without the goddess-damned princess.

"Three days before the solstice, you portal to Hawthorne Manor. Agreed?" Galean moves his fingers in an intricate pattern, summoning a shimmering portal between us.

"Agreed," I sigh. "Three days before the solstice."

"No later, Nova." With a sharp huff, he steps through the portal and disappears.

I exhale slowly, smoothing out my skirts before stepping back into the parlor.

"Well?" Ophelia asks, her expression unreadable. "Will he help us after all?"

"It's taken care of. We just need to map out our journey." I wave a hand dismissively before turning to Ryvvik. "Would you mind running into town? I left some money and a list on the counter."

He barely needs prompting. "Skalanis, what do you say? We

can grab cold cuts for a late lunch while we're there."

Skalanis grumbles but gets to his feet. "Sure, why not."

As soon as they leave, I turn back to Ophelia, an idea already forming in my mind. The Shadow Moon is coming up during the summer solstice—the same night the Shadowbound Blossom is supposed to reveal itself. If we time it right, we can sneak into the palace disguised as priestesses.

Let's be honest—priestesses don't just seek entry for blessings and prayers. A flirtatious look here, a well-placed word there, and the guards will let us through without question.

And if that fails?

Well, I have my lucky charm. One that can send out a swirl of persuasion and make us even more irresistible.

I smirk. "Well. That went well."

A chorus of groans answers me, but it doesn't matter.

There's only one course of action now.

Screw Galean.

I'll find my own way into the cemetery—using my wits and tits.

CHAPTER 18 - TWISTED PIXIE

Ryvvik

Bevan is overcrowded today, making it harder for me to slip unnoticed through the market. Still, I manage to sneak off, claiming I have personal errands to run. I sent Skalanis to Trix's with a special request and a list of things to collect for Nova—enough to keep him busy while Beatrix's crew whips up our order. Once he picks it up, he'll hitch a ride back to the manor.

I, however, have other things to do.

Navigating through the flood of people heading to the market for their daily shopping, I keep my hood pulled low. The alley I'm searching for isn't in the nicer part of town, and I'd rather not be recognized. The west corner of the market—better known as the slums—is home to all manner of unsavory characters, but it's also where I arranged to meet her.

I take a sharp right, cutting through a side street that will get me there faster. By the time the market bells chime again, signaling another hour lost, I've reached my destination: *The Twisted Pixie*. A local dive bar. The kind no respectable citizen of Bevan dares to enter.

I duck my head as I step through the door, making my way straight to the booth in the back. It's positioned near the bar, giving me a full view of the entrance and anyone who might be watching. The room is thick with the acrid scent of cigar smoke, laughter, and curses flying across the space from a lively card game in the corner. Nearby, a group of men argue over something trivial, their voices rising in drunken bravado.

In another corner, women draped in scandalously little clothing perch on the laps of men old enough to have sired them. Their giggles carry across the room as they play their game, whispering sweet lies to loosen purse strings and secure a night upstairs.

I clench my fists beneath the table. It isn't my fight today.

I don't have to wait long—thank the fucking goddess—before she strides through the door.

She moves with quiet precision, slipping into the seat across from me. A dark green cloak wraps tightly around her, and the hood dips to conceal her face. She wastes no time.

"Report?"

"It's getting worse," I say, keeping my voice low. "The executions have doubled in the last six months compared to before. Something shifted, though I'm not sure what. The crown seems to be handling the news well, all things considered. We've developed a course of action to see that the crown reaches its throne."

She digests the information, her fingers lightly tapping

against the table.

"You'll take the proper precautions, I assume? You know what will happen if you fail." Her voice is sharp, a warning wrapped in silk. "And what of the shield?"

"I have for fifteen years, haven't I?" I say tightly, irritation flaring at her continued mistrust. I exhale, forcing the tension from my shoulders. "No new developments regarding the shield."

She watches me for a beat, then slides a small pouch across the table. "Perhaps you'll need this after all."

I take it without question. She wouldn't tell me what it is anyway.

"I'll let you know when the time is right. For now, keep it hidden. Locked away. It's too potent to use more than once."

I nod, tucking the pouch inside my cloak.

"And what of your sister?"

"I'm due for a visit today. I'll have more answers next time."

She considers this, then shifts the conversation. "What are the plans regarding the crown?"

"The plans remain unchanged. The crown is aware of the Silver Devil's movements. She shows promising compassion toward our cause." The code phrases slip easily from my lips. "The crown is angry."

Her lips curve slightly. "Anger is good. It will help with what must be done." She leans back, voice softer but no less firm. "The crown and the shield must be prepared. See to it that they are ready."

I nod. Our meeting is over.

She slides out of the booth, pausing to say, "Let's hope things have progressed next time we speak. I'll light candles in the temple for your sister."

I bow my head in acknowledgment. "Yes, my lady."

She nods once before disappearing into the bar's chaos.

A barmaid approaches, setting down a mug of ale. I take it gratefully, flipping her an extra few coins for the pitcher. I drink deeply, refilling my mug again and again until the tension in my chest dulls to a manageable ache.

When I slide out of the booth and toss more coins on the table, I'm buzzing just enough to keep my emotions at bay.

I step into the alley, scanning my surroundings to ensure I'm alone. Satisfied, I take a deep breath, releasing the tension from my shoulders. I close my eyes, reaching deep into myself, summoning the shadows that curl and slither at the edges of the natural world.

They respond eagerly, wrapping around me like an old friend.

The shift happens in an instant—the familiar pull of space bending, the world tilting—before I'm standing in a dark-toned throne room.

Kieran is already waiting.

"Cousin." He descends the dais with effortless grace. Olive-toned skin, ebony hair, and silver eyes that glint with mischief. He's amused, no doubt ready to reprimand me for how long I've stayed away.

"Kieran." I cut straight to the point. "How is she? Has anything changed?"

He rolls his eyes, smirking. "Oh, I'm *fine*, thank you for asking. I'm doing just *splendidly*." His voice drips with sarcasm, but he doesn't make me wait. "She's still much the same. No changes, I'm afraid."

Guilt claws at my ribs, momentarily stealing my breath.

"I'm sorry, that was rude of me. How are you?"

He snorts. "Fine. Same as always. Just another day in my gilded cage."

Right. There's not much I can say about *that.*

He sighs, rubbing a hand over his face. "I'm only snarkier than usual because I'm not sleeping again."

I don't have a response for that either.

We walk in silence, passing through opulent halls of black and gold, with dark wooden beams that hang high in the ceiling etched with designs of every fantastical creature of Eventide. It's an architects dream, or so Kieran tells me. All too soon we come to the great hall, and I gape in shock at the sight before me. The great hall is lined with rows of beds, each occupied by a figure lost to an endless sleep. Priestesses in white robes move between them, checking for changes that never come.

We stop at the third row, moving several cots down.

She's there. Right where I left her two weeks ago.

Nothing has changed.

I knew that it wouldn't be different. I *knew* that. And yet, the frustration flares hot in my veins, the pain of that night slamming into me all over again. If I hadn't been delayed, if I'd gotten there *sooner*—

I grit my teeth, forcing it all down. Violence won't bring her back. Wishing won't wake her.

I exhale slowly. "You'll summon me if anything changes?"

Kieran inclines his head. "Of course."

I nod once, turning away before the grief can take hold, and call forth the shadows. I step into them, letting them swallow me whole. "Elowyn Jade, I swear to you—I'll find a way."

* * *

The Ghost

I watch as Ryvvik leaves the bar, his shoulders squared, his steps full of purpose. Foolish boy. He thinks I don't know who the Shield is to him. He's mistaken. Gravely.

The Shield has always been the logical one. The scholar. The strategist. Control is essential to her—but knowledge? Knowledge is her obsession. Oh, what fun it will be watching her chase her own tail!

Ryvvik believes he's the only one capable of getting close. I nearly laugh. How arrogant. How naïve.

I roll the thought away, exhaling through my nose as I flick my fingers over the rim of my cloak. He didn't even question the pouch I gave him. Not a single hesitation. Disappointing. I had hoped to watch him squirm.

Still, the prismbloom mixture is potent. Lethal if misused. Even he won't be foolish enough to waste it. The timing isn't right—not yet. But when it is, oh, it will be perfect.

Across the street, Ryvvik vanishes into the shadows. I grin. My job is done.

I turn and slip into the crowd, weaving through drunken patrons and weary shopkeepers. The stench of piss and stale beer clings to the air, thick enough to taste. A slumped-over man reeks of rot, his breath a putrid cloud of decay and fish. I wrinkle my nose, stepping past him with practiced indifference.

This part of town is filth. But filth has its uses.

I've yet to get close to the Crown. Or the Herbalist. Yet.

But that is about to change.

I pivot down the next alley, the pieces of my plan already falling into place. This will be risky. Dangerous. But the reward? Oh, the reward is worth everything.

So lost in thought, I don't see the towering figure in front of me until I collide with him, my momentum breaking against his chest.

A low chuckle rumbles in his throat as he steadies me. "Is it done?"

"It is." I brush imaginary dust from my sleeve, then glance up at him with a smirk. "But I have a new plan. One that will get us exactly what we came for."

He frowns, gray eyes flickering with unease. "What plan?"

I tap a finger to my lips. "Don't worry. It's going to work out perfectly."

His jaw tightens. He knows better than to trust me completely. But he also knows he won't stop me.

Sighing, he takes my hand, guiding me down the street. "I would ask, but you'll do what you want anyway."

I grin because he's right.

And as we step into the open field, I know the real game is about to begin.

CHAPTER 19 - PRISMBLOOM'S & SHADOWBOUND. OH MY!

<u>Elrond</u>

The stench of rot and decay thickens with every step I take through the dungeons. Filth. The incompetent fools among my guards have captured another one, dragging it here to wither in chains.

"Imbeciles, the lot of them," I mutter, leaning heavily on my cane as I stalk through the final corridor. The twisted remains of my once-great power flare with every step, a cruel reminder of what was stolen from me.

Because of her.

The treacherous bitch.

Siofra. My deceiving, scheming wife. I curse the day she betrayed me, the day she defied me in an act so blasphemous that the gods themselves saw fit to obliterate her into dust. Not even a scrap of fabric remained to claim—such a pity. If I'd had the chance, I would have made her suffering legendary.

I reach the last chamber, and the two guards outside scramble to attention, fumbling to unlock the door.

"Well?" I snap, my patience razor-thin. "Am I to stand here all day, or must I do everything myself?"

They flinch, springing into action. The heavy iron door groans open, and I step inside without glancing at the fools.

The sight before me fills me with satisfaction.

Suspended from shackles, the creature dangles in the center of the room. Its spindly arms stretch painfully above its antlered head, its gray-mottled fur hanging in slimy, ragged clumps. The thing should be afraid—it has gone from hunter to hunted. And yet, those sickly yellow eyes glare at me with silent, simmering rage.

Good. Let it rage.

"My king."

Ithil, my Head Torturer, steps forward with a flourish, bowing deeply. "The creature is prepared."

His voice drips with reverence, but I barely acknowledge him. My attention is already drawn to the gleaming instruments arranged on the table beside me—an exquisite selection of tools crafted for pain. My fingers trace over the cold steel, the familiar weight of knives in all shapes and sizes. Each blade is honed to perfection, suited for the art of agony.

Further down the table, a series of whips lie coiled, their dark leather supple from use. I select one with practiced ease, letting its weight settle in my palm. Black leather, braided for precision, its handle fitting perfectly into my grasp. A sigh of contentment escapes me. It has been far too long.

Fleeting memories stir, remnants of another life—one I have

long since discarded. There was a time when I moved unseen, slipping through the dark, hunting my prey carefully. How sweet their screams had been, a symphony of terror that heightened my senses and fed my power. The shadows have always craved fear as much as I do.

Oh, how I have missed this.

I take a step forward, rolling the whip between my fingers.

"I've been told you are... uncooperative." My voice is a low purr, mocking pity. "A shame. I had hoped we could do this the easy way."

A lie. I am practically salivating at the thought of breaking it.

The creature hisses, its lips peeling back to reveal jagged fangs. Its glare is unwavering. Defiant.

How delightful.

I lift the whip, letting it coil through the air before striking. The sound cracks like thunder, splitting across the beast's torso. It howls in pain—a sound so rich, so perfect, that pleasure coils in my gut. It's music to my ears.

I smile. "Shall we try again?"

The creature growls, its breaths ragged. And then, it speaks.

"We were summoned."

The words slither through the room, hissing from its throat like venom.

I pause, tilting my head. "Summoned?"

The thing remains silent. That is unwise.

The whip whistles through the air again, lashing across its spindly arms. The next scream is sharper, rawer, filling the chamber with its delicious echo.

Yes, I have certainly missed this.

＊ ＊ ＊

My hands are slick with thick, rancid blood. As I wash them off, my mind drifts back to the confrontation in the dungeon— it ended far too quickly for my liking.

The beast refused to tell me anything worthwhile, speaking in riddles, constantly referring to itself as "we." A hive mind, perhaps? If they share a collective consciousness, then eliminating one does little good. I scowl, tossing the bloodied linen aside before storming out of the dungeon, my cursed cane slowing pace again.

Climbing the stairs, I go straight to my study, the echoes of my steps swallowed by the grand halls. Then, as if to taunt me, an old memory slithers into my mind—*our wedding feast.* I haven't thought of that night in years, but it claws its way forward like a festering wound that refuses to heal.

Esmyra. That wretched woman.

I snarl, pushing open the heavy study doors and heading straight for the table lined with bottles of Eventide's finest brandy. I pour myself a glass, inhaling the rich scent of cedar, vanilla honey, and warm cinnamon-spiced with nutmeg. The first sip floods my senses with heat, its sweet burn chasing away the lingering filth of the dungeons. But one glass is never enough when ruminating on the past.

I drain the rest in a single gulp and pour another before returning to my desk, my eyes landing on *her* journal.

Eowyn.

Before our last child was born, Eowyn had been onto something. It was my fault she died; my failure that led to Eowyn's demise. I had once believed she could be an ally, that she would see reason. But like her sister, she was a *reckless, blinded* fool.

The journal was where I left it before heading to the dungeons. I flip through its worn pages, scanning her erratic handwriting. It was the beginning of her descent into madness. She raved about a prophecy, hidden truths, and a kingdom stolen.

My fingers tighten around the edges of the pages as I remember the bedtime stories she used to weave for our children —tales of Prismblooms, Shadowbound Blossoms, heroes, and tyrants locked in battle. The boys had adored her stories and hung onto every word. She knew how to work a room and spin myths into something *tangible.*

I skim ahead, stopping at the passage I had read before the dungeon interrupted me. Leaning back in my chair, I take another swig of brandy and read it aloud:

"One child blessed in moonlight.
One anointed as the morning star.
One locked away, bound till she came of age.
In duty, she is bound by great sacrifice.
Truths hidden shall be uncovered.
Her Kingdom stolen by a ruthless crown.
Injustice, strife, and scorned are they.
Long forsaken, a hope-filled whispered dream.

When darkness meets light.
Earth will meet fire.
Water will meet air.
When a Shadowbound Blossom blooms.
A mistake is made.
An offering given will break her bonds.
Her rage unleashed will set them free.

Queen of Night, she will be crowned.
Bathed in darkness and starlight.
Swathed in death and deep eventide.
Death dispatched, they will cry!
Righteous Morningstar, Astraea chosen!"

I slam the journal shut, my grip tightening around the leather binding.

That night. The wedding feast.

Esmyra thought she could kill me. The treacherous bitch had been poisoning me for an entire week leading up to the ceremony. If not for Galean's meddling, she might have succeeded.

And then—her.

The moment Esmyra presented her daughter, I knew. The silver hair. My damned eyes. The simmering power beneath her skin.

Siofra had hidden her from me until that night.

I had done what any man in my position would have. I sent a warning—a lesson for all to see.

Esmyra's death was that warning. And my daughter has heeded it—until now.

The deathlings. The prophecy. Her. It's all connected. I can feel it, like a blade pressed against my throat.

Only time will tell how.

And when it does—I'll be waiting.

CHAPTER 20 - I SHOULD'VE LISTENED!

<u>Nova</u>

The missive lies scattered across Seraphina's desk, and each glance I spare in its direction sends another ripple of anxiety through me.

I snatch my satchel, sling it over my shoulder, and rush down the hall, my boots barely skimming the floor. Taking the stairs two at a time, I nearly trip over my skirts in my haste.

Ophelia's going to be pissed—really pissed.

But if there's even a shred of a chance to help Kara, I have to take it. Even if it means starting another argument.

I skid to a stop in front of Ophelia's door and all but collapse inside. She startles, her wide-eyed expression a mix of alarm and irritation.

"Dammit, Nova! You scared the fuck out of me! What's going on? Why are you out of breath—and for fuck's sake, why do you look like you've seen a ghost?" Her gaze sweeps over me, wary and suspicious.

"We have to go. Now." I grab her wrist and yank her toward the door before she can protest.

"Nova! Where the fuck are we going? What the fuck—"

"Not now!" I snap, pulling her down the grand staircase, Ophelia sputtering behind me. "I'll explain when we get there, but you're going to have to trust me."

She says nothing, biting her lip instead, but her violet eyes flash in warning. She'll trust me—for now—but I won't get away with keeping her in the dark for long. I sigh, glancing over my shoulder before finally blurting out, "I got a summons —a call for aid. Frostmere is under attack. We don't have time to waste."

Ophelia relents, shooting me a glare that could freeze fire. I barely spare her a glance before rushing down the steps and out the front door.

The moment we reach the manor's front lawn, I throw my hands up, fingers moving in intricate, blisteringly fast patterns. Energy crackles in the air, a shimmering green portal bursting to life before us. It hums with raw power, the edges pulsing like a living thing.

Satisfied, I seize Ophelia's hand and yank us forward.

The moment we step through, the world folds in on itself. Inky darkness clings to us, pressing and pulling, stretching time and space until—

We're flung out the other side.

We hit the ground hard, landing in a tangled heap in the frigid snow. The sharp bite of cold barely registers as the acrid scent of smoke fills my lungs. My breath catches.

The city is gone.

Everything has been torn asunder—blackened ruins, scorched earth, nothing but ashes and bones. The smell of battle lingers, thick with decay, a heavy pall of death hanging over the ruins. It wraps around me, sinks into my skin, stealing the air from my lungs.

If I weren't already buried knee-deep in snow, I would have fallen.

Pain lances through me, sharp as a blade to the chest. This once-thriving city is nothing but ruin, death, and despair. The grief is a hollow thing, a cavernous void that threatens to swallow me whole.

Ophelia's gasp barely registers, nor does the weight of her arms around me. I can hardly breathe, my soul breaking into a million pieces with every sob. The pristine lake, once a place of beauty and enchantment, flowing endlessly in harmony through snow and ice, now lies ruined. Bodies litter the shore, lifeless and cold, scattered like discarded remnants of something too pure to deserve this fate.

Bodies. The bodies of *my* people.

It's too much to bear. The sobs, the aching weight of grief, the gut-wrenching guilt clawing at me—if only I'd paid attention sooner. Kara's last messages had been filled with warnings, desperate cries for help. She'd spoken of dreams—violent, horrible dreams—that tore her apart every night, keeping her awake in terror. I should've seen it. I should've known.

Why didn't I *fucking* listen?!

I should've listened to her warnings. I should've come sooner. We should've met, gone over the dreams, worked through this together. But I was too fucking distracted. Goddess-damnit, this is all my fault.

Ophelia's arms tighten around me, offering solace so gentle

it feels like a lifeline, a quiet strength that seeps into me. I lean into her, clutching her like a drowning woman grasping for the only thing tethering her to the surface. My fingers dig into her as though she's the last shred of stability in a sea of chaos. She's my anchor, my calm in the storm that's raging inside me.

And then— a scream. A scream so terrible, so soul-shattering, it sends a jolt straight down my spine. In an instant, I pull away from Ophelia's arms and spring toward the sound. Just past the wreckage of the town, the meeting hall's crumbling remains come into view. There, lying on the shattered steps, is Kara.

Blood coats her skin, mingling with dirt and a thick layer of black grime that smells like decay and death. My heart drops, the sight of her nearly too much to bear.

I shudder, my knees buckling as I collapse beside her. I gather her into my lap, the warmth of her body conflicting with the cold reality of the scene. Ophelia stands behind us, frozen, wide-eyed, her hands twisting in helplessness as though she's unsure what to do.

I don't have the time to coddle her. Kara is my priority.

Her breath rattles in my ears, each gurgle a painful reminder of how little time we have. The wheeze is so deep it sends a shiver down my spine.

"Kara..." My voice cracks, and tears fall freely down my cheeks. "I'm so sorry."

"Save it," she rasps, her storm-gray eyes locking with mine, wide with frantic desperation. The scar running across her eye is a brutal reminder of the battles she's survived. If anyone can tell me what happened here, it's her.

"What happened?" I whisper, my fingers trembling as I brush the strands of her dark brown hair from her face.

"We were attacked... These decaying creatures, they came in the night. Seemed like they were looking for something. They scorched everything. Everyone. It was madness... We never stood a chance, Nova." Her voice cracks, and the sob that follows cuts through the cold air, a sound so raw it shatters something inside me.

Ophelia's hand finds mine, her fingers gently squeezing, though the tightness of her grip doesn't alleviate the weight in my chest. She's watching me closely, her lips pressed together, as if holding back words. I barely register it before Kara's next breath snaps my focus back to her.

"I tried to save them... I tried—but we failed... I failed." Her voice wavers, ending in a terrible, wet-sounding breath.

The death rattle. I knew it was coming, but that does nothing to soften the crushing weight pressing against my ribs.

"Kara..." I whisper, grief wrecking through me like a storm. My sobs break free, and I clutch her hand even as the light fades from her storm-gray eyes. With trembling fingers, I close them, pressing my palm against her heart.

"I will make this right," I vow, though the promise feels hollow in the face of such senseless loss.

The silence that follows is suffocating—oppressive. It coils around me, sharp and unrelenting. Kara's death is a knife buried to the hilt in my chest, splitting me open with grief and guilt.

Ophelia shifts beside me, her eyes never leaving my face. Concern flickers in her gaze, but there's something else there too—doubt. I feel it before she even speaks. The unspoken questions press against me like a blade at my throat.

"Nova," she says carefully, her voice tight. "I know you're grieving, but you need to start talking to me. I'm not blind—I see the things you're not saying."

I swallow hard, my throat thick with emotion. "Not now," I manage, voice raw.

"Then when?" she snaps, stepping back. "After the next body drops? After more people die and you tell me it was 'too much' to say anything? This was her home, Nova, her people, and I didn't even know she existed until today."

The words cut, but I can't blame her. I've kept too much hidden—protected her from truths that should have never been mine to conceal. But I can't crack open those wounds now. Not yet.

Untangling myself from Kara, I take a steadying breath. I cross her arms over her chest, placing two golden coins over her eyes. A silly superstition, but I do it anyway. She deserves this honor.

"Help me?" The plea escapes me, fragile and broken.

Ophelia's sharp gaze softens, but I can still feel her tension, the wariness in her movements as she steps forward. "Of course."

With her help, I lift Kara onto a canoe—one of the few not destroyed in the wreckage. My fingers tighten at my sides, magic simmering at my fingertips as I summon fire. A brilliant burst of flame engulfs the boat, and I watch as it drifts across the lake, setting the waters aglow with its golden light.

"Until we meet again, my friend," I whisper, tears falling freely down my cheeks as the lake takes her home.

"Nova." Ophelia's voice is low, edged with warning.

I shake her off, forcing one foot in front of the other, each step toward the town hall pressing the weight of my own failure deeper into my chest. This is my fault. All of it.

A sharp sigh escapes Ophelia as she falls into step beside me.

I don't have to look at her to feel the frustration rolling off her in waves. The stiff set of her shoulders, the clench of her fists —she's barely keeping herself together. She's wound too tight, ready to snap over my secrets, and I know the next push— whatever it is—will set her off.

Good. Let her snap. Maybe then she'll understand.

Something is here. A whisper at the back of my mind, a pull in my gut. I can feel it—the presence of something left behind, something meant for us.

A shiver runs through me, but it's not from the cold.

Kara would have known. She would have told me. If I had just *fucking* listened.

Your fault.

I push the thought away, nearly tripping over the shattered steps as I rush into the ruined hall.

＊ ＊ ＊

Ophelia

There's something she's not saying, and I'm determined to get it out of her. Frustration is clawing at my insides, and I'm wound so tight I feel myself beginning to snap.

I'm so sick of the fucking secrets.

I thought we were past this already. I should've known bet- ter. An ugly feeling of hurt twists its way through my body, niggling like doubt hiding in the shadowed recesses of my mind.

It's enough to make me want to throw something.

"Nova," I snap, my voice edged in frustration. She stops mid-step, her shoulders rigid. "Who was she?"

Her back remains turned to me, but I see the slight tremor in her hands. "She was my friend, and a great soldier in the rebellion," she says, her voice tight and controlled. "That should be enough."

It's not. Not for me. Not after everything.

I scoff, the sound bitter. "That should be enough? Are you fucking kidding me? You dragged me out here, gave me half-assed answers, and expect me to just go along with it?"

Nova whirls on me then, her eyes flashing with barely restrained fury. "I didn't drag you anywhere! You followed me because you trusted me!"

"Yeah? Trust goes both ways, Nova!" I throw my hands in the air. "And right now, it feels pretty fucking one-sided. You keep me in the dark, you push me away, and then expect me to just fall in line?"

Her jaw tightens. "This isn't about you, Ophelia."

"Like hell it isn't! You pull me into your chaos, but the second I start asking questions, you shut me out. You don't get to do that! Not anymore!" My voice cracks, and I hate the way it sounds—like a plea, like something desperate and raw.

She stares at me, her breaths shallow and uneven, fists clenched so tight I half expect her knuckles to split. "You don't understand," she grits out.

"Then make me understand!"

For a moment, I think she might. But then something shifts in her expression—an iron wall slamming into place. She exhales sharply, turning away. "Not now."

Anger burns hot in my chest, but before I can press further, a gust of frigid wind howls through the broken hall, and I feel it —something waiting in the shadows, something watching.

And then I see it.

Near the ruined dais, half-buried beneath a collapsed beam, a strange marking is scorched into the stone. A sigil, its edges curling like the petals of a star-shaped flower. A prickle of unease runs down my spine.

Nova sees it too. Her anger fades in an instant, replaced by something colder.

Another secret she still won't share.

CHAPTER 21 - GO ON A HIKE, THEY SAID. IT'LL BE FUN, THEY SAID.

Ophelia

We've been trekking through this gods-forsaken forest for three days now. Three. Fucking. Days. And it's all starting to blur together—same gnarled trees, same tangled underbrush, same sludge sucking at my boots like it has a personal grudge. It's enough to drive me insane.

Nova's incessant chatter about the local flora is a close second.

It's cute, sure. I'm glad she knows so much, but for the love of the goddess, I wish she'd just hush.

I'm covered in mud, twigs, leaves, bug bites, and gods-know-what else. I'm irritable, exhausted, and dangerously close to losing it. A hot bath, the comfort of my bed—they've never felt more like a distant dream.

And the worst part? We have another week of this.

I slap away another winged menace, cursing when I trip over a tree root. The last thing I need is to fall flat on my face in front of her. Again.

"Fucking Astraea's sake..."

"...And that's why the Shadowbound Blossom is one of the rarest flowers in Eventide." Nova's voice breaks through my grumbling like a splinter in my mind. "It just so happens—"

"Wait. Shadowbound Blossom?"

Nova shoots me a sharp look, the kind that dares me to keep being this distracted. "Were you even listening?"

I wasn't. Not even close. I don't have the energy to pretend.

She mutters a few choice words under her breath, then forges ahead. "Shadowbound Blossoms are extremely rare. They only bloom once every fifty years, and only under the light of the Shadow Moon. According to ancient texts, they only bloom when a royal spills their blood on an altar in the royal cemetery during this moon.

More importantly, the flower is said to be a key ingredient needed to unlock a shadow gate."

The words hit me like a cold wave. I exhale sharply, unwilling to let the weight settle. "Why do I get the feeling you're about to tell me something I don't want to hear?"

"Well... if I'm right, the next Shadow Moon is in nine days. Just in time for the Summer Solstice, which happens to be one of the most powerful moons in over a hundred years."

I stop mid-swing, the realization crashing through me like a brick. "Of course it is."

I should've known. This is Nova. Always chasing something bigger, something magical. No matter how many warnings I give her, she's always two steps ahead, pulling me along with her. And now, this. She was so eager to leave Frostmere, so quick to dismiss Kara's warning.

Nova shrugs, that same infuriating calm in her voice. "Hey, I don't make the rules. You know as well as I do that we don't control fate's destiny—just the path we take to meet it."

I can feel my fists tightening at my sides, my succubus stirring restlessly beneath my skin, clawing for release. "Fucking fates..." The words come out in a hiss, like acid. I scrub a hand down my face, trying to steady myself. "So let me get this straight. We have to sneak onto the palace grounds, break into the cemetery, pray I can find one of these damn flowers, and —if we're lucky—hope some mysterious, magical fountain actually reveals itself? Or is this just my mother sending us on a wild goose chase?"

Nova nods with that too-casual air, like she's already dismissed my doubts. But it's more than that. She's moved on, buried the anger and *everything* we should've talked about back in Frostmere. *That* sight. The blood, the way Kara's body had been left for us to find. The sigil. The silence that followed.

But that's just it. Nova's pretending it never happened. She won't say a word about it, and I'm *sick* of pretending that I'm not disturbed by what we witnessed. That *I'm* not disturbed by it.

I grip my dagger so tight my knuckles pop, fighting the urge to lash out at her. At everything. The betrayal I feel, the questions about the sigil—*none of it* is resolved. It's like Nova's pretending none of it matters, like she's already moved on while I'm stuck, spinning my wheels in the mud.

I take a long breath, forcing myself to speak through the anger, through the hurt. "Fucking fantastic."

But the silence between us is the worst part. Nova doesn't argue. She doesn't offer me an answer. She just *lets* it hang there, heavy and cold. That's the thing about her: she's so good at shutting down. At hiding her secrets in plain sight.

She has her reasons, I know that. But what about mine? What about the things I can't bury? The things I can't just leave behind?

I bite back the words threatening to escape. The ones that will tear her walls down. I tighten my grip on the dagger, taking it out on the vines, feeling the sick satisfaction as they snap and fall.

Nine more days of this.

I'm going to lose my mind.

* * *

We finally cut through the last stretch of forest and reach its edge. It's a slight relief—but a relief nonetheless.

After nearly a week of fighting through tall grass, swatting away insects, and hacking through hanging vines, the winding dirt road ahead feels like a gift from the goddess herself. Adria. Small though it is, the thought of reaching it sends a spark of energy through my exhausted limbs. A bath. A real meal. A bed. Fucking fates, I might actually cry.

"Ohhhh, do you think they'll have pie?" I ask, suddenly ravenous and craving something sweet—my mouth waters at the thought of warm apple pie smothered in caramel sauce.

"In Adria?"

"Where else?"

Nova exhales sharply, the weight of her frustration already creeping into her voice. "Forgive me, but I think you have forgotten the urgency of our journey. Pie, for goddess's sake." She shakes her head, picking up the pace, taking the lead like she's already made up her mind about everything. "We'll be lucky if we find a place willing to take us in—much less one that serves sweets."

"Insufferable," I mutter under my breath, irritation bubbling up like a constant thorn in my side. That's Nova—always so damn calm, like everything can be brushed aside with a half-smile and a quick word.

She grumbles something under her breath, the fabric of her skirts swishing as she pulls out a map. We've reached a small fork in the road, and after a moment of scrutiny, she decides we'll go left.

"I think you've been away from Astra too long," she murmurs, folding the map. "You've forgotten how tight the king's grip on the land is—how hated magic has become here. Small towns like Adria, especially those near the capital, aren't friendly to our kind. I can pass for human most of the time, but you?" She gives me a once-over, grimacing at the filth caking my skin. "They'll know what you are when they look at you."

My patience snaps. "Your point?"

She hesitates before speaking again. "My point is that maybe I should glamor you." She tilts her head, almost like she's trying to convince herself. "It might be easier. Safer."

I feel the frustration surge within me like wildfire. I don't need her magic to pretend to be something I'm not. But it's the way she just glosses over things. The way she can't even acknowledge what we've been through. Kara's body. The sigil. The goddamn fight we never finished.

Without another word, I snatch the map from her hands, my fingers burning as I grip it tightly, and storm down the muddy road, letting the irritation spill over.

"The nerve of her," I mutter to myself, more to drown out the silence between us than anything else.

"Stubborn succubus..." Nova mutters behind me, amusement lacing her tone, as if my mood doesn't matter in the slightest. As if nothing matters except her precious plan.

I flip her a middle finger over my shoulder. Her soft laughter trails behind me, and the need to turn around and wipe that smug grin off her face is nearly overwhelming. But I don't. Because Adria beckons.

I glance down at the map, tracing the winding curve of the road. Markings line the edges—symbols I don't recognize, scribbled hastily over Nova's notes.

"For fuck's sake..." I slow, turning a frown in her direction. "What the hell are these markings?"

She smirks, closing the distance between us and snatching the map back. Her eyes dance with amusement as she makes a show of examining it, drawing the moment out just to piss me off.

I roll my eyes, tapping my foot in annoyance, but she doesn't care. She never does.

Then—

"Princess of Shadowssssssssssssssssss..."

The voice slithers out of nowhere, the chill in the air slicing through me like ice. My skin crawls.

Nova freezes beside me, her eyes wide like mine. A sharp awareness snaps through her that matches the sickening feeling spreading inside me.

My pulse slams against my ribs, a sick rhythm that won't

stop. The forest has gone still. There's no wind, no rustling branches. Even the insects have quieted. *This isn't right.*

The scraping sound follows—a harsh screech that sends a tremor down my spine. Then, a thud. Another dragging noise, that sounds like something heavy is being pulled across the forest floor.

Instinct screams at me to run. But I don't. We don't.

I won't hide again.

But Nova's anger is palpable, crackling beside me. It's the only thing sharper than my own fear.

She looks at me, her gaze flickering with a wild, reckless energy I've never seen before.

I nod. We're not going down without a fight.

The creature emerges from the shadows at the road's edge.

It's massive, its body a grotesque patchwork of matted black fur and mottled gray skin. The stench of decay hits me like a blow to the gut. I nearly choke on it. Long, spindly arms drag the carcass of a fallen doe, blood trailing behind it like a macabre procession.

Its head—long and bone-white, jagged teeth dripping fresh blood. Then, it's head, antlers made of bone with strings of hair and fur dangling like trophies.

And its eyes—yellow, burning, and locked onto me.

"At lasttttttttttttttt…" it hisses. "I will be rewarded deeply for finding you."

My heart slams against my ribs, but I force myself to stand still. It's all I can do.

My grip tightens on my sword, the hilt burning beneath my palm. Behind me, Nova's magic stirs, the ground trembling as if it knows the storm coming.

Then— The creature lunges, racing toward us.

Nova doesn't hesitate. A jagged chunk of earth rips free, floating in the air before her. She catches my eye—grinning, the reckless fool—before hurling it forward.

The creature smashes through it, abandoning its kill as it surges toward us.

I react instantly. My dagger flies through the air, slicing into its yellow eye. The monster screeches—an ear-splitting, bone-shaking wail that rattles my skull. But it doesn't slow.

If anything, it charges faster.

I unsheath my curved dual blades, steel flashing as I brace myself.

Twenty feet.

Nova's vines lash up from the earth, wrapping around its legs. The beast rips through them.

Ten feet.

I inhale. Exhale. Focus.

Two feet.

The monster swipes.

Talons clash with steel.

Its rotting face is too close, breath putrid with death. I shove back with all my strength, sending it stumbling sideways.

But it's fast.

Slash. Strike. Parry.

We weave in a deadly rhythm, steel against claws. Nova chants behind me, her voice rising, the ground trembling beneath our feet.

Then—the creature pounces.

It slams into me, knocking me to the ground.

The breath leaves my lungs in a painful whoosh.

Talons rake across my cheek. I thrash, trying to throw it off—

"Audit terra clamantem, audi vocem meam!!" Nova roars.

"Terram convellere, totam deglutire! Obsecre te!!!"

The earth shatters–a deep fissure cracking open beneath us.

The creature flinches, momentarily distracted—just long enough for me to plunge my blade into its exposed abdomen.

The sickening squelch of flesh and muscle rips through the air. Blood and entrails spill over me and I gag, my nostrils burning at the stench.

But the beast doesn't let go.

Its ugly snout inches closer, preparing to sink its teeth into my neck.

Desperate, I twist the blade deeper, ripping it upward. A wet tear, followed by blood, viscera, and rotten flesh. I wretch violently, barely managing to turn my head before I empty my stomach onto the dirt.

The ground beneath us crumbles further, and the monster slides toward the gaping fissure, dragging me with it.

Its talons dig into my leg, a searing pain that has me screaming.

Nova shouts my name, but I don't spare her a glance. I can't, every bit of my concentration is required.

I strike with the hilt of my blade, bashing its skull. It rears back—just enough for me to kick, sending the monster plummeting.

But its talon is still embedded in my leg. Pain explodes through me again, sending a fresh wave of nausea roiling through me.

I lose control.

Dark energy surges through me, pouring from the creature's dying form into mine. White flames erupt across my skin, burrowing into the beast with force.

The beast screeches, writhing, burning from the inside out,

its life force flooding into me.

I rip the talon from my flesh, hurling its charred corpse into the abyss.

The stench of death and burnt flesh clogs my throat, and I wretch violently, inky grime spilling onto the ground before me.

Nova calls my name, but it's distant, fading.

The world tilts and spins.

Then—everything goes black.

CHAPTER 22 - CHECK–MATES?

<u>Ophelia</u>

I wake up gasping for air, drenched in sweat. My heart pounds wildly in my chest, my breath coming in ragged gulps as I struggle to shake off the weight of unconsciousness. It takes a few moments to calm the racing panic, my pulse steadying as my vision adjusts to the dimly lit room.

A fire crackles low in the hearth. Sheer curtains veil the window to my left, letting in just a sliver of moonlight.

The bed I lie in is small, the mattress thin, yet the warmth of the blankets clinging to my skin feels almost suffocating. A desk sits to my right, cluttered with what looks suspiciously like tonics and poultices. The sharp scent of herbs lingers in the air.

I groan as I throw back the covers and attempt to sit up. As I move, the bed creaks beneath me, but my legs betray me the second I try to stand. The world spins, and a wave of nausea slams into me so violently that I fall back onto the mattress in a heap.

The door creaks open.

"You're awake!"

Nova's voice is thick with relief as she rushes into the room. She crosses the small space instantly, pressing the back of her hand to my forehead.

"Thank fucking Astraea, the fever finally broke."

I swat her hand away with a scowl, but when she moves to help me sit up, I grudgingly let her. My limbs feel like they've been replaced with lead, and my throat is raw when I rasp, "How long was I out?"

She hesitates. "Two days."

I swear.

"We still have time," she says quickly, sensing my growing frustration. "We're close—closer than before. But I had to get you somewhere safe, and Adria..." She trails off, chewing her lower lip. "You would've died if we stopped there."

I tense. "Nova..."

"I had no choice. I had to get you to Galean's manor."

I glare at her, my jaw tightening.

She winces but pushes forward. "We're just outside Astra at Hawthorne Manor. A two hours ride to the palace at most."

Another string of curses leaves my lips. "How the fuck did you get me here?"

Her teeth catch her bottom lip again. She's hiding something.

I narrow my eyes. "Nova."

She sighs, stepping back. "It's easier to show you."

A vibrant green glow floods the room, so bright I have to shield my eyes. When it fades, I lower my arm—and my breath catches in my throat.

Where Nova stood just moments ago is now a towering, magnificent Sphinx.

My mouth parts in shock as I take in the sheer size of her, the powerful musculature beneath sleek white fur. Her massive paws flex against the floor, her tail flicking idly behind her. A pure white mane cascades over her shoulders, framing a lioness's face that watches me with piercing blue eyes. She stretches out white feathered wings, wings that I ache to touch.

She's breathtaking.

"You're a shifter," I whisper.

She dips her head in confirmation, stepping closer. Without thinking, I reach out, threading my fingers through the soft fur at her neck. She rumbles low in her throat and nuzzles into me, and something in my chest shifts.

A rush of power surges between us, invisible threads of energy weaving together, green entwining with purple. My pulse pounds in sync with hers.

Something primal, something ancient, hums in my blood.

Mate.

The word crashes through me with the force of a tidal wave, stealing the breath from my lungs.

I remain utterly still as she shifts back into her human form. Her luminous blue eyes meet mine, searching, waiting, hopeful.

"You're my mate." My voice is barely above a whisper.

A slow, knowing smile spreads across her lips. "Took you long enough."

I huff a breath of laughter, cupping her cheek. Then, before I can second-guess myself, I kiss her.

It's soft at first—hesitant, testing. But then the dam breaks. A flood of emotion crashes through the bond, too vast to separate hers from mine. Fear. Relief. Longing. A deep, unshakable love that has been waiting—patiently, silently—until this moment.

When I finally pull away, she searches my face with quiet reverence.

"Why didn't you tell me?" I ask.

"And scare you away?" She scoffs. "You practically ran like fire was licking at your heels that day in the market."

I wince. "...Fair point."

Her smile falters, and she looks away, but I catch her chin, tilting her face toward mine. "What is it?"

Her throat bobs with a swallowed sob. "I almost lost you."

I feel her words like a blow, and I can't help but flinch. There's a weight in the air now, a tension thick with unsaid things.

But then she looks at me with those eyes—so full of pain and raw emotion—and I know she's struggling too. I reach for her, my hand trembling slightly, but she pulls away, as though the connection between us is something too fragile to bear.

I want to reach out. I want to comfort her, to take away that look of torment. But I can't. Not when all I can think about is Kara.

"You didn't fail her." My voice cracks. "And you didn't fail me."

Her eyes flick to mine, searching. Slowly, her lips parted, and she spoke with an almost reverent softness.

"I know. But I *almost* did."

I squeeze her hand, the weight of Kara's death still heavy

between us. "You didn't fail her, Nova. You didn't fail me," I repeat, more for her than for me.

Nova's eyes widen slightly, but she doesn't say anything. Her gaze flits to my legs, the bandages still covering most of the damage. She starts to peel them away with delicate care, revealing the work she'd done to save me. Thin pink scars line my legs, and the memories of the battle—of everything—simmer just beneath the surface.

"I did what I could," she murmurs, her voice tight with guilt. "But even my magic has limits." She hesitates, then pulls away the last of the bandages, revealing my foot. The jagged scar. The bruises. "This was the worst of it."

I don't speak. There's nothing to say. She did what she could. She did everything she could.

But some scars linger longer than the flesh.

Her hands tremble as she works, but she stays steady. She finishes quickly and moves to clean up the remnants of her work. But I can see how her fingers linger and her gaze flickers back to me like she's afraid I'll vanish.

"Nova," I murmur, my voice rough.

She stills, then turns to me, her eyes soft and full of something I can't name.

I reach for her hand, drawing her closer. Her fingers shake as she meets my touch. A single tear slips down her cheek, and I wipe it away, pulling her into me.

"We're okay," I promise, my lips brushing her temple. "I'm okay. Thanks to you."

She exhales shakily and nuzzles into my neck. We sit there in silence, the weight of everything slowly settling, but there's an unspoken understanding between us now—one that didn't exist before. One that won't break.

And then, as if the floodgates open all at once, I pull her down into the bed. Our lips crash together in a searing kiss, desperate and fervent. She melts into me, fingers tangling in my hair, her breathless surrender echoing in the bond. I trail kisses along her cheek, forehead, and nose, chasing away every lingering fear, every dark thought.

We move together, silent but for the rhythm of our breath. Touching, seeking, needing. No words spoken, none needed.

She is mine. I am hers.

My mate. My mate. My mate.

The words pulse in my blood, echoing in every fiber of my being.

Tomorrow, the weight of the realm will return.

But tonight—

Fuck the ream. Let destiny be tomorrow's problem.

✳ ✳ ✳

The following day, Galean enters, seething over his new tenants.

I'm seated in the parlor, an ostentatious-looking room filled with a ridiculous amount of baubles and knick-knacks, watching as he paces back and forth like a caged animal. His fury is palpable, radiating off him in waves. Meanwhile, I roll my foot around, stretching the tendons. Thanks to Nova's healing tonics and my own abilities, I can ride this afternoon. We have no choice—we must reach Astra and the palace grounds.

A fact Galean is not happy about. A fact Nova and I have argued over all morning.

She insists we take the south wall, the middle entry point closest to the royal cemetery. This is a solid plan, except for one glaring issue: The king's guard watches the south wall heavily.

Personally, I don't think smashing our way through an entire regiment is the best idea. Not that I mind a little bloodshed.

"The timing couldn't be worse," Galean snaps for what feels like the thousandth time, raking a hand through his chestnut-colored hair. "Really, Nova? When I said you needed a new course of action, this is not what I meant. You were supposed to be here three days ago. Alone. What happened to portaling at the earliest convenience?"

"I couldn't leave her behind knowing that vengeance is partly hers to take," Nova replies, shooting me a pointed look that all but begs me to keep my mouth shut.

Interesting. She doesn't want him to know my blood is the key to unlocking the mystery of the shadow gates. And judging by his reaction, Galean hadn't wanted me involved. Is this what their spat was about? Is this the *real* reason we had to take that hike through the woods?

Fucking hell.

"Vengeance? Seriously? Are you insane?" Galean snarls. "And bringing her here—for the love of the goddess. Our plan took nearly a decade to perfect. You said it had to be impregnable. Unbeatable. This?" He gestures wildly. "This is a fool's errand! You're practically signing your own death warrant attempting this tonight."

"I'm fully aware of that, Galean." Nova pinches the bridge of her nose—a sign that reminds me so much of Seraphina that I almost laugh. But it does nothing to quell the tempest inside me.

"In case you haven't noticed, the plan has changed," I say

through gritted teeth. "We need a way in. And we need it tonight."

Furious, his head snapped toward me, and his amber eyes burned with rage. "And you! I sent her to find you to protect you!" He whirls back to Nova, his voice rising. "When you said you needed a way into the cemetery, I agreed because I assumed it was just you. Do you not understand how this compromises everything? She's not supposed to be here. I can't risk someone figuring that out before we bring him down. And she's *especially* not supposed to be sneaking back into the castle to steal some magical artifact or whatever her goddess-damned mother wants you to locate. You're ruining everything we've worked for by including this naive child in our business. It's ridiculous. Insufferable—"

My fist collides with his face, and a satisfying crunch fills the room.

Blood gushes from his nose, and I don't bother hiding my feral grin. "You broke my nose!" he bellows, snatching a handkerchief from his pocket to stem the bleeding.

"I'll do more than that if you insult my mother or me again." I crack my knuckles. "I'm not an invalid. I can handle myself. And I'll be damned if I sit back and play damsel while everyone else gets to stick a knife in that twat."

Nova's jaw practically hits the floor.

Galean and I glare at each other, neither willing to back down. And then—Nova laughs. A full-bodied, cackling fit that leaves her doubled over, gasping for breath.

I scowl.

Galean glares at her.

"Oh, this is too rich," she wheezes between bouts of laughter. "Finally, Galean. You've finally met someone impervious to your bullshit. And you know what? It's glorious. Fucking amazing." She wipes a tear from the corner of her eye, still chuckling.

"What a way to take the fun out of it," I grumble, flopping onto the couch.

Galean mutters another curse, storming out of the room and barking at a servant for a towel and a bowl of water. When he returns, cleaned up but still scowling, he folds his arms and fixes us both with a hard stare.

"If you two are so hell-bent on taking this path, I suppose I have no choice." He exhales sharply. "We need to find you a safe way in. Since the original plan is no longer viable, I can only help so much now. I'll be expected back at court by dinner, so whatever we do, we must do it quickly."

For the next hour, we dissect every strategy, fallback plan, and worst-case scenario.

Despite my initial reservations, we land on the south wall. Galean will create a diversion, though he's less than thrilled about it, considering how much he's risked to sow the seeds of rebellion within the court. Our presence here jeopardizes everything.

The Summer Solstice celebration will be in full swing—that will be our opening.

Nova and I will glamour ourselves as priestesses of the goddess and slip through the south wall gate. Galean's distraction should keep the guards preoccupied, making it easier to slip inside unnoticed. If we're captured, we fight our way out. If things go south, Galean will blow his cover and intervene. Our rendezvous point is outside the castle grounds.

It's a solid plan for the most part.

"Are we all in agreement?" Galean's voice is tight with frustration.

I glance at Nova. She's already made up her mind. She nods at me, her expression firm.

"Agreed," I say. "Let's get this shit show on the road."

As the conversation simmers down, I catch Nova's gaze. There's an intensity in her eyes, a weight she hasn't let slip until now. The silence between us stretches, and I feel the tug of something unresolved, something she's not saying.

"Nova..." I murmur. She doesn't respond right away, but I catch the way her shoulders tense. "What about Kara?"

Her lips press together, and the corners of her mouth tremble. "I couldn't save her, Galean," Nova whispers, her voice breaking. "We were too late. She was a goner before we could even get to her."

Galean's expression hardens, though there's a flicker of something in his eyes. "I knew Kara," he says quietly, the weight of her death sitting heavily on him. "She was a good soldier, one of the best. She knew the risks, but the rebellion was her life. And if she knew she was taking a last stand for this cause, she'd have done it without hesitation." He pauses, a long breath escaping him. "But we can't let that cloud what we need to do now."

Nova's hand trembles in mine, and I feel the pressure of her grief—grief that's been held back until now. "I should've gotten to her faster..."

"You did what you could, Nova," I murmur. "No one failed her—not you, not me, and not Galean. We didn't fail her." The words feel hollow, but they're the truth.

Galean nods, his expression softening briefly, a gesture that catches me off guard. "Kara wouldn't want this," he says quietly, his voice heavy with unspoken grief. "She'd want us to stay focused on the bigger picture. The mission is all that matters now."

I take a step closer to Nova, wrapping her in a quiet embrace. We don't speak for a long while, but I can feel the weight of the death we couldn't stop. The mission continues, but in this moment, it's just us—struggling through the aftermath.

Finally, we turn our attention back to the task at hand. There's no time to dwell. There's only the mission, and the mission must continue.

CHAPTER 23 - MIRRORS? WHAT MIRRORS?

<u>Ophelia</u>

The ride to the capital is quick, hard, and dirty. And not in the way I'd prefer.

By the time we reach the wall, we're both drenched. The storm has raged the entire way, and I can barely see a foot in front of me, let alone the moon. Finding what we came here for in this mess will be a nightmare.

Lightning cracks. Thunder rolls in the distance.

Nova glamours me first, leaving me speechless at the illusion she creates.

Ruby-red robes flow behind her, her dark brown hair cascading over her shoulders. Her eyes match—warm brown, utterly human. A diadem of garnet and gold rests atop her head, completing the picture of a high priestess.

I step back, and wait for the storm to pass.

Something prickles at the back of my mind, a nagging sense that the night is far from over. Kara's death lingers like an unseen shadow, haunting me at the edges of my thoughts. I can't escape it—not that I want to. But it's Nova's grief that I hear most clearly in my mind. She hasn't said much since we left Galean's manor, but I know. I see it in the way her jaw clenches, and her eyes shift when they flicker over me.

She holds herself together, but the guilt... the weight of her guilt nearly crushes me. It hangs heavy between us, as though the air itself is too thick for either of us to breathe properly.

"Your turn," she says, her voice low, pulling the hood of her cloak over her head.

Her hands move with practiced precision, weaving an intricate pattern through the air, her lips whispering incantations that vibrate in the stillness. Magic curls around her fingers, weaving its way through the storm-saturated air, settling over me in a way that feels like a breath held too long. A moment later, she exhales in satisfaction, and we resume our grim march through the mud, the weight of the storm pressing down with each step.

My pulse races as we near the towering structure of the gates. They stand before us like sentinels, cold and unforgiving, shimmering with the faint glimmer of a force field that cuts through the darkness. Nova's breath catches, and a curse slips from her lips.

I swallow hard, my voice barely a whisper. "So... what now?"

"We wait." Nova jerks her chin toward the top of the wall, where a small balcony juts out into the black sky.

Through the storm's relentless rage, I can just make out two figures, their outlines faint against the downpour: guards. In that instant, the weight of what we're doing sinks deeper into my bones.

Fucking fantastic.

I brace myself, every muscle coiled, ready for a fight. But just as I tense, the gates slide open without a sound, a sudden, eerie quiet sweeping over the space.

"Follow my lead," Nova murmurs, her tone hard with determination. "And whatever you do, do not let go of my arm. It's easier to maintain the glamour that way. And bow your head to anyone we meet. For the love of the goddess, don't look anyone directly in the eye. They'll think your eyes are green from a distance, but up close, the purple around your irises will give us away. And—" she pauses, giving me a hard look "—keep your smart mouth shut."

I scowl, irritation flaring, but the truth of it hits too close. She's right.

"Oh, don't look at me like that," she teases, her voice soft but firm. "It's a beautiful mouth, my love, but if you open it to the wrong person, we'll be dead before the night's out, and all this will have been for nothing."

I huff, frustration and the weight of the situation settling into my chest, but she isn't wrong. So, I clasp her arm, and with a shared breath, we step forward.

A guard greets us on the other side, his grin lopsided and too eager, the kind that signals he doesn't know what he's dealing with. Oberon, according to Nova, and our lax patrol that Galean acquired. He's all chatter, leading us with a bounce in his step, oblivious to the tension coiling in the space between Nova and me. The storm continues to rage around us, but for the first time, the oppressive quiet of the palace grounds feels heavier than the storm itself.

Finally, we reach an archway of black granite, its doors carved with depictions of the moon's phases. At the top, three moons crafted from selenite gleam in the stormlight—one full in the center, flanked by opposing crescents.

Nova thanks our guide, promising to give Lord Hawthorne a glowing report, but I barely hear her.

"That's selenite," I whisper, dread pooling in my stomach. "The last time we found selenite—"

"I know," she murmurs, voice tight. "I had the same thought."

"What if—"

"Shhh! Not here. Not now." She gives a barely perceptible nod toward Oberon's retreating figure.

I swallow hard. "Fine. Let's go," I say, bracing myself for whatever nightmare awaits on the other side.

* * *

Unsurprisingly, after about an hour of searching, we found nothing remotely close to what we were looking for.

It's not like I'm any closer to figuring out what I'm supposed to be looking for, either.

We wander through the crypts, past rows of headstones and intricate gardens, finally stopping at the cemetery overlooking the Celestia Sea.

Its waves crash against the jagged rocks below, and I inhale the sweet scent of salt. The experience is heady and almost relaxing, a fleeting moment of reprieve that clears my mind.

"We're going about this the wrong way," I say, turning to Nova as an idea strikes me. "My mother said it would be revealed under the moon's light, but she didn't specify how. So I think—what are we missing? How else can you see the moonlight? Aside from conjuring it, I suppose..."

I fall silent when she doesn't answer, my mind racing over what we've already passed. Nothing. Not a single thing stands out.

I could scream in frustration.

"What if you're right? What if it is artificial moonlight?" Nova's eyes gleam with realization.

My brow lifts, skepticism prickling my thoughts as she grabs my hand, and we race across the grass.

We stop at one of the gardens, its ornate fountain striking even in the darkness. At the top, the goddess stands, arms raised elegantly above her head, a full moon held triumphantly in her palms.

And her crown—selenite.

Its sharp points glow softly, thrumming with a quiet hum.

"A thought struck me by the sea..." Nova says, walking toward a mirror I don't remember seeing. "I recalled this spot, with its glass hanging in the trees and its odd mirrors placed at random. But now..." She turns the mirror to face the fountain. "Now, it doesn't seem random at all."

The mirror catches the faintest glimmer of moonlight and shoots out a beam that perfectly aligns with the selenite crown.

My pulse quickens.

I sprint to the next mirror, yanking it down and angling it into place.

Nova has already reached the third. With a final, determined tug, she aligns it—and light explodes.

The brightest beam of moonlight erupts from the goddess's

crown, illuminating the full moon in her palms. A deep, resonant hum fills the air, reverberating through my very bones.

The ground quakes.

I grab onto the nearest tree, steadying myself as the fountain shifts. The earth splits open beneath it. Stone grinds against stone, revealing a staircase swallowed in darkness.

Nova gasps, excitement radiating from her. She rushes forward—

"WAIT!"

She halts, turning to me with a glare. "We just unearthed the most significant discovery in my magical career and—"

"We don't know what enchantments protect this place." I step in front of her, my jaw set. "Please, let me go first."

Nova crosses her arms but begrudgingly nods.

I exhale sharply, then descend into the darkness before I can second-guess myself.

The shadows move, coiling around my legs, and brushing against my skin like a whisper, like an embrace. A strange sensation crawls up my spine—not quite fear, but something else. Something familiar.

I reach the bottom, unsurprised, to find nothing but an empty stone chamber. Of course. Nothing about this journey has been simple. But at least nothing has tried to kill me—

Yet.

"It's clear!" I call up, running a hand along the chamber walls, searching for something, anything.

Something calls to me.

The magic hums beneath my skin, whispering in my blood. *"Blood."*

The realization is instant. Instinctual.

I draw my dagger, steel glinting in the dim light, and slash my palm.

Warm blood wells, sliding down my fingers. My breath hitches as I press my palm to the cold stone.

The earth shakes. Magic erupts, slamming through me in a violent wave.

I freeze—trapped, pinned in place as raw power courses through every nerve, every vein, every molecule of my being. The force is unbearable, searing.

I try to scream, but the sound is swallowed before it leaves my throat.

"Ophelia!!" Nova's voice reaches me, but it's distant—too distant.

I want to turn. To call out. To fight.

But I can't.

Another surge crashes into me.

I'm ripped apart, my body convulsing as my bones snap, twist—reforming.

My wings burst free, unfurling into the thick, magic-drenched air. My canines lengthen, sharpening in my mouth. The transformation is violent and primal.

Another blinding surge of power crashes through me, and I collapse.

I hit the floor hard, pain ricocheting through me, my vision darkening. The edges of my sight flicker, shadows creeping in.

Somewhere beyond the pain, beyond the trembling earth—I see it.

A garden bathed in moonlight, shimmering with a celestial glow. Rows upon rows of flowers stretch before me, their petals star-shaped, shifting like constellations.

The colors—midnight blues, deep purples, shadowed blacks—flicker like the night sky, as if the flowers themselves are woven from darkness.

And at the very center—two onyx pillars.

Sleek. Towering. Ancient.

They pulse, calling to me—a silent song threads through my veins, through my bones.

A promise.

A warning.

Then—nothing.

Darkness claims me.

CHAPTER 24 - A LEAP OF FAITH

<u>Ophelia</u>

E verything. Fucking. Hurts.
Pain reverberates through every inch of my body, relentless and consuming. My lungs scream for air, and when I finally inhale, dust coats my throat, sending me into a violent coughing fit. A shiver racks my frame as I gasp, my heartbeat thundering in my ears.

Then it all floods back–the journey. Nova's screams, and the agony that held me hostage. The blood, and those strange flowers.

And–those fucking pillars.

I force my eyes open. My vision is blurry, and I blink

rapidly, testing my limbs. Fingers, toes, arms, legs—everything moves, though each motion sends me a fresh jolt of pain. Nothing broken, as far as I can tell. But something is... different.

A hum pulses beneath my skin, not just a sensation but a force, rippling like disturbed water. My breath shudders as I blink again, and the world sharpens into focus this time.

Except—I'm not in the chamber anymore.

The garden stretches around me, glowing in the dim light. The strange flowers glitter with an otherworldly luminescence, their petals shifting like captured starlight. The twin onyx pillars stand tall and foreboding, and between them, a shimmering, violet light flickers like ocean waves. The sight stirs something deep in my blood, an aching call that thrums in time with the magic beneath my skin.

I shudder.

Where is Nova?

She should be here. Should've found me by now. Should be chastising me for being reckless—

A fresh wave of pain crashes through me as I push onto my elbows, dragging myself upright inch by agonizing inch. My muscles scream, but I grit my teeth and rise to my knees. Then, with the grace of a newborn fawn, I stagger to my feet.

For a moment, the world sways. Then—
A flicker.

Energy surges through me, bright and electric, instantly wiping away exhaustion. My body crackles with power, and when I stretch my fingers, white-hot currents arc between them.

"Well… that's probably *not* normal," I mutter.

The garden pulses in response, the strange flowers swaying toward me as if drawn by the same unseen force pulling me toward the pillars. The urge to touch them —to connect—is overwhelming. My pulse pounds in my ears, my instincts screaming louder than reason.

Like calls to like.

I take a step forward, my fingers reaching—BOOM!

I jerk at the sound, whirling around—nothing--not a single rustle or shred of movement.

Swallowing hard, I turn back to the pillars. Their presence is magnetic, thrumming in sync with my heartbeat. My breath catches as my fingers graze the cool stone. Relief washes over me, like something deep inside has finally settled into place. Runes flare to life, glowing in intricate patterns along the pillars' surface.

I don't recognize them. But I wish I did.

A violet light blooms between the structures, shimmering like liquid starlight. I ache to touch it, to step forward and—BOOM!

The ground shudders beneath me. Dust and stone rain from above, and I barely have time to throw myself aside as a massive slab of rubble crashes down where I stood. I hit the ground hard, coughing as a thick cloud of dust billows around me.

When it settles, a figure stands across the clearing, silhouetted by flickering light.

Nova.

Her eyes blaze like lightning, her expression torn between fury and relief.

"YOU!" she shrieks, stabbing a finger in my direction.

Fun fact, a witch pointing at you is never a good thing.

I swallow thickly. "Me."

Her lips tremble, her bright blue eyes shining with unshed tears. And then, before I can react, she launches herself at me.

I barely stay on my feet as she crashes into me, her arms locking around my shoulders, her breath ragged.

"You stupid, STUPID—twat," she breathes against my lips before claiming them in a bruising kiss. She clings to me like she's afraid I'll disappear again, her body shaking.

"I'm okay," I whisper against her hair, pulling her closer.

I get three seconds of peace.

Then—fire.

She shoves me back and plants her hands on her hips, fury replacing relief.

"You should've never attempted that alone! What the fuck were you thinking? Oh, and let's not forget the fact that you VANISHED into thin air—"

I cut her off with another kiss, pouring every ounce of reassurance into it.

She exhales sharply, pulling away as her gaze lands on

the twin pillars behind me. Her jaw drops at the sight of the glowing flowers surrounding us.

"Ophelia... this is enough to bring an entire army through one of those things."

"There's more," I say quietly.

She turns just as the magic crackles across my skin again. Energy dances along my fingertips, shifting into white fire that licks up my arms and across my body. It doesn't burn. It feels right.

I exhale, and the flames vanish.

Nova's eyes widen. "Your bonds..." She grins, awe breaking through the lingering anger. "They're broken!"

I flex my fingers, the power still humming beneath the surface. "I think... I think my blood was the key to unlocking this place. And the spell tied to my blood demanded a price."

She shivers. "And you think the price was your bonds?"

"It seems so."

Her gaze flickers back to the pillars, and she exhales slowly. "That's... powerful magic. I'd expect nothing less from Queen Siofra. But still..."

"I know."

She takes a few steps away, and an eerie silence surrounds us. I let her work, my attention drawn back to the towering pillars. The way the light ripples between them is mesmerizing, almost hypnotic. It calls to me again, that unbearable ache to reach out and touch them.

I nearly do.

My fingers twitch at my sides, but I clench them into fists, resisting the pull. Instead, I glance at Nova, gauging how much longer she'll need. She moves quickly, collecting a generous handful of Shadowbound Blossoms—the key ingredient she believes will unlock the gateway.

I exhale slowly, turning back toward the blast zone Nova left in her wake. The destruction is vast, the earth scorched and split apart. A sickening feeling coils in my stomach as I take in the jagged ruins and smoldering embers.

Something isn't right.

My skin prickles, goosebumps racing down my arms. The air shifts, thickening with an unnatural weight. Every nerve in my body screams at me, my instincts on high alert.

Then I see it.

Dark tendrils of shadow snake through the gaping hole in the ruins.

"Fuck," I mutter, the word barely audible over the sudden rush of energy in my veins.

I don't hesitate. My body responds instantly, my human façade shedding like a second skin as my true form takes over. My wings burst free, spreading wide in a protective shield. My canines sharpen, a primal growl vibrating through my chest as I brace for whatever is coming.

Another figure emerges from the darkness.

A towering man built like a mountain, his pale skin bathed in the flickering glow of the ruined chamber. Midnight-blue eyes lock onto mine, burning with something indecipherable. Power radiates off him, thick and suffocating.

Nova stiffens behind me. I instinctively shift, positioning myself between them.

"So, the rumors are true," he muses, voice smooth yet laced with something dangerous.

A slow, vicious smile spreads across my lips. "That depends. Which rumors?"

I don't get an answer—only the sound of steel slicing through the air.

He moves faster than I anticipate, closing the distance in a heartbeat, his sword raised for the kill.

Instinct takes over.

I call on the crackling power beneath my skin, summoning it in a desperate burst. A bolt of white-hot fire erupts from my palms, blazing toward him.

He dodges effortlessly, his sword cutting through the air with deadly precision.

I barely have time to unsheath my blades before he's on me. The force of his attack rattles my arms, but I hold firm, meeting his relentless strikes head-on.

He fights like no one I've ever faced—unpredictable, unrelenting, each movement different from the last. Even my years at Raven's Hall weren't enough to prepare me for this.

Another powerful strike, this time aimed for my chest. I barely block in time, my dual blades locking against his.

We're close now, his breath warm against my face. For a fraction of a second, confusion flickers in his eyes. Then it's gone, replaced with pure disdain.

"Who are you?" he demands.

I smirk. "Wouldn't you like to know?"

Then I slam my knee into his ribs.

He grunts, dropping slightly, and in one swift motion, I flip my blades, pressing them to his throat.

"I don't think that's any of your business," I taunt, baring my teeth.

His chuckle is slow, dark. "Foolish girl. You have no idea who you're dealing with."

"Oh?" I tilt my head mockingly. "By all means, enlighten me."

His smirk widens. "Arax. Prince of the Realm, Enforcer of Eventide, Protector of Astra, Guardian of Astraea—"

"Okayyy, we get it." I roll my eyes. "You're a big, bad, mighty *warrior*."

My heart stutters. Fuck. Double fuck.

Arax.

I should have recognized him sooner, but I was too focused on survival. I steal a glance at Nova, our unspoken understanding passing between us. We need to leave. Now.

No time for reunions.

Especially not with a brother who would sooner drive a blade through my heart than embrace me.

"Well," I say, tightening my grip. "Lovely meeting you,

Arax, but we really must be going."

His smirk deepens. "Oh, I don't think you'll be going anywhere."

Before I can react, he jerks free, knocking my swords from my hands. They clatter across the floor.

Fuckity-fuck-fuck-fuck.

Desperation surges through me. I unleash my succubus side, summoning every ounce of energy ruthlessly trying to drain him.

For a moment, it works.

He falters, a sharp inhale rattling his chest as his strength seeps into me. His power is unlike anything I've ever tasted—rich, electric, intoxicating.

Then, something shifts.

His eyes ignite, burning like molten steel. A pulse of cobalt energy crashes into me, knocking me backward.

I barely manage to grab Nova before we hit the ground.

Dust swirls around us—the air crackles. A new sound rumbles above—low, guttural, ancient.

A shadow moves through the haze, and I catch sight of wings. My breath catches as scales gleam in shades of the sea.

Nova stiffens beside me, tension rolling off her in waves.

"Phe..." she whispers. "Do you trust me?"

"With my life."

"When the dust clears," she says, gripping my hand tight, "strike the ground with everything you have. Pull from me if you must, but whatever you do—don't let go."

Shit. This is so not good.

She starts chanting in a language I don't recognize, her voice rising in a desperate plea. The only name I catch is Astraea's.

A heartbeat passes. The dust still rages.

Another heartbeat. The wind dies for a breath—then roars again.

One more. The dust settles.

I don't hesitate. I slam my power into the earth, every ounce of electricity crackling through my veins, spilling outward.

The entire chamber lights up. And where Arax once stood...

A dragon hovers in his place.

Holy. Fucking. Shit.

Majestic doesn't even begin to cover it. He's enormous, his wingspan alone casting the entire garden in shadow. His scales ripple like liquid starlight, and his midnight-blue eyes burn with fury as he locks onto me.

Then, he opens his jaws.

Astraea help us.

This mother fucker is going to turn us into dinner.

Nova cries out, her chant reaching a fever pitch as she slams her hands to the ground. A wall of shimmering green energy erupts before us, catching the dragon's fire just in time.

"It won't hold for long!" she shouts. "We have to do

something reckless."

I don't like the way she says that.

Her gaze flickers toward the pillars, and I shake my head violently. "NO."

Another explosion rattles the barrier.

"It's our only chance, Phe," she pleads. "He's too powerful. We have to go."

"We don't even know how to use the fucking thing!"

Another blast, and this time the force field flickers.

"We'll figure it out." She squeezes my hand. "If I'm right, it should take us to Aetherlight Hall."

Should, being the key word.

Fuuuuuck.

"Fine," I mutter. "But when we end up in the nether regions swarmed by darkness, I blame you."

She smirks, yanking me forward and we make a mad dash toward the pillars.

The dragon roars, slamming his body against the shield. A few more hits, and we're dead.

I don't wait–I grab Nova, beating my wings furiously, and launch us toward the pillars.

A final crash shakes the world, but I can't stop. I beat my wings harder, launching us closer and closer.

Finally, we land in a heap in front of them, just as a roar fills the chamber. I reach out, gently pressing my fingers on the pillar—the runes *ignite.* The energy shimmers, warm and velvety against my skin. An understanding settles over me.

I was meant to use this gate.

I steal one last glance at the dragon, nearly sputtering in disbelief.

Time seems to have paused. I turn to Nova, her expression a mix of awe and fear. "Ready?" I ask.

"Y-yes," she stammers.

Then, I take a breath—and step through.

※ ※ ※

Time, space, the present, past, and future meld together in a symphony of visions flitting around us.

Nova is beside me, tethered, yet we float.

We drift in a sea of starlight and darkness—an eerie calm, the kind that lingers just before a storm. The shadows call to me, soothing, a balm to my frayed edges. My body hums with a dangerous temptation, an invitation to stay.

No. We can't.

We have to go home.

I summon the vision of Aetherlight Hall, nestled in the valley where sunset and starlight dance across the sky. The lake shimmers in the dying light, and warm golden glows flicker in the windows. Seraphina, Ryvvik, and Skalanis wait at the doors, their silhouettes etched in welcome.

Then—I feel it—the path to the gate.

Blinding white light explodes in front of us. The door appears.

We made it!

I yank the tether between us, dragging Nova forward. We crash through the force field at neck-breaking speed, landing face-first on the cold stone floor of a chamber deep within Aetherlight Hall.

I suck in a sharp breath, my heart hammering. We did it. And more than that—we did it without spells, potions, or rituals.

"HOLY FUCKING SHIT!" Nova barks out, her voice bouncing off the walls.

A wheezy snicker slips from my lips as I roll onto my back.

My gaze flickers to the gate behind us, still glowing faintly. Its magic pulses in time with my own. How did we make it across? I don't know, and I don't care. It's a miracle we made it across the kingdom in one piece.

Then—voices.

"I'm telling you, everything is fine!" Seraphina says, her voice tinged in frustration.

A garbled male response follows, and I barely hold in my laugh as their footsteps grow closer.

The selenite-covered door swings open, revealing Seraphina mid-argument, only for her words to die in her throat when she catches sight of us.

"What in the—what the FUCK happened to you two?!"

she shrieks.

Behind her, Ryvvik looms, his sharp gaze instantly assessing.

"Well... ya see..." I start, then sigh. "It's a long fucking story, and I really just want a scalding bath and a few moments alone with my mate."

Dead silence.

Fuck.

Their heads snap toward me in unison. I almost groan. Curse my big, fat mouth.

I can kiss my peace goodbye.

Seraphina narrows her eyes. "I think you better start talking. Then—er, yes, maybe a bath. You stink." She waves a hand in front of her face dramatically.

And so, begrudgingly, I do.

I recount everything. Our departure. Frostmere. The fight in the woods. The palace. The gate. The blood. The shadows. Every harrowing detail.

Ryvvik listens like the general he is, dissecting each moment.

Who did we talk to? What exactly did we see? What happened in Frostmere? What does the sigil mean? Why did my blood unlock the chamber? Why did it lock Nova out? How long before we were forced to fight? Why did the Shadow Gate let me through?

By the time I finish, my head is spinning. Nova stiffens beside me, her grip tightening in silent support.

Finally, Ryvvik is satisfied. Seraphina touches his arm

before moving toward us, her healer's eyes scanning for injuries. Thank the goddess, nothing was broken, but we've both seen better days.

She leads us to the library, where we collapse near the hearth. The fire crackles, its warmth sinking into my bones. I stare into the flames, my mind circling back to the gate. The pathways. My blood. Me being the fucking key to salvation.

It's too much.

Nova's fingers tighten around mine, pulling me from my thoughts.

I turn to her—and freeze.

Her eyes are glazed over, an eerie, milky white.

A chill skates down my spine.

The temperature in the room plummets.

Her grip tightens—tighter, tighter—pain lances through my hand.

"Nova?" My voice is barely above a whisper.

She doesn't respond. Then—

"Youuuuuuuuuuuuu..." she hisses.

A sharp, inhuman sound comes from Nova, sending sharp fear roiling through my body.

My breath catches, and a chill runs down my spine. In a blink, she's on me, thrashing, fists pounding my body in wild, erratic bursts.

Fuck—

I grapple for her wrists, twisting away, scrambling toward the library doors—my pulse hammers.

This is Nova—my *mate*.

She wouldn't hurt me.

"Queennnnnn of Nightttttttt," she snarls.

My stomach drops, my knees shake, and I nearly crumple in the floor.

Steel flashes in her hand–a dagger I didn't even know she posessed.

"Fuck."

She lunges, her arms raised high, and swipes the dagger in my direction.

I sidestep at the last second, kicking the dagger from her grip. It clatters across the floor.

A guttural roar tears from her throat as she shakes her head violently like she's trying to fight something off.

"She's fighting for control," I murmur, panic climbing my throat. "SERA!! RYVVIK!!!"

My succubus call laces my scream, desperate, urgent.

I reach for the dagger in my boot, my fingers wrapping around the hilt as I force myself to breathe.

She charges, her speed unnatural, inhuman.

I have one second to act.

I move at the last possible moment, spinning behind her. My dagger hilt cracks against the back of her head.

She drops, hitting the floor with a sickening thud. I wince as her face connects with the floor. Well, that wasn't the plan.

"Damn," I mutter. "Isn't this just fucking fantastic."

"WHAT... THE ... FUCK?!" Seraphina's shriek pierces the

air.

I turn, glaring at the two of them, completely and utterly exhausted. "We have a fucking situation, and if either of you breathe a single word, I swear to the goddess, I will lose my shit right here, RIGHT NOW. And trust me, you don't want that."

Seraphina and Ryvvik are frozen, and their mouths agape.

I don't care.

My mate has been fucking possessed.

Astraea save us all.

Seraphina's eyes widen in horror as she takes in the entire scene. It's enough to send another vortex of panic swirling through me.

I force three deep breaths. "Unless you two want to try your hand at her, I suggest we bind her hands. Quickly. She's not… herself."

Seraphina stiffens. "What do you mean? What aren't you telling us, Ophelia?"

"Like I said—a fucking situation." My voice is razor-sharp. "Now move before she wakes up."

Goddess help us.

CHAPTER 25 - SUCH A FUCKBOY...

Arax

I'm seething. No, raging in cataclysmic proportions is probably a better definition.

I *had* them. I was so fucking close. And then—nothing. A blank space where a memory should be. One moment, they were right there, and the next... *gone.* No trace of how they vanished, no flicker of where they might have gone. Just a gap in my mind, an emptiness that *shouldn't* be there.

The king will not accept, *"I'm sorry, I have no clue what happened."* That excuse won't save me from his wrath.

I scan the strange pillars, searching for any clue they might have left behind. But they've disappeared as if the ground itself swallowed them. The only proof they were even here is the disturbed earth, scattered footprints in the dirt, and the crumbled wall across the meadow. I clench my jaw. *How?*

Morningstar Palace is full of secrets, its corridors whispering with the echoes of generations before me. But this? This place was unknown to me. And if it was hidden from *me*, it was hidden from nearly everyone. The king *never* tells me anything, not unless it benefits him.

My eyes drift to the flowers growing in the meadow. Their petals shimmer in shades of deep purples, blues, and blacks, like pieces of the night sky scattered along the ground. They pulse faintly, almost like they're alive, calling to something unseen.

I don't know why I take them. But I do.

Scooping up a few of the glittering flowers, I tuck them carefully into the pocket of my breeches, an instinct whispering that they might prove useful. Then, without another glance back, I stalk across the meadow, slipping through the jagged hole in the wall and ascending the hidden stairs.

The moment I step outside, the night air hits me. It's thick with the scent of damp earth and the distant salt of the Celestia Sea.

I shift without hesitation.

Magic ripples through my veins, instant and seamless, and in a blink, I'm airborne, my dragon form taking to the skies. My wings catch the next updraft, propelling me higher until the world below becomes insignificant. The royal cemetery shrinks beneath me, the trees mere specks. Usually, I'd find a sense of solace in flight, in the vast openness above. But not tonight.

I don't have time for distractions.

Morningstar Palace looms ahead, a fortress of black stone and deep purple banners, its towering turrets catching the moonlight. It sprawls across fifty acres of land, nestled along the coast, its walls symbolizing dominance. A place I've called home my entire life.

But it hasn't felt like home since my mother died.

I dive low, angling toward the central courtyard. As soon as my feet hit the ground, I shift back and swiftly climb the steps, eager to get this over.

The doors swing open before I can push them.

Barnaby stands there, ever the dutiful attendant. "Good evening, Your Highness," he greets, his voice smooth but edged with curiosity. "Shall I send someone to attend to you? The celebration is well underway, but I can have a man—"

"No." My response is clipped as I shrug off my cloak, dropping it into his waiting hands. "Is the king in his study?"

Barnaby bows. "Yes, Your Highness."

I don't waste time.

Moving past him, I stride through the dimly lit halls, the weight of the impending confrontation settling in my chest. Lessons from my childhood echo in my mind—*never delay facing the music. Never let him think you're hiding.*

Straightening my shoulders, I push open the heavy ebony doors.

My father sits at his desk, a glass of brandy in hand, the amber liquid swirling as he stares into it, lost in thought. He doesn't acknowledge me.

I clear my throat. "Father, I've returned. There's news—"

"Oh, so you've *finally* come to tell me that intruders infiltrated palace grounds, managed to slip into the royal cemetery, and possibly made off with priceless artifacts?" His voice is calm. Too calm. He still doesn't look at me. "Tell me, did they also unearth a monumental discovery?"

My blood runs cold. How the fuck does he already know?

"I only just returned." My teeth clench, irritation clawing beneath my skin. "I came straight here."

Finally, his gaze lifts, pinning me with a look that's far too knowing. *Predatory.*

"Were you at least *successful* in capturing the trespassers?" His words are laced with quiet menace, each syllable a test.

That familiar childhood instinct kicks in. The one that warns —*don't flinch, don't stammer, don't show weakness.*

"No, Father." The admission tastes bitter. "But I *did* collect what they were after." Carefully, I reach into my pocket and pull out the flowers. "I thought it best to have them tested."

I place them on the desk, and the effect is immediate.

His entire body becomes rigid. His fingers tighten around the glass, nearly shattering it. His gaze locks onto the flowers, and his breath momentarily hitches.

"Where did you get these?" His voice is sharper now, the brandy forgotten as he snatches the delicate blooms from my hand.

"In the cemetery," I reply. "Beneath the Garden of Mirrors, there's a hidden entrance—an underground meadow." I hesitate. *Do I tell him about the pillars? About the way they disappeared?* My gut screams *no.* "That's where I found them."

He says nothing for a long moment, his thumb running absently along the petal of one flower. Then, without looking at me, he says, "I'll send them to the priestesses at the temple." A pause, then. "That will be all."

Just like that–I'm dismissed.

I swallow back the urge to press for answers. He won't give them. Not unless it serves him.

So I bow. "Yes, Father."

And then I turn, walking briskly from the room, shutting the heavy doors behind me.

The moment they click into place, I let out a slow, steady breath. My hands flex at my sides, still tight with tension.

As I make my way to my chambers, my mind spins with everything that's happened.

They got away. I don't know how.

But I do know one thing.

For the first time in a long time, I'm grateful for a *stupid little flower*.

* * *

The celebration is in full swing. Lively music fills the ballroom, weaving through the mingling voices and the scent of roasted meats, spiced wine, and honeyed pastries. The plum and black décor gleams under the golden chandeliers and the air hums with anticipation.

Thankfully, my father is nowhere to be seen. Instead, Lorne has taken over the ball, lounging in the throne-like chair set on the stage at the end of the room. He looks entirely too pleased with himself, reclining as if he's already king.

The room is filled with our guests, all dressed in their finest silks and embroidered velvets for the Summer Solstice. They are the heads and heirs of the nine noble families, each carrying the weight of their respective realms. Every house has its purpose, its power, its place.

The Aetherlight and Stormsong families rule the water realm, their magic shaping the tides and summoning storms —a force no navy would dare challenge. The Flintvale and Rivershade houses govern the earth realm, their influence deeply rooted in agriculture, trade, and stability. The Emberweaver and Astralis clans wield dominion over the fire realm, a place of perpetual heat and grandeur, where flame-dancers turn destruction into spectacle. And then there's the air realm, ruled by the Lunara and Duskweaver families, their magic as sharp and biting as the ice-capped mountains that guard our northern borders.

Each of them are a critical piece of Eventide's foundation. And then there is my family—the ruling house of Morningstar —who hold the throne itself.

This means that remaining inconspicuous at these events is impossible despite my best efforts.

I barely make it twenty feet into the ballroom before I'm surrounded by a cluster of women and their mothers.

"Prince Arax!" An older woman calls my name, waving frantically from the side of the crowd. Her silver-and-gold hair is pinned in an elegant bun at the nape of her neck, and she gestures toward the young woman beside her—one who can't be more than twenty. "You simply must meet my granddaughter." She beams, pushing the girl forward. "Prince Arax, allow me to introduce Lady Rosalie Aetherlight."

Rosalie steps forward, brown eyes wide with a practiced innocence. The rest of the ladies sigh and flick their fans, their impatience barely concealed.

If I want to escape, there's only one option.

"Lady Rosalie," I say, dipping my head. "May I have this dance?"

A ripple of disappointment passes through the crowd as she takes my hand, and we step onto the floor. Her deep red gown swishes behind her as we move, a stark contrast against the sea of dark color tonight. No doubt, this was a deliberate choice meant to make her stand out.

"Are you enjoying the celebration?" I ask as I spin her effortlessly into the next movement.

"Oh, very much so, Your Highness." She smiles, cheeks tinged pink.

"Wonderful."

The song draws to a close, and I dip her low to finish the dance. Her breath catches as she rights herself, her fingers lingering on my arm. She looks at me expectantly, but if she's waiting for an offer for another dance—or something more—she will be disappointed.

I might entertain her if I had any interest in securing an alliance. But I'd rather spend the rest of my night drinking my brother out of his money. Or, if I'm feeling particularly reckless, finding a priestess to keep me company in the pleasure gardens.

"Thank you for the dance, Lady Rosalie," I say with a stiff bow. "Enjoy your evening."

I don't wait for a reply before turning on my heel.

Lorne was still seated the last time I looked, lazing about as he ordered a servant to bring him more grapes. But when I glance toward the makeshift stage, the throne is empty.

That's never a good sign.

Sighing, I make my way toward the back of the stage, pushing through the curtain to the dimly lit hallway beyond.

And that's when I hear it. A choked sound, followed by muffled sobs.

I move swiftly, my steps silent as I approach the end of the corridor. The sight that greets me ignites a sharp, sudden fury that threatens to consume me.

Lorne has cornered one of the staff against the stone wall.

His hands grip her arms too tightly, his mouth curled into something grotesque.

Indignation surges through me like wildfire, and before I can think, I move.

I yank him back by the collar of his doublet, tearing him away from the terrified girl. "What the fuck are you doing?" I snarl, my voice low and lethal. "It's the night of the Summer Solstice, and you can't wait until after the party to get your fill in the pleasure quarter? If our father catches wind of this—"

Lorne scoffs, trying to wrench free, but I slam my fist into his jaw.

"Go," I command the girl, not looking away from my brother. "Find Caecinnia in the pleasure gardens. Tell her I sent you."

She hesitates only a moment before fleeing, the click of the door behind her echoing in the corridor.

Lorne barely has time to recover before I throw him to the ground and drive my boot into his ribs. He gasps, rolling onto his side, blood smearing his chin.

"This will stop," I growl. "Do you hear me? You're the fucking heir, for Goddess' sake."

He grins through the blood, spitting onto the stone. "What Father doesn't know won't hurt him, Arax."

He wipes his chin, wheezing as he drags himself to his feet. He's leaner, a head shorter than me, built like our father. His green eyes gleam with barely contained rage.

"You'll pay for that interruption, *brother*," he hisses.

He lunges, throwing a sucker punch that clips my nose. I rear back and slam my forehead into his face, grinning at the satisfying crunch.

Lorne howls, swinging wildly, but I sidestep the blow with ease. I kick out his knee, sending him crashing to the floor. Before he can recover, I grab a fistful of his hair, forcing his head back.

I should be ashamed. But I'm not.

A hand clamps down on my shoulder, yanking me back. I whirl around, only to come face to face with Galean Hawthorne, my personal advisor.

He scowls, shoving me aside before offering Lorne a hand. "At least someone has some manners around here."

Lorne dusts himself off, adjusting his dark green doublet. "If you need me, I'll be in the pleasure gardens. Clearly, I've worn out my welcome."

He stalks off, leaving me with Galean, who levels me with an unimpressed stare.

"Do I even need to ask, or is randomly attacking the heir just something we're doing now?" His voice is eerily calm. "Was it absolutely necessary?"

"It was," I smirk.

He sighs, dragging a hand through his chestnut hair. "I suppose I'll have some smoothing over to do." He pauses. "Can you at least try to pretend like you respect him? That you're loyal to him?"

"I interrupted him mid-attack on a defenseless staff member. Was I supposed to let him continue?"

"No," Galean mutters, pinching the bridge of his nose. "No, of course not. If I'd stumbled across him first, I can't say I wouldn't have hung him up in the air before punching him in the dick."

A strangled laugh escapes me. "At least we agree on something."

He grins, offers a slight bow, and disappears through the servants' entrance.

I sigh. Someone has to play host tonight. And since my brother is licking his wounds, the honor falls to me.

CHAPTER 26 - SQUARE ONE

Nova

It's only a matter of time before I lose my strength—and my sanity—completely.

I don't think I ever really made it out of the Shadow Gate. Not truly. My body might have escaped, but my mind? My soul? They're still trapped in the endless dark, drowning in the echoes of something ancient and rotten. The taint of that place clings to me, thick as grave soil, and I know—deep in my marrow—I won't make it out of here without losing a piece of myself.

I've been shoved into some twisted, hidden corner of my own mind. Locked inside, screaming, beating my fists raw against the walls, scratching, kicking—nothing gives.

And the thing that did this to me? The fucking deathling?

It's beyond terrifying.

This is the creature from the road to Adria. The one that

nearly killed my mate. The nightmare I thought I'd left behind, only to find it's been waiting for me all along.

I don't know how much longer I can fight like this. I don't even know how to fight back. I never imagined these creatures could breach the stronghold of a mind, let alone invade it so wholly. I was blindsided. Arrogant. Weak.

I let her down. I let them all down.

Ophelia—Godess, my Ophelia. The thought of never seeing her again is a blade twisting in my ribs. She must be furious. Devastated and worried sick. And I can't even tell her what I found, what I know to be true.

The Shadowbound Blossoms don't just power the pathway for non-magic users. They're tied to the curse. A curse that demands the blood of the Morningstar line to break. And a cure—if I'm right—one that could save all of us from sharing my fate.

A curse and a cure. How fucking ironic.

I have to get out of here.

Another scream rips from my throat, wild and raw. I thrash against the unyielding walls, fury crashing through my body in waves. My magic rises like a storm—power thrumming beneath my skin, thick with the scents of rain, wildflowers, and earth.

I don't hold it back.

The first strike of energy slams into the stone with a deafening crack.

Satisfaction burns through me as another surge barrels forward, then another, each one splintering the surface, carving through my prison. I don't stop. I don't hesitate.

The wall shatters.

And then—I step through.

* * *

The first thing I register as I claw my way back to consciousness is the sound of arguing—loud, heated voices overlapping in a chaotic blur. The second is the sharp bite of rope against my wrists, binding me to a chair. And third—my head. It feels like an entire fortress has been dropped onto it, every sound too sharp, every flicker of light stabbing through my skull.

"What... happened?" I rasp, my throat dry as the Perinise Desert.

"You're back!" Ophelia's voice is a breath of relief before she's at my side, hands cupping my face, her touch careful but frantic.

Her stormy gaze searches mine, worry bleeding into something more—panic.

"I'm sorry..." The words slip out, hoarse, and weighted with guilt. "I don't know how it happened."

"It's not your fault." She grips my chin, forcing me to meet her eyes before pressing a soft, desperate kiss to my lips.

I try to reach for her, only to be yanked back by the bindings. The second I realized it, so did she, and she stepped away. Not far, but enough. The space between us stings more than it should.

I flex my fingers, rolling my shoulders against the ropes, an edge creeping into my voice. "Why do I get the feeling I'll be tied to this chair for a while?"

"We need to be sure..." Seraphina murmurs from my left, voice barely above a whisper.

Ryvvik shifts his stance subtly to shield her, one hand resting on the hilt of his sword. His posture is coiled and ready. Ophelia turns away, silent tears slipping down her cheeks.

The sight guts me. Whatever happened while I was... *gone*, it wasn't small.

I force myself to look at the fire instead of the broken expressions around me, grasping at the tattered remains of memory, trying to piece together how I lost control.

"You don't need to worry about it happening again." My voice is iron now, leaving no room for doubt. "If you want to save yourselves—if you want to save all of Eventide—you'll untie me so I can fetch the queen's journal from my riding bag. Otherwise, we're all fucked."

Ophelia hesitates for only a moment before slicing through the ropes. The relief is short-lived when I see the storm raging in her eyes. She's furious—about my secrets, about everything —but I don't have time to care.

I rub my wrists absently before grabbing my bag and turning it over, letting its contents spill across the floor. My fingers find the journal instantly, trailing over the worn leather before flipping to a passage burned into my memory.

Clearing my throat, I read aloud:

"My priestesses have finally found the ancient knowledge I've been searching for. Caecinnia has uncovered something almost unbelievable that matches the prophecy Niahm delivered. This child I carry... she is blessed, but she is also cursed. And I must take extreme measures to ensure she survives long enough to do what must be done. We have dissected and studied the Shadowbound Blossoms at full capacity, and we are on the right path. I have begun the process of creating tinctures infused with

*their power—combined with Morningstar blood. The re-
sults have been astounding. Not only have we expelled
the invaders from the body, but the shifter has become
stronger and more resistant to the effects of the gate. I
have trusted only Caecinnia and Niahm with the full details of what must be done. They will keep the tinctures
secure and store them safely within the temple until the
time comes. They know the signs. Astraea help us."*

Silence falls as they absorb the words.

I shut the journal. "We need to contact the temple. In the
meantime, I'll use what's here to replicate the process at Aetherlight Hall. And now that I know I'm vulnerable to being—er
—possessed, I'll take every precaution to ensure it doesn't happen again."

Ophelia remains still, unreadable, but her shields are up,
locked tight. *Good.* One less thing to worry about when
Skalanis starts training us. He's a genius when it comes to
mental defenses.

She exhales slowly, voice heavy with frustration. "So we're
right back to square one." A humorless laugh escapes her.
"I know nothing about priestesses or temples. And I doubt
Galean is particularly thrilled with me after our last encounter." She cringes at the memory.

I smother a chuckle. "Leave Galean to me. He owes me a
favor."

Her eyebrow arches at that, but she says nothing.

Seraphina clears her throat, her voice softer than usual. "You
can use anything in my laboratory. And... if you need my help,
you have it."

Ryvvik stays silent, but his energy shifts, taut and barely
restrained. I can *feel* the dragon in him churning beneath the

surface. Protective. Possessive.

Interesting.

"Ryvvik…" I draw out his name, a slow grin spreading across my face. "Something you'd like to share with the class?"

His gaze snaps to mine, then to Seraphina. His jaw ticks. "No."

A low growl rumbles in his throat, but I don't miss how his arm tightens around Seraphina's waist. *Oh, this is priceless.*

I let out a full, delighted laugh. "Well, well. Looks like I'm not the only one who's found their mate. Congratulations, my friend."

Seraphina's eyes widen, flicking to Ryvvik in question. He hesitates, then gives her a slight nod, a flicker of a smile. And just like that, his arm curls more securely around her.

I may have forced his hand—okay, I *definitely* forced his hand —but seeing them like this? It's worth it.

Ophelia shakes her head, amusement slipping past her exhaustion. A genuine smile tugs at her lips as she hugs her sister, whispering something I can't catch.

Seraphina blushes furiously.

Ryvvik cups her cheek, brushing his lips softly over hers, and I suddenly find myself searching for *my* mate across the room.

She's watching, a quiet smile playing on her lips. Her onyx hair glows under the firelight, the shimmer catching just right as it cascades down her back.

Goddess, she's beautiful. But there's no time for this. Not yet.

I force myself to turn away, my mind already shifting to what needs to be done. Letters must be written—plans set in motion.

Ophelia is going to *hate* what I'm about to ask of her.

I've dragged her into my world of deception, and I should feel

6021211411114211111111

guilty for it.

But I don't.

Because without her, without us standing together—all of Eventide will fall.

CHAPTER 27 - AN IMPOSSIBLE CHOICE

<u>Ryvvik</u>

Waiting is brutal, especially where she is concerned. There's never any clear indication of when she will show up, only the certainty that she won't leave me dangling at the edge of a cliff... yet. At least until I prove myself no longer useful.

The Twisted Pixie is overcrowded, so I've perched on a stoop hidden in the alley beneath the overhanging bridge. Its shadows provide an aura of anonymity that she will, at the very least, appreciate.

Footsteps fill the underpass, echoing off the stone walls. I turn as she beckons me forward with a wave of her hand. I leap off the stoop, striding toward her with purpose and ease. "You summoned me?" The words fall from my lips in a whisper.

"Yes," she murmurs, her cloaked head tilting past me toward the Twisted Pixie, "and why couldn't we have met inside?"

The tone has a bite to it, like she can't stand the choice I made. Typical. I should have known better.

"In case you didn't notice, the bar is crowded," I hiss, shifting slightly to block her line of sight, "this seemed like the best second choice."

She tenses, as if listening for something, before checking over her shoulder. I start to protest, but she snaps a finger up in my direction, silently ordering me to halt.

My senses go on high alert, my dragon stirring restlessly beneath my skin. He's pissed, and rightly so—if even she is wary.

She sucks in a breath before snapping her attention to mine. "Forgive me, I thought I saw something. It must be my imagination."

The words don't feel entirely true, like there's more she'd like to say but can't—or won't. Does it really matter?

"I need you to pay your cousin's realm a visit," she says, slipping a package toward me. It's a small, black, ordinary-looking velvet pouch, and I'm tempted to peek inside. Before I can, she speaks again, pulling me out of my thoughts. "There's a man there... angular features, thick brows, golden hair..."

"And?" I ask, curiosity piquing in a way it never has before.

"This tincture is a secret, you understand?" Her tone is low, commanding—an ever-present reminder of the oath I swore to her.

I nod, giving my agreement easily. It's not like she couldn't force me if she wanted to. "Does this man have a name?" I ask, my tone like ice.

Just because I'll follow doesn't mean I have to like it.

"That is entirely irrelevant and *way* above your pay grade, soldier," she snarls, checking over her shoulder again.

"How the hell am I supposed to pinpoint one man based on

such a vague description?" I snap, dragging her attention back to me.

Her next words are visceral, laced with poison sharper than any blade. "If you would learn an ounce of fucking patience—Astraea's sake. He has a scar on his right cheek, cutting straight across in a deep line."

Feeling properly chastised, I nod, stick the pouch into one of my innermost secret pockets, and wait for her instructions.

"The elixir in this vial can only be used once, Ryvvik. Do you understand?"

I frown, not fully grasping the weight of her words—until her next sentence cuts through me like a blade from navel to throat.

"This elixir will wake him up, and you will use this as a bargaining chip with Kieran. Have I made myself clear?"

Sweat lines my palms, my heart hammering erratically in my chest. "Wake him up? No one can wake those people up. This is a goddess-damned fool's errand!"

The words end in a shout, one that bounces back at me off the stone walls, making me cringe at my slight misstep.

She grabs my arm with force, yanking me toward her in one swift motion. "*Foolish boy*! Keep your voice down," she hisses, pressing her lips close to my ear. "You will do as I ask. Stop questioning me, or I swear I will make you use the other one on the shield out of pure spite. Got it?"

I grit my teeth, jerking myself free of her hold. If what she says is true—Elowyn Jade. My throat thickens, and my heart races again, though for an entirely different reason this time. Through clenched teeth, I force out, "Understood."

"Go. *Now*." She jerks her thumb toward the end of the tunnel, giving me just enough room to call forth the magic of the shadows.

I don't spare her a fucking glance. I'm too furious, and lingering here will only make my situation worse. Cool, shadowy tendrils coil around me, and in an instant, I'm gone—leaving the streets of Bevan behind.

✳ ✳ ✳

As soon as my feet touch the ground, I stalk toward the throne room in search of Kieran. My stomach clenches, anxiety rising in a wave that threatens to bowl me over. *Where the fuck is he?*

"Cousin?" A sleepy voice greets me from behind, and I suck in a breath, my rigid posture easing instantly.

"There you are." I stride toward him, not even bothering with formalities. There's no time. "I have to do something— Kieran..." The words die on my lips.

How can she expect me to ask this... of him? Of all fucking people. Has he not suffered enough? His people?

My mouth tastes like ash.

Shrewd silver eyes glint in the flickering gaslight, staring straight through me, like he can glimpse my very soul. Shuddering, I close the gap between us, the words cloying my mouth like grains of sand.

"What is it?" he asks, sharp, alert, ever watchful.

"I think... I might have a cure. I'm not sure what she wants with you—"

The words are cut off by a snarl that crashes through the room, rattling the stained glass. "What. Do. You. Mean? What the fuck have you done, Ryvvik?"

I gulp, shifting slightly as nervous energy rushes through my body. "I've been searching for a way to wake them up, Kieran."

He startles, his silver eyes widening in disbelief. He swears under his breath, muttering something that's surely an insult, before returning to me. "Are you sure?"

"We won't know until we try it," I say, albeit a bit begrudgingly.

He doesn't even hesitate. There's a newfound determination igniting inside him, burning bright and unwavering. He doesn't care that I've probably made a deal with the devil to get this.

Hope.

The thought comes unbidden, followed by a swell of something I'd rather not put a name to. Hope, while beautiful, can be a dangerous thing.

In what feels like no time at all, we arrive at the rows of sleeping patients lining the once-great hall. I scan the rows, searching for the person she instructed me to wake. My jaw clenches, but my eyes betray me, wandering of their own accord to the spot that houses my slumbering sister.

My twin. The other half of my soul, lost to me for what feels like an eternity.

Gritting my teeth, I change course, heading straight toward the cot that has housed her for the last six months. A priestess scuttles by me, and without fully thinking it through, I reach out and catch her sleeve.

She startles, her brown eyes crinkling at the corners as she narrows her gaze at me, cutting right fucking through me.

"Apologies," I mutter. "Can you help me with something?"

Her gaze softens, and she glances at Kieran behind me. Right.

Of course, she would need to defer to him.

He nods at her, and she follows me down to Elowyn's cot. "What would you like me to help with, Lord Ryvvik?" she asks softly, smoothing stray white-colored hairs away from her face. The action is tender, and it fills me with unexpected gratitude for the care Elowyn has received while here.

"Can you raise her head for me and help me get this vial of liquid into her mouth?"

She eyes me suspiciously, like a mother hen guarding her clutchlings. "It's okay, Theia," Kieran reassures her, nodding again before turning to me. "Let's hope this works."

Quickly, I retrieve the velvet pouch from my pocket, emptying the tiny vial into my hands. The liquid has a light shimmer to it, almost as if it's glowing from within. With shaky hands, I pop the cork, praying to the fickle goddess above.

"Please don't let this be a mistake," I whisper.

CHAPTER 28 - HIDDEN AGENDAS

<u>Galean</u>

After interrupting what was sure to be yet another fiasco between the two princes, I had taken off searching for my mate.

Briar's quarters are in the military wing of the palace, accessible only through the servants' entrances. I take a left, descending a long flight of stone stairs. At the bottom, I turn right, striding down the dimly lit corridor leading to the barracks.

Briar is one of Eventide's top commanders—a force of nature on the battlefield and one of the most powerful warlocks I've ever encountered. His mastery of weather magic is unparalleled, securing his rapid rise through the ranks. It's also earned him plenty of enemies.

Few know the extent of our relationship. Briar fought tooth

and nail to get where he is, and I refuse to let anyone discredit his achievements by claiming he only holds his position because of who he's fucking.

I stop before a polished ebony door, straightening my clothes —a nervous tick, really—before stepping inside.

The moment I enter, my eyes land on him.

Seated by the window, Briar is engrossed in a book, his sharp mind lost in whatever pages captured his attention. His blue eyes, flecked with black, lift to meet mine, and the slow smile that spreads across his face makes my stomach flip.

His dark hair, streaked with silver, tumbles over his forehead, a testament to the power that crackles just beneath his skin. The first time we met, I reached for him, and sparks leaped between us. It had been instant. I had known, from that moment, that he was mine.

He's my one bright spot in this wretched kingdom. It's the only thing I genuinely fear losing.

"Galean, love," Briar greets, closing his book. "Didn't expect you this early. Everything alright?"

"Yes and no," I reply, heading straight for the brandy. "But first, I need a drink."

Briar watches in amusement as I pour myself a generous glass.

"I had to create a distraction tonight," I continue, swirling the amber liquid before taking a long sip. "One that I'm sure you've already heard about."

"I knew you set that fire in the foyer," he smirks. "Brilliant move. But did you really have to hit the tapestries? You do realize those were priceless artifacts covered in our history?" He shakes his head in mock devastation. "I was translating them in my spare time, you know. Now, what will I do for a hobby?"

I snort, leveling him with a knowing look. "Please. As if you have the patience for that."

Briar grins. "Alright, you caught me. That was actually what High Priestess Niahm was hollering about earlier. Quite the dramatic display, really." He stands, closing the distance between us and looping an arm around my waist. "So? Tell me. What's the worst part?"

I groan as he tugs me onto the couch, where I settle into his warmth.

"The king cornered me after it happened," I admit. "His paranoia is getting worse—but this time, he was dangerously close to being right. I had to distract him with something else... someone else."

Briar arches a brow, mischief sparking in his eyes. "What did you do?"

I roll my shoulders. "Prince Arax was sent to investigate the cavern under the cemetery. Somehow, the king knew the fire was a diversion. So, I gave him a new obsession—I told him that Arax would return with a rare flower. One that could aid his experiments with the creatures he's been researching." I fix Briar with a pointed look. "You still don't know anything about those?"

"Let me guess." Briar smirks. "After you dangled that little tidbit, he was practically salivating over the chance to get you into his bed?"

I scowl. "I'm serious, Briar. Do you know anything? I'm not asking as your mate—I'm asking as the Prince Warlord's advisor."

His smirk fades into a resigned sigh. "No. I don't know any more than you do. But there's something strange about them, and I know for a fact the king is keeping everything under lock and key. It's been harder than usual to sneak around."

That doesn't sit well with me.

I exhale slowly, letting my thoughts turn over in my mind.

"So..." Briar drawls, breaking the silence. "How bad was it this time?"

I glance at him. "Do you even have to ask? He cornered me. Grabbed my dick. Mild, in comparison to what his son pulled tonight."

Briar stiffens, his entire expression darkening. "That fucker."

I shrug, forcing down the sick feeling that always lingers after those encounters. "It's nothing new. Besides, I'd rather distract him than let him get too close to my real secrets. This time... he came too close."

A shiver works its way down my spine.

Briar immediately quips, "That's what he said."

I choke on my brandy, sputtering as I glare at him.

"Too soon?" he asks innocently, lips twitching.

I shake my head, snorting before a deep laugh rumbles out of me. Briar joins in, his warm laughter filling the chamber, and just like that—he's erased the tension.

It's one of the things I love most about him. He knows how to pull me out of my own head and drive away the lingering filth of moments I'd rather forget.

Yes, Briar is my one constant in this cruel, ever-changing world.

I press closer, resting my head on his shoulder, letting myself sink into his warmth. And when he tilts my chin up and claims my mouth in a searing kiss, everything else fades into nothingness.

* * *

"There now, be a good boy and come here."

The voice slithers through the air like smoke, thick and cloying. I know it too well—it haunts my dreams and taints my already blackened soul. No matter how many times I fight or how many times I will my body to resist, it never listens.

My feet move of their own accord, the cold iron collar biting into my skin as I turn my head toward him. King Elrond stands before me, his silver eyes gleaming like polished steel. The heavy chain attached to my throat rattles as he yanks it hard, dragging me forward with a sickening scrape of metal on stone. My knees buckle, and I slam face-first onto the cold, unforgiving floor. The impact sends a sharp burst of pain through my jaw, the chill of the stone seeping into my bare skin like icy fingers.

A sound—a whimper, barely more than a breath—catches my ear. My body turns toward it on instinct, my breath lodging in my throat the moment I see him.

Briar.

He's manacled to the ground, his body battered and broken. Blood stains his pale skin, dark bruises blooming across his face and chest like the petals of a rotting flower. His usually piercing blue eyes, now swollen and red, flicker weakly toward me. He tries to speak, but all that comes out is a wet, ragged cough.

Magic surges in my veins, an instinctive call to fight, but it dies before it can spark to life. The iron band around my neck thrums with power, leeching away my strength and essence. I snarl, my teeth bared, the taste of blood sharp on my tongue.

"Let us go," I seethe, forcing my head up to glare at the monster before me.

Elrond smirks. He steps closer, slow, deliberate, his polished boots clicking against the stone. The sound is deafening in the silence. He crouches before me, his gaze searching, peeling me apart layer by layer. He always does this—always looks for the cracks in my armor.

His hand moves, fingers grazing my cheek with the mockery of a lover's touch. My skin crawls—the air shifts, thick with something oppressive, something suffocating. The caress turns brutal in an instant—his grip tightens, yanking my head closer until our faces are mere inches apart.

His breath is warm, laced with the faintest hint of spiced wine. His eyes—cold, sharp, dissecting—burn with something between revulsion and hunger. My stomach churns, bile clawing up my throat, but I refuse to give him the satisfaction of seeing my disgust.

The first strike comes without warning. His fist connects with my temple, white-hot pain bursting through my skull as I collapse to the floor again. Before I can breathe, a boot drives into my ribs. A sickening crack echoes in the chamber. I gasp, the pain like lightning in my side.

The next blow is a bite—sharp teeth sinking into the flesh of my shoulder. I choke on my own cry, the agony twisting through me in waves. Then it begins—a vicious, merciless cycle of fists, kicks, pain, pain, pain—until I can no longer tell where one strike ends and the next begins.

Briar screams.

A guard grabs my head, forcing me to watch.

I vomit. The acrid burn coats my throat, but I barely notice because Elrond is looming, smiling, taking what he has no right to take from Briar. My mate's strangled sobs rip through me, and I thrash against my restraints, clawing at anything, anyone—desperate to stop this, desperate to kill him.

But I am utterly powerless.

I scream, a sound that feels like it's been torn from the deepest part of my soul. Briar's cries fade, swallowed by the heavy silence that follows. And then—

Stillness.

His body crumples to the ground in a twisted, lifeless heap.

I stare. My mind refuses to understand, refuses to accept what I'm seeing. His blue eyes, dull and unseeing, are locked onto mine. A void opens in my chest, something vast and hollow, a grief so consuming that I can't breathe, can't think—

"What have you done?!" I sob, pounding my shackled hands against the floor. My voice is raw and desperate, but Elrond only laughs, his smile one of pure satisfaction.

A blade flashes, and cold steel bites into my throat. And then...

Darkness swallows me whole.

* * *

"Galean!"

A deep timbre, rough with concern cuts through the haze. Familiar, rough hands shaking me, grounding me to the moment. My eyes snap open, searching for the source.

"Briar," I rasp.

I see his face, his beautiful, whole, *alive* face, hovering above me. He's real. He's here. A choked sob rips from my chest as he pulls me into his arms, his warmth instantly chasing away the phantom chill of the dream.

"Another nightmare?" he asks softly, shifting so he's behind me. He tucks me against him, wrapping his arms securely around my torso.

I nod, unable to speak. My hands clutch at his arms, as if afraid he'll disappear if I let go.

"The same one? Or was it different this time?" His breath is warm against my neck, his lips pressing a gentle kiss there. The tenderness of the gesture sends a shiver down my spine.

"The same scene... but you were there this time." The words come out barely above a whisper, as if speaking them aloud will somehow make them real.

He doesn't say anything at first. He just holds me, giving me time and space. He knows better than to rush me.

"You died," I finally admit, my voice cracking. "Right before my eyes. I couldn't do anything but watch. We're playing a dangerous game, Briar, and I'm afraid..." My throat closes, a sob clawing its way up. "I—I don't know how much longer we have."

His grip tightens. "It was just a dream, my love," he murmurs, his lips brushing against my temple. "You're safe. I'm right here."

The sobs come anyway. I can't stop them. I don't want to. Briar holds me through it all, whispering soft reassurances as I cling to him like a man drowning.

Even as exhaustion finally pulls me under again, the dream lingers. A shadow that refuses to be ignored.

And I can't help but wonder—how long before it becomes a reality?

CHAPTER 29 - BACK IN THE GAME...

<u>The Ghost</u>

The stink of stale ale, body odor, and cigars lingers in this accursed excuse of a tavern. I rap my fingers impatiently against the worn wooden table, waiting for Ryvvik to make his grand entrance.

Any moment now, he should be striding through the door, informing me of the progress he's made. Another bolt of nervous energy crawls through my belly, sinking its teeth in, gripping me in its wake.

Like clockwork, he strides through the door, startling me out of my thoughts. I have only a moment to compose myself, and I clasp my hands in front of me, schooling my expression.

He takes a seat across from me, his stance rigid as ever, his face unreadable.

"What game are you playing at?" The question is calm, laced with a lethal energy so unlike Ryvvik that it takes me by surprise.

"Before I entertain this line of questioning," I reply, my voice equally calm, equally lethal, "care to explain?"

"It didn't fucking work!" he hisses, rage flashing in his emerald green eyes.

Something in his expression has me shifting in my seat, scrutinizing my next words with great care before I speak. "Ryvvik, darling… please tell me you weren't so foolish as to waste the one batch I gave you?"

His eyes widen slightly, as if he's only just now realizing the gravity of his mistake. He doesn't speak for a moment, his gaze darting around the room nervously.

It's enough to have me gripping the edge of the table in frustration. "Ryvvik…" I warn, my voice dangerously low.

He finally turns his attention back to me. "I had to try."

The words slam into me, unleashing a rage so hot it burns like a volcanic eruption. "*Elowyn,*" I seethe.

I knew this was always a possibility—one I had planned for in the event he would double-cross me. "You gave her the tincture, didn't you?"

"Yes—and I don't fucking regret it either!" he snarls, his voice raw with defiance. Anyone in their right mind would cower, would run for cover at the first opportunity.

I'm too furious to entertain the thought.

"Do you have *any* idea how long it took to get my hands on that?!" I whisper-shout, barely restraining the fury threatening to consume me.

He has the good sense to look ashamed, squirming in his seat like a child being scolded by their mother.

"You're lucky I even have another one already in the works—"

He interrupts me, a storm destroying everything in its path.

"What fucking good is another tincture when the first one didn't work at all? You. Lied. To. Me!"

I shake my head, already growing weary of this conversation —just when I had been starting to enjoy our rendezvous. "I never said how *long* it would take for it to work, Ryvvik. Only, that it does." The words are tipped with steel, just enough of a bite to have him gasping.

The pieces shift into place—I see it the moment realization dawns on him, the exact second he understands what I've been saying all along.

"You mean…" he whispers.

"Yes! You *fool*!" I snarl, nearly scaring the poor barmaid who chose that exact moment to bring us a round of piss-flavored ale.

She gives me a glare before setting a mug in front of us both, quickly turning her attention back to more pleasant customers than myself. I sigh, fixing a glare on Ryvvik. "Not only have you cost me precious time, resources, and money… now? You're going to owe for it too, Ryvvik."

He glares at me, clearly unimpressed. No matter.

"You will return, you will use another tincture on the correct person this time, and you will follow my instructions from here on out—to the fucking letter." I snap, taking a sip of the poor substitute for my usual drink. Sighing, I set the mug back down on the table. No matter how many times I try, the damn ale never tastes the same.

"What would you have me do?" he asks finally, eyeing me warily."You'll see," I mutter, not giving him the satisfaction of a direct answer. The wheels in my mind are turning, and then —inspiration strikes. The corners of my mouth twitch into a smirk. "The next time you return to the Shadow Realm, you'll take the shield *and* the crown with you."

His head snaps up, frosty green eyes locking onto mine with open contempt. "No," he says, fiercely, his tone edged with defiance.

"You will," I counter, my smirk widening. "If you want me to help you save your cousin's people."

He swears, clutching the edge of the table so hard I half expect it to snap in half beneath his grip. A shiver of anticipation runs down my spine—I have him exactly where I want him.

"If you thought I was letting your little transgression go unpunished, you were sorely mistaken. I suggest you get your shit together. Speaking of the crown and shield—update. *Now*. And Ryvvik, darling, don't lie to me this time."

"The crown is progressing well. There have been some minor setbacks… nothing it cannot withstand. As for the shield, well. There's nothing to tell."

The lie rolls off his tongue too easily, but I know better. I can smell the bond he's so desperate to hide.

I chuckle, the sound dark and knowing. "Does she know she's your mate?"

He falters, his expression shifting from surprise to guarded in an instant.

"That's what I thought." I mutter, shifting in my seat so that I lean over the edge of table, closing the distance between us so that he feels the weight of my words. "Give me the truth, Ryvvik, or I swear to the goddess herself, I'll cut your balls off, and offer them to her as penance for your lies. Tell me the truth."

He hisses, an overwhelming and primal instinct to protect floods my senses and I know it's his emotions I'm feeling. "I suspect the shield is as powerful as the crown." He says finally, teeth clenched, like he can feel me pull the truth from his lips.

"There now, was that so hard?" I smirk, leaning back in the booth. "I'll return soon with another vial, and when I do… I expect you to return to the Shadow Realm immediately with the crown and the shield in tow. Since you failed to complete your first task, and completely disregarded direct orders, *you* get to deliver the message to the shadow prince that he will have to wait to save his kingdom. Oh, and Ryvvik? If you ever disobey me again… I'll make sure you wish you'd never been born. Understood?"

"Understood." The growl leaves his lips, and in an instant he's up and searching for the barmaid to refill his mug.

Satisfied, I slip out of the booth, and leave the tavern behind, seamlessly slipping into the crowd and weaving my way toward my final destination.

✳ ✳ ✳

Ryvvik

"Vera!" I holler, not even bothering to glance in the barmaid's direction. Dropping onto a stool, I slap a few coins on the counter. In an instant, she slides a mug of what might as well be piss down to me. I down it greedily, wiping the foam from my mouth with the back of my hand. "Much obliged," I murmur before heading straight for the door.

I hurry down the alley, pushing past people with more aggression than is probably necessary. It barely registers—my dragon is furious, still seething beneath my skin over her threat. The beer did nothing to soothe him or to quench the fire burning inside me.

Something flickers in my peripheral vision at the next crossing, snagging my attention. A dark cloak billows behind a small, womanly frame before vanishing into the crowd. My gut gnaws at me, pulling me toward the alley. Before I fully realize it, I'm already moving, trailing behind her at a safe distance.

She slips through the alley's end and veers right. I wait a few moments before following, my pulse spiking with the thrill of the chase. She manages to slip me again, forcing me to pick up the pace.

I catch sight of her at the next corner, barely missing an overturned cart. Ducking behind it, I hunker down quickly before she spots me. She stands at the next crossing, wringing her hands with obvious worry as she waits.

A towering figure stalks toward her, cloaked in dark gray. Impatient. Agitated. Their hushed conversation is too low to catch, but their body language says plenty. I swear under my breath—there's no real way for me to inch forward without revealing my position.

The man turns, waving his arms in the air, and soon, a glimmering silvery portal opens in the middle of the dark alley. He ushers her through, lingering at the edge for a moment. It's like he can sense me in the shadows, watching.

His hood slips back, revealing a chiseled face framed by gray eyes and dark brown hair. He looks familiar, but at this distance, it's hard to be sure. His gaze sweeps the alley once more, his eyes narrowing as they land near my hiding place. Gooseflesh prickles my arms as he stares at the cart shielding me.

I hold my breath, gripping the pommel of my sword tightly.

The towering male scans the perimeter again before seeming satisfied. He turns, giving the alley a final glance before adjusting the ties on the weapons strapped to his back and stepping through the portal.

And that's when I see it—the dark, inky tattoo of swirling tentacles coiled around his right arm.

I nearly gasp and have to work hard to keep the noise from escaping my lips. It can't be. My heart races, galloping in my chest like a herd of wild horses. My mind works to make the connection, dreading it all the same.

Lots of people have tattoos like that—right?

"Looks like I'm not the only one keeping secrets," I grumble, straightening as I turn back toward the market.

Despite my reservations, now that I know she isn't working alone, I have a little leverage to use against her.

And just like that, I'm back in the game.

CHAPTER 30 - THE CALM BEFORE THE STORM...

Ophelia

This morning, the training yard, which is really our back lawn, offers a breathtaking view of the lake. Our three suns are already rising, their conjoined light shimmering over the restless waters. The trees sway in the breeze, and the sky is a rolling canvas of soft clouds. It's peaceful—at least, it should be. But peace is the last thing I feel.

Anxiety pools deep in my stomach, heavy and unmoving. It's been a week since Nova's last possession, and the tension between us has only worsened. I don't know where we stand. I don't know what secrets she's keeping. And I have a sinking feeling she won't make this easy.

I sigh and step toward Skalanis. He stands facing the lake, back straight, arms crossed. He doesn't turn when he speaks. "You're up early." His voice is quiet, but there's an edge to it—

like he already knows why.

His stark tone startles me for a moment before I regain my composure. "I couldn't sleep," I admit, my gaze flicking back to the lake. The surface ripples, catching the morning light, but it only reminds me of my unrest instead of soothing me.

Skalanis hums knowingly. "Seems like that's a trend lately. Especially with a certain shifter." His voice is laced with amusement, and the trace of a smirk is evident even without looking at him.

I scowl. *So much for peace.* "Can we not?" I snap. "I'm not in the mood. And don't you have better things to do than pry into your sister's love life?"

He chuckles. "She means well, you know. Not that I was going to tell you to forgive and forget." He shoots me a sideways grin. "Nova deserves every bit of ire you're throwing her way."

"Sure you weren't," I say, rolling my eyes. "You wouldn't have brought it up if you didn't want to meddle."

He sighs, finally turning to me. "Maybe you should just *talk* to her."

I scoff. "And miss a chance at kicking your ass? Not a chance." Smirking, I stride toward the training ring, a rough circle of stones marking the battlefield.

Skalanis shakes his head, following. "Alright, then," he says, stepping inside with a smirk. "Put your money where your attitude is."

I drop into my stance, palms open, weight shifting lightly between my feet. My dual blades rest against my back, ready. Skalanis moves like liquid, circling me with light-footed ease. He feints left, aiming for my wrist—I deflect, twisting out of reach. He sweeps low, trying to trip me with his staff, but I flip backward, using my hands to propel me away.

Before I can counter, he shifts—feinting left but striking right, his elbow ramming into my ribs.

"Shit." I stagger back, a sharp ache spreading through my side.

"Tsk, tsk," he chides, smirking. "Barely ten minutes in, and I already have you stumbling."

I grit my teeth, drawing both blades in one smooth motion. His staff meets them with a sharp *clang* as I push forward, knocking him back several feet. A sliver of wood splinters from his staff where my blade struck, and I nearly grin when he snarls.

"You're *cheating*," he growls, his eyes flashing.

I twirl my blade in my grip. "You have a staff. It's only fair that I have my swords."

With a burst of speed, I spin and land a quick jab to his face before he can dodge.

He stumbles back, cursing. "You're supposed to be using your hands! Not every fight is fair," he teases. "What were they even *teaching* you at Raven's Hall?"

He lunges—staff aimed for my torso, whirling like a storm. I barely evade the strike before twisting midair, my boot snapping up toward his chin. He dodges, but only barely.

We exchange another flurry of blows—him pushing forward, me darting away. When he overcommits on a swing, I seize my chance. I duck low, pivot, and send a sharp kick straight to his backside.

He crashes to the ground.

"At least I used my *foot* this time," I say, smirking.

Skalanis rolls over, sitting up with a dazed yet exasperated expression—half impressed, half irritated. Finally, he grins. "I have to give it to you. That was quick thinking."

I offer him a hand, hauling him to his feet. "It was hilarious, actually."

He chuckles. "Aye. A little bit funny."

"I'm a riot, I know," I say, flashing my most innocent smile.

He scoffs and pulls over two large rugs. "Sit."

I drop onto the oval rug, mimicking his posture as we begin our meditation session. We've been doing this for three days now, training my body and my mind. Surprisingly, I don't hate it.

"Deep breath," he instructs. I inhale, exhaling on a count of three. His voice guides me further into stillness.

"Now, clear your mind. Picture your aura—your energy. What does it look like?"

I used to think my aura was roses and thorns. But looking now, I realize I had been lying to myself. It was never that. It was always *shadows and white fire*.

"Shadows and fire," I murmur.

"Good. Now, feel the walls you've built. Can you sense my presence?"

I do. There, at the edge of my mind—a presence pressing against my shields.

"Yes."

I reinforce them instinctively. Dark shadows weave through blazing white flames, sealing the cracks.

Skalanis tests them, sending sharp mental spears toward the barrier, but they bounce harmlessly off.

"Very good," he says approvingly. "You learn fast."

I grin, victorious. But the triumph fades when a familiar scent—vanilla and warmth—hits me like a punch to the gut.

Nova.

I tense as she approaches. I don't even need to turn around to know it's her. Her energy invades every sense, distracting me from every thought I had.

"Brother," she greets Skalanis warmly. "I see training is going well."

"Aye," he says, a mischievous glint in his eyes. "Would you like to start *your* lesson, or is there another reason you're here?"

The meddling prick.

She sighs, glaring at him before turning to me. "Actually, I came to speak with you. Walk with me?"

I exhale sharply. "Fine."

We walk along the lake in silence, the wind picking up, the storm on the horizon creeping closer.

"I sent a letter to Galean," she finally says. "I can't get the ingredients to mix correctly. Everything I've tried has been a disaster." She sighs, pulling her cloak tighter. "I have so many questions for the priestesses."

I stop walking. "That's what you wanted to talk about?"

"Of course that's not *all* I want to talk about!" she snaps.

"Then *talk!*" I whirl to face her.

She falters, her eyes widening.

But then she straightens. "There are things I *can't* tell you, Ophelia. Secrets I swore an oath to protect." Her voice tightens. "Breaking that oath could get you killed."

I stare at her, shock giving way to frustration. Then frustration turns to anger.

"When are you going to realize that I don't *want* you to keep me safe?" I demand. "That's not what I *need*."

"Ophelia, I'm not—"

"Then what the *fuck* do you call *this?*" I cut her off.

"It's *not* that simple!" she cries. "I've already pulled you too deep into my world. You're going to have to *trust me.*"

The rain is pouring, soaking through my clothes, but I barely notice.

I shake my head. "If you won't let me in, then I don't see the point in this."

And I walk away.

* * *

Dinner is one of the most awkward affairs I've ever endured.

Nova sits across from me, Ryvvik to her left, while Seraphina presides at the head of the table. As always, I'm seated at her right, with a grumpy Skalanis beside me, which suits me just fine. No one speaks. The tension is so thick it could be sliced and served as a side dish.

I'm still seething from our argument in the training yard and not remotely ready to talk to Nova. The silence between us has made the atmosphere unbearable, not just for us but for everyone else. She stabs at her roasted chicken with surgical precision, and if I weren't so furious, I might have laughed. Instead, my appetite is nonexistent.

It's a shame, really. Luca's roasted chicken is one of my favorites—the blend of herbs and the secret glaze she swears has been in her family for generations. She's never revealed the full recipe, but I always catch hints of oregano and lemon, the citrus cutting through the richness in just the right way. Usually, I'd savor every bite. Tonight, I push it around my plate with a sigh.

Seraphina mutters something under her breath. I shoot her a

sharp look, followed by a mental command: "Don't even start."

She grimaces and downs a long swig of wine. I grab my own glass and drain it in one go, setting it down with a loud *thud.*

Nova's chair scrapes against the floor as she pushes it back. "Oh, for fuck's sake." Her voice is low, tight with frustration. "If you'll excuse me, I'm suddenly feeling exhausted."

She stands, strides to the doors, and slams them behind her.

I nearly sag back in my chair, exhaustion and anger tangling in my chest.

Seraphina, however, is not having it. She jabs a finger in my direction. "Fix it."

I glare at her. "I'm not the one keeping secrets." My hands grip the edge of the table as I shove myself up.

"Sit back down, for goddess sakes!" she snaps. "I don't care who's keeping secrets or why—just fix it already. It's been a week. Aren't you tired of fighting with her?" She gestures toward the door with her wine glass. "Did you ever stop to think she might have a good reason?"

"A good reason?" The rage bubbling in my chest spills over. "Goddess, Sera. Would that be the same reason everyone—including *you*—has used my entire life?"

"Ophelia—"

"No! Don't do that. Don't act like I'm overreacting." My breath comes sharp, my pulse pounding in my ears. "You don't get it. I've *always* been kept safe, kept in the dark. My entire life, I haven't been given a choice. I've had every single decision made for me, and I never questioned it—until now. But I'm not a child anymore, Sera. I don't need constant protection. And I sure as hell don't need people deciding what I *should* know."

I take a breath, but the fury won't fade.

"I want my revenge." My voice trembles, raw with conviction.

"I want to look that bastard in the eye as I sink my blade into his chest. I want to watch him bleed out onto the ground until there's nothing left. And then… I will march straight to Morningstar Palace and *burn it all down* if I have to. I am *not* some damsel in distress, and I refuse to be handled like one."

Silence.

I don't hear Seraphina's response and don't care to listen to the others pleading with me to stay. Instead, I shove my chair back and stalk toward the door, letting it slam behind me.

I'm *done* being treated like a fragile thing locked in a glass case. If they won't tell me the truth, I'll find it myself.

Before I know it, I'm down the hall, standing before our ancestral library.

The doors swing open with more force than necessary as I storm into the library, letting them slam shut behind me. My feet carry me straight to Seraphina's desk, guided by an instinct I can't explain.

I sit. And then—I start rifling through her papers.

I don't even know what I'm looking for. All I know is that something is pulling at me, an unseen force whispering that I'll find what I need here.

Most of the documents are meaningless. Old letters from my time at Raven's Hall, outdated correspondence from the palace, requests from Bevan's villagers—pleas for leniency on rent, calls for healers. *Nothing.*

I exhale in relief—until my fingers brush the hidden compartment.

It slides open with a quiet *click,* revealing two portraits I found weeks ago. I pull them out, my breath catching as I take them in again. My mothers. Their bright eyes, their smiles frozen in time.

A lump rises in my throat. "It's not fair," I whisper.

The words crack something inside me, and suddenly, it all rushes out.

The grief. The anger. The loss. The exhaustion of trying to hold everything together when I feel like I'm falling apart. I miss Esmyra, even though I'm furious at her for lying to me. I miss the simplicity of my life in Bevan. I don't know how I'm supposed to *rule* an entire kingdom. And Nova—*my mate*—feels so distant, so unwilling to *trust* me, and it *hurts.*

Tears spill over, and for once, I don't fight them. I let them come and carve through me like rivers through stone.

And then, finally, I let them go.

I breathe in, breathe out. One by one, I discard the thoughts I can't control, sifting through the wreckage of my emotions. When my heartbeat slows, I lean back in Seraphina's chair, propping my feet up on the desk.

My gaze lands on the bookcase to my left, which hides the shadow gate.

The anger still simmers under my skin, but curiosity takes hold.

I rise, striding to the secret wall. White flame flickers to life in my palm as I pull the hidden lever. The door groans open, stone grinding against stone.

"I don't think I'll ever get used to that," I mutter as I descend the staircase.

At the bottom, the selenite-covered door gleams. I press my palm to the rune at its center. It instantly recognizes me—Queen Siofra's daughter—light pulses from the carving, illuminating the chamber as the door opens.

And there it is. The shadow gate.

Twin onyx pillars frame the swirling violet force field. Beyond it, the obsidian glass pathway shimmers faintly in the dim cavern. The closer I step, the more the pillars *hum*—not a sound but a vibration in my bones, a resonance in my blood.

Something compels me forward.

I lift my hand.

The violet shimmer brightens. The runes on the pillars ignite, their glow rippling outward. The cavern vibrates with energy.

I should stop. I *should.* But I don't.

I press my palm to the force field.

Light *erupts*—so bright I have to squeeze my eyes shut. A sound like clinking glass fills my ears.

And when I open my eyes again—the gate is *clear.*

A dark landscape sprawls beyond it, stretching into the unknown.

My heart pounds. A voice in my head whispers, *This is a mistake.*

But another voice, quieter, more certain, whispers back: *Or it's the beginning of everything.*

I take a deep, steadying breath, and then—I step through.

✳ ✳ ✳

I whooped in excitement the moment I stepped through the gate, nearly exhaling in relief when my boots hit solid ground. But as I blink, adjusting to the dim landscape before me, the excitement fades into something more uncertain.

Darkness stretches in every direction; the sky painted in deep purples and navy hues without a single star to light the way. In the distance, jagged mountains of gleaming obsidian loom, their sharp peaks cutting into the endless night. The air is stale, carrying the faint scent of something long abandoned. Around me, gnarled trees with skeletal branches twist toward the sky, their roots tangled in patches of dead, waist-high grass that sways despite the lack of wind. There is no water. No sun. No moon. Just an unnatural stillness that settles heavily over the land.

I turn back quickly, relief swelling in my chest when I spot the shimmering violet portal behind me. Through its glassy surface, I can still see the cavern beneath my home, its soft glow promising a way back.

"Well, it's now or never," I mutter, brushing the dust from my cloak. I summon my white flame to my palm, the flickering light illuminating the barren ground at my feet. Only then do I step forward, leaving the gate—and the safety of home—behind.

Each footstep crunches against the earth, the sound far too loud in the oppressive silence. I listen for movement, for any sign of life—or threat—but the world around me remains eerily quiet. I press on, walking straight, keeping my path simple. If I don't stray, I'll know how to get back.

It's fine. I'm just going a little further.

But the further I go, the more unease slithers up my spine. I don't recognize this place. I *shouldn't* recognize this place. So why does it feel like I was *meant* to be here? The thought gnaws at me, my fingers tightening instinctively around the flame in my palm.

A faint snap echoes behind me. A broken branch. A footstep.

I whirl around, scanning the shadows, but nothing moves. The gnarled trees stand motionless, their twisted limbs reaching like grasping fingers. My heart kicks up a notch, but I force myself to breathe through the tension coiling in my gut. It's nothing—just my imagination.

Still, I grip the flame tighter and walk faster.

Then I feel it.

A pull.

It's subtle at first, like the tug of an invisible thread at my core. Then, all at once, it's overwhelming—dragging me to the left, veering me off my carefully chosen path. My feet move of their own accord, drawn forward by an unseen force. I don't fight it. I *can't* fight it.

The path beneath me shifts, smooth obsidian emerging from the earth, runes carved into its gleaming surface. It leads me into a small clearing where a single, enormous tree stands.

It is ancient and towering. Its sprawling, thick, gnarled roots stretch for nearly half a mile, gripping the land like skeletal fingers. The trunk is massive, and its bark is a strange ashen gray, blackened in places as if it had once been struck by lightning. There are no leaves or blossoms, just bare, twisted branches reaching skyward in silent agony.

An ache blossoms in my chest. Sadness. Grief.

I don't know why, but I *mourn* for this tree.

Without thinking, I slash my palm, the sting barely registering as blood wells to the surface. I press it against the bark, offering what little I can. My tears fall freely now, mixing with the droplets of crimson sinking into the wood.

Then—

"Ophelia..."

The whisper is soft. Feminine. It rides the wind like a ghost's sigh, chilling me to the bone.

I freeze, my breath hitching. The sadness in my chest twists into something sharper. Heavier.

"Hello, daughter... I've been waiting for you."

A luminous lilac light spirals around the tree, glowing brighter and brighter, encircling me in its eerie embrace.

Something inside me cracks open. I don't understand it, but I *feel* it—like a door deep in my soul has been unlatched.

I spin, searching wildly for the source of the voice, but there's nothing. Just the lifeless land stretching endlessly around me.

Panic slams into me, shattering whatever trance had taken hold. My feet move before I can think—I'm *running*, sprinting back the way I came, lungs burning, heart hammering.

The obsidian path reappears beneath my feet, but I don't slow. The gate is close—I can see its violet glow flickering through the gloom.

Twenty-five feet.

Fifteen.

Ten.

The runes along the pillars are still lit, and the shimmering veil between worlds remains intact.

I don't stop. I don't look back.

I *throw* myself through the gate, my breath ragged as I collapse onto the cold stone floor of the cavern. The portal flickers shut behind me, sealing away the dark world I had just left.

For a long moment, I kneel there, shaking.

Then, a nervous laugh bubbles up in my throat, escaping before I can stop it. "Thank the fucking goddess."

I don't know how I made it back. I don't even fully understand *where* I was.

But I do know one thing—I did it. I used the gate on my own.

I proved I *could*.

"I have to tell Nova," I murmur, pushing myself up on unsteady legs. She'll—

I stop.

We're still fighting.

My excitement deflates as reality crashes back in. My sister. My mate. Their constant need to protect me. Their endless secrets. And now, my own.

Shame settles in my stomach, twisting like a blade. I was reckless. Stupid. I *know* that now.

And yet, as I quietly make my way back to my room, exhaustion finally dragging at my limbs, I can't shake the feeling that I've set something in motion.

I stare out the window, watching as the crescent moon hangs low in the sky, its dim light barely illuminating the land below. The three suns will rise soon.

But I don't sleep.

Instead, I whisper into the silence, my voice hollow.

"I'm no better than they are."

CHAPTER 31 - FUCK! THAT ESCALATED QUICKLY.

<u>Ophelia</u>

The following two weeks pass in a blur. I'm still avoiding Nova, and I've taken to having dinner sent to my bedroom chamber in the evenings. Training has gone the same each day, though it's brought me little respite.

If anything, Skalanis has gone harder on me the last few days, seemingly just as irritated as his sister. On the other hand, she has gone out of her way to show up at every training session just as I'm about to leave. Every time, I think she'll break the silence, and each time, she ignores me completely. It's like she's pretending I don't exist. It's enough to grate my nerves, even though I know I'm doing the exact same thing.

I don't know why it's so hard for me just to close the gap and explain what I'm feeling. Betrayal is an ache that keeps burning in the middle of my chest, effectively rendering me breathless. But it's more than just that—it's fear. Fear that she'll say exactly what I don't want to hear. That she won't care as much as I do and that I'll be left standing there, vulnerable, with nothing to show for it.

Get a fucking grip, Ophelia.

That thought has me bounding down the stairs, heading toward the library for the good brandy. I slide down the banister, gliding gracefully—until Nova comes around the corner unexpectedly. Her eyes widen as she sees me flying straight toward her. I don't have time to stop.

We collide hard, crashing onto the floor in a tangled heap, both of us groaning in pain.

"What the fuck did you do that for?" she growls, clutching her side and wincing.

"I didn't mean to! I didn't know you were coming this way." I grimace, rubbing my head.

"Right, of course not. Because you've been too busy avoiding me like the damn plague." She rolls her eyes and pushes herself to her feet. Then, after a beat, she extended a hand toward me. "Momentary truce?"

I hesitate, eyeing her warily before finally clasping onto her outstretched hand. "Fine."

She hoists me up quickly, but the second I'm steady, she lets go—like she can't stand to touch me for too long. The loss of contact is a slap to the face.

"I was actually coming to find you," she says, shifting uncomfortably. "I was hoping we could talk."

"If you won't answer my questions, what's the point?" I shoot back before I can stop myself. My frustration bubbles to the surface, clawing at my throat.

Nova's jaw tightens. "Damnit, Ophelia! Why must everything be so damn hard with you? Can you really not trust me to tell you everything when the timing is right?"

Her eyes shine with unshed tears. "Please," she whispers. "Just trust me."

And then she kisses me.

Her lips graze mine, hesitant at first, but when I don't pull away, she deepens it—her fingers tangling into my hair, her arm winding around my neck, drawing me closer.

I should resist. I should shove her away. I should hold onto my anger, my hurt. But when her tongue sweeps inside my mouth, plundering, claiming, I feel myself unraveling. She tastes like pomegranate, smells like vanilla, and the last traces of summer. Her fingers scrape down my back like she's trying to fuse herself to me, as if she's terrified to let go.

Her fists clench in my tunic, as if torn between pushing me away and pulling me closer. My emotions swirl in a violent storm, twisting and fraying, but for one fleeting second, all that exists is *her*.

Then, I bite her lip. Hard.

She groans, not in pain but in something dangerously close to pleasure. That sound alone makes my head spin.

And just like that, I hate how much I want her.

Nova breaks away first, breathless, searching my face with worry. "I'm sorry," she whispers.

Reality slams into me like a tidal wave, crashing through the haze of lust. I take a sharp step back, chest heaving.

"What is it you wanted to talk about?" My voice is hoarse, my pulse hammering in my ears.

Nova exhales shakily, wringing her hands. "We can't just

leave things like this."

I cross my arms. I don't trust myself to speak—not when my emotions are still clawing at my insides, not when I can still taste her on my lips.

She hesitates before finally whispering, "There are things about my past. Things I've done... I'm not proud of them. And I can't tell you, because it's not just my story to tell."

I want to stay mad. I want to hold onto my rage. But the way she says it, the way her voice trembles, chips away at my armor.

"That, I understand, Nova." My voice is quieter now, but the frustration still laces every word. "But what I don't understand is how you've kept so much from me—like trekking through the forest, lying about Galean offering help only if you took the mission, and hiding that journal from me when you knew how desperate I was to hold onto anything of hers. I trusted you with everything. Why can't you trust me to take care of myself?"

The weight of all the secrets she's been carrying settles between us, a ghost hovering in the air. I can feel the silence pressing on my chest, thick and suffocating. The way she's withheld things—how she kept me in the dark about Kara, about the rebellion, and the manipulation behind her actions —all of it circles around us like a storm waiting to break.

"You should have told me," I add, my voice barely a whisper. "I could have handled it. I should have known what was at stake."

Her gaze shifts to the floor, guilt flickering in her eyes. It's not the first time I've caught that look, the one that betrays her even when she tries to hide it. I want to believe her, but every lie, every half-truth, makes it harder to trust that she's been honest with me about anything.

"It's like you don't trust me," I whisper, the weight of the words pressing heavily on my chest.

After everything we've been through—after the lies, the betrayals, the desperation for answers—this feels like the breaking point. I don't know where to begin with the chaos that's been bubbling beneath the surface of my heart, everything I've held back and everything I've forced myself to push aside. But the distance between us, the way she's hidden things from me, kept her secrets tight to her chest as if I'm some helpless child incapable of understanding the weight of our world—it all feels like too much.

"I do trust you!" she cries, her frustration almost palpable as she pushes her hair from her face. "I just—" She sighs, searching for the words. "I can't bear to lose you, Ophelia. I almost did once already, and I haven't forgiven myself for that. I'm terrified of what will happen if you're caught."

My chest tightens. Her vulnerability slams into me, and I flinch, the weight of her fears gnawing at me. She doesn't realize how much I understand, how deeply I've been caught in the storm of guilt, doubt, and fear too.

"Nova..." I try to soften my voice, but she won't let me.

"No!" she interrupts, her voice rising as the anger bleeds into her tone. "You're the princess, Ophelia. You don't understand just how important you really are—"

"Everyone keeps telling me how important I am, yet no one wants to give me a chance to prove what I'm actually capable of!" I explode, the words ripping from my chest like a firestorm. "I don't need a protector, Nova. I need a mate. I need you to stand by me, not in front of me. If you can't do that—then get the fuck out of my way."

Nova's eyes widen, and for a heartbeat, I think I've lost her completely.

Her whole body stiffens, as though my words have physically struck her. Her jaw clenches, and I see the old familiar flash of defiance in her gaze, mixed with the sharpness of something darker. Something she's buried so deeply, even I can't fully understand it. She opens her mouth, then closes it again, and through gritted teeth, she says the words that cut deeper than anything else: "As you wish."

And just like that, she's gone.

She turns on her heel, walking away slowly, deliberately, each step taking her farther from me. My chest feels hollow. My heart clenches like it's being torn apart by invisible hands. The warning bells in my head scream at me to call out, to stop her, to hold her, to make her understand... but I can't. I won't.

I don't move. I stand there, frozen, as the space between us widens, until she's out of sight, and I'm left standing in the hollow silence of my own making.

The ache inside me is sharp and relentless, a raw wound I'm too afraid to acknowledge. And as I watch the last trace of her disappear, something inside me cracks violently, leaving a void that I don't know if I can ever fill again.

* * *

Dinner is another sordid affair, filled with silence so thick it suffocates. Tension mounts with each clink of silverware, each shift in the air a reminder of the words still lingering from earlier.

I swirl my fourth glass of brandy, its warmth doing little to ease the hollow ache in my chest. The venison on my plate sits untouched, my appetite long gone, but the wild berry tarts catch my eye. I reach for one simultaneously as another hand, fingertips grazing against mine.

My breath catches. Nova.

Her gaze meets mine, and something like hurt flashes in those stormy blue depths before she jerks her hand away, as if my touch burned her. "All yours," she murmurs, her voice strained.

I hesitate, then pick up the tart and lean forward, setting it on her plate instead. A small, hesitant smile flickers across her lips, and she takes a bite. The simple act loosens something in my chest, and for a fleeting second, I wonder why we're even fighting.

Clearly, the brandy is going to my head.

Nova lifts her glass in a silent toast, and despite myself, I snort, biting into my tart with unnecessary enthusiasm. Across the table, Ryvvik and Skalanis exchange a knowing look, one that screams they've placed bets on our argument.

I choke on my brandy, laughter bursting free before I can stop it.

"A mooncoin for your thoughts?" Skalanis asks, his grin wide and far too amused.

"I just hope you bet on the right horse. This one has a stubborn streak." I smirk, tossing a pointed look at Nova.

Her gaze sharpens, shifting between her brother and Ryvvik, suspicion creeping into her features. Then she turns to me, her eyes narrowing as realization dawns. Color flushes her cheeks, and anger crackles in the air like a brewing storm.

"You're joking about our fight?" Her voice is low, deadly.

Shit.

Ryvvik and Skalanis go still, their amusement evaporating. I throw them a murderous glare, but it's too late.

Nova shoves back her chair, palms slamming onto the table as she stands. "Since our relationship is such a hot topic of conversation, how about I fill in the gaps?" Her voice is saccharine, laced with venom. "She's mad at me. I'm equally pissed at her. She told me to fuck off, so I did. End of discussion. Are we clear?"

Her breath is ragged, blue eyes flashing with a fury that could incinerate the entire goddess-damned room. And fuck if I don't find it ridiculously attractive.

I push to my feet without thinking, something unspoken passing between us. She lingers just a second before turning sharply on her heel, excusing herself. I shamelessly follow.

We don't even make it past the staircase.

The moment we reach the bottom steps, Nova fists her hands in my hair and yanks me to her, crushing our mouths together. The kiss is rough and punishing, sending my pulse into a frenzied gallop. Her nails scrape down my back, her bites sharp enough to sting, and *I fucking love it.*

"What the fuck was that about?" she mutters against my lips, nipping my lower lip hard enough to make me hiss.

I don't answer. Instead, I grip a handful of her curls and yank her head back, reveling in the sound of her gasp.

She retaliates. Hands sliding down my chest, she cups my breast through my tunic, squeezing just hard enough to send heat pooling between my thighs. Then, without warning, she grabs my tunic and rips it straight down the middle.

My breath stutters.

She doesn't stop. Her mouth finds my nipple, hot and insistent, sucking hard enough to make my knees shake. Her hands roam my body, mapping every inch with a possessive hunger that leaves me lightheaded. I arch into her, letting her take what she wants, letting her claim.

But she's still angry—I can feel it in the sharpness of her touch, the way she bites instead of kisses, scratches instead of soothes. It fuels me, fanning the fire already burning in my veins.

I slip my thumb into her mouth, laughing darkly when she bites down. My succubus stirs, clawing its way to the surface, drawn by the intoxicating mix of anger and desire crackling between us.

She sees the shift in my eyes and smirks. Knows.

Then, suddenly, I'm on my back, her weight pressing into me, her hands fumbling with my belt. The wind is knocked out of me, but fuck if I care when her mouth trails lower—

Nova's tongue flicks against my clit, and my world shatters.

A strangled groan tears from my throat, my back arching against the steps as heat coils tight, coiling tighter and tighter until—

She stops.

I snarl, a feral sound escaping my lips as I snap my eyes open.

Nova is laughing. That awful, wretched, delighted laugh bouncing off the foyer walls.

My succubus takes over before I can think. My human form sheds in an instant—dark wings unfurling, incisors sharpening. In a blink, she's beneath me, her gown ripped, her bare breasts heaving with each rapid breath.

I growl.

Her lips part, her pupils blown wide with expectation.

My mouth devours her, tasting every inch of soft, fevered skin. She writhes beneath me, fingers sliding over the sensitive webbing of my wings, and I shudder violently. Too sensitive.

Her nails drag over the tips, and my hips jolt forward, a sharp gasp ripping from my throat.

She takes advantage.

Suddenly, I'm the one on my back.

Nova wastes no time, her tongue finding my clit in quick, devastating strokes. My thighs tremble, pleasure building unbearably fast. I clutch the steps, desperate for something to ground me, but there's nothing—just the relentless, fucking perfect torment of her mouth.

Until—

I break.

A cry tears from my lips, my body locking up as I come apart beneath her. My wings tremble, every nerve ending in my body alight with raw, burning pleasure.

Nova grins, a smug expression tugging at her lips.

That's the last straw.

In a flash, she's on her back, skirts shoved up, her thighs trembling as I settle between them. My mouth claims her, my fingers sliding inside inch by agonizing inch. She gasps, writhes, begs—

And *godess*, I drink it in.

Her release is violent, her body locking around my fingers as she cries out, her pleasure searing through me like a brand. I let her ride it out, savoring every broken sound, every shudder of her body beneath mine.

Then—reality slams back in.

I shouldn't have done that.

I shouldn't have fucking done that.

Shame knots in my chest, hard and unrelenting. I sit up, grabbing my torn tunic and pressing it to my chest like armor–

like a shield.

"That can't happen again." The words slip out, sharp and final.

Nova's eyes flicker with confusion; her lips still parted in the aftermath of her pleasure. "*What*?"

I don't let her finish. "Not until we fix whatever the fuck this is."

Her expression shatters, sending a wave of dread through my stomach.

"You're serious?"

"Dead serious."

I don't wait for her response.

Instead, I turn and leave, climbing the stairs two at a time and leaving her behind.

CHAPTER 32 - OOPSIE! DID I DO THAT?

Ophelia

The dark landscape greets me once again, obsidian peaks glinting in the distance, jagged and foreboding against the endless void of this accursed land. I slip away from the gate, following the glass pathway as before. But this time, I don't know how I got here. I don't remember stepping through the gate. I only know that I am here, drawn back as if by some unseen force.

Another week of silence. Of waiting. Of burning questions left unanswered. It's enough to drive me mad, and perhaps that's why I'm here again—because madness thrives in stillness. I don't do well in silence. I never have.

My footfalls are soft against the glassy path, each step swallowed by the abyssal quiet. I shouldn't be here. I should be in bed, resting my aching limbs after the brutal training session Nova put me through.

Nova.

I grimace, recalling the way I left things on the stairs. Heat coils in my chest, something tangled between longing and frustration. I shake it off. Focus. I came here for a reason—curiosity, maybe, or stubborn defiance.

The tree—that twisted, *lifeless* tree haunts my thoughts. How long has it stood in this forsaken place? Why is it alone? Why did I hear that voice? The questions circle relentlessly, a loop with no exit.

The landscape refuses to change. The same blackened ground, the same swirling gray sky, as if I haven't moved at all. If not for the gate shrinking in the distance, I'd believe I was walking in place.

Something isn't right.

I feel it like a splinter beneath my skin—a quiet, gnawing wrongness—a whisper at the edges of my senses, urging me to *pay attention*. I slow my steps, scanning the barren expanse, searching for... something.

And then, I see it.

A break in the path. It's a narrow, winding passage lined with gnarled trees that shouldn't be here, their skeletal limbs stretching toward me like grasping hands. The air thickens, pressing against my skin, yet I move forward.

I step between the twisted trunks, their bark cracked and peeling, revealing something darker beneath. The scent of decay lingers, not strong, but present enough to make my stomach turn. Every instinct I have is screaming at me to turn back.

I don't, instead padding softly along ignoring every warning.

The obsidian pathway appears ahead, gleaming with a soft glow. Runes swirl across its surface, silver symbols shifting like liquid starlight.

Those weren't there before. Were they?

The tree looms in the clearing, unchanged—its bark ashen, its twisted branches stark against the empty sky. It stands alone, a monument to something long forgotten. And gods help me, but I feel... sorrow.

My chest tightens as I approach. There's something about this tree, something that *calls* to me. It tugs at a place deep inside, a place I don't understand, a place that feels *ancient*.

Without thinking, I unsheath the draconian dagger Ryvvik gifted me. The blade is curved, dark as midnight, the obsidian gem in its hilt gleaming under the eerie light. I press it against my palm and drag it across my skin. Warm blood wells, a crimson offering against the cold air.

I press my hand to the bark.

"May this blood give you life," I whisper, voice trembling. "So that you may be fruitful once more. So... *thrive*."

The moment the words leave my lips, my succubus stirs.

Power surges through me, bursting past my barriers, flooding into the tree like a river breaking free of a dam. A lilac glow pulses from my palm, spreading across the bark in a ripple of iridescent light.

And then—

A white-hot burst of energy explodes from my hand.

I stumble back, eyes wide as the glow wraps around my arm, spiraling up like living fire. Panic lances through me, sharp and immediate.

"Fuck! *Shit!*" I flail my arm, but the light only climbs higher, creeping toward my shoulder. My heart hammers. My breath shudders. My magic *reacts*.

A voice cuts through the chaos, calm and steady.

"Hello, my child. Welcome back. I've been waiting for your return."

The feminine voice is warm and familiar, making my stomach clench with something close to fear.

No. No, it's not possible.

My magic flares wildly in response, panic igniting a white inferno that engulfs me whole. Flames sear across my skin, too bright, too hot—I slam my eyes shut against the blinding light.

"Ophelia... be still."

That voice—

"Who... who are you?" My voice wavers, barely more than a whisper.

Silence stretches. And then—

"Astraea."

My breath hitches. My heart pounds so violently that I think it might shatter my ribs.

No...it can't be.

The name echoes in my skull, reverberating through my bones. A high-pitched buzzing fills my ears, drowning out everything else. My entire body vibrates, my teeth chatter, and my vision blurs.

My skin is *burning*.

I collapse to my knees, palms slamming against the scorched ground—a scream tears from my throat, raw and unrelenting. Energy erupts from me, violent and unchecked, ripping through the air with blistering force.

For a moment, I think I'll tear this entire plane apart.

And then—

Silence—A deafening, eerie silence.

I open my eyes, blinking through the haze. Cinders float around me, shimmering embers drifting like dying stars. The lilac glow still shrouds the tree, pulsing softly, alive.

I look down at myself—

Stark. Fucking. Naked.

My breath catches. "What the *fuck* was that?"

My fingers tremble as I press them against my bare skin. My leathers—gone. Completely incinerated.

"Well, there goes my favorite outfit," I grumble.

A shaky laugh escapes me, bitter and disbelieving. I wrap my long onyx hair around my shoulders, shielding what little I can, and rise on unsteady legs.

The obsidian path glows beneath my feet, silver runes dancing in the air, twirling like stars caught in a silent waltz.

I don't understand this place. I don't understand *any* of this.

But I know one thing—I can't keep this to myself. I need to tell Nova. I need to tell *Seraphina*.

I need answers.

Still, the thought of speaking it aloud, of voicing the impossible, makes my chest tighten.

Not yet.

Later.

For now, I have a mystery to unravel.

One jump at a time.

CHAPTER 33 - FORGIVENESS
& REVELATIONS

Ophelia

Another week turns into two, then three, and before I know it, another unfruitful month has passed. Autumn looms on the horizon, the harvest season creeping closer, and yet I've left so much hanging by a thread where Nova is concerned.

We've been locked in a silent stalemate for weeks, neither willing to be the first to break, or end the other's suffering.

It doesn't help that I've snuck out at least ten more times since that first night—each time enduring the same grueling process, only to be met with the same endless expanse of darkness. No answers, no revelations. Just silence.

The guilt I feel gnaws at me, twisting its way through my chest. That righteousness I clung to so fiercely now feels hollow.

I'm miserable, and everyone can see it. Though only two are foolish enough to interfere.

Seraphina and Skalanis.

Those busybodies have taken it upon themselves to hound me for the past week, convinced that I need to "make things right." As if I'm the one being unreasonable, like I'm the one dragging this out.

I exhale a long, shaky breath, the cold evening air biting at my skin as I run my hands along my arms, trying to summon even a spark of warmth. There's so much I want to say to Nova, but I've bottled it up for so long that I fear when I finally do let her back in—

No.

I shake my head, cutting the thought off before it can spiral.

There's no time for me to sulk. There is no room for self-pity.

Not when the weight of my secrets keeps stacking higher, pressing down on me. Keeping things from Nova is unbearable enough. But from Seraphina? From Skalanis?

I've never been good at hiding my emotions or keeping my thoughts from slipping through the cracks. And yet, even in my exhaustion, I keep my mental shields fortified. It comes at a cost, though.

If Skalanis has noticed the strain wearing me down during our training sessions, he hasn't said. But the sleepless nights spent traveling to that strange, forsaken realm—practicing my magic in the oppressive void—are taking their toll.

There's something about passing through that gate that drains me.

I still don't know why I can use it. Or how.

But one thing is clear—the places I visit are all part of the same realm. The same dark landscape greets me each time. The same lifeless terrain. Some features never change, no matter where I land.

I've even seen *The Dark Tree* again.

Left another offering of blood, experiencing a wave of power I've never felt before.

But nothing seems different about the tree. No signs of life returning, and no whispered secrets from the shadows. Just my name, spoken into the silence, as if that alone should be answer enough.

I grit my teeth, shoving the frustration aside as I make another sweep of the perimeter, scanning the looming darkness. Aetherlight Hall stands quiet. Still, I can't shake this nagging feeling.

It's been clawing at the back of my mind for days.

The darkness is waiting.

For what, I don't know.

But it lingers, patient and watchful.

So, I wait, too.

Night after night, I keep vigil. I watch. I listen. And when the suns begin their descent, I slip away through the gate, letting the strange, quiet void be my only reprieve.

It's strange how much I've come to crave it.

The stillness.

The isolation.

It gives me time to sift through the tangled thoughts in my head, to make sense of the things I've seen in that realm.

I sigh, realizing my patrol is nearly over. My steps slow as I approach my favorite fallen log, settling onto it just as the last sliver of sunlight dips below the valley. I let myself get lost in the moment, in the shifting colors of the sky, in the way the wind stirs through the trees—

A twig snaps behind me.

My muscles tense, instincts flaring as my head snaps around —only to find Nova standing there.

I huff, turning back toward the fading sunset, scowling as I force myself to remain still while she takes a seat beside me.

The hurt I thought I'd buried surges up, clawing at my ribs, but I shove it back down where it belongs.

After a long moment, I glance at her, arching a brow.

"I assume you need to speak with me."

She sighs, as if my coolness toward her is wearing thin on her patience. I should feel ashamed that a small, petty part of me enjoys it. I should… but the pettiness in me won't hear of it. It's ironic, considering the mountain of guilt lodged like a stone in my chest.

"Since you've avoided me—" she raises a hand to cut off my obvious rebuttal— "I thought it best to come to you. I know you're upset, and I know you're angry that I kept things from you. I understand, and I don't blame you. But the least you could do, as my mate, is hear me out. Then, decide if I deserve this silent treatment."

Guilt and shame resurface tenfold, hot and sour in my throat. I've been too hard on Nova. I know that. She's my mate, and I'm not the only one suffering in silence. Now, it's just my pride keeping me from admitting it.

"Fine."

The tension in my body uncoils slightly, and she doesn't waste the moment. She exhales, resigning herself to what she has to say.

"The truth is, I was afraid I'd never get to tell you. And if I did, I wanted it to be in private, where we could work through things together. That night… it haunts my dreams."

She turns to the fading sunset, gathering strength from the last slivers of golden light. It paints her in a halo of fire and shadow. Only when our triple suns disappear completely does she speak again, her voice barely a whisper. Even with my heightened senses, I have to strain to hear.

"I've played that night repeatedly in my mind, trying to understand why it happened. I think I broke free because of the witch's blood in my veins. Though, now, I can't be sure. When I woke up, bound… it brought back something worse. A vision that plagues me, plagues my dreams. In it, I am a prisoner. My choices are not my own. Being tied to that chair rekindled every ounce of that panic. And I know you had no way of knowing that storm was raging inside me. How could you when I haven't been entirely forthcoming about my past? Or my involvement with the rebellion?"

She laughs, but the sound is hollow, foreign on her lips.

"Haven't you ever wondered why I'm always sending missives by raven? Or why I travel with such a small group? Or why I rushed off to Kara's side without even thinking twice? I'm not just the leader of *this* faction, Ophelia." Her voice cracks, and she swallows hard, fighting back tears that hover at the edges of her control. "I'm the fucking leader of the entire rebellion. And I know that's not the truth you want to hear."

My breath turns to lead in my lungs, my ears ringing as white flecks swarm my vision.

"If you want to walk away, I'll understand," she whispers. "If you choose to stay, I'll tell you everything. Even the classified information Queen Siofra entrusted me with before her death."

Shock settles like a heavy stone in my gut, followed by anger. Then sorrow.

I was ready for a confession. But not this.

An awful, gnawing feeling coils low in my belly, and I swallow against the bile in my throat. I've held her to an impossible standard—demanding honesty when I've kept my own secrets in the dark.

My heart aches for us, for the danger we will face for the rest of our lives if this fails. I'm still furious with her, though I know I have no right to be.

But none of it matters anymore. I can't stand the distance between us.

The scent of vanilla wraps around me, warm and familiar. I don't hesitate.

I pull her to me, crushing my mouth to hers. Our teeth clash, a desperate, wild thing between us. I hold her tightly, deepening the kiss until we're both gasping for air. When I finally pull back, I refuse to release her completely.

"I'm sorry," she whispers, resting her forehead against mine.

"I know," I sigh. "I'm sorry, too. And I'm still ridiculously furious with you. But you wouldn't be the person I fell in love with if you weren't the damn leader of the rebellion. I should have known. And I'm annoyed that you hid it so well."

She chuckles, nestling into me for warmth. The stars have begun to appear, glinting in the crisp night sky. We sit in silence, letting the moment stretch between us.

After a long pause, I finally asked, "Have you ever met her... the queen?"

Nova stiffens. Sighs. Then says, "Twice. Though the first time, I was barely three. Queen Siofra visited our court often—up until she met your mother. She and my mother were thick as thieves, or so I've always been told."

She smiles, remembering a simpler time.

"She wanted a future where all magics could blend together. She knew she had to make sacrifices to see that dream through. The first was accepting her rightful place as queen when the Morningstar appeared to her."

"She didn't know she was a descendant of Eowyn's line?" I ask, my mind spinning.

"She did. But she didn't realize her mother was a devout fanatic of the faith. Queen Eowyn waited for a sign before naming her heir—a sign that came on the night of the Reaping. The Morningstar flitted across the sky just as the Blood Moon rose into place."

"The Reaping?" I echo, curiosity sharp in my veins.

Nova sighs wistfully. "The Reaping is how we would have met in another life. A festival of magic, pleasure, and fate. Witches gather to find their mate, or—" she smirks "—to offer themselves in exchange for powerful magics bestowed by the goddess Astraea."

"So, my mother... she was one of those offerings?"

"Yes. She entered the rite willingly. She offered her body to a masked male, and together, their magic bled into the land, making it fertile for nearly a decade."

A realization strikes me like a bolt of lightning.

"The Morningstar chooses the next queen, doesn't it?" I whisper.

"It does," she says, squeezing my hand. "And yes, before you ask, it appeared on the day of your birth."

My stomach twists.

"Damnit. And here I thought the goddess made a mistake."

Nova snorts.

I exhale sharply. "How did you become part of the rebellion? Better yet, how did you end up leading it?"

Her expression darkens. "Because King Elrond took someone dear to me. And killed them for their power."

The words slam into me, sharp as a blade. I want to demand who, but the raw grief in her voice stops me. Instead, I take her hand, letting her know she doesn't have to say it. Not yet.

"Ever since the day my father died, I've worked tirelessly to find a way to stop him. I guess that's why, when Queen Siofra approached us, I knew we were fighting for something worth it."

Gobsmacked, I let out a nervous chuckle, my head reeling. "She approached you?" My palms are sweating, and I can't help but fidget as I wait for her response.

"Yes and no," Nova says, shifting slightly. "She approached the faction itself. At the time, Ryvvik was acting as my representative, the rebellion's figurehead. I was keeping secrets from everyone, my mother and Skalanis most of all. I couldn't risk being recognized." She hisses. "Though, of course, Skalanis figured it out quickly—especially after Siofra crashed one of our meetings and confronted him personally." A flicker of anger tightens her features.

I take a moment to absorb everything she's just admitted, then let out a dry, incredulous laugh. "The real irony? I somehow managed to fall in love—and mate—with the elemental witch who's going to help me burn it all down."

Her laughter rings out into the frosty night. "Astraea seems to have an incredible sense of humor where we're concerned, my love."

We sit in silence, both of us needing time to process. Nova's confessions prove she truly wants to put the past behind us. But it offers me little comfort, considering the secrets that still weigh like a noose around my neck.

316

I try to reconcile the enormity of everything—who I am and what's expected of me. A queen meant to lead Eventide into the light. My life was never my own, and the sudden realization makes my magic surge in frustration. My skin crackles with energy, white-hot flames licking at my fingertips.

Nova doesn't miss a thing. She reaches for my hands, cradling them between her palms. Her touch is grounding, and just like that, my magic sputters out.

"I know your mother asks too much of you," she says softly. "And I know I've asked too much of you by pulling you into this. I'm sorry that your path was decided by the fates themselves. I pray the goddess won't demand sacrifices you can't live without." She pauses, searching my face. "You've already lost your home, your family. You've bled for this cause. But this isn't just about our kingdom, Phe. It's about the entirety of Eventide. And when this is over, you can do whatever the hell you want. If you choose to abdicate, I'll stand by that choice."

Her words hit me like a physical blow.

She's offering me an escape—An everyday life fading into the background and spending our days in Bevan, serving the city instead of a kingdom.

It's a dream I desperately want. And one I know I don't deserve.

My throat tightens. "You know I can't do that," I say, the weight of it pressing down on my chest. "As much as I'd love to disappear and let what's-his-face take my place, I could never forgive myself if I didn't fight to make things better for the people of Eventide."

Nova smiles—soft, knowing. Pride shines in her gaze.

"I will follow you anywhere, my queen."

I scowl. "Don't get ahead of yourself. We still have a king to overthrow and a legion to face in battle."

"That reminds me," she says excitedly, "Galean answered my summons. We're to report to Hawthorne Manor within the next three days. He'll help us get into Morningstar Temple."

"Fabulous." The sarcasm slips out before I can stop it.

"Please, Phe, try not to smash his face in again," she says with a grimace.

"I'll play nice if he does," I growl.

"This is going to be a nightmare, isn't it?"

"As long as he keeps his snide remarks to himself, he'll have nothing to fear," I smirk. "But if he can't, I'll be happy to remind him of his manners."

"Somehow, I don't doubt that," she sighs. "At the very least, can you wait until after he gives us the rendezvous point? Otherwise, you'll just make this unnecessarily harder for both of us."

I roll my eyes but nod once in concession. "I'll behave."

"I didn't miss the eye roll," she huffs. "If you want this information, you'll have to play nice for now. Smash his face in after if that makes you feel better—I don't give a fuck."

She groans when she sees the devilish grin spreading across my face. "Oh, for fuck's sake. I was just about to tell you the fun part. Now? Maybe I won't."

"Fine. I'll wait until we get what we need. Now, what's the surprise?" I laugh at her scowl.

"I'm not telling you now. You're going to have to be surprised." She smirked and rose from the log as if heading back to the manor.

"I can make you tell me," I smirk back, knowing I've hit the mark when her lips part in surprise.

A saccharine smile spreads across her face. It's the kind of smile that makes my fingers twitch with the urge to smack her ass in punishment because she can't possibly be up to any good. I'm so caught up in wanting her that I almost miss it when she says, "You'll have to catch me first."

"With pleasure," I murmur, gripping the log to hoist myself up—

Roots snap out in all directions, wrapping around me and forcing me back down.

I growl. "That's cheating!"

"I never said I fight fair." She giggles, her voice growing distant as she sprints toward the manor.

A genuine smile tugs at my lips—the first I've had in weeks. Flames dance across my skin as I cut through the roots, their ashes drifting away in the wind.

If my mate wants to play, I'll play.

I let my succubus rise to the surface. My wings unfurl, spreading wide. My ears and horns sharpen to their points. My incisors lengthen, my body thrumming with raw power.

I grin, giving her a few more moments to think she's safe. Then, I take off, soaring over the ground.

I catch up to her in seconds.

She squeals in delight as I grab her, lifting her into my arms and climbing higher above Aetherlight Hall, heading back toward the lake.

"You didn't really think you were getting away, did you?" I ask, my voice thick with satisfaction as she reaches out and strokes the inside of my wing with her fingertips.

She smiles mischievously. "I was thinking... you should fuck me with your wings out. Again."

Her fingers skim the sensitive webbing, and I nearly lose control. A whimper escapes before I can stop it.

We almost crash into a tree.

Her cheeks redden, but she's trying to hold back a laugh.

I scowl. "I'm guessing you forgot that a succubus is... sensitive... about their wings."

"Nope." She grins. "But I can say you were so distracted that we almost took out a tree." She bats her eyelashes, feigning innocence.

I cackle, my laughter ringing in the night. We reach the manor too quickly, landing on the dock. Our boots crunching softly against the planks as we cross.

"I was serious about the wing comment, you know." She purrs, trailing a teasing finger along the inner curve of my wing.

I nearly snatch her wrist and bend her over my knee—the ornery wretch.

"I know," I smirk, pretending her touch doesn't make me want to yank her head back and claim what's mine. "Such a shame."

"Hmm? How so?"

I don't give her time to think about it. I tug her toward the nearest tree, shoving her against the bark with a wicked grin.

"That wasn't very nice," I tut, pinning her wrists above her head.

"I knew you could handle a few roots," she says sweetly, pretending she doesn't know exactly what she did. But her body betrays her, arching into mine, seeking more.

I growl and claim her mouth in a possessive kiss.

She nips at my lower lip, a soft growl escaping her own throat as my tongue sweeps through her mouth.

We claim one another, growing more desperate with every maddening second. Her hands slip free, tangling into my hair, stroking along my wings.

By the time we break apart, we're both panting, breathless.

"I don't think I'll ever grow tired of this," I whisper into her hair.

"Neither will I," she sighs, hugging me tightly. "I'm not ready to return to Hawthorne Manor if I'm being honest."

We both know the risks ahead—the enemies we'll make. And I—I've already compromised myself by demanding answers from her.

The weight of my own secrets presses down on me.

I force out a dark chuckle, tracing my fingers along her cheek. "You already know how I feel about that."

Her expression turns serious. "Whatever comes, promise me one thing."

I tense.

"Promise me we'll work through it together. No more hiding. No more avoiding confrontation just because you're angry with me."

My heart drops into my stomach. But I smile anyway, kiss her lips lightly, and say, "I promise."

"Good." She grins, shivering as she rubs her hands together. "Now, can we please go inside before we freeze our tits off?"

I laugh, taking her hand as we head back to the manor.

But as we reach the entrance, the shadows stir.

A whisper rides the wind, sending a prickle down my spine.

I pause, my hand lingering on the door, scanning the grounds behind us. Nova calls to me from inside, but something—something was here. A flicker of shadows, and now it's gone.

That thought unsettles me more than its presence ever could.

With one last sweeping glance over the lake, the trees, and the empty darkness beyond, I scurry inside, plastering a smile on my face as I take my seat beside Nova at the dinner table.

She gives me a questioning look that I pointedly ignore.

No sense in worrying them.

There was no sense in burdening them with the weight pressing down on my shoulders.

We'll be fighting for our lives soon enough.

So, tonight, I eat. I talk with my newfound friends, my sister, and my mate. I let the worries fade.

Tomorrow... Tomorrow, I'll tell them.

Tonight, I just want to enjoy their company.

Goddess knows if we'll all be here again the day after tomorrow.

CHAPTER 34 - FIRE?! WHERE'S THE FIRE?

<u>Ophelia</u>

When I wake up, my first thought is that something's wrong. Seriously… seriously wrong.

Thick smoke chokes the air, curling through my bedroom like a living thing. My throat burns as I cough violently, struggling to clear it. *How long has the manor been on fire? Too long*, my mind screams.

Beside me, Nova stirs, her breathing shallow and ragged. Panic spikes through me. I shake her hard. "Nova! Wake up!"

"What's… gggoo…?" She slurs, barely coherent.

No time. I throw clothes onto the bed, and my backup bags are already packed. My hands move on instinct—leathers, boots, blades, all strapped into place in record time. But Nova—*fuck.* Her movements are sluggish, her limbs trembling. She's inhaled too much smoke.

Another cough racks her body, violent and wet. *Too much.*

BOOM!

The foundation shudders. The walls groan. My heart slams into my ribs as a fresh wave of fire explodes from below. The whole manor shakes like a wounded beast.

"Fuck!" I curse, grabbing Nova's dress. But when I shove it into her hands, her fingers barely curl around the fabric.

"No, no, no—stay with me." My voice cracks as I yank her forward, half-dressing her myself before hauling her to her feet. She stumbles, barely conscious, and I don't hesitate—I throw her over my shoulder, my muscles burning as I drag her toward the door.

The second we step into the corridor, the heat intensifies. Flames crawl up the walls, hungrily devouring everything in sight. The ballroom, kitchens, and servants' quarters are already gone—reduced to a roaring inferno. And the fire is spreading. *Fast.*

Nova slumps against me, her head lolling.

"No!" I hiss, shaking her again. She barely reacts—my pulse hammers in my ears.

I can't fly—not in this. Not when the ceiling is collapsing in chunks.

I'm out of options.

Then—movement. A blur of shadows coming straight toward us, and I nearly cry out in relief.

Ryvvik. Skalanis. Seraphina.

They barrel down the corridor, Seraphina's furious gaze locking onto mine. Without a word, I reach for her, our hands clasping together. She squeezes my palm once, grounding me for half a second.

Then Ryvvik rips Nova from my grasp, lifting her effortlessly into his arms.

"Let's go," he grits out.

Skalanis takes point. Seraphina and I fall in behind him, Ryvvik bringing up the rear. We move fast—too fast, yet not quick enough.

The staircase looms ahead. Flames lick the railings, hungrily devouring the wood. The heat is unbearable.

I grip Seraphina's wrist and brace myself—then *dodge* as a chunk of burning debris collapses inches from my head.

We're running out of time.

By the time we hit the last steps, my lungs are screaming. I stumble—Seraphina nearly goes down with me—but Ryvvik's steady hand yanks us upright before we hit the ash-covered floor.

The front doors are in sight. *We're so close.*

"Where are the servants?!" Seraphina calls out, her voice nearly lost in the roar of the flames.

No response.

Not enough time.

I tug her toward the door. "We have to go—now!"

I reach for the knob, twisting hard.

Nothing.

"Fuck!"

Skalanis pushes past me, moving with an eerie, inhuman grace. He slams his fist against the door—once, twice. Testing it.

Then, satisfied, he throws himself against it.

Wood splinters. He slams into it again. And again.

The fire howls behind us, and the ceiling groans.

One last impact—and the door explodes outward.

Skalanis vanishes into the dark, and we don't hesitate.

We follow.

* * *

"Sweet, blessed air!" I croak, collapsing to my knees. My palms slap against the cold, wet ground as I cough violently, the acrid taste of smoke clinging to my throat. Each gasp of air burns, but the fresh night breeze sweeps through my lungs, clearing my mind. The relief is dizzying.

"What the fuck is going on?!" Sera snarls beside me, her voice sharp enough to cut through the chaos.

I whip my head toward her, still catching my breath. "The manor is on fucking fire! Isn't that obvious?!"

"I KNOW THAT!" she snaps, eyes flashing. "I want to know HOW! How the fuck did this happen?!"

Before I can answer, she turns away, fury radiating off her in waves. Water surges from her outstretched hands, colliding with the inferno. Steam billows into the sky, thick and suffocating, before clearing to reveal nothing but a pile of smoldering rubble.

My chest tightens. A memory slams into me—the prickling sensation from last night, the feeling of being watched. No. It couldn't be... could it?

"Sera..." My voice is hoarse, barely above a whisper. "I think someone was watching us last night."

She curses under her breath, raking a hand through her silver hair.

Another realization crashes through me, colder than the night air. Where are the servants?

"Where's Luca? Where are the others?" My pulse pounds,

dread pooling in my stomach.

"They're over there, my lady." Skalanis gestures toward the lawn, his tone calm and careful, not wanting to stoke the fury barely leashed beneath my skin.

I follow his gaze and nearly collapse with relief. Luca stands at the center of the gathered staff, her expression thunderous as she barks orders. Even in the dim light, I see a stablehand stumble, only to be met with a glare so cold it could freeze the air itself. I almost laugh. Almost.

"Who would dare attack our home?" Seraphina seethes, her siren purring in fury.

Who indeed.

"No one knows we're here except Galean." My voice is sharp with suspicion. "If he—"

"If he so much as thought about double-crossing me, I swear to the goddess I'll castrate him myself."

Nova's voice cuts through the night, fierce and unwavering. My head snaps toward her—she's standing tall, her breathing steady, eyes blazing with raw fury. My relief is so overwhelming that I nearly whimper.

She strides toward me, wrapping her arms around my waist and pressing a kiss to my temple. I sag into her embrace, whispering into her ear, "Don't you *ever* scare me like that again."

She nuzzles into me, stroking my hip in silent agreement before pulling back. Her gaze shifts to Skalanis, then to Sera.

"I don't like this," she admits, "but we have no other choice. It looks like we're all making this trip."

She turns to Sera, her voice softer now. "I know you didn't ask to be dragged into this war, and I can't promise to keep you safe..." Her grip on my hip tightens, grounding herself. "But if you choose to fight with us, it would be my honor. And... I'm sorry my wards failed."

Tears spill down her cheeks, and I feel it—her pain. It crashes into me, wrapping around my ribs, squeezing the breath from my lungs. Her wards were supposed to protect us. She had woven them carefully, with all her strength, and still... they weren't enough.

Seraphina looks atRyvvik. He gives her a silent nod—your choice.

She rolls her shoulders, and I know her answer before she even speaks. She will fight. Not just because it's right, but because Aetherlight Hall—whether it was ever ours—was still our home.

And no one fucks with our home.

"I'm in." She grins, her razor-sharp teeth glinting in the firelight. Her siren purrs in anticipation.

My beast stirs beneath my skin, humming with the same hunger for vengeance. "Then what are we waiting for?" My voice is thick with rage.

"It might be a trap..." Skalanis warns, pulling our attention back to him. "We don't know what we're walking into."

"I've got a bone to pick with Galean," I growl. My beast rumbles in agreement, craving blood.

Skalanis smirks but remains firm. "Aye, I imagine you do. But we can't go storming in like a pack of rabid wolves. We need a strategy. One shot. No room for error. If Galean betrayed us, fine—but we don't know who else is involved."

Damn him. He has a point.

"How are we traveling?" Nova asks, cutting through the rising tension.

"The quickest way is by portal, but it could be traced." Ryvvik glances at Skalanis.

Skalanis strokes his beard, considering. "Too risky."

"What about by air?" I suggest, an idea forming.

He shakes his head. "They'd see us coming. If Hawthorne Manor is under Elrond's control, we'll fly straight into an army."

"Not if she glamours us." I tilt my head toward Nova.

Her lips curve into a wicked grin. "You clever, clever girl."

I turn to the others. "If we combine Ryvvik's elemental air magic, my shadows, and moonlight, Seraphina's light and persuasion magic, and Nova's glamour, we can bend the light around us. We'll be invisible."

Skalanis exhales, rubbing his temples. "It could work..." He hesitates, then fixes his gaze on Nova. "But can you maintain the glamour for that long? It's a three-day flight. You'll drain yourself."

Nova's confidence falters. I grip her hand, already knowing the answer.

"We could complete the mating ceremony." My voice is gentle, giving her space to process what I'm suggesting. If we bond completely, she'll have access to my seemingly endless energy reserves. Our magic together could bring an entire kingdom to its knees.

Tears well in her eyes, but she closes the distance between us, pressing a soft, chaste kiss to my lips.

"Are you sure?" she whispers, resting her forehead against mine.

"I've only ever been sure of one thing in my life," I whisper back, tightening my hold on her. "And it's us. All that I am—all of it—is yours."

"OW!"

A loud yelp startles us. I whip around to find a pained Ryvvik rubbing his arm while Seraphina stands before him, hands planted on her hips, molten silver eyes blazing.

"When were you going to tell me about this official mating ceremony?" she growls, her voice edging between accusation and disbelief. "You were going to tell me, right?"

Ryvvik sighs, pinching the bridge of his nose. "For Astraea's sake, woman! You've only just come to terms with the fact that I'm your bloody mate—why would I want to scare you off for good? Especially with a mating ceremony that's been outlawed for nearly fifty years." He flicks a pointed glance at me. "A point, I might add, that seems to have escaped your sister's attention."

I grimace but don't bother denying it. Technically, he's right. It *is* outlawed. But... since when have I given a shit about that?

I'm the *queen*. What I say *goes*.

Seraphina chews her bottom lip, her anxiety leaking into the air. She shoots me a look, and I confirm it with a slow nod.

Ryvvik exhales and takes her hands in his, his expression softening. "Love, I want it all. I'm a greedy bastard when it comes to you. So let's do the fucking ceremony—who gives a shit if it's outlawed? I want a future with you." His voice dips, reverent. "I even want the gaudy dragon tradition of The Revealing so that I can show you off to my kin. I want you by my side. And, goddess willing... one day, a little dragon boy and maybe a feisty little siren girl just like her mother."

I blush, feeling like an intruder in their moment—especially when Seraphina *climbs* Ryvvik like a damn tree. If there's one thing about dragons, it's that they are *passionate*, and clearly... there's no shortage of that here.

A surge of energy crackles through the air, thick with their desire. My beast stirs, sensing it, drinking it in greedily. My skin prickles, and I clench my jaw to keep from shuddering. Power is power—I'd be foolish to waste it, even if it *is* my sister's lust. *Yuck.*

"Double ceremony, then?" Nova calls out, amusement lacing her tone.

Seraphina startles, cheeks flushing as she untangles herself from Ryvvik. He almost nods but hesitates, looking at her in silent question.

"Oh, for fuck's sake, *come off it!*" Skalanis growls. "We all know you're meant to be together. Any flaming idiot could see that. Now." He holds out a hand expectantly. "Someone give me a bloody knife, and let's get this over with. You can plan your parties later."

Ryvvik snorts and tosses him a dagger with a sapphire-studded hilt.

"You sure?" he asks Seraphina, his voice lower, more serious. "There's no going back after this."

She lifts her chin. "You're a fool if you think you're getting rid of me that easily." A slow smirk tugs at her lips. "I'll drag you down to the watery depths of hell before I let you escape me. You're *stuck* with me."

Ryvvik chuckles, but there's something fierce in his gaze—something *claimed.*

Skalanis steps between us, eyes sharp as he gestures for us to stand before our mates, palms up. "Hold still," he instructs.

With swift, practiced movements, he slashes each of our palms, carving the necessary runes into our skin. He then binds our hands together with leather strips, cinching them tight so that our mingling blood drips onto the earth—an offering, a promise.

I meet Nova's gaze, warmth blooming in my chest.

It feels... right.

"Now," Skalanis says, clasping his bloodied hands behind his back. "Say the words."

Our voices rise in unison, the ancient vows ringing in the crisp night air:

"From my blood, I give you life.
From my blood, I give you my soul.
From my blood, I give you my magic.
With my blood, I promise to protect your life with my own.
With my blood, I bind my soul to yours.
With my blood, I bind my magic to yours.
With our blood, we offer these solemn oaths to the goddess. With our truth, be satisfied.
Amarie!"

A brilliant light erupts between us, engulfing our bodies in a silvery-blue glow. The magic settles into our skin, leaving a sharp, almost stinging sensation in my palm. As the bindings fall away, I look down to find a glowing, *humming* rune in the center of my hand—an earthy green star thrumming with power.

Nova stares at her palm, disbelief written across her face. "Astraea... she..."

I swallow hard, my breath catching. There, glowing in the center of *her* palm, is its twin—only this one pulses with my violet energy, answering each beat of my own.

Skalanis exhales, his usual steel-like composure shifting. "Seems Astraea not only accepted but *blessed* your bonds."

"She *blessed* it?" Seraphina echoes, turning her hand over, mesmerized by the swirling gold energy in her rune.

"Well." Ryvvik chuckles, rubbing his thumb over the silvery mark on his palm. "Guess that locks things in, then."

"Aye." Skalanis nods. "Now... what do we do with them?" He jerks his chin toward our staff, still huddled together against the frigid cold.

"They can go to Bevan for now," Seraphina suggests. "We have the funds. It's more than enough for several lifetimes, honestly. They deserve to rest somewhere *safe*." She twirls a strand of hair around her finger, thoughtful. "And we'll need shelter for the night, too."

Nova glances over her shoulder at the humans, still shivering on a bale of hay. "A night in Bevan would do us good. We should leave tomorrow, just after sunset."

"So, it's settled then," Skalanis says, giving a curt nod. "We go to Bevan tonight. We fly out tomorrow evening when Ophelia's power is at its strongest." He glances up at the night sky, exhaling. "Thank the fucking goddess, it's not storming."

And just like that, Astraea changes the game again.

I can't help but wonder—what *else* does the goddess have in store for us?

CHAPTER 35 - SURPRISE!

<u>Ophelia</u>

After securing our staff's lodgings and filling their purses with as much coin as possible, we left Bevan behind.

The night air whips through my hair as we soar high above the land, the vast stretch of wilderness unfolding beneath us. I don't regret leaving immediately, even though it wasn't part of the original plan. I couldn't sleep there. Not even with Nova beside me could I find rest. I doubt I'll sleep tonight, or any night, until I know we weren't betrayed.

Luckily, neither could anyone else.

A pulse of affectionate energy flares through my mating bond, followed by a very vivid image Nova plants in my mind—one that leaves nothing to the imagination. Her desire for me in this form makes my mouth water.

This witch will be the death of me.

I laugh at the thought, knowing I'd die happily in her arms.

I tilt my wings, slicing through the air as I race toward the front of the formation, where Ryvvik stubbornly holds position. He insists it's for tactical reasons, but really, I think he just likes to show off like a peacock. Though to be fair, his golden dragon form is a sight to behold. Massive even by dragon standards, with sharp horns, jagged spikes running along his back and legs, and a venomous dagger-like tail—he's easily the last dragon I'd ever want to tangle with.

Seraphina sits atop him, nestled in a saddle he had made for her. The silver-threaded embroidery glints in the moonlight, intricate designs of roses and leaves woven into the leather—an unmistakable homage to Aetherlight Hall. She catches me staring and flashes a brilliant smile before lifting her arms, letting the wind whip through her hair.

She looks so carefree, weightless, and joyful that I smile. For a moment, I forget the mission.

Almost.

But Ryvvik's following words snap my focus back into place, his dragon voice reverberating in my mind like rolling thunder. *"I bet you can't beat me to the Shadowy Peaks."*

A slow grin spreads across my face. *"Bring. It. On."*

Seraphina must hear the challenge because she leans forward, gripping the pommel of the saddle.

Now in her majestic sphinx form, Nova flies up beside us, carrying an utterly exasperated-looking Skalanis. *"Ryvvik... I swear to the goddess, you better not."*

Ryvvik snorts—or at least, the dragon equivalent of one.

"Oh, for fuck's sake," Skalanis mutters, crossing his arms.

I nudge Nova playfully, and she practically purrs in anticipation. I meet Seraphina's gaze, waiting for the signal.

She grins, mischief dancing in her eyes. *"On the count of three!"*

"One... Two... Three!"

In a flash, we take off, wind howling past as we streak across the sky, soaring over towns whose names I can't remember to save my life.

Ryvvik is faster than I expected, his wings cutting through the air with precision, gaining ground; I refuse to let him keep. I push harder, beating my wings furiously, slicing through the currents. The Shadowy Peaks loom ahead, jagged and ominous.

Seraphina declares it a tie.

But I *know* I beat Ryvvik by a second. Maybe even two.

So, naturally, I call it a win. *"See? I told you I was faster."*

Ryvvik grins, shaking his head. He doesn't argue. This wasn't really about winning—it was about the distraction. A moment to let go of the weight pressing on all of us. And it worked.

The anxiety coiling inside me finally unravels, releasing its hold. I take a slow, deep breath, centering myself. There is no sense in carrying doubt. It will only lead to mistakes. And mistakes will get us killed.

I won't allow it.

"How much further until we need to make camp?" I ask once my pulse settles.

"At least a few more hours," Skalanis answers. *"Best to rest during the day. We can figure out the watch rotations once we stop."*

We land briefly, taking fifteen minutes to drink, stretch, and gather our bearings before pressing on.

The next stretch passes in a blur. When we finally reach the dense forests near the Dark Whispering Woods, exhaustion weighs heavy on my body, and I know I'm not the only one.

We covered more ground than anticipated, putting us ahead of schedule—not that it brings me much comfort.

Because once we arrive, there will be *more* to deal with. More plans, more threats to dismantle. More treachery to uncover.

And I am *still* seething over that self-righteous prick who dared to betray my mate.

Sighing, I rummage through our supplies before settling on a makeshift pallet beside a weary looking Nova. She's still beautiful, but I know she's just as drained. I offer her a piece of dried venison, and she takes it without a word.

Ryvvik tends the fire while Seraphina curls into their bedding. Skalanis and Ryvvik have taken the first watch, standing guard at the cave entrance. I don't argue. They know these forests better than we do, and the creatures lurking here are no joke.

Our last venture through these woods? It was *far* from triumphant.

So, for now, I let it go.

For now, I pull Nova into my arms, holding her tightly as the weight of the night settles over us.

Sleep won't come easy. But at least, for a little while, I can pretend we're safe.

✳ ✳ ✳

The next several days settle into a simple rhythm. We sleep through the daylight hours to regain our strength, then fly as fast as our wings will carry us through the night. After what feels like an eternity, we finally arrive at the edge of Hawthorne Manor's grounds.

As much as I loathe to admit it, the bastard has taste.

Hawthorne Manor overlooks a town that bears its name—a bit pretentious but undeniably picturesque. Nestled in a valley at the foothills of the estate, Hawthorne Grove is a charming mix of magic and wealth. The cobblestone streets bustle with beings of all kinds, their clothes woven from the finest fabrics I've ever seen. Shops and cottages, built of sturdy brick, line the streets, their windows glowing warmly as they showcase enchanted wares. There's an easy rhythm to the town—laughter spills from market stalls, friends chatter as they browse, and for a moment, I catch myself wondering...

Does Galean rule these people with fairness? Are they truly this content, or is it all a carefully spun illusion?

I shake the thought away. I have bigger concerns than the ethics of a town that isn't mine to rule.

With a subtle signal, I let the others know it's time to move. Nova strengthens our glamours and wards, shielding our approach, and together, we ascend, flying high above Hawthorne Manor.

Scouting the town first had been my idea—I wanted to assess any military presence. But as we close in on the manor and find none, I'm unsure whether to be relieved or wary. From above, the obsidian spires of the estate gleam under the moonlight, dark and regal. It's a breathtaking sight in its own eerie way, and if I weren't seething with fury, I might admire it.

"Any sign yet?" I reach out to Ryvvik through our mental link.

"Nothing. We move forward." His deep voice rumbles in my mind, and I signal the others.

Adrenaline surges as we push forward, wings slicing through the cold night air. The scent of the Celestia Sea drifts up from beyond the cliffs, salt, and brine mixing with the damp earth of the manor grounds. We bank and swoop low, scanning every inch of the estate.

"No guards," I murmur through the link, feeling the first true prickle of unease.

Ryvvik and Seraphina touch down beside me, just as Nova and Skalanis land on my other side.

"Definitely promising," Nova smirks, shifting back into her human form. Her pale blue eyes glint mischievously as she winks at me.

"Promising," I agree, *"but don't get comfortable."*

Skalanis steps forward, voice sharp as steel. *"Galean didn't rise to power by being careless. He's a tactician—he'll have planned for every possibility and set contingencies in place. We don't let our guard down for a second."* His gaze sweeps over us, deadly serious. *"At the first sign of trouble, use the link. Do not engage unless you are absolutely certain you can neutralize the threat quietly. Otherwise, find cover and signal the rest of us."*

I nod, shoulders tensing as he continues.

"We split up from here. I'll take the barracks and stables—if his personal guards are anywhere, they'll be there. Ryvvik, you, and Seraphina go through the kitchens and his private rooms. Ophelia, you and Nova take the servants' quarters and lower levels. Move carefully. If anything feels off, you signal."

"Understood."

The word echoes in unison, and without another moment's hesitation, we vanish into the night.

✳ ✳ ✳

The eerie thing about this entire experience? The manor is dead silent.

We arrived just as the suns began to set, and I know we couldn't have spent more than an hour at Hawthorne Grove. So...

Where is everyone?

We've searched the servants' quarters and combed through the lower levels—tunnels, storage rooms, and an extensive wine cellar that's almost impressive—and yet, we haven't seen or heard a single soul. It's unnerving enough to make me want to turn around and get the hell out of here.

I'm a bundle of nerves by the time we reach the main entrance. Even Nova, usually a wildfire of motion and sound, is quiet, though I can feel her fury simmering just beneath the surface.

"Nothing," I say through the mind link, scanning the grand foyer of Galean's home. My unease won't settle until I hear from the others.

"Clear." Ryvvik's voice rings in my head.

A moment later, Skalanis confirmed his area was clear, and soon, we were all standing in the middle of the foyer, regrouping.

I cross my arms, leaning against the south wall. *"This feels like a trap."*

Skalanis narrows his eyes, scanning the darkness. *"It does, doesn't it?"*

Nova snorts. *"I'll make that fucker eat his dick."*

It takes everything in me not to burst into laughter—such violence in such a tiny package. Sometimes, I'm convinced

Astrea handpicked this woman just for me. She's my match in every way—right down to the bloodlust.

Before I can tell her how much I'd enjoy assisting in that endeavor, a deafening crack fills the room.

Bolts of red energy explode around us, crashing into the floor and walls in a chaotic, unpredictable storm. The magic doesn't follow a pattern—there's no way to anticipate where the next strike will land. It's pure, unbridled chaos, and for one terrifying second, I'm convinced we're about to die right here.

A bolt crashes dangerously close to me. Instinct kicks in. I yank Nova against my side and dash toward the opposite end of the room. The swirling energy moves as if it has a mind of its own, drawing all its power inward.

In a flash, a sphere begins to form at the center of the room, and the air crackles. My skin tingles and heat pricks my arms. The wind howls, pressing us back against the walls and stealing my breath.

A high-pitched hum builds—piercing, vibrating in my bones —and then a blinding flash of white light explodes through the space.

Then... silence.

I blink furiously, my heart pounding as I strain my senses. My vision is still hazy, but my hearing sharpens. Footsteps. A single person.

Another heartbeat, and my sight clears.

I nearly growl when I see who stands before us, wearing an impossibly sour expression.

"About time you got here! What the hell is going on?" Galean scowls, giving us a once-over. "I thought you were arriving by portal today. I even sent my staff and guards to the festival in a neighboring town—bought their silence with a night off on my coin. And you all look like shit, by the way."

For a moment, none of us move. None of us speak.

We thought our worst fears had been confirmed. But... could it be true? Did he actually not betray us?

Galean throws up his hands. "Is anyone going to fill me in, or are you all just going to stand there like statues all night? I'm on borrowed time as it is."

I narrow my eyes, searching his face. "You didn't send someone to kill us by fire?"

His expression twists into something between offense and disbelief. "What... You can't possibly be serious."

"I am." My voice is low, wary. "You made it clear you don't care for me. And you live the life of a double agent well—almost too well."

Galean scoffs, rolling his eyes. "Insufferable. Absolutely ridiculous—I don't—" He gestures wildly, cloak billowing. "Honestly, why do I even try? You're a bloody simpleton. A foolish girl who has no business running a kingdom, I swear—"

A sickening crunch fills the air.

Galean reels back, blood gushing down his face, his amber-colored eyes burning.

I stare, wide-eyed, entirely caught off guard.

Skalanis just punched him square in the nose.

I should stop him. But, truth be told? I'm enjoying this far too much.

"Let's get one thing fucking clear." His voice is a low growl, deadly and sharp. "Don't ever speak about my queen that way again. You haven't even given her a fucking chance! So, what gives you the right to even speak on her character? Speak of her like that *one more fucking time*, and I'll rip your goddess-damned throat out. Show her some fucking respect."

Galean's amber eyes burn bright for a moment—glowing with barely restrained fury.

I hold my breath.

Then, he blinks. The glow fades, and the fog lifts. He exhales sharply, wiping his bloody nose with his cloak. "What is it with you people and throwing punches?" He scowls. "Sucker punch me again, and you'll be missing your hand."

He straightens, clearly irritated but not ready to push his luck. "Unfortunately, as she is *yet* to be crowned, she's still just a princess—no real power of her own. Until we unseat that bastard on the throne, she's no different than you or me. You're all losing your minds, and we haven't even started the fucking war."

Nova pinches the bridge of her nose. "That's why we came here, you twat. We have a fucking plan."

I snort, failing miserably at holding back my laughter. Her exasperation is almost too much.

Galean sighs dramatically, shoving back a few wayward locks of hair. "Finally, someone is going to tell me what's going on." He turns on his heel, muttering as he strides toward the hall. "Come on, then. We'll finish this in my study. I need a cup of brandy after all that... fuss."

And so, we follow.

Each of us settles into a chair while Galean gathers glasses. After two rounds of brandy and a full debriefing, we finally dispersed to our assigned rooms for the night.

Galean portaled back to Morningstar Palace, assuring us we wouldn't be disturbed. No concrete plans yet, but he's promised to figure out how to get us into the temple.

After days of traveling and all the stress, it's no wonder I'm out the second my head hits the pillow.

CHAPTER 36 - DRUNKEN DEBAUCHERY

Ophelia

The manor is too quiet as I walk down the dimly lit hall toward our guest room. On one hand, I'm grateful there's been no sign of Galean while we've been holed up here the past few days. But on the other, the waiting is starting to gnaw at all of us.

And that's when the idea struck me—an idea I can't shake no matter how hard I try.

I fling open the bedroom door, letting it bounce off the wall with a thud. "We need to get out."

Curled in a plush wingback chair, Nova glances up from her book with an arched brow. She's wearing a deep indigo gown, the flowing bell-shaped sleeves draping elegantly over the chair's arms. Her expression is a mix of confusion and mild amusement.

"I'm sorry... *what?*" she asks, setting her book aside and turning to face me fully.

I grin, dropping onto the chaise lounge and kicking my feet up, boots and all. "There's a festival in town. I say we go. As a family."

Nova gives me a look that practically screams *seriously, Ophelia?* But I see the flicker of curiosity beneath it.

"And what, exactly, do you think we'll find at this festival?" she asks, humoring me.

I smirk, knowing I have her now. "Apparently, Galean's little town is famous for its yearly Ale Festival. Rumored to be one of the best in all of Eventide."

I watch as interest sparks in her eyes. Then, finally, she exhales a laugh, shaking her head. "Alright, I'll bite. Want to go round everyone else up?"

"I *thought* you'd never ask." I leap to my feet, adjusting the clasp of my cloak before sauntering toward her. Leaning down, I press a lingering kiss to her forehead before tossing over my shoulder, "Oh, Nova? You might want to wear some of my clothes."

She frowns. "Wait... why?"

I flash her a wicked grin. "Because there's an archery competition. And some axe throwing." A beat of silence. "I may or may not have entered us both."

Nova's eyes widen in disbelief, but before she can argue, I snicker and slip out the door, shutting it behind me on her undoubtedly bewildered expression.

* * *

We practically bounce down the cobblestone streets of Hawthorne Grove, all of us with a single thought in mind—find the ale, drink it fast, and throw axes while shitfaced. A flawless plan, if I do say so myself.

The air thrums with excitement, the scent of roasted meats and spiced cider weaving between bursts of laughter and lively music. The town is alive with festival energy, a welcome contrast to the stuffy, silent manor in which we've been holed up for days.

Shops line the street, displaying handcrafted treasures—silk scarves billowing like captured whispers, paintings bursting with every color imaginable. Each storefront brims with something unique, something made with care. I let my gaze wander, taking in the artistry, until something down the street catches my eye.

An open structure, more workshop than shop, stands at the end of the road. Its high vaulted ceiling stretches toward the sky, and dark beams crisscross overhead. A massive metal door rolls up, revealing the artistry within—sculptures of gleaming steel and intricate jewelry, each piece crafted with a precision that makes my fingers itch to reach out and touch it.

Drawn in, I drift away from the group.

At the back of the shop, a towering man—easily seven feet tall—hunches over a steaming vat of molten metal. Sparks fly as he hammers away at a blade, the rhythmic clang of metal on metal echoing through the space. I'm so entranced that I don't notice the woman approaching me until she speaks.

"Can I help you find something?"

Her voice is soft, yet it carries an unmistakable confidence.

She's tall—taller than me by at least a foot—with auburn hair cascading down to her waist. Her hazel eyes glimmer with quiet amusement, and her smile's warmth is immediately grounding.

"No, I wasn't looking for anything," I admit, still enjoying the shop's beauty. "But these... they're incredible."

Her smile deepens. "My husband, Xetizar, crafts the sculptures and forges the blades. I focus on the finer pieces—rings, necklaces, engravings. I'm Miret." She inclines her head. "Welcome."

Something in the way she says it makes me pause, but she continues before I can dwell on it.

"I think I have just the thing for you."

Swishing her deep burgundy skirt, she glides toward the counter, the movement as effortless as breathing. The glass display cases on either side house delicate rings and necklaces, most designed with intricate floral motifs. But my attention snags on something else.

A ring—set with a black opal that catches the light like the heart of a dying star. Onyx diamonds form tiny points around it, resembling a celestial crown. The deep blues, purples, and reds shimmer against the dark metal, mirroring the sunset as it fades into night.

I barely have time to process my fascination before Miret plucks it from the case and beckons me closer.

"This one," she murmurs, holding it out. "Go on."

Drawn in by something I don't understand, I slip the ring onto my finger. The cool metal sends a faint tingle up my arm, and the black opal glows in the dim candlelight, as if alive.

"It's beautiful," I breathe. "But I can't accept this."

Miret simply shakes her head, her expression unreadable.

"I'm afraid that once you try it on, it's yours. These rings are crafted with intention and a touch of magic." She folds her hands in front of her, observing me. "They're enchanted to find the person meant to wear them."

A chill races down my spine—not of fear, but of something more profound. Something ancient.

"I—"

"This is a gift," Miret continues, her voice softer now. "One I hope you'll wear with pride in the coming months." She dips her head slightly. "You bring great honor to my family by gracing us with your presence."

My pulse stutters.

"I think you have me confused with someone else."

She smiles, knowing and unwavering. "No. I know exactly who you are."

My breath hitches.

"We've long hoped the rumors of your death were untrue," she says gently. "I would recognize your hair and eyes anywhere. You're the image of your mother." Her gaze softens. "She was a kind soul. She often spent her summers here, learning to craft jewelry. Not exactly a suitable pastime for a princess, but... I couldn't refuse her."

I can't breathe.

"This ring..." She gestures toward my hand, where the opal still gleams like captured starlight. "She designed it. Forged it with her own hands while I enchanted it."

A sharp ache blooms in my chest, tightening my throat.

"She saw what the future could be," Miret murmurs. "A vision of peace, of unity. This ring was her hope. The future she dreamed of." She pauses, then, softer still, "That hope now falls to you."

Tears blur my vision. I swallow hard, forcing down the emotions clawing at my throat. "Thank you," I manage. "For this piece of her."

Miret presses a hand to her heart before wrapping me in a gentle embrace.

"You will not be alone," she whispers. "There are more of us in the shadows, waiting. When the time comes, all you must do is call."

I nod, unable to speak, and let her go.

Turning, I find Nova waiting nearby. The moment she sees my face, her brows knit together. "What's wrong?"

Wordlessly, I lift my hand.

She inhales sharply, eyes darting between the ring and my expression. Then, in true Nova fashion, she whirls toward the shop. "Why didn't you say anything?! We *must* go back—I need to browse pretty jewelry for a change!"

Despite the whirlwind of emotions still coiling in my chest, I can't help the breathless laugh that escapes me.

"I—Nova—"

Too late. She's already dragging Seraphina toward the shop, chattering excitedly.

"Did you know there's jewelry in the back?"

Just stepping out, Seraphina blinks in confusion. "Wait... no? What?!"

Nova grabs her by the wrist. "Let's go see!"

Seraphina fumbles with her belt, cinching her too-big pants tighter before getting swept up in the chaos.

"Oh, for fuck's sake," I mutter, exasperated—but when I glance down at the ring, the weight of my mother's legacy resting against my skin, I can't help but smile.

CHAPTER 37 - IS THAT.... PIE?!

<u>Ophelia</u>

T he night carries on in a haze of laughter as we wander down cobbled streets, our hands brushing over trinkets and our eyes constantly drawn to something new. The scent of powdered sugar-dusted cakes and spiced apple ale drifts through the air, teasing my senses.

We round a corner and find ourselves in a bustling square filled with food stalls. There are caramel-dipped apples, golden-brown pretzels glistening with butter and salt, and endless pints of ale frothing over the rims of wooden mugs. My stomach growls loudly, earning a smirk from Ryvvik.

"Is that... pie?" he asks, sniffing the air like a bloodhound.

I grin, grateful the dragon shares my love of sweets. "I think so. Let's go grab a slice."

We saunter over, leaving Skalanis, Nova, and Seraphina to hunt for drinks. In no time, we carry plates of warm apple pie drowning in caramel sauce, the ice cream melting into golden rivulets over the flaky crust.

The others have claimed a small round table, just big enough for five. We settle in, and I groan in pure bliss as soon as I take my first bite. "This... is... so... good."

"It reminds me of Mom's," Seraphina says, her voice soft with nostalgia as she washes down a bite with crisp apple ale.

"It does," I murmur, savoring the blend of cinnamon, nutmeg, and perfectly sweet apples.

"Aye, the best damn pie I've ever had." Skalanis practically inhales his slice before draining his ale in one go. He sets the empty mug down with a decisive thunk. "Alright, when's this bloody competition starting?"

"Oh! Look!" Nova nudges me, eyes alight with excitement. "They're setting up for the axe throwing." Then, she turns to me with a smirk that immediately puts me on high alert. "You know I'm going to win, right?"

Skalanis snorts. Seraphina giggles.

I narrow my eyes at my mate, accepting the unspoken challenge. "As if."

Draining the last of my ale, I grab her hand and pull her toward the stage.

A crowd has already gathered, the energy buzzing with anticipation. I barely register the announcer—an older gentleman in a red vest, a handmade black shirt, and a cane topped with a silver wolf—before Nova wraps her arms around me from behind. Her breath is warm against my ear as she nuzzles into my neck.

"We could make this... interesting," she murmurs, her lips grazing my skin.

"Interesting. How?" I arch a brow, already suspicious.

She leans in just enough that only I can hear. "If you win, you can claim me right here in the street. If I win…" Her lips curve in a wicked smile. "I claim you."

A sharp bolt of heat shoots through me, but before I can respond, she kisses my cheek swiftly and saunters toward the stage like she hasn't just set my blood on fire.

The announcer raises his voice over the cheering crowd. "Welcome, one and all, to our annual axe-throwing competition! And to start us off, we have a couple who promises to be quite entertaining."

I shoot Nova a withering glare. She only chuckles.

"Wicked thing," I grumble as we take our places.

The announcer hands us our first axes, laying out the rules. Three throws each. Whoever lands closest to the bullseye wins—unless someone strikes dead center on the first try.

"Begin!"

I gesture toward the target with a smirk. "Ladies first."

Nova rolls her eyes, but she's already stepping up, as fluid as ever. In one smooth motion, she lifts the axe and throws. It spins end over end, sinking into the wood barely an inch from the bullseye.

She glances at me, smirking, before accepting her next axe.

Again, her throw is devastatingly precise—close but never quite hitting dead center—and the third lands precisely like the first two.

She's doing it on purpose. She wants me to work for it.

I grin, stepping up to the line. Testing the axe's weight, I roll it between my hands, feeling its balance.

"Quit showing off," Nova teases.

I throw the first axe, watching it sink just on the edge of the bullseye. My second throw lands just above the first. Too close but not quite there.

Damn it.

I exhale, grounding myself as I take up the final axe. The world narrows—no crowd, no sounds, just me and the target. One breath. Two.

On the third, I let it fly.

The axe slices through the air, and when it lands, the crowd erupts into cheers.

Bullseye.

"Yes!" I whoop, throwing my fists into the air before turning to Nova. She's already watching me, eyes dark and filled with something decidedly dangerous. Then, she smiles.

Molten heat pools deep in my belly, spiraling downward in a relentless ache. My breath stutters, my thighs clench, and my mouth waters at Nova's knowing smirk. Her lips part slightly, curling at the corners with wicked intent before she turns on her heel and bolts.

Her plum-colored cloak billows behind her as she dashes off the stage, a flash of dark silk disappearing into the festival crowd.

I don't hesitate.

I'm after her in an instant, weaving between laughing onlookers and dodging vendors, my pulse hammering with something far greater than the thrill of the chase. Dimly, I hear the announcer making some jest behind us, but the words don't register. Nothing does. Not the revelry, bright lanterns swinging overhead, or distant music lacing the night air.

All I see is her.

Nova turns sharply into a shadowed alley but isn't fast enough. I catch the trailing edge of her cloak and yank, spinning her back to me. She barely has time to gasp before my mouth crashes onto hers.

She meets my hunger with equal fervor, her hands fisting in my hair as I press her against the rough brick wall. The world outside ceases to exist. My fingers make quick work of her belt; my touch is urgent as her hands tug at mine, both of us fumbling, frantic.

I tear her tunic upward, my mouth finding the soft swell of her breast. She hisses, arching against me, her nails digging into my scalp as I flick my tongue over a taut peak.

"Godess! Ophelia..." Her voice is a rasp, a breathless plea.

I answer with my mouth, trailing heated kisses down the length of her stomach, savoring the way she quivers beneath me. Her pants are undone in seconds and shoved down as I sink to my knees.

The moment my tongue meets her sex, she gasps, fingers tangling in my hair. I don't relent, teasing, tasting, drinking in every cry that escapes her lips. She's exquisite like this—unraveled, undone, lost to the pleasure I give her.

Her thighs tremble. Her breath hitches. Then, with a sharp cry, she breaks apart, her release rolling through her in shuddering waves.

I don't let up. Not yet.

A wicked chuckle escapes me as I press a teasing kiss to her still-sensitive clit, reveling in the way she squirms.

"Stop it," she breathes, but the fire in her eyes tells me she doesn't mean it.

My only answer is another slow, deliberate stroke of my tongue.

Her second climax crashes into her just as swiftly, and only then do I allow my succubus nature to unfurl, drinking in the intoxicating energy of her pleasure.

She sags against the wall, panting, but I don't give her long to recover.

Nova moves with a predator's grace, flipping our positions before I can protest. My back meets the wall, and she's on me in an instant—lips, hands, body pressing flush against mine.

I shudder as her fingers slip beneath my waistband and tugs my pants down with impatient hands. Then she lifts my leg over her shoulder, looking up at me with that wicked gleam in her ocean-deep eyes.

I groan, the sound breaking into a sharp gasp as her tongue flicks over my clit.

"Nova..." I choke out, fingers gripping her hair, hips bucking into the devastating rhythm she sets.

I'm lost. Entirely, wholly lost in her.

The pleasure builds impossibly high, tightening like a bowstring drawn to its limit. When it finally snaps, the force nearly breaks me. My unrestrained, unrepentant scream echoes off the alley walls.

Stars explode behind my eyelids. My body pulses with a fierce bliss that leaves me boneless, trembling, and weightless in its wake.

Nova rises, her lips brushing mine in a kiss so soft, so reverent, it nearly undoes me all over again.

But we are not finished. Not yet.

A hunger still burns between us, raw and insatiable, born from the knowledge that our time together—here, like this—has an expiration date.

So, with the last shreds of my focus, I call upon the shadows, pulling her into their depths.

And then I lose myself in her all over again.

* * *

<u>Seraphina</u>

Ryvvik's fingers tease me beneath the table, a slow, deliberate torment that sends heat pooling between my thighs. The thick material of my pants dulls the sensation just enough to make me desperate for more. I bite my lip, struggling to keep my breathing even, grateful that the rest of our group is nowhere in sight.

"Let's take this somewhere quiet," he murmurs against my ear, his breath hot and teasing. A delicious shiver runs down my spine.

He takes my hand, leading me away from the table and into the crowd. We weave through the throng of festival-goers, the music and laughter around us starkly contrasting the tension between us. The anticipation is thick and intoxicating, wrapping around us like a spell.

The alley we slip into is dark and deserted, hidden from prying eyes. The moment we're alone, Ryvvik wastes no time. He pushes me back against the rough brick wall, his lips crashing into mine in a fierce, possessive kiss. His hands roam my body, igniting fire wherever he touches.

With practiced ease, he works at the belt of my breeches, his fingers moving with the same controlled precision he uses in battle. A swift tug, and the belt falls away. My pants follow. I barely have time to register the cool night air against my skin before he lifts me effortlessly, pressing me against the brick. Instinct takes over—I wrap my legs around his waist, threading my fingers through his hair.

His growl vibrates against my throat as he finds me slick with arousal. "So wet," he murmurs, his voice rough with need. His fingers slide over my aching center, teasing, tormenting.

"Please..." The word escapes in a whimper, my body arching into him.

Ryvvik answers with a deep, approving sound, his grip tightening as he positions himself. I work frantically at his belt, my fingers fumbling in my urgency. In one swift motion, he's inside me, stretching me with a deep, claiming thrust. I cry out his name, muffling the sound against his shoulder as he moves, each stroke sending pleasure spiraling through me.

"Mine," he growls against my lips, swallowing my moans with a kiss.

"Yours," I whisper, breathless, lost in how our bodies move together.

His hand finds my throat, not squeezing, just holding—a possessive touch that sends another wave of arousal crashing through me. His thrusts quicken, each one raw, desperate, pushing me higher and higher. My back scrapes against the brick with every movement, the slight bite of pain only adding to the pleasure. His thumb finds my clit, circling in rhythm with his strokes.

The tension coils tighter, unbearable until it finally snaps. My orgasm crashes over me in waves. My cries are muffled as his lips claim mine. Ryvvik follows moments later, his release shuddering through him as he groans against my skin.

For a moment, we just breathe, bodies tangled, hearts pounding in sync. He kisses my hair, murmuring something in a language I don't understand.

I smirk, still catching my breath. "What is this spell you've woven on me?" he whispers, his fingers trailing along my jaw.

I tilt my head, running my nails down his back. "I could ask you the same thing."

"Witch," he mutters, the word laced with fondness. His still half-hard length twitches inside me, making me groan softly.

I slide off him, sinking to my knees. His breath hitches, his eyes darkening as I trail my tongue along his length. He tastes like salt and sweat, and the throaty moan that escapes him is music to my ears.

He fists my hair, guiding my movements as I take him into my mouth. He thrusts deep, making me gag, tears pricking my eyes. The sound spurs him on, his hips moving in a desperate rhythm. Our eyes meet—his gaze is blazing, wild, possessive. I shudder, pleasure building all over again as I touch myself, matching his pace.

"Faster," he commands, his voice tight with restraint.

I obey, working my fingers in time with his thrusts. My second climax crashes over me just as he groans my name, spilling into my mouth. I swallow greedily, delighting in the way his body shudders with pleasure.

When he pulls me to my feet, my legs are unsteady. As we hurriedly redress, the world outside the alley feels distant and unreal. Heat floods my cheeks when we realize where we are, but Ryvvik grins as he tightens my belt for me.

"We should probably head back," he muses, lacing his fingers through mine. "I lose all common sense when it comes to you."

I laugh softly, squeezing his hand. "I could say the same about you."

As we step back into the festival, the crowd's energy sweeps over us—music, laughter, the scent of ale and spiced pastries. Everything is vibrant and alive. Another competition is underway, cheers erupting as a new winner is declared.

And then I spot them—Ophelia and Nova emerging from a neighboring alley, looking just as disheveled as we probably do. I smirk, nudging Ryvvik. He chuckles, shaking his head as if to say, *looks like we weren't the only ones.*

Laughter bubbles up in my chest, light and carefree. The festival is still in full swing, and the excitement is infectious. Then, the music shifts—lively and intoxicating, with a melody so catchy that my feet tap before I even realize it.

Around us, people pair off, twirling into the open square. The joy in the air is undeniable, and before I can second-guess myself, I grab Ophelia and Nova's hands, dragging them into the crowd.

We're laughing, stumbling into the rhythm, our movements clumsy but free. We sway, spin, and trip over our own feet, but none of it matters. No one cares that we're terrible dancers—everyone is too lost in the moment, too caught up in the music and the magic of the night.

For the first time in what feels like forever, I let go. I dance until my muscles ache, until the stars fade into the first streaks of dawn.

And I know, deep in my heart, that this is a moment I will hold onto. A bright, fleeting ember of joy before the coming darkness.

CHAPTER 38 - A LEADER IS BORN...

<u>Ophelia</u>

It's been several days since the festival, with the infectious energy doing its job—solidifying the bonds we've built. So when Nova mentioned an errand that would carry me back toward Xetizar and Miret's shop—Celestial Metals—I didn't hesitate.

I'm anxious to see Miret again and thank her for the delicate ring now on my left hand. It is a reminder of my legacy, one I hope will mark the birth of a new golden era for Eventide.

As we near the familiar shop, I'm surprised to see a gathering of people on an otherwise empty street. The hour is relatively late, and suspicion starts creeping into my bones.

"Nova," I warn, my voice low. "What's going on?"

"Shh, just wait a moment, will you?" Nova quips, tossing me a mischievous smile over her shoulder.

I scowl.

She chuckles but turns her attention to the crowd. "Everyone, if you'll please. I believe Miret and Xetizar Veydris have taken care of all our needs."

With that, the small group of people enter the shop—disappearing before my eyes. I blink, sure I'm mistaken. Nova grins, tossing me a saucy wink before stepping inside.

Exhaling a shaky breath, I step closer to the edge of the workshop. A faint shimmering blue light swirls before me, moving like dust caught in a sunbeam. I reach out, testing the edge with my palm, marveling at how it glitters and shifts under my touch.

Sucking in a breath, I step through the veil, slipping easily into the true space of their shop.

At least several dozen pairs of eyes stare back at me—some hardened, some filled with curiosity, and some brimming with hope.

The energy in the room is palpable, suffocating in its layered tension. I gulp, my gaze darting around, searching for the only set of eyes that might bring me calm.

I find her standing next to Ryvvik, Skalanis, Seraphina—and even Galean, though the latter looks downright furious.

"Ah, there you are," she says, turning to me with an outstretched hand. I move warily toward her, taking her hand in mine. The moment our palms connect, I feel a caress down our mating bond, sending the strength I desperately need.

"I asked you all here tonight so that we might plan our course of action. We have a plan. Your queen has a plan. May I introduce Ophelia Xamira Morningstar—future Queen of Eventide."

Gasps ripple through the room, a mix of shock, disgust, and outrage. It's enough to send a shiver of fear skittering down my spine. I snap my gaze to hers, silently begging her to spare me a glance, but she doesn't. She only presses forward.

"You doubt me?" she challenges, scanning the crowd, holding each person in a snare before swiftly moving to the next. "I have seen what's to come. I have seen how our future unfolds without her behind our cause. And we have found information that just might change the tide in the coming war. Let's state the elephant in the room—war *is* coming. Whether you want it or not, it's already on your doorstep. Now, if you'll give Her Majesty your attention, please."

I gulp, heat creeping up my neck. I'm sure I've turned three shades of red. *I'm going to wring Nova's neck.*

Drawing in a steadying breath, I shift my attention to the gathered crowd, stepping away from her as I let my gaze settle over them. A man at the front with blonde hair, honey-brown eyes, and a steeled expression catches my attention. The tight set of his jaw makes his frustration with this turn of events clear.

"What she says is true," I begin, returning my focus to the rest of the room.

I let my defenses down, relaxing my stance, adopting an air of confidence I didn't even know I possessed. "We've been searching for something to give us an edge in the coming months, something that will help us against the true evil in this realm. I'm sure you have faced hardships I can't even begin to understand or make right. But if you'll have me, I'd like to try."

I sweep my gaze across the room, meeting each person's eyes, letting sincerity drip from every word.

A commanding voice cuts through the room, laced with bitterness that's impossible to ignore. "Forgive me, *Your Majesty*," the voice practically drips in sarcasm, and I whip my head toward the sound.

The same honey-brown eyes snare me, contempt simmering within them. "I don't know you, and as far as I'm concerned, the *princess* died in her infancy. What I would like to know is what you plan to do about the loss of my brother—for their losses!" He hisses, sweeping a hand toward the rest of the crowd.

A murmur of agreement sweeps through the room, and Nova's gaze hardens. She steps forward until she's only a few feet away from the gentleman.

"Talon's death was a travesty. There's nothing I can say or do that will ever change that. But that doesn't erase the fact that a leader who craves change just as desperately as the rest of us stands before you—willing to do what needs to be done. Tyverian Vale, you are one of the strongest men I know, and I'm grateful to have you on our council. If you can't trust her, can you trust me? At least for now."

A sad smile tugs at the corners of her mouth, but she doesn't back down. If anything, she straightens to her full height, meeting his scrutiny head-on.

"Fine," he relents, stepping aside so Nova can retake the floor.

"It's no secret that news of Frostmere will have reached your cells by now." Another murmur of discontent rolls through the room. "I arrived too late to be of use, and I will carry the regret of that mistake every day for the rest of my life. Before Kara's passing—"

A keening wail cuts through the air, sharp and raw. My eyes instantly find the source.

A woman with dark brown hair, piercing blue eyes, and an eerily familiar face drops to her knees. A string of howls follows, filling the room as several men and women fall to their knees in support.

Their hands clasp onto her back, shoulders, and head, and the howls resume for several long minutes. The hauntingly beautiful sound fills the room, and tears prick at the corners of my eyes. Thick and cloying grief stings my nostrils, painting vivid imagery in my mind—a dark gray wolf with piercing gray eyes running with its pack.

The tears roll down my cheeks. I can't stop them, even if they're not wanted, and I can't stop the pull I feel to join them. My feet move of their own accord, and I kneel in front of the young woman sobbing the hardest. I hesitate, glancing behind me at my mate, who nods in silent approval, her eyes shining with unshed tears.

Placing my palm on the woman's shoulder, I lift my voice to the heavens with them, though my attempt is a poor one at best. No one snickers, no one questions it—they only join me in a new chorus, our voices ringing into the rafters.

Ice-blue eyes meet mine as the final echoes of our song fade into the silence. The connection hits me square in the gut.

"Thank you, Your Majesty," she whispers before kissing each of my cheeks. "You honor my sister's memory with your voice. Kaela Stormblade, at your service." She bows deeply in respect —taking me completely by surprise.

A red-hot blush creeps up my neck, and I awkwardly step back. "I may not have known Kara, but my mate believed her to be a person worthy of her loyalty—I promise you, her death will not go unpunished."

The words are edged with an unfamiliar steel, and I find myself rising once more.

A murmur ripples through the crowd—one that can only be described as a collective understanding. Maybe not quite respect, but something adjacent. I can work with that.

"We've all been brought here for the same purpose. The goddess placed us on this path for a reason. I don't believe the things happening are mere coincidence—if anything, they're a sign of what's to come if we fail. I can't promise to lead with poise or the grace of a seasoned general, but what I can promise? To earn your respect, to give you mine."

I pause, letting the words settle, my gaze sweeping the crowd again. "To hear your concerns, and to make them *mine*. I will fight by your side and *die* for a cause I know is worthy."

Miret steps forward from the crowd, her smile shining brightly. "I will fight with you, my queen." Placing a palm across her chest, she kneels to the floor. "I pledge myself to your cause, your fight, and may the goddess shine upon your reign."

Thick emotion stings the back of my throat, but her words are all that's needed. One by one, they kneel—wave after wave —pledging their hearts and loyalty. All for one, except Tyverian.

I meet his gaze and offer a small smile. I won't push him, but I won't wait for his approval either.

"Please, rise. There's no need for all this," I say to them, "We have a plan, one that will require a great deal of help down the road, and we need solutions. Prepare your messengers and select your generals. We regroup in ten."

⁂

Tyverian Vale, despite his reservations, is proving to be quite the strategist. Kaela is equally adept at planning, her voice carrying weight despite her young age, at just twenty. Galean even surprises me with his quick thinking and ability to pivot while maintaining his integrity.

The actual wild card comes in the form of Lysander Roane— shifty as a fox, with auburn locks that stop just shy of his neck. His hazel-green eyes never stop assessing the situation, yet–he has yet to utter a single word.

Veyra Morvain is probably a close second. She's a siren like Seraphina, though unlike my sister, she embraces the darker side of her nature, making me uneasy. And the fact that she's rumored to be a powerful seeress who's already seen how the war ends?

Yeah, no thank you. I'll stay in my corner over here. It's enough to give me the heebie-jeebies.

Which leaves Jax "Boom" Redthorne—a stocky, short man with a reddish beard streaked in gray and green eyes that dance with mischief. An explosives expert with a penchant for making things blow up in Astra that shouldn't be.

I was immediately sucked in by his harrowing tale of a jewel heist gone wrong.

"I'm telling you, we need to strike now! While we have the element of surprise."

The words jolt me out of my thoughts, and I narrow my gaze at the voice. *Tyverian.*

"And I'm telling you that Xetizar will need time to manufacture enough weapons to equip our people!" Nova's sharp tone cuts through the air, slicing through the fog clouding my head.

"We're going to lose momentum if we wait forever! I say we use the power bestowed upon us by Astraea herself. What's stopping us from smiting him outright?" Tyverian argues, narrowing his gaze at my mate.

Rage slithers through my body, and I step toward Nova, placing a hand on the small of her back. She leans into my touch —her only acknowledgment of the strength my presence lends her.

I don't bother casting a glance in her direction. Instead, I take the reins. She can fight her own battles, but I refuse to let grief be the reason we rush into a war we can't possibly win—not without weapons.

"Do you think for a second I'm going to agree to send *anyone* to their deaths just because you're so clouded by grief?" The words are sharper than intended, but they all hit the same mark.

"Magic is not enough! If you haven't noticed, the king hasn't held his throne for this long without learning how to quell the masses. He will be five steps ahead of us no matter what we do. That's why it's important for us to get this right, *now!*" I hiss.

"*Excuse me?*" Tyverian chuffs, his eyes flashing with rage.

"TYVERIAN!"

The sharp feminine voice startles me, and I jerk at the sound.

He glares at Veyra, but she doesn't shrink. In fact, her diminutive stature seems to expand. Her fiery amber gaze and stark white hair add an edge to the smirk dusting the corners of her mouth.

"If you don't shut the fuck up and open your damn ears to what everyone around you is saying, then get... the... fuck... out." Her words are visceral, laced with venom, and dangerously low.

"You're not helping, you're hindering, and I swear to the fucking goddess I'll gut you myself. I came here to *listen* and take my orders, fulfilling my role and purpose for our cause.

Get in line, *or ship out!*" she hisses at him before stepping to my side.

"Excuse him," she quips, tossing an exasperated glance toward Tyverian. "His brother's death has made him bitter. He's not usually this pigheaded."

Red washes over Tyverian's face, but it does nothing to quell the snickering that ripples through the room.

"Alright, enough!" I yell, cutting through the murmurs. We're not ready for a full-scale war, despite what Tyverian believes," I say, shooting him a withering glare. Our cell still needs to retrieve the information necessary to protect us from the creatures that destroyed Frostmere. They're *nothing* like you've ever seen."

"What are your orders?" Skalanis asks, breaking the tension in the room. He nods—silent confirmation that he has my back every step of the way.

I sweep my gaze across the war council, meeting each person's eyes before speaking. "For now, gather your soldiers, ready your provisions, and prepare for multiple contingency plans. Galean has already been working on finding us a way into the temple grounds, one that will provide secrecy and help us conceal our movements. Stealth is our priority. Mask your movements, code your messages, and for fuck's sake... keep your shit together. After this mission is complete, we'll regroup and plan for a precision strike. For now, lay low, be safe, and may the goddess grant mercy on our souls."

CHAPTER 39 - HERE WE GO AGAIN...

<u>Ophelia</u>

After a week of lounging around Galean's manor—while avoiding him like the plague, especially after that disastrous war meeting—I shiver at the memory. The mounting tension, the frosty glare Tyverian gave me before storming out...

It doesn't matter.

I've proven myself, given orders to ensure our success, and secured my role in the rebellion. The only thing that matters now is getting the one thing that might help us in this accursed war.

Galean's finally figured out a way to get us into the temple. It's not foolproof, but it's our best shot. The only catch? We'll have to separate to pull it off.

Nova, Seraphina, and I will travel together. Galean has procured proper temple attire for us, and we've taken every precaution with our glamours. The men, Galean included, will enter through the pleasure sector, where the temple caters to visiting dignitaries. Posing as members of King Elrond's court, they'll pretend to seek a night of indulgence with the priestesses—who, in recent years, have become just as skilled at seduction as they are at their sacred duties.

It's no secret that a growing sect within the temple is more interested in courting powerful men than in fulfilling their divine obligations. Something I fully intend to change when I take the throne. But that's a battle for another day.

Once the men have gained access to the temple grounds, we'll regroup in the central gardens near the High Priestess's private chambers. Then we'll send a raven to the rest of the rebel cells. It's the least conspicuous meeting point, as the priestesses often take their evening strolls there after completing their rituals.

Galean steps into the hall, his expression tight with urgency. A glowing crimson portal hums to life before him, pulsing with raw energy. He sweeps his gaze over us, his voice firm. "Is everyone clear on the plan? There's no room for hesitation. My cover at court depends on this."

"Ready." The word leaves my lips without hesitation, but my stomach twists uncertainly.

With one last glance at the others, I step into the portal, hoping we're walking toward salvation rather than our doom.

✳ ✳ ✳

Sneaking into the temple grounds is more manageable than

I expected. It makes me wonder—are they truly lax in security, or are they so assured of their safety that they don't bother with tighter measures? As we move unhurriedly, blending in among the visitors, I see why people might be drawn to serve this place. The sprawling grounds are paved with pristine white marble, framed by towering columns, and filled with open spaces that invite tranquility.

As we pass a corridor overlooking the east garden, my steps slow. There's an undeniable beauty to it, one that tugs at something deep inside me. The garden seems to embody the element of Earth—flourishing with a perfect balance of vibrant flowers woven together in careful harmony. Weeping willow trees are nestled in the courtyard, their delicate limbs swaying with the breeze. A few priestesses rest beneath them, lost in quiet contemplation.

I smile and nod at them, feigning casual interest as we approach the central garden. With so many breathtaking sights, it's easy to pretend I'm merely admiring the temple's splendor.

But all too soon, we reach the entrance to the central garden, where two guards stand posted along the hedges. They greet us with warm smiles, offering the usual Emberfall Festival blessing.

"By the leaves and their falling grace, do we look forward to the rebirth that darkness will bring. Merry meet, and Astraea blessed are we."

"Merry meet, may the goddess bless you," I murmured, lowering my gaze as we passed through.

The moment we step inside, I know this garden is different. It isn't just the presence of all four elements coexisting in perfect harmony or the masterful way each is showcased through intricate designs. It's something else—something familiar, tugging at me like a half-forgotten memory just beyond reach.

Priestesses move through the garden, tending to their daily duties, but my attention is drawn elsewhere. My feet move of their own accord toward a stone bench before a magnificent fountain. Made of pure selenite, its pool is deep and wide, with a striking figure at its center—a woman sculpted from the same luminous stone, cradling a lyra. If you look closely, you can see it's her playing that gives birth to the world. The sight is so peaceful and mesmerizing that I almost don't notice the older fae woman entering the courtyard.

She moves with a quiet grace, her white linen robe flowing as she walks. Dark gray hair peppered with silver frames her aged yet regal face, and her pale silver eyes twinkle with wisdom. A strange feeling grips my chest. Those eyes... remind me of Esmyra.

"That has to be her," Seraphina's voice slips into my mind through our bond.

"Aye. I'm certain it's her." Skalanis' agreement is tinged with excitement.

From the south garden, just as planned, Galean and the others make their entrance. They look drunk—whether that's good or bad, I can't be sure—but luck is on our side. They've managed to charm a few priestesses into accompanying them, laughing and stumbling toward the courtyard.

"I'm going to try to speak with her. Give me ten minutes," I say through the bond, smoothing the crimson velvet of my dress. I adjust the golden diadem of moons atop my head before stepping forward.

I approach with feigned curiosity, trailing my fingers along the fountain's edge, pretending to admire the craftsmanship.

When our eyes meet, something flickers in her gaze. Recognition?

"Have we met before, my dear?" she asks, her voice soft and warm—grandmotherly.

"I can't be certain, but I believe you knew my mother very well," I answer carefully, hands wringing in my lap as I wait for her reaction.

She stiffens. Her breath hitches, eyes widening as if she's seen a ghost. I know then that my glamour has slipped. A quick glance at Nova confirms it—she knew I needed the illusion to fade before I did.

"Oh my..." The woman clutches a handkerchief to her heart, tears welling in her eyes. Slowly, she bows her head in respect.

"My darling girl, I've waited a long time for this moment. I see you've finally found your mother's journals."

Her palm cups my cheek, warm and trembling. She chuckles softly, though her sniffles betray the emotion brimming beneath.

"You... you knew of me?" My voice barely escapes in a whisper.

"Darling girl, I'm your grandmother. Of course I knew you were alive. I've carried that secret for nearly three decades, intending to take it to my grave. Esmyra, my sweet and lovely Esmyra... she loved you so much, as did Her Majesty."

The words strike me like a bolt of lightning. My grandmother?

I struggle to process the revelation, but I push forward. "Niahm—I mean, High Priestess Niahm—do you know where we might find Caecinnia? We need the elixir she's been saving for me."

"Grandmother will be just fine," she corrects gently, patting my hand. But then her expression darkens. "Ophelia, my girl, you must stay for a moment. There's something you need to hear—something your mother wanted to tell you but never had the chance."

She sighs, gripping the handkerchief tightly as though steadying herself.

"When you were born, Elrond became furious. He had high hopes that his sons would inherit the kingdom. He grew paranoid, seeing enemies everywhere. And one night..." she hesitates, her gaze flickering toward Galean and the others.

"Grandmother," I press, bringing her attention back.

She exhales sharply. "Esmyra caught him standing over your cradle. If she had been a moment too late, he would have succeeded in killing you."

A chill runs down my spine.

"Your mother made a deal that night. If you ask me, a deal with the devil, though she never told me the particulars. Only that we were never to mention it or the Shadow Realm again, but I know this—until you fulfill her bargain, you will never truly be free. Not from Elrond, and certainly not from the darkness that calls your name. If you do not, you will be the kingdom's damnation."

My breath catches. "Then what do I do?"

"Your only hope is to cross into the Shadow Realm. Perhaps there, you will find the answers you seek."

I sit frozen, reeling—the prophecy. I knew it hadn't told the whole truth. There was always going to be a cost—something I'd have to give up.

"You said the realm has been forgotten... why?"

"Because your mother made sure of it. She used Shadow Flame to strip Elrond of his power, but the price must have been steep. Afterward, she ordered every entrance to the Shadow Gates blocked and guarded day and night. No one was to enter. No one was to speak of it again."

A strong male voice cuts through the garden.

"Galean!"

My head snaps toward the sound. My stomach drops all the way to ground.

"Oh, for fuck's sake," I mutter.

"Ophelia, darling, take this," Niahm says quickly, grabbing my attention. She presses an old map into my hands. It's covered in names, spells, and unfamiliar landscapes.

"It has the incantations to unlock the Shadow Gate beneath the temple. You'll find the entrance in my office—take the stairs down. You can catch Caecinnia on the way; she's tending to Prince Lorne in the pleasure garden."

I grip the map, nodding. "Yes, Grandmother."

Before I can move, she squeezes my hand once more.

"Oh, my darling girls. My heart is full seeing you together. Light and dark, shadow and starlight. Twins, destined for a great purpose."

Twins?

My breath stalls. "Grandmother—"

"No time. Go, child. Take your sister and leave this place. Restore the balance. Go swiftly... and give your sister my love."

I rise to my feet, urgency coursing through me like wildfire as I stride toward Seraphina and Nova, my mind link flaring to life.

"I have the map and the directions to the gate. If we hurry, we can catch Caecinnia along the way."

My thoughts are still reeling, tangled in the bomb our grandmother just dropped on me. I'm a fucking twin. A prophecy that had never told the whole truth. And now, a race against time to secure what we need before everything collapses.

"Can't."

Galean's clipped answer is enough to snap me back to the present, grating against my last fraying nerve. My head whips toward his direction, fury igniting like flint on steel. I quickly turn my head back toward Seraphina and Nova, staying the course.

"Can't? Or won't?" I challenge, voice like ice. *"Surely you can give your little friend there the slip."*

He hisses. *"He wasn't supposed to be here. I'm trying to keep his attention on me and off you. Otherwise, you're going to blow my cover. It's not just Arax; Lorne is here too."*

A muscle in my jaw twitches. *"Thanks, my grandmother already told me."* My voice is a low seethe. *"I'm pretty sure he's holding Caecinnia in the pleasure garden. We need her elixir if we're going to have a fighting chance against King Elrond and the deathlings."*

Galean curses, the sound muffled in my head. *"I understand that, but if you don't let me divert his attention—fuck. He's spotted you."*

I don't need to turn to know that we've been made. The atmosphere shifts, tension thickening like a storm cloud rolling in.

Then I hear it—heavy boots striking against stone—a snarling voice, sharp as a blade, cuts through the air shortly after.

"YOU!"

The priestesses scatter, their delighted squeals turning to hushed whispers as Prince Arax storms toward us, dragging Galean and Ryvvik in his wake. His grip on Galean's shirt is ironclad, and Galean is visibly struggling to loosen it.

"We can explain... Your Highness, please!" Galean chokes out, coughing as Arax finally releases him. He stumbles but quickly rights himself, adjusting his black tunic with a sharp exhale.

"Explain it then." Arax growls, his molten gaze snapping to me. "Why are they here? And how the fuck is it that you know who they are?"

A heavy silence settles over us.

Galean hesitates, then shifts his gaze to me.

And in that instant, I know.

He's going to tell him.

My heart plummets, sweat dampening my palms.

"Your Highness," Galean says carefully, squaring his shoulders. "I think it's best if we just come clean. You've been searching for a way to take out your father. And, well... I've found our solution."

Arax's eyes narrow.

Galean gestures toward me. "Meet Princess Ophelia Xamira Morningstar." His voice is calm, unwavering. "Your sister."

The world seems to stop.

Arax stares at me, eyes widening, his expression frozen in disbelief. His lips parted slightly as if forming words that never come.

Then—his jaw clenches, his entire frame locking with tension. His fingers twitch at his sides, curled into tight fists.

Then, with a low snarl, he wrenches Galean up by the front of his shirt again.

"That's *impossible*." His voice trembles with fury. "I watched my father *murder* my sweet sister nearly twenty-seven years ago. I watched, completely and utterly powerless. I was a little boy no more than five, and couldn't stop it. And you're telling me that this—*this fraud*—is my long-lost, very *dead* sister, and heir to the kingdom?"

Galean barely manages to keep his footing as Arax shoves him back.

I steel my spine. "He's telling the truth." The words taste bitter and reluctant, but undeniable. "As much as I loathe to admit it, you're my brother."

His expression flickers, something unreadable crossing his face.

I push forward, seizing the moment. "Look at me. Really look." My voice lowers, controlled. "My eyes. My hair. I remind you of her, don't I?"

Arax takes a shuddering breath, his gaze locking onto mine. Something falters in his stance, a shadow of hesitation.

But then—

He exhales, slow and measured, and his expression hardens into something ice-cold and ruthless.

"I don't care." His voice is low, quiet, and lethal. "I don't fucking care if you're actually her."

The air stills, heavy with the weight of his following words— like a knife to my chest.

"You know nothing of what I've endured to get here. You know nothing of this kingdom. And you sure as fuck aren't ready to run it." He steps closer, towering over me. "No. This is ridiculous. The plan stays the same, Galean." His voice sharpens. "Get rid of her."

I stiffen. "Excuse me?"

"Take her back to whatever hole she crawled out of. I don't want her here, and she sure as fuck isn't getting anywhere near our plans." His glare is razor-edged, cutting straight through me. "If my father catches wind of this, everything I've worked for is lost. All of it. I won't waste our one chance taking a gamble on some fucking imposter."

His gaze flicks back to Galean, something dangerous simmering beneath the surface. "And don't think for a second that I'm letting this go unpunished."

Galean tenses. "Your Highness—"

Arax silences him with a raised hand, his head tilting slightly —listening.

Then I hear it.

A bloodcurdling, marrow-deep scream that sends a sharp jolt of fear through my bones.

Another follows, even more chilling.

"Skalanis!" Nova cries, eyes wide with terror.

We don't waste a moment.

In an instant, we're moving—racing toward the pleasure garden.

My heart hammers against my ribs as another agonized scream echoes through the temple grounds.

A silent prayer slips past my lips, a desperate plea to the goddess.

Please. Don't let us be too late.

CHAPTER 40 - OH, FOR FUCKS SAKE...

Skalanis

I can't explain the pull I feel... It gnaws at me, an invisible force dragging my attention away when I should be focused on running interference for Galean, on keeping the prince occupied. But something is calling me back toward the pleasure gardens.

The sensation intensifies—an electric hum beneath my skin, a whisper in the marrow of my bones. Then, I catch it. A scent. Sunshine and cinnamon, rich and intoxicating. It coils around me, seeping into my lungs, drowning out every rational thought.

Before I realize what I'm doing, my feet are moving, my body following the scent like a man possessed. I barely murmur an excuse before slipping away, my pulse quickening with each step. The further I go, the stronger it gets until I'm practically running down the long corridor, my heart hammering with an urgency I can't explain.

Then I hear the screams.

It's a woman's voice, filled with raw terror.

I break into a sprint, my boots pounding against the stone. I round the corner, eyes scanning frantically until—

A petite red-haired woman is shoved against a pillar, her skirts bunched in a desperate grip. A blonde man leers over her, his nasally voice sneering as he wrenches at her clothes. She thrashes, her fists flying, her knee jerking up in a desperate attempt to fight back—his hand cracks across her face, stunning her for just a second too long.

A red haze blurs my vision.

"Keep your mouth shut, you filthy whore! You asked for this, you—"

"GET OFF HER!" My roar fills the garden, shaking the air as I lunge. My fist connects with his nose in a sickening crunch. He reels back, blood spurting as he stumbles against a marble column before crumpling in a heap, unconscious.

Chest heaving, I turn to the woman. She trembles, her green eyes wild, and her breath comes in shallow gasps. Her hands shake as she smooths the crumpled fabric of her emerald skirts, dazed and unseeing.

I approach slowly, hands up in a placating gesture. "Are you alright?" My voice is softer now, but she doesn't seem to hear me.

"He's never... I never..." She trails off, tears spilling down her cheeks.

Hesitating momentarily, I reach for her hands, wrapping them in mine. Her skin is ice-cold, and her delicate fingers twitch under my touch. I squeeze gently. "You're safe now," I murmur, and the moment the words leave my lips—

Something surges through me.

A rush of blistering heat, a fire curling in my gut, wrapping around my ribs like an unbreakable chain. Sunshine and cinnamon flood my senses, swallowing me whole. I can barely think, can scarcely breathe.

Protect.

Mine.

She's mine.

The realization slams into me, staggering in its force. But before I can understand it, her eyes go wide with terror.

She screams.

A shadow looms behind me.

Pain explodes across my skull as something cold and sharp slices through the air—a dagger. I barely manage to grab the blade before another one crashes against the side of my head, sending me reeling.

I don't even hit the ground before the next blow comes—a fist to my jaw. Then, the stone floor rises to meet me, my body collapsing in a heap.

I struggle to rise, but something heavy pins me down.

Pain lances through my chest.

I choke, coughing wetly as fire spreads through my ribs. My vision blurs, the edges tinged with red. A fucking dagger. Lodged deep in my lung. That's why I can't fucking breathe.

"Fuck," I rasp, blood bubbling at my lips.

Dark spots dance across my vision, the weight on my waist pressing harder, suffocating me. My body protests, but I can barely lift my arms.

Another blade. It plunges deep into my arm, the pain blinding. I bite down on my tongue to keep from screaming, the coppery taste of blood filling my mouth. I spit it in his face, throwing a wild punch with my free arm.

It does nothing.

He just keeps going.

More steel. More pain. My body jerks with every stab, warmth spilling over my skin, soaking the ground beneath me. My limbs grow heavier. The sounds around me—yelling, fighting, chaos—start to fade.

Then I hear it.

"SKALANIS!"

Nova's voice. She's close. But she sounds so far away.

I want to answer. To tell her I'm still here. But my lungs are filling with blood. It drowns my voice, drowns the world, drowns everything.

Even as hands rip my attacker away, even as Nova's magic floods through me, I feel it.

The darkness. It's waiting. It's calling my name.

I don't fight it.

I let it take me under.

* * *

Ophelia

I can't breathe.

The scene before me is pure chaos. Blood, screams, the clash of metal—it's overwhelming. My mind struggles to make sense of it all.

A petite, trembling woman stands in the corner, wringing her hands. "Help him!" she squeaks, her voice barely audible over the madness. She points toward the center of the room—toward Skalanis.

He's sprawled on the floor, pinned beneath a blonde man who's straddling him, stabbing him over and over—a new blade for every strike.

Skalanis is pale. Blood oozes in thick pools around his body. He hacks up a mouthful of it, crimson staining his lips.

"SKALANIS!" Nova screams, the raw agony in her voice cutting through the chaos like a blade.

Arax moves first, throwing himself at the attacker. He wrenches the bastard off Skalanis by the collar, hurling him across the room with inhuman strength. "WHAT THE FUCK, Lorne?!" he snarls. His voice is a storm, vibrating with barely contained fury. "I'm assuming this is your mess?! What the fuck were you thinking?! It's not enough to get your jollies with the whores in the pleasure sector—you have to maim a priestess and kill someone too?!"

Lorne staggers to his feet, wiping the blood from his split lip. He doesn't even look remorseful. Just annoyed. "I was simply taking back what was owed to me." He shrugs, flicking a hand toward the woman in the corner. "I paid for her. She tried to go back on our arrangement, and this *idiot* decided to play hero." His lip curls in disgust as he gestures toward Skalanis.

I don't hesitate.

In an instant, I'm on him, grabbing him by the throat. My fist crashes into his face, once, twice—satisfaction surging with every crack of bone against my knuckles. He staggers, but I don't stop. I sweep my leg under his feet, knocking him flat onto his back. Before he can react, I straddle him, driving my fists into his face again and again.

Arax pulls me off him—only to slam his own fist into Lorne's already ruined face.

I grin, wild and unhinged. Watching Arax beat the bastard until his features are barely recognizable is *almost* satisfying enough.

Almost.

A shrill scream rips through the air, snapping my head around.

My blood turns to ice.

A deathling has the priestess in its clawed grip, yanking her toward its jagged teeth.

I don't think. I act.

My dagger leaves my hand in a blur, striking true—embedding itself in the demon's right eye. The beast screeches, thrashing in pain as it releases its captive.

Its head jerks toward me, fury radiating off it in waves.

Good.

We begin to circle each other. I manage a few quick slashes with my blade, but the creature moves like liquid shadow, dodging and weaving before its claws catch my face, raking across my cheek.

Arax steps in before it can strike again, unleashing a torrent of blue dragon fire.

The beast shrieks, its body engulfed in flame as it drops to its knees, writhing in agony.

I don't give it a chance to recover.

With one clean swing, I bring my sword down, severing its head. It hits the floor with a wet *thud*, rolling across the blood-slicked stone.

Arax prods the twitching corpse with his boot. "What the fuck *is* that?"

"The stuff of literal nightmares," I mutter, suppressing a shiver.

Instinct takes over. I open my palm, and white flames lick up my fingers, dancing along my blade. I plunge the weapon into the demon's chest, watching as the fire spreads, consuming its body until nothing but ash remains.

Arax stares, wonder flickering behind his midnight-blue eyes. "How'd you know to do that?"

I shake my head, gripping my sword tighter. "I don't know," I admit. "Just... a feeling."

Before I can turn back to Skalanis—before I can even process Nova sobbing as she pours healing energy into him—I hear it.

A low, guttural growl.

Then another.

And another.

Heavy footsteps echo in the corridor. The sound of something *coming*.

Arax stiffens beside me, his hand tightening on his blade. "What was that?"

Then we see it.

A deathling rounds the corner, its eyes locked on us with ravenous hunger.

Then another–and another.

And then *dozens*.

They fill the corridor, a writhing mass of death and hunger.

"Oh, for fuck's sake," I mutter, before I toss myself into the melee.

CHAPTER 41 - WHERE'D YOU GO?

<u>Seraphina</u>

It's absolute fucking madness.

The temple gardens are overrun with monstrous creatures, their guttural snarls mingling with the terrified screams of those caught in their path. The air is thick with the scent of blood and the acrid stench of burning flesh. Fear coils deep in my gut, but there's no time to dwell on it—I'm too busy fighting for my life.

I cut down the last of the snarling beasts in front of me, their patchy tufts of fur slick with dark, putrid-smelling blood.

Block. Strike. Parry.

The rhythm is ingrained in my body, honed since childhood. But the heavy folds of this godsdamned gown are slowing me down, making each movement sluggish and clumsy. A feral growl rips through the air, and I whirl just in time to see a creature lunging for me, claws swiping dangerously close. I pivot, but my feet tangle in the cumbersome fabric—my balance wavers.

I hit the ground hard.

A breathless curse escapes my lips as I scramble backward, my hands digging into the dirt. Three of them rush toward me, their jerky, unnatural movements twisting my stomach. The lead one, eyes burning like embers, opens its maw, revealing rows of jagged, yellowed teeth.

Lightning crackles through the air.

Galean's magic slams into them, sending them sprawling, buying me precious seconds. Heart pounding, I push myself up and sprint toward the garden's edge, my slippered feet slipping against the grass. My lungs burn as I reach the wall—a towering structure of brick and vine—a dead end.

"Shit."

A guttural snarl behind me sends a spike of dread down my spine. I whirl, throwing out a pulse of ice magic. Jagged shards pierce a deathling mid-stride, splitting its chest wide open.

But it's not enough.

More of them are coming.

Galean hurls crackling bolts of energy, and two priestesses join the fight, their hands ablaze with elemental magic as they fling it toward the onslaught. My muscles tense, readying another blast of ice, when—

"Sera!"

Ophelia's warning comes just as a deathling lunges at me from the side. A searing streak of white-hot fire slices through the air, incinerating the beast instantly.

There's no time to thank her, so I nod my head before turning my attention to the creatures that have swarmed me.

More creatures surge forward, relentless and hungry. My

siren senses latch onto the fear thick in the air, drinking it like a heady elixir. Power thrums through my veins. I throw my hands forward, summoning a brutal wave of ice. It crashes into the nearest group, slicing through flesh and bone, their entrails spilling onto the blood-soaked ground.

But for every one I kill, three more take their place.

"Ryvvik!" I scream, my voice barely cutting through the chaos.

Three deathlings have me cornered, their grotesque forms blocking any chance of escape. Another two surge in from the right, their claws glinting wickedly under the moonlight.

Ryvvik's fire scorches through the air, striking the nearest one and forcing the others to hesitate. It's the only opening I need—I drop into a roll, slipping beneath a vicious swipe before scrambling back to my feet.

Then I see it.

A hooded figure lingers at the edge of the pleasure garden, untouched by the carnage surrounding us. Still. Watching.

Fury ignites in my veins.

"There!" I shout, pointing toward them as I sprint across the bloodied grass.

"Who the fuck is that?" Ryvvik growls, yanking me out of another creature's grasp, his grip firm and grounding.

"I don't know! They've been standing there—watching," I yell back, breathless. "I think they're responsible for this!"

His answering snarl is lost to the clash of steel and the screeching of the beasts. He flings another wave of fire behind us, clearing a path as we weave through the throng of priestesses who have joined the battle.

A guttural roar rips through the night. My gaze flicks to Ophelia as a monstrous, horned beast lunges at her from behind.

"Ophelia!" I hurl an ice dagger, the blade slicing deep into its ribcage. It wasn't fast enough. The creature's claws rake down her leg, and she stumbles, crimson staining her skirts and cloak.

I grit my teeth, but there's no time to check on her. The hooded figure still hasn't moved. They're waiting for something.

Or someone.

Ryvvik and I push forward, dodging and cutting down anything in our path. But the moment we break free from the worst of the fray, the figure finally reacts.

They run.

"Not a fucking chance," I snarl.

I release a torrent of ice in their direction, jagged shards glistening as they tear through the air. The figures twist at the last second, their movements impossibly quick. They dodge every blade, careening right before vanishing into the maze of columns leading to the central gardens.

I surge forward, but Ryvvik curses behind me—he's locked in battle with another deathling, its putrid breath inches from his face.

I hesitate.

Do I stay?

Or do I go after the answers we desperately need?

It's a snap decision. I run, sprinting towards them with everything I have.

The figure is fast, slipping through the gardens like a shadow, but I push harder, my gown a tangled mess around my legs. I hurl another barrage of ice daggers—miss. Again.

They zigzag unpredictably, doubling back, trying to lose me.

I slam into a column, gasping as pain lances through my shoulder, but I shove forward.

Then—a blur of motion, and the hooded figure flickers. Vanishing into thin air.

I skid to a halt, blinking furiously.

What in all the hells—

A bellow tears through the night.

I whip around just in time to see Ryvvik go down.

A hulking beast looms over him—massive, muscled, its wolven head twisting toward the kill. Ryvvik struggles, scrambling back as the creature lifts its clawed hand.

Something inside me shatters.

"No!" The word is torn from my throat, but it's more than a scream. It's a command.

Magic surges, raw and unfamiliar. My voice twists into something otherworldly, resonating with the air itself.

"Stop."

The beast freezes.

I gape, my heart hammering. Did I just—?

Ryvvik doesn't waste the opportunity. He lunges, the blade slicing through the creature's throat in one swift, brutal motion. Its head rolls to the ground with a sickening thud.

But I barely register it.

A scream rips through the battlefield—sharp, shattering, filled with soul-deep agony.

Nova.

A chill runs down my spine. I don't think. I run.

Ryvvik is beside me in an instant. We fight as one, pushing through the horde with perfect, instinctual harmony—fire and ice, slicing and burning, cutting them down ruthlessly.

A priestess crumples near me, blood pooling beneath her

body. Her blonde hair is matted, her hands clutching at her stomach as her insides spill out. I drop to my knees, reaching for her, but it's too late. Her chest rises—falls—stillness.

I swallow against the bile rising in my throat: so much death and so much destruction. Then—

A sound that guts me, sending a wave of dread through me. It's a wail, raw and keening, so powerful that it's echoing throughout the entire garden.

"NOOOOOO!!!!"

My sister's scream captures my attention, and I snap my head up, my pulse hammering.

And then I see it. My breath catches, my body locking up in horror. I'm too far away, I won't make it in time.

Ophelia is closer.

Please, for fucks sake Astraea, let her reach them in time.

CHAPTER 42 - WHAT GOOD IS POWER, IF IT'S LEFT TO ROT?

The Ghost

These wretched creatures might just be the death of me.

I shiver at the garden's edge, watching as the battle rages around me. Despite the chaos, the Crown and the Shield are holding their own. I'll give them one thing—they certainly know how to adapt. Even after years of power suppression, they wield their abilities with an ease that is, admittedly, impressive.

I shouldn't linger. I shouldn't be watching. Yet, something keeps me rooted to the spot.

The Shield is backed into a dead end, scrambling for footing against a horde of deathlings. The wall behind her is covered in thick vines, useless as an escape. She scrambles, then finds her footing and charges back into the chaos. I observe how they move and fight together; each one focused solely on bringing the creatures down. It's... fascinating.

And yet, I don't have time for this.

I need to reach the High Priestess's office before I'm discovered, preferably before the battle is over.

Forcing my attention away, I slip into the shadows, darting down an open corridor and keeping to the thick columns for cover. The yells of combat grow distant as I move with practiced precision. Every step is calculated. Every breath is controlled. But just as I'm about to round the final corner—

"Shit."

I've been spotted.

I freeze, torn between abandoning the mission entirely or pressing forward. My hesitation costs me. When I glance back, my stomach tightens—

The Shield is barreling toward me. And Ryvvik is right behind her.

I don't wait. I run.

My cloak billows behind me as I tear across the garden, slipping between columns and dodging fallen priestesses. I don't need to look over my shoulder to know she's throwing everything she has at me. I can feel it in the sharp zings of magic whizzing past my head.

An ice dagger slices through the air, missing me by mere inches, sending adrenaline hurtling through my body.

Luck. Or perhaps divine intervention. Either way, I use the opportunity to my advantage, quickening my pace as I zigzag through the central gardens. The energy crackling at my back is relentless, but I don't stop. I can't.

I sprint toward the next corridor, lungs burning. I'm almost there. Almost—

A sharp cry echoes through the air—a pained, visceral sound.

I risk a glance back—

Ryvvik is locked in combat with a monstrous creature, one that sends a chill crawling down my spine.

The Shield hesitates.

And that's my opening.

With a final burst of speed, I push forward, feeling the familiar tug of my tether. That brilliant blue thread calling me back. I reach for it, grip it tight—

The shift is immediate.

I snap back into my body with a force that steals my breath.

"Dammit," I hiss, blinking away the dizziness.

A deep voice cuts through my disorientation. "I take it things didn't go according to plan?"

I whip around, my heart still racing. The Commander leans against the doorframe, his usual smirk in place. His gray eyes gleam with amusement, but the humor doesn't last long.

"What went wrong?"

I exhale sharply, fingers absently toying with the end of my braid. "The Shield spotted me in the garden. I never made it to the High Priestess's office."

"The creatures swarmed?"

"As expected."

He nods, considering. "Directives?"

"We stay the course."

Without another word, he turns and strides out of the room, leaving me alone with my thoughts.

I knew this mission was a risk. I knew there was a chance I wouldn't make it in time. Still, frustration coils tight in my chest. The information I seek is so close—just out of reach.

I push to my feet, abandoning the cushions on the floor as I move toward the window. The market below is alive with blissful ignorance.

They titter from place to place, oblivious.

Like lambs to the slaughter.

They have no idea of the dangers lurking beneath their feet. No idea of the disaster creeping ever closer due to generations of negligence.

What good is power if it's left to rot?

The thought burns, igniting something bitter inside me.

Turning from the window, I drift toward the oak desk, its surface cluttered with scattered papers, books, and scrolls— each one a fragment of my research. So much time was spent searching. And yet, still, nothing.

My gaze shifts to the decanter sitting on the wooden table nearby.

Without hesitation, I pop off the cap and pour myself a drink, the rich aroma of sangria filling the air. I take a long sip, letting the citrus and spice dull the sting of failure.

I despise failure. I take another sip, then another. Still, the fury lingers.

I glance at the scrolls, at the secrets buried within them.

One way or another, I will find the truth.

Even if I have to tear their world apart to do it.

CHAPTER 43 - THE BEGINNING
OF THE END...

<u>Ophelia</u>

It's complete and utter fucking chaos.

Once they start pouring in, it's like a dam has shattered, flooding the temple grounds with deathlings. I can't tell if we're winning or losing—the battle ebbs and flows, a relentless tide of screams, snarls, and searing magic. The sounds will haunt my nightmares for years.

I pivot to dodge one creature, only to find myself face-to-face with another. It's endless. How much longer can we keep this up?

Arax is locked in battle with one of the biggest deathlings I've ever seen, his muscles straining as he wrestles it into submission. He hurls another one my way like it weighs nothing, and I don't hesitate. White fire erupts from my hands, consuming the beast in a brilliant inferno.

"Incoming!" he bellows.

Ryvvik slams another deathling toward me, and I strike before it can lunge. The creature lets out a guttural screech before bursting into black ash.

"Two o'clock!" Ryvvik warns.

I spin left, narrowly avoiding claws that would've taken my right arm clean off. "I'm rather fucking partial to that arm!" I snarl, thrusting my hand forward. Fire erupts from my palm, burning flesh and bone until nothing remains.

Seraphina flings another beast my way, and I meet it with a tumbling wall of white fire. She moves like a dancer, cutting them down with a deadly elegance that almost looks like art. An ice dagger flies from her fingers, embedding itself into a creature's throat just as Galean sends a crackling bolt of energy at another one barreling toward her.

More priestesses have joined the fray, their elemental magic streaking through the battlefield like falling stars. Seraphina hesitates for a split second, before hurtling more ice daggers into the fray—until another bone-rattling screech pierces the air.

A deathling with a rack of jagged antlers charges toward her.

"Sera!" I shout, flinging a hand out. A white-hot blaze roars to life, colliding with the beast before it can reach her.

I barely have time to register her frantic nod of thanks before another creature descends upon me. Its wings are slick with black grime, its skeletal frame a grotesque imitation of something that once lived. I duck beneath a swipe of its claws and drive my blade into its chest, pinning its wings to the ground. Magic surges through me, and I channel a stream of fire down the steel. The smell of charred flesh and decay makes my stomach heave, but I yank my blade free and whirl back into the fight.

"RYVVIK!" Seraphina's voice cuts through the night, sharp with urgency.

I don't have time to look. I have to trust him—to trust that he'll protect her, to trust that he'll make it through this.

Galean steps into Ryvvik's place beside me, and we move in perfect tandem, cutting the creatures down one by one. There's no hesitation, no room for doubt—only fire, fury, and the unrelenting need to survive.

"To your right!"

Galean snarls the warning as he sends a lightning bolt straight through a deathling's skull.

I leap over a fallen priestess. Her lifeless eyes are still open, her mouth frozen in a silent scream. *Not now.* I shove the grief away, lock it down tight, and unleash a stream of white fire at the creature clawing toward me. It's gone in an instant.

Then something *yanks* my cloak.

I hit the ground hard.

"Ophelia!" Arax calls, his voice strained, but I don't have time to look for him.

A deathling looms over me, talons reaching for my chest, its beak snapping in an attempt to rip my heart out.

I grab its wing, twisting violently to avoid its snapping jaws. It shrieks, thrashing, trying to break free. I snarl, channeling raw power into its body and sending it crashing to the ground. The second it hits, it turns to ash.

I push myself up, heart hammering, and scan the battlefield for Arax.

There—in the center of the pleasure garden.

He's shifted into his dragon form, but even then, the creature he's fighting is bigger.

The deathling's wings stretch twice the size of his. Its jaw alone could fit around Arax's head. One of its eyes is missing, a hollow socket where flesh and tendons should be.

Terror digs into my ribs, sharp and unrelenting.

I run.

I dodge bodies and attackers, pushing through the chaos. Arax and the beast are locked in a brutal, merciless fight, each trying to tear the other apart.

I barely sidestep a horned deathling before it can impale me. Pain lances through my leg as it nicks me, but before it can strike again, Seraphina's ice dagger finds its mark—the beast stumbles just enough for me to send another wall of fire slamming into its chest.

I don't stop. I can't stop.

I'm almost to Arax when I hear it—

The roar.

I turn just in time to see Arax fall—human again. Vulnerable.

Above him, the monstrous deathling dragon opens its jaws.

Black fire.

A storm of it rushes toward him, burning everything in its path.

I don't think. I move.

I thrust my hands out, and white fire erupted from my palms. I built a shield between him and the oncoming blaze.

Galean throws himself into the fray, hurling bolt after bolt at the beast. The creature screams in fury, flinging itself skyward, circling us.

I sprint to Arax's side, grab his arm, and haul him up.

We run.

Black fire rains down behind us, but I throw another wall of white fire up, blocking the attack.

Arax pants, staring at me like he's never seen me before. "Ophelia... you saved my life."

"Later!" I hissed, shoving him aside just as another deathling lunges. Twin blades in hand, I strike, severing its head clean off. Flames rush down my blade, sinking into its chest until nothing remains but ash.

Then—a scream.

Raw. Broken. Agonizing.

"No! No, no, no!"

Nova's wail rips through the garden.

I turn, dread pooling in my belly, and the breath is knocked out of my lungs.

She's clutching Skalanis's *body.*

I hit my knees.

The battle fades around me. The screaming, the magic, the blood—all of it blurs into something far away, something I can't process.

Seraphina and Ryvvik are still fighting, but I barely see them.

The south side of the garden is in chaos. Galean is outnumbered five to one. Arax is faltering. The redhead is still hurling spells, and the priestesses are still falling.

And Nova—

Nova is sobbing over Skalanis.

A deathling lunges for her.

"YOU CAN'T HAVE HIM!" she shrieks, hurling a boulder with raw, desperate magic.

It barely slows the creature.

I move.

"NO!"

I slam my hands into the ground, pulling from everything.

White fire explodes from me in a shockwave, burning

through the battlefield.

The creatures scream.

But I don't stop.

I pour every last drop of magic into the earth, sending it out in pulsing waves. My lungs *burn.* My muscles *shake.* My eyes blur with tears, but *I don't stop.*

Not until there's nothing left.

Silence.

Seraphina rushes to my side, pressing a wave of healing magic into me. It cools my veins and steadies my trembling hands.

"Did... are they gone?" I whisper.

A hand lands on my shoulder. I jerk, twisting—

"Woah! Easy there," Ryvvik's voice is calm, but there's a flicker of surprise in his golden-green eyes as I instinctively twist his arm behind his back.

I let go immediately, stepping away as shame burns up my throat. "I'm sorry." The words feel hollow.

Ryvvik chuckles, bumping his shoulder against mine in easy camaraderie. "It's been a long day. You're allowed to be on edge. After that display, I'd bet the priestesses will be buying you drinks tonight in thanks."

I don't smile. "They're gone then...?" My voice comes out quieter than I expected.

"It would appear so."

Arax joins our circle, and his face is shadowed with exhaustion. He fidgets with the straps of his leathers, hesitation tightening his features. "Lorne is gone. I—I don't know when he disappeared. It must've been during the chaos."

Galean swears. The sharp, venomous bite of his voice makes nausea churn in my stomach. "Goddess, damn it." He kicks at a pile of ash, frustration seething beneath his usually controlled exterior.

I exhale sharply, already dreading the inevitable fallout.

Arax shifts beside me, something unreadable crossing his face. "Ophelia... I think I owe you an apology."

I blink, startled.

He presses forward, voice lower now. "I can't promise I'll be successful, but I'll try to cut Lorne off before he reaches the king. At the very least, I can buy you some time—"

A scream rips through the air, so raw and visceral that it skewers me straight through.

My head snaps toward the sound.

Nova is cradling Skalanis in her lap, her body hunched protectively over him as if she can shield him from the inevitable.

The fiery redhead—the healer—is at her side, frantically summoning reinforcements.

"Oh my goddess..." Seraphina's voice breaks, and Ryvvik pulls her into his arms before I can even turn.

I hear it before I see it—his ragged breaths.

No.

I can't move. I can't think.

The weight of reality slams into my chest, crushing the air from my lungs.

Skalanis can't be dying!

He *can't*.

A strangled sound escapes me, a broken, shattered thing that barely scratches the surface of the storm inside me.

Nova's wails match my own, both of us crumbling beneath the grief as they lift Skalanis and carry him away.

Regret. Guilt. Shame.

It coils tightly around my ribs, suffocating me.

"This is all my fault." The words slip out before I can stop them, thick with devastation.

My body moves before my mind catches up, stumbling toward Nova. I wrap my arms around her, holding her as tightly as I can as she sobs uncontrollably.

She clings to me just as desperately.

And all I can think is—

What the *fuck* have I done?

CHAPTER 44 - FUCK!

Ophelia

I pace outside the healing quarters, unable to sit still.

No matter how hard I try, I can't stop moving, can't force my body to rest. Not when Skalanis's life hangs in the balance. Not when none of us know if he'll make it through the night.

Lorne—the vile, sadistic bastard—used twenty-three poison-tipped blades. Each one meant to tear him apart slowly.

The thought makes me murderous all over again. My fists clench at my sides, fingers aching with the need to hit something, to burn something, to hurt something. I force myself to stay still. Barely.

Arax left not long after they carried Skalanis down here, vowing to track Lorne's movements. His last words still ring in my ears, and I don't know how to process them—not after everything.

Hope for the future is bleak.

Galean's cover is likely blown. We may have just started a war we can't possibly win—not yet. Not with two enemies closing in, and one of them damn near indestructible.

Ravens have been sent to the other cells, instructing them to lay low and to keep us apprised of the king's movements. It's not enough. None of it is enough. But there's nothing else I can do.

My magic is nearly spent, my body is exhausted, and yet, I can't rest. Every little sound sets me on edge. The battle still rages in my head, playing in an endless, looping nightmare.

The screams.

They won't stop.

The priestesses' cries—their terror, their agony, their last breaths.

My fault.
My fault.
My fault.

The words drum through my skull, over and over, until it's all I can hear.

I should have done more. I should have saved them.

My legs threaten to give out beneath me, but I won't fall. So, I pace.

I pace to keep from collapsing. I pace to keep from screaming. I pace because I might never get up again if I stop moving.

Nova is curled up beside Ryvvik, while Seraphina rests in his lap. The three of them cling to each other, waiting, hoping.

I swallow hard and swipe at the tears burning my eyes. Not now.

Across the room, Galean paces too. He should have been

back at Morningstar Palace hours ago, but until we hear from Arax... sending him into the unknown is a death sentence.

I've lost track of how often I've walked this hall when I hear soft footsteps approaching.

I stop.

The red-haired woman—the one from the temple—appears, her expression grim.

She hesitates, her eyes rimmed red and her voice unsteady.

"I'm so sorry about your friend. This is all my fault. He saved me... you all saved me. I can't thank you enough for everything you did back there."

Her voice shakes.

"I'm in your debt. I'm Caecinnia Emberweaver, one of the healers in the palace."

She takes a breath. Her throat bobs.

"Your friend... he sustained fatal injuries."

My knees buckle.

Nova's sob pierces the silence, raw and broken.

Seraphina wails, clutching Ryvvik's tunic, while his sobs echo through the chamber.

It's like the world tilts. The air thickens.

The moment Caecinnia's words register, everything sounds underwater.

Distant. Warped. Wrong.

"FUCK!"

The world tilts again. And then—

Everything goes black.

ACKNOWLEDGEMENT

I never dreamed this book would make it past the first ten chapters. Somewhere along the way, Ophelia's story became my greatest obsession.

One I couldn't have imagined would become so big.

Through so many sleepless nights, Sunday meetings, and brainstorming sessions, an epic story was born.

To my husband: I can't thank you enough for standing by me. For putting up with my long hours and nights.. I know there were a lot of them. I hope you know how much you mean to me, and how thankful I am for all of your support. Thank you, for always beliving in my crazy ideas, and for pushing me to reach for every single dream I've ever had. You're the best babe. I love you, with all my heart.

To my Beta Girls: Each and every single one of you have had a hand in helping me develop this book. Each of you have been such a bright spot in my life, and I'm thankful for you. Thank you all for your amazing feedback, and for following along every step of the way. I couldn't have done this without you!

(Shana Rhodes, Charletta Marie, Erynn Kessler, Kayla Vaught, Amanda Long, Shannon Alderman, Kelsey Perkins, Jamie Taco, Felicia Smith, Krystal Lowe, & Kristina Smith)

To my ARC readers: You all were so amazing, and I can't thank you all enough for diving into my story, and all your hard work. You guys rock!

To my mom: Thank you for always reminding me that I can do anything I set my mind to. I love you. Please don't read this book.

To my sister: Thank you for being my best wingman, my best hypeman, and the best sister I could ever ask for. I hope you know how much I love you, and I can't thank you enough for always pushing me to do what makes me happy. I love you, sippy!

To my author friends: Amy Akers & Yvonne Hamilton - Every single sunday meeting will forever live rent free in my head. From every goofy moment, to the best brainstorming of our lives. I'm grateful for both of you, and the community we have built. I love you ladies, and am so thankful for you both.

To Racheal & Shell: Thank you ladies for all your encourage-ment, friendship, and every bit of love you've sent my way. I'm so thankful for you both!

To Letta: Thank you for every bit of encouragement and friendship. Having you be a part of this process has been so special to me, and even more so getting to share Ophelia with you from day one. I love you!

To Amanda & Erynn: I love you both so much, and am so glad I got to share this moment with you. I cannot believe we're finally here ladies. Thank you both for devouring this book, and for giving me all the love. You both are the best!

To Kayla: Thank you for taking the vision in my head and making it one of the coolest covers I've ever seen. I'm so ridiculously proud of it, and can't thank you enough! It's so special to me, and I'm so glad I got to share this with you. I love you so much, and am beyond grateful for you!

Lastly, to my readers:

Thank you. Thank you for giving this book a chance. I hope you loved Ophelia's story as much as I do. From the bottom of my heart, thank you. I'm so grateful for each and every one of you. Love you all!

- B

ABOUT THE AUTHOR

B Wills

B is a devoted wife and dog mom, who has always loved writing. When the opportunity arose, she channeled all her energy, and passion into creating an immersive world that captivated readers from the very first page. B loves traveling, reading, photography, and videogaming with her husband. She actively shares her journey on social media, connecting with readers, for Shadows & Starlight.

www.ingramcontent.com/pod-product-compliance
Lightning Source LLC
Chambersburg PA
CBHW051057030726
47504CB00006B/1671